Stars and Soil
Scions and Shadows
Dax Murray

KRAKEN COLLECTIVE

Copyright © 2023 Dax Murray
All Rights Reserved.

No part of this book may be used or reproduced by any means, graphic, electronic, or mechanical, including photocopying, recording, taping, or by any information storage retrieval system without the written permission of the author except in the case of brief quotations embodied in critical articles and reviews.

This is a work of fiction. Names, characters, businesses, events, and incidents are the products of the author's imagination. Any resemblance to actual persons, living or dead, is purely coincidental. Opinions, sentiments, or actions of the characters should not be conflated with those of the author. In fact, there are many characters that the author wishes a very pleasant 'never creep out of the book and into real life.'

This book depicts consensual sexual activity and tackles difficult and sensitive topics, such as abortion, pregnancy, religious abuse, rebellions, violence, and execution. **Reader discretion is strongly advised.**

Dax Murray
www.daxmurray.com

Kraken Collective Books
www.thekrakencollective.com

Cover Design: Sarah Waites of The Illustrated Page
Interior Illustrations by Etheric Tales

Interior Design by Dax Murray

Contents

	IX
PART ONE	1
1. Priests and Protestors	3
2. Princes and Parties	27
3. Fights and Friends	43
4. Royals and Rebels	63
5. Physicians and Fires	93
6. Love and Lies	127
7. Assignments and Assassins	151
8. Dangers and Dukes	173
9. Splinters and Sisters	195
10. Premonitions and Promotions	215
11. Flowers and Foes	233
12. Weddings and Widows	251
PART THREE	275
13. Deeds and Desires	277

14. Thieves and Threats	313
15. Treason and Truth	339
16. Rituals and Rites	363
17. Fathers and Fears	389
18. Betrayals and Birthdays	403
PART FOUR	425
19. War and Wounds	427
20. Reunions and Revelations	447
21. Keys and Clues	475
22. Dungeons and Discoveries	495
23. Flames and Futility	523
24. Partings and Promises	545
25. Hope and Home	557
Also By Dax Murray	569
About Dax	571
Kraken Reads	573
Kraken Reads: City of Strife	575
Kraken Reads: A Promise Broken	577
Acknowledgements	579
Coming Soon: Smoke and Steel	581

Dedication

For Didi.

You were absolutely the best cat and writing partner.
Thank you for all of the spilled coffee.
I miss you every day, my darling demon daughter.
2011 - 2023

Content Warning List

This is a work of fiction; the behaviors, actions, and views of characters should not be conflated or confused with the author's opinions and beliefs. The presence of these darker themes in this work is not an endorsement of them. This list is as complete as the author can make it.

- Consensual Intercourse,
- Abortion, Infertility, Pregnancy, Childbirth,
- Violence,
- Murder, Execution,
- Revolution,
- Domestic violence,
- Arson,
- Assault,
- Torture,
- Blood,
- Religious abuse,
- Consumption of alcohol

PART ONE

ONE

PRIESTS AND PROTESTORS

Caitlin does not want to leave Whick. The autumn air is warm and full of salt, and the quay is loud: as many ships making port as leaving. For a place where no one stays long, Caitlin wants to stay forever. Yet the letter in her hand tells her that she must do just that.

Business, such as it is, changes far faster than most would like. Brocade is out of fashion before one can fill their shop with it; gold-trimmed flatware is yesterday's fad before one can make their first sale. Her family's business is not any different. Caitlin knows she should be happy about this change, and yet. It should satisfy her that her family's business is so profitable now that they need a permanent placement at the capital. And yet.

Someone will have to go to Eoi to establish that new headquarters, to that city on the other side of Fayn, to that city where all that people speak of is the prince and his newest paramour; the merchants there talk of Lady Shennen Ahernn and how scandalous it is that Prince Cian is courting a Calla lady who is distantly related to a Suan noble family without their permission. The vendors ponder why he left Amelia Devlin, the Marquess of Muiris. The traders there gossip about the Duchess of Clare, Lady Clare, and why she once again snubbed a marriage proposal, this time to Lord Tynen, the Earl of Berach's son. And, and, and... Information that is ultimately meaningless to Caitlin.

But sometimes they do speak of more critical issues; how favorable the ambassador from Garcelon is in the eyes of the king; if tensions are still fraught with Janeuq; if the riots of the lower classes are impeding trade; if these uprisings are growing larger and more violent or are waning and now easily contained; if the recent death of a Tsvetokrasan noble was the work of mysterious assassin Fiadh Róisín? That city is so full of overt etiquette and comportment, but lurking beneath that is rumor and underhanded dealings that Caitlin knows she cannot navigate, seeing as she spends much of her nights in taverns with sailors or traders with questionable obtainment methods. Or, at least, she used to. She used to go with xir and gamble and sing and drink.

A residence needs to be found and purchased. A decision needs to be made on who will live there. Living in a city where the buildings are brick, or sometimes marble, not limestone; where half of the houses have elaborate crown molding of pure gold, and the other half crumbling from neglect.

All the documents for such will require reading and signing, enacting, and enforcing. While Caitlin knows how to write a contract for selling and buying merchandise, she does not know how to navigate real estate. She has never had to. After she married, her fathers gifted her a small house. This purchase now involves an entire estate and office space. An estate is nothing like spider silk. No doubt, Caitlin will do these tasks. She stares out at the shores, the piers, the vast, turquoise ocean on the horizon. The sights that do not exist in the city. The river that runs through Eoi cannot compare to the sapphire jewel she spends so much time admiring from her office window.

She is leaving this port city, leaving the humid air on summer mornings and the crack of lightning on spring nights. The stinging crispness of winter. The radiant sunsets in autumn: burning fire on water.

She sets the documents down again and paces back and forth, running her hands through her hair and stitching them together behind her head. Her thoughts skit away from xir, xir name, xir face, xir scent. *No*, she tells herself. It is Whick that she does not want to leave; it is nearly thirty years of habits that she does not want to break; it is leaving behind the years of wishing to leave, the thoughts of a teenager dreaming of adventure. It is falling in love with this city after realizing there is no adventure beyond the gates. It is the comfort she has found in her small home. Her home. Their home.

"It is not about leaving xir," she says aloud, only the scraggly tabby in the open window for an audience. The stray yawns, stretches, and leaps outside. "It is not about leaving xir. There is no reason to want to stay only for xir. Shouldn't I want to leave old ghosts behind?"

Old ghosts. Xir ghost. Though, Caitlin knows that xir people don't believe in ghosts.

It is her fathers, Teige and Rían of the Peddigree Trading Company, and the closeness to them that she now has, having outgrown the desperation in her youth for them to leave her alone, to let her live her own life. But now she has learned to love her parents in ways that are only learned after spending her teen years believing they were holding her back. They are the first people she goes to with a problem, both before xir and now after xir.

She pounds her fists on the desk. No, it is not about xir. It cannot be about xir. Xie cannot be the reason Caitlin wants to stay; xie *can't* be the reason; it makes no sense for xir to be the reason she wants to stay.

She can't leave. She can't live without xir. She will not live without xir.

It is not about xir.

It is the friendship Caitlin has found with all the regular sailors and merchants. Yes, that is the reason. Surely that is the reason. She wants to drink with these friends until the dawn, for fun... at least, at first. But then to drown out the memories.

She scrunches the papers in her hands and then incinerates them in her fireplace. It can't be because of xir. Anyone in her position would want to leave this town of sorrow and memories.

There is a tradition in these ports. No one knows how it started. For being such a large port, there is not even a monument to the god Iden, so it is not a tradition of His. There is a fountain at the center of Whick with the shells and wave emblem of the goddess Muriel. Perhaps this tradition belongs to Her. Regardless of which god can claim this rite as theirs, it starts with still-wet shells collected at dusk. It requires small bowls forged with sands from the shore, filled with seawater on the night of a new moon. It ends with a song.

It isn't because she wants to carry out this ceremony once a month, every month. Even the ones where the cold might freeze the water before she arrives at the grave. Xir grave. If she leaves this city, she can't do that anymore. And that is a silly reason to not want to leave.

So, it can't be that.

Xie told Caitlin about the last rites for xir people—there is a cycle for xir people, and what happens at the end of this cycle. It starts with a child appearing at the base of a tree, a metal bracelet on their wrist. And later, a journey to shape that bracelet into something personal, something meaningful: a circlet of impossible, unearthly beauty to adorn their head. They call it *ahnhörn*. Magic and intuition; magic that only xir people know. Xie told Caitlin that when xir people die, they disappear back into the *aclaere;* the life force of the planet. And then they will be born again one day, again materializing from the currents of the *aclaere* at the base of a sacred tree. Xie told Caitlin how important it is that they go back when they hear the spirits say it is time to return to their birthplace. But Caitlin knows it is too late and carrying out this last rite is impossible. If she leaves, there will truly be no way to see this cycle to its end. But that is in the past, a truth that she has accepted. It can't be because of that.

It is not because she won't be able to carefully run her fingers over the indented words; the letters spelling out xir name, and the numbers the day xie died. The day her wife died. It is not because she doesn't want to leave the home they shared, to pretend every night that she doesn't hear xir close the door gently behind xir when xie comes home, pretend she can still find xir fingerprints on the mirrors, xir warmth on the pillow next to hers. That is not the reason she cannot leave.

She must let her fathers know that she wishes to stay here, that she will not be moving, and provide a list of candidates for the new role in Eoi.

She cannot leave this place. But it has nothing to do with xir. It has nothing to do with Brenna. Her Brenna. The beautiful *Ástfriður* she called her wife.

She collapses into her large desk chair, dips her quill into a nearly empty ink bowl, and lets her fathers know that she will start planning for her move to Eoi promptly.

The townhouse is larger than her home, but it is claustrophobic. She feels hemmed in, as though the brick walls are shrinking in on her. It is several stories high, the first two of which will be used by the business for office and inventory storage. The top three are hers to arrange as she pleases. Even with only a fraction of the home at her disposal for personal use, it is still larger than the home she shared with Brenna.

A winter storm is rolling in. The coachman had mentioned that winter comes late in Eoi, but when it does, it rolls in fiercely. She fears she will never grow used to the shrill howl of the winds here and resents that the air tastes stale rather than salty as the sleet comes down. She fears she will only become depressed by living in a city with dull and dark buildings rather than the bright white limestone of home. Madness will take her before she can accustom herself to the constant smell of refuse that seeps out of the streets and into the walls.

She deemed it more efficient to furnish her new home when she arrived rather than to move all of her belongings with her. A sly lie to herself, that. She left her home just as it always had been; frozen in the single moment before she got that letter from her fathers; that letter that led her here. Locked in time until she returns. She brought only a few trinkets with her; Brenna's *ahnhörn* included. If she could not carry it back to xir birthplace, Caitlin could at least keep it with her. Hidden. Safe.

Her fathers say they will keep the house clean and free of dust and mold. She wants to refuse them. She wants the air inside to have been air Brenna might have breathed, the stray hairs in the carpet, ones that might have been xirs. With each cleaning, a little of xir is being cleared out. Caitlin couldn't share these thoughts; not wanting to dwell on them longer than she had to, embarrassed for even having them.

"Follow me, and I will show you the kitchen," Rían, her 'Pa', says. The townhome is chilly as her fathers give her the tour, and she wonders how long it will take for the hearth to warm her new dwelling.

It is different, and living in that difference, rather than appraising it, is uncomfortable. This is not her warm hearth; it is not her—their—soft bed. It isn't a home to Caitlin. Business has had her stay overnight in various inns across Fayn. That was temporary; that was a night or two; always knowing that there was a home waiting. Brenna was waiting.

She makes notes in her head of what she can move and re-arrange. Maybe even replace. Her fingers graze the marble counters, eyes land on the oddities, her skin trying to adjust to the dryness of the air. "And this is your office," Pa says. He has the mannerisms of his usual spark, but Caitlin knows it is an imitation. Teige, her 'Da', stoic as ever, turns away, shoulders slumping, to look out the large window into a meticulously kept courtyard.

"This will do," Caitlin says, turning away from both, not wanting them to see any more of her sorrow.

Da grabs her arm. "Caitlin. I know, I know you don't want to be here. I understand."

There are a thousand words she wants to say to him, words that have been building in her stomach for months. Words that she needs to tell him. She looks at the floor, then back at Da. "You don't, though."

Outside, the rain turns to snow.

Whick has just two temples; one for the Order of Muriel and one for Iden. Eoi, however, has several dozen; multiple Temples for each member of the Tudáe pantheon. It is the towering Temple of Culain, patron god of the Royal House of Fola, that overlooks the bustling market square in the Saibh district.

Caitlin had not meant to get so caught up in work that morning, but she did. The last nine months have been day after day of her not meaning to get so caught up but doing so anyway. And now she must battle a crowd at the market, all of the choice meat and produce long since plucked from the stalls and stowed into bags by the early risers. At least the chill of dawn has left, and it is a pleasantly warm and clear autumn morning.

"Our people are being misled by unholy miscreants who preach idleness and slovenly attitudes," a priest cries from a dais raised in the center of the market square. "Culain calls upon the people to show their dedication to Him through work, and in doing so, He will bless them with wealth!"

Acolytes of the god surround the dais, all wearing the snow-white robes with high collars and cuffed sleeves that mark them as Culain's devout, distributing pamphlets to any who catch their eye when walking past. Caitlin lowers the brim of her sun hat, hoping they will not notice her. She has no such luck. "Beautiful lady," an acolyte says, blocking her path. "Do you know of the grace of Culain?"

"I am not interested, thank you." She attempts to maneuver past him.

"But you should be! It is no mistake that King Tarmon and Queen Isleen have chosen Culain as their patron deity. He has rewarded the entire Fola line for their devotion. He ordained and blessed their rule."

"That is all very nice, but I must be getting back to—"

"Please, do take this. Honor Him with hard work and dedication to the righteous path, and he shall grant you all the riches you desire."

"I have no need for riches, thank you."

"Are you devoted to a different god?"

"I do not have time for this. I am sorry."

She elbows past him, ignoring him as he makes one last attempt to engage her, and pushes to the front of a farmer's stall. "How much for a dozen this morning?" She picks up the eggs, examining them for any cracks.

"Five daels. But if you get two dozen, it's eight daels and I'll throw in a pint of butter."

Caitlin fishes some coins from her pocket, her mouth a thin line. "They were only two daels for a dozen three weeks ago."

"Can't help it. Lost half my hens and don't know when I'll have the means to replace 'em."

"I am sorry to hear that." She hands over the money; there's a time to haggle, and this isn't one of them. With her basket now full, she makes for a bench on the outskirts of the square, savoring the smell of fresh baked goods wafting across the square and listening to the gossip.

"Princess Daya's sibling has disappeared. Do you think there was a fight about...?"

"The prince has taken another lover! Captain Alice Halloran. Yes! The High Admiral's daughter!"

"...you can't go to work all beat up like that, especially for the wage you make! There's a cheap clinic...."

"...The Marquess of Muiris has rejected yet another suitor!"

"But why? Is she hoping the prince will come back to her?"

"...can't help it, ma, I need to do another day a week at the factory. Can you watch Mal and Lorne or not?"

"King Tarmon has made Sir Seamus Connal a baron, Baron Rivers! Apparently, the ambassador suggested it..."

"Please, miss, do you have a dael to spare?"

Startled out of her reverie, she takes in the disheveled woman before her. Clothes no more than rags, deep lines on her forehead, and dark bags under her eyes. Without hesitation, Caitlin hands the woman the last few dael in her purse. The woman thanks her and hurries away.

"What are you doing?" An acolyte approaches her. "That woman does not need help. She needs Culain! Please, you are doing her a disservice by giving her your money."

"What? She was hungry."

"We have offered her our services many, many times. She still will not renounce some of her wicked ways, and so she cannot receive our charity. She also refuses to work, another way in which she could honor Culain. You are only enabling her."

"Wicked ways?"

"You are truly as lost as she is. Please, take this. Our Temple is hosting our weekly worship tomorrow morning. I hope to see you there."

The follower gestures from his chin to the sky and resumes mingling with the crowd while the priest on the dais continues his proselytizing.

Caitlin has never cared for politics except inasmuch as she must care about taxes and having business paperwork in order. She has never cared for foreign affairs unless it impacted importing and exporting luxury items. And until today, she had never had a firm opinion on religion.

The idea of having a strong enough opinion one way or another seems too strange. She still cannot adjust; adapting to an environment that has frequent enough unrest and more than enough gossip.

The unrest here is unlike anything she experienced at home. This is not the brawls that sometimes happen when rivals make port simultaneously; a flash of violence and then quite glowering at the tavern. This is something larger but much more silent. Much more serious. She has never felt this out of her depth before.

She doesn't have anyone to whom she can ask questions; how to live here, how to survive here. Someone she trusts enough to explain life here, what is normal and what is not. Three seasons without laughter at a tavern, lunches on the pier, games of cards with friends. Friends that came and went, and then came again as ships left and returned, and left again. But always friends.

Rains came and went; sweltering dry days passed by, and when the snow came back around, she still did not know how to live in her new residence. Home is a word reserved for a place that is now an old myth, so ephemeral that she is not sure if it ever existed. The entire world has changed, and each season brings a fresh set of differences she must adapt to.

An entire year has passed since she moved to Eoi, and she is still a stranger.

She makes her way around the buzzing market, a soft wool scarf obscuring her features and protecting her from the bite of the winter afternoon. The dreary weather does not deter the farmers and craftspeople from shouting their prices, nor the musicians from playing and the priests from proselytizing, it does not stop the smell of candied applies and roasted meat from permeating the square and tempting passersby.

"Businessmen are working their employees to the bone," someone behind her says.

"They should stop complaining and work harder, as Culain instructs them to."

"Serfs in the country are being killed by their lords," an apprentice trader says to his employer.

"They owe a great deal to their lords for allowing them to work those lands. It is as Culain, in His divine wisdom, has ordained it."

She determines that she can do without eggs today and should hurry home before the sleet worsens.

"Factory workers are working in dangerous conditions," an elderly man says.

"If they were truly so dangerous, why would the factory owners allow it? They wouldn't do that. The workers are just lazy," a youth replies.

She doesn't need bread, either.

"There are more and more people begging on the street."

"They should get a job, not make demands on the sovereign. To work is to be closer to the gods."

She ignores them; these conversations, ignores everything around her, and trudges back home.

"My apologies, ma'am!"

Oblivious to her surroundings, she bumps into someone, causing her basket to drop and its contents to scatter on the streets. "Oh, no, I am at fault. I was not watching where I was going," she says to the man. He is tall, almost inhumanly so, but thin, and for all that his stature is imposing, he looks like one more inclined towards anxiety than aggression.

"Let me help you," he says, setting aside his umbrella and placing the bruised produce back in her basket.

Caitlin packs the last of her items back in the basket. "Thank you, sir. I am sorry to have caused you any inconvenience."

"Let me escort you," he says, holding the umbrella above her head.

"I couldn't possibly impose on you. I am almost home, anyway. Just one more block."

"Oh? You wouldn't be Mistress Peddigree, would you?"

"How—yes, I am."

"Ah, then we share a destination!" He beams the smile of a child on the face of a grown man. "Now, you simply must let me escort you. After you," he says.

She allows him to accompany her home. "How did you know who I am?"

"I asked around, wanting to make a good impression, so… Some people gave me more information than I asked for."

"I see," she says, turning the key and opening the door. "You have business then?"

He stomps the snow off of his boots, sets his wet umbrella on the stand next to the door, and removes his jacket. He looks as though he attempted to dress the part of a businessman, but none of the items match; the seams are worn, and everything is a bit too baggy. The only item that could be considered professional is the golden pin he wears over his heart, a blooming lily. "Yes. I am here on business. Are you purchasing carpentry items?"

"That depends." She motions to her desk in the back corner. "Can you provide me with business credentials? And more specifics of what exactly these items are?"

He chuckles. "And how do I do that?"

"Do you have any paperwork about the wares you sell and what you wish to sell them for? The articles filed for incorporation as a business?" This man does not need to know how little she actually cares for articles of incorporation or permits or any other paperwork at all. She buys from whomever she chooses, from whoever has the best items. But she has learned, in the year that she has now lived here, that purchasing from pirates and brigands is quite frowned upon, and while she could get away with it in Whick, business done in Eoi must at least look official, even when it isn't.

He slouches. "He never tells me these things. I'll be back, I guess."

"The weather is only going to get worse. Please, stay at least long enough for it to pass. I have tea or coffee if you would like."

"Now it is my turn to decline assistance. I have other pressing business I must still attend to."

"Before you go, please tell me your name and when I can expect you back."

"Diarmuid Marr," he says. "And probably next week."

"I'll see you then."

Marr? She's heard the name before. An extremely talented craftsman, one who is also extremely reclusive. But she was sure that his name was not Diarmuid. A relation, maybe? If this were concerning the person she thought it was, it would be an excellent stroke of luck for Peddigree Trading, especially if they could make an exclusivity contract. She notices too late that he forgot his umbrella. With no other information about him, though, she must hope he sticks to his word and returns.

A week passes, and then two, and then more. Caitlin forgets about the anxious man as surely as he forgot about his umbrella, and sellers who don't keep their word aren't worth the space in her mind, no matter the value of their wares.

"Hello? Mistress Peddigree? Are you open? I am back." The wind outside rushes in as Diarmuid steps through the door, and with it comes the songs of the protests several miles away, loud enough to carry on the clear, chilly winter afternoon.

"Oh, that's right. Mr. Marr, I'd thought you wouldn't return."

She leads him to her back for more privacy, waving off her assistants, and gestures for him to sit in her cramped and disorganized office. He runs a finger across the edge of her mahogany desk, laughing to himself. "I hope these are the right papers," he says.

The papers are dog-eared and, in many places, smudged and torn, the scent of varnish and coffee clinging to them. She rifles through them, glancing at Diarmuid.

"You are the craftsman, then?"

"No, that would be my father, Seth. He is the owner of the business. I am just his errand boy."

"These papers will suffice." Her chest tightens. She does not know what half of these papers even say, and she does not care; he has confirmed that she could indeed make a deal with the reclusive but talented carpenter. These papers could say he was a convicted felon, and she would not care. To have Marr pieces in their inventory… "What sort of commerce are you looking for?"

"My father can't sell his furniture, even though it is the best in the city. He wants to sell it fairly, but only the nobility and aristocrats can afford it. They come asking, but rarely. He has heard that you have an extensive network, and maybe we could work out an agreement."

"I see." She puts the papers back in the folder; there is no point in attempting to read the poor handwriting on the yellowing paper of the few pages that weren't stained. "I trust these are handcrafted, then. Would you like us to purchase some of his stock and sell it abroad? Foreign markets? Or here? Are they all unique? Does he take custom orders?" She tries to speak slowly; letting her excitement get the best of her would not be conducive to sealing this deal.

His head droops, and he sighs, rubbing the back of his neck. "Yes?"

"Which one?" She taps her fingers on the table.

"All?" He shifts in the chair.

"Alright." If she didn't pity the man, she knew she could swindle him. "Are you authorized to sign contracts? I can have our lawyer draft one up."

His eyes widen.

"Is there a problem? We can go over all of the details with the lawyer, but if you would prefer to use your own lawyer present, too, we can wait. We don't have to figure out all the details right now if we get a rough overview of what—"

"No, no, no. It's not that. I'm just not sure if I can."

She cocks her head to the side. "You aren't authorized to conduct these sorts of transactions in the paperwork?" She pulls the folder back towards her, flipping through the pages. Again, it matters little to her. It matters very much to the lawyers and judges who are now her neighbors.

"No, the thing is, my father is terrible at this. He barely got the legal part of making a business, and as you can see..." He motions toward the papers and sits back in his chair.

"I see."

"Officially, I'm not even an employee," he chuckles. "I tell him all the time he needs to actually find someone to do the business side of things, but all he wants to do is build."

"But he ropes you into it?" She laughs. That is how she originally started working in the business.

"Rarely, but when he does, it's stuff way over my head. I am a physician! I'm not even good with people most of the time. Terrible bedside manner and all. I don't—"

"I understand all too well."

"That's right, you're the daughter. I take it you enjoy this, though? That's why you're still doing it, right?"

"I suppose," she says. "I'm good at it."

"Not what I asked. But I won't pry. Anyway, what do I need to do next?"

"Get you authorized to conduct business on behalf of your father's company or bring him in himself to draw up a contract. Would you like to work with your own lawyer or ours?"

"How much does your lawyer charge?"

"She would help you at no cost. I will tell her tomorrow to draw up the paperwork, and then I can bring it by, or you could stop over to sign it. But we do need your father's signature on the authorization form."

"That is awfully generous of you. It sounds almost too good to be true."

"I am not about to swindle you. Do not fear."

"Do you want to start the paperwork now? I can fetch Mistress Clermont now."

"I should probably speak with my father first, and it is almost dinner, besides."

"Here," she says, pulling a document from her desk drawer. She wants to find a way to at least pin him down a rough idea of his fathers desires. She fears that if he leaves now, he won't come back at all. "This is an example of what our standard contracts look like for various arrangements."

"Most helpful. I'll get these to him. Speaking of dinner, though, would you like to get some with me? Tonight?"

"Tonight?" She blushes. Meals with clients and associates are common, but he hasn't even committed to that much. "Well...I have not the faintest idea of where to go, though. I do not get out of my office except on market day."

"I know just the place, then. Let's go."

"Excellent," she says. The work she still needs to do for the day can be put off until tomorrow; this deal is too good to let slip away.

Their journey to the tavern is cut short by the sound of loud screams and chants.

"No... why are they heading in this direction?"

"A riot or protest?"

He sighs. "You shouldn't be caught up in it. Can we postpone our dinner until another day?"

"Of course. Will you be alright to make it to your home?"

"Oh, I am going to my clinic. There will probably be injuries among those in the protest. I want to be prepared."

"You agree with the rioters?"

"Why should I deny medical care to someone based on their beliefs?"

"I see... well, good luck. I shall see you again soon. And this tavern better be worth the wait."

"Oh, the beer certainly is. The food? Not so much. The company? More than worth it." He winks and sprints away from her, waving over his shoulder.

She laughs for the first time since she moved to Eoi over a year ago. She does not make it home before finding herself caught between the rioters turning down her street on one side and the King's Shield appearing out of nowhere to flank them on the other.

The sound of metal clashing echoes as she hurries towards home, hoping to make it before the chaos reaches her. She grabs ahold of her skirt tightly and dashes, trying to ignore the yells of the protesters crying for better working conditions and more reasonable rents, trying to ignore the stringent smell of freshly lit torches, trying to ignore the clatter of hoofs as the King's Shield advances, trying to ignore the taste of blood as she bites her lip in concentration.

She jams her keys into the keyhole, turning it so hard she almost breaks it. Safely inside, without hesitation, she locks the doors, closes the blinds, and goes upstairs to wait, distract herself, and pretend that the calamity outside is the familiar brawl of two enemy pirate gangs and the colleagues who took bets on the winners. Nevertheless, she keeps glancing down at the protest from the second-floor window.

By now, she knows what they do; corral the protesters from all sides, pinning them in. They arrest as many as they can; destroy whatever belongings they have, kick and punch, and hit the protesters until they are barely conscious.

She didn't think she would ever have an opinion on this; it never seemed to be her business. Whatever they are upset about has very little to do with her. But watching the royal guard run their horses over the protesters, swing torches at them, lock them in like this... If this is how terribly the king treats his dissenters, she wonders what he has done to earn their dislike. But she does not want to care about these things. All she wants to concern herself with is if the king has raised taxes on imports.

One by one, foot soldiers grab protesters, forcing them to the ground and binding their arms behind their backs. Once or twice, as she peers out the window, she swears she sees the insignia of the King's Shield flash on the hilt of a soldier's sword. The elite of the elite selected warriors who are more weapons than humans.

Some protesters slip away, pulling others behind them, evading the guards, knights, and soldiers, and running down allies. Some shopkeepers surreptitiously pull people inside. There is no keeping count of who escapes and who is taken away in iron and chains.

The afternoon becomes evening and then twilight. The clash dies down as more protesters either flee or are apprehended. And now it is silent. Burned-out torches discarded, fliers scattered, glass adorning the street.

She spots Diarmuid turning the corner, limping as he makes his way back and knocks on the door. *Why does it feel as though doom is standing there on the other side of the door?*

She goes downstairs and lets him in.

"I'm so sorry about that interruption," he says, removing his hat. "Do you think it's too late for dinner now?"

"Excuse me? You cannot be serious." She crosses her arms, eyebrows raised.

"I am quite serious. I've attended to all the emergency patients for the evening, and now I want a full dinner with good company. Shall we?" He holds out his hand in invitation.

"I suppose I can. You better not be lying about the quality of the beer." She laughs, taking his calloused hand and hoping it will make the nervous knot in her stomach disappear.

TWO

PRINCES AND PARTIES

*Á*STFRÍÐUR ARE NOT RARE *in Fayn, but they are not common either. Skin that shines like diamonds; the people from a far-off archipelago; a people that are reclusive and secretive; a people wrapped in rumor in superstition. Their ahnhörns; a glowing horn upon their head, sets them apart, marks them as beings outside of the laws of the wo rld.*

Their songs are like chimes, and their movements are like liquid copper. They sing of the waves that brought them here, and the clouds they say will call them home again. The Isles of Ástfriður are home to many clans, tribes, and factions. However, the traditions of all those who live in the Valley of the Veil are united in their distaste for anything that outsiders have touched. Even their own children: once one of their own leaves those glittering shores, no matter the reason, they cannot return until they hear the song that beckons them back into the aclaere for their reincarnation.

Only one clan allows outsiders; traders may land at one port, and that port only. Those outside of those Isles prize their gemstones, their metals, their stones, and granite and marble. Kings send their treasurers to that port to procure the most beautiful gemstone, lovers save for years to buy a real Ástfríður diamond for their sweethearts. Blacksmiths value the strength of Ástfríður metal, and jewelers value the pliability. These unworldly beauties are trivial to the Ástfríður, the flawed rejects of their harvests, for they save the best for themselves. People speculate that if what they trade are discarded defects, what they keep for themselves must be fatally resplendent. When Caitlin's fathers asked about the veracity of such rumors, Brenna would smile and say with a shrug, "Maybe."

There are attempts to raid the islands, but suspiciously well-timed, vicious storms always rise to meet these plunderers, harsh winds, drowning waves, and lethal lightning. Caitlin saw many come and go at her ports, boasting that they will be the ones to take the spoils of the Isles for themselves. But only one member of one ship came back from those attempts in all her years overseeing the ports, rescued by more scrupulous traders on their way back to Whick. The would-be thief rarely spoke of what they saw except to say it was a nightmare.

Every time she heard someone speak of the sacrilege of spoiling another's home, of coveting what they had never even seen, wanting what they could speculate existed, she wondered at what could possibly be worth the crime. What could make someone willing to risk the lives of their crew and be ready to take the lives of others? Was it worth it? The treasures thought hidden under those boughs, concealed on those islands? Was it worth more than a life; Lohyue, Qatu Calla, or Ástfríður?

How much is a life worth?

How much was Brenna's life worth?

"Caitlin, we will visit soon for a few weeks," the letter read. "Don't worry, we've obtained our own lodgings. We will be hosting a few parties while in town with potential clients and customers of the respectable sort." She had waited for them to call on her, or at least visit the office. But a week went by, and then another. Her invitations for lunches went unanswered. But she kept waiting.

That waiting harbored a thousand thoughts. If they are coming here and meeting with the upper echelons and in such settings, maybe they have reconsidered who to station in Eoi. She had gotten used to living here, used to the way people talked, lived, and thought, but she would still jump at the chance to return to Whick.

With the friendship she had found in Diarmuid, she had noticed herself no longer depressed. Since she had met him a few months ago, Diarmuid had introduced her to many other people, equal parts potential friends and potential business opportunities. She could introduce her fathers to him, introduce them to all of her new professional relations, and then go back to Whick. Go back home.

And now her daydreams will be real. Wringing her hands, anticipating the joyous news, she opens the door for them. Before they have even removed their jackets and closed their umbrellas, she ushers them upstairs and into the formal dining room, hoping that the steak and vegetables are not already cold.

"Sorry we are late," Pa says. "The food smells wonderful, though." Da pulls out the chair for Pa before settling into his own.

"What is going on?" she asks, not even wasting time with the usual small talk. Her stomach is in knots, but she picks up her fork anyway.

They stare at each other in solemn silence. Pa fiddles with his wedding ring. "The business is extremely profitable now, all due in part to your work here," he says. "A business that can continue to expand and grow should have primary operations here. We will make Eoi the new headquarters for Peddigree Trading."

"You want me to go back to Whick? You move here, and I go back to Whick?" She is going back home. She is going home!

Neither of her fathers speak.

"You... you are moving here, aren't you? You're the founders and owners. You should be the ones here."

"We want to retire," Da says.

"When?" Not the news she had been hoping for or expecting.

"Within the next few years. But we want enough time to hand it over to you gradually."

Her fork clatters to the floor. "Now?" Thoughts of returning to Whick, all the daydreaming of returning to her small house on the shore... "I see."

"Caitlin. You have seen the books, you've done the inventory, you've made large deals, you've made important deals. You've made us quite successful; the profit we needed to expand further," Pa says.

Caitlin looks to Da, hoping he sees the desperation in her eyes, hoping he sees how much they are asking of her. But he turns away and looks out the window at the radiant evening glow.

"You need to be the face now," Pa says. "You need to be socializing; you need to be overseeing the managers we've stationed at all other ports. And you need to be gaining the trust of the nobility. That is how we continue to expand. That is how we get new ports built; that is how we can sell higher valued items; that is how we will afford to go to even more distant lands. Hire a few more people to help you out at this office, someone else to take over your duties here while we find—"

She throws down her napkin. Somewhere between her move here and now, a small seed was planted in her heart. And today, that seed blossomed into a blood-red rose, emotions she had never thought to have, had never believed herself capable of. Anger that she did not want to admit to, anger at all the times her life veered off-course, forced to change and adapt when all she wanted to do was go back to Whick, to sleep next to Brenna... "You want me to take over and uproot my life again. 'Find someone else' for here? Where are you sending me to this time?"

"Caitlin," Da says.

"Don't 'Caitlin' me. You've been distant this whole trip. And now you drop this on me. I went along with it when you gave me responsibilities as a teenager; I happily accepted all of the promotions you gave me afterward. Happily, I managed all of Whick while you came and went in your dealings. And I came here when asked, even though it broke my heart."

"We understand…" Da says.

"You don't!" She does not want to hold back the thorns of that anger. All of the changes that they have demanded of her, a rose in a garden she did not know she had been tending. "I'm a widow, and you asked me to give up the home Brenna and I had built. I could have quit, you know? I could have refused, found myself another vocation. But I have been a loyal daughter. And you avoid me for weeks and then tell me you want me to, yet again, uproot my life?"

"It wouldn't be too far. You'll still be Eoi, but we have found a better location, a larger one, and it's in the Saibh district. Once it's ready and set up—"

"Are you kidding me? Are you actually saying this to me? Did you just hear what you said? It wouldn't be too far? That doesn't matter! That still means changing everything!"

"You never—" Da tries again.

"I've been trying this week to introduce you to my friends, to the people I have bartered and traded with here, with the other merchants with homes here, with so many people that trust me. That know me. And you would not meet them. That is not just poor business; it takes no interest in what I, the one you want to hand the reins to, have done here personally. The ways *I* have adapted to fit *your* business needs."

"There's a social event we are hosting—" Pa says.

"Oh! So, I shall meet *your* friends."

"Caitlin, you will run this business soon; we need this time to pass on our knowledge, to show you how to run the entire operations we have built."

"Get someone else to do it." Words that she had never dared herself to even think, suddenly on her tongue. All of the times she had said 'yes,' to them, but not this time.

"Your father and I—" Da cut in.

"That's just it, isn't it? You built this together. Husbands and business partners. You grew up together and grew this business together and had a family together."

"If this is about Brenna…"

"Do. Not. Say. Her. Name."

"I'm sorry." Da looks down at his plate. The energy Pa came into this dinner with is now gone, abdicating to the gentler nature of Da.

"You are asking me to rebuild my life. Again. You are asking me to take on the responsibility that you two shouldered together. And not just that, you are leaving it to me larger than when you started. Do you realize the responsibilities you are asking me to take on? The magnitude?"

"We don't trust anyone else, though."

Caitlin retrieves the fork from the floor and cleans it with her napkin. "Too bad. Find. Someone. Else."

"Will you at least come to the party we are having? We have some dresses for you to try on, shoes, someone to do your hair…" Da says.

"You are truly set on impressing them." She turns away from them to carry her plate back to the kitchen, not knowing how to both scream and cry, at least not knowing how to do it while not making a sound.

Da follows her. "I know we haven't been as supportive of you as we could have been. We loved Brenna, too, you know. We didn't know what to do, how to help any more than we did."

"No, your help was what I needed. That isn't what this is about, though." She knows she cannot endure yet another upheaval. Another uprooting. Another change she had never agreed to and never wanted. Every time her life has changed, she has adapted, despite wanting desperately to cling to what she truly wanted. She has learned to live here, despite it all, to make a small amount of happiness in this part of Eoi. It still might be Eoi that they are asking her to live in, but it's a different Eoi entirely.

Da tries to take her into his arms. "You always put us first; you always put the business first. We demanded that of you, though. We asked because we trust you. Because we know you can carry out the job responsibilities."

"You do not understand. I don't want more responsibilities!" She steps back, holding her hands up. "I am happy with what I am doing now. I am happy with what I've found. It isn't the happiness

I wanted; it isn't the happiness I dreamed of all those years ago…" She lets out a sigh; she knows what will happen next. She knows that she is not, despite everything, going to shirk this request. She has always known this was coming. She just thought it would happen differently.

He sighs. "I hear you."

"I'll do it." She slumps down into a chair in the kitchen's corner. The anger is gone, spent. The only one left standing in the fight is Da. "I will take over for you when you retire."

"And the party? When I said I wanted you at the party, I meant it personally, not as a calculated business maneuver. I really would like you there to spend more time with me. We have been so busy; after the party, it will just be the three of us for a week. You can take me on a tour; introduce me to the people here you spend time with."

"May I bring a friend?"

Brenna would have laughed at this dress; the crushed velvet, the fluttering sleeves, the way that it slowly fades from the color of grape wine to lilacs. Caitlin runs her hand along the soft fabric; it is not the sort of attire Caitlin would wear normally, not even to a wedding. Brenna would have laughed and asked Da if he could get xir a matching tailcoat. No, she can't think of xir right now. Can't think of Brenna. But Brenna is all she has thought about since the fight with her fathers.

The house they have been staying in is far nicer than the townhouse Caitlin is living in, and that's already far grander than the small house in Whick. It feels even more uncomfortable than the townhouse when she first moved in. She cannot believe the sprawling grounds that surround it, the gardens and ponds and marble benches. Inside, she scans every inch, nose crinkling. The grand staircase, the gold molding, the glittering chandelier. This might be her residence soon. She shies away from the thought; the neighborhood here is too pristine, the guests too perfect. Certainly not the people she would ask to throwback ale and play poker with her.

Looking around, she wishes once again that Diar had accepted her invitation. When she asked, he rubbed his hands together and said that he had a patient in critical condition and he needed to be nearby in case the patient took a sudden turn for the worse. He has become her friend, accompanying her to lunches after business meetings or asking her to stop by his clinic after hours to go out for dinner. He is terrible as a poker partner but makes up for it by being a good drinking buddy. But he isn't here. She's alone, once more, in a situation she doesn't like.

She retreats to the bedroom she is staying in, needing another moment. She finds Da waiting for her, staring out the open window into the clear night sky. "Join me," he says. "It's way too stuffy in the ballroom. Thank you for coming. I understand that you feel less than happy about this. So, thank you. Here." He pulls a simple brown box out of his pocket. "Open it."

Opening the box, a thin gold chain falls out: elegant but not ostentatious. The perfect necklace for the night. Understated beauty. "Oh, thank you."

"Do you like it?"

"Yes," she says, putting it on.

"Then let's go." He escorts her out to the ballroom but soon leaves her to mingle on her own. She sips her wine, savoring the nutty aroma, enjoying the lively waltz that the band is playing, and tries to navigate the highly choreographed chaos engulfing her. She doesn't know the language of the nobility; she doesn't think she can master or adapt to it; she certainly does not think she can learn it before her fathers pass the reins to her. There are some who find comfort in the rules and formalities of politeness, or at least the facsimile of it. Caitlin knows now that she is certainly not one of them. The politeness of a business negotiation is far different from this.

She downs her drink in what she knows is a very unladylike manner; a server immediately appears to offer her another, but she waves him away and steps back, bumping into a gentleman speaking to a large group of nobles, all clearly hanging on his every word. His eyes are almost translucent blue, and his long hair is unnaturally blond. There is something that feels almost wrong about him, not quite human, but also more mundanely human than anyone else in the room.

"I'm sorry," she stammers.

"And who are you?" His eyes travel down and then up again, grinning while he motions for another drink for himself.

"I am Caitlin Peddigree, sir."

"Oh! Mistress Peddigree! The lady of the house herself. Where have your Teige and Rían been hiding you?"

"They haven't; I prefer to stick to the accounts and inventory side of the business."

The man's companions follow his lead, surveying Caitlin. Some grin, some roll their eyes.

"Ah, you should come out more often. It is a pleasure to meet you, Mistress Peddigree." He takes her hand and kisses the back of it.

"The pleasure is mine." She waits for him to offer his own name. One of his companions taps him and whispers to him. "Excuse me," she says, her heart pounding in her ears. "I think my father said he had someone he wanted to introduce me to, and it looks like he's with her now."

"I hope to see you again." The man winks and slowly turns back to his cadre with a chuckle. She turns on her heel and doesn't waste a second in finding Pa.

"How much longer will this last?" she asks.

"Not too much longer. Here, let me introduce you to Emily Namara. Mistress Namara is a trader we met recently while overseas in Sua. It was so comforting to have another Fayn to talk to."

"Our competitor, then." Caitlin laughs.

"If you want to see it that way," Emily replies., blushing.

Emily's hands grab the hair at the nape of Caitlin's neck. Caitlin is mesmerized by her; her face brutally beautiful in the rays of moonlight, her choppy the light breeze in her golden hair smelling like lavender and thyme. Her arms snake around Emily's torso, wanting to pull her lips toward hers, wanting to pull the gorgeous woman down onto the plush bed with her. But Emily is quicker, pulling away and shoving Caitlin back down. "Not yet," she says, her voice silky but commanding.

Squirming, writhing, reaching. Emily smirks. "I said: not yet." Emily's knee presses into Caitlin's chest, and she releases her hair from her grip, equal parts firm and gentle. There is a moment where Caitlin thinks she may free herself. But she doesn't try, or at least not in earnest; instead, she lets Emily quickly pin her hands above her head.

"Shh, shh," Emily purrs. Her fingers lightly trace along Caitlin's cheeks, skipping down her neck, and grazing past her collarbone. Caitlin moans, hoping Emily will keep going further down.

"Shh," she sighs. She lingers between Caitlin's breasts, quickly leans forward to take each nipple into her mouth, a gentle lap of her tongue, quick enough to for Caitlin to want more, not long enough to savor it.

Caitlin tries to encourage Emily's hand, pushing into it, trying so hard not to scream out in need.

"Oh, my darling. Tell me what you want," she whispers into Caitlin's ear as her hand finally reaches its destination, hovering ever so slightly, so very close and impossibly far away.

Darling. My Darling. It is not Brenna's soft tenor voice saying the words. Caitlin looks up into Emily's wood-brown eyes, lost words, dying words. They aren't Brenna's eyes; they are not the ever-changing green-gold gems that she used to get trapped in.

"Use your voice, pet. Speak up."

Caitlin twitches and squirms, aching. Trying so hard not to thrash wildly, wanting to cry in grief and pleasure.

"Tell me," Emily says.

"Please," is all Caitlin can manage. "Please!" She bites her lips to keep herself from calling out her wife's name.

"Hmm." She pulls her hand away. "If you won't tell me, I don't know what to do."

Caitlin whines. Words she has not said in years. "Please. Please take me."

Words she regrets immediately.

She sits down for breakfast in the morning. Emily slipped out quietly before the crisp spring dawn, kissing Caitlin's forehead and commenting about doing business in the future.

They both knew it was a fleeting moment of shared needs, a night of meaningless indulgence, pretty words spoken as the final coda to their short song. Caitlin is glad it was nothing more than that, a fleeting comet in the sky.

This is the first time she has had sex since Brenna died. She tries to ignore the guilt, the shame, the hollowness that always bubbles up. Every ounce of unexpected happiness had been met with a pound of guilt for enjoying something, enjoying anything without xir. The guilt the first time she had genuinely smiled since moving here, the shame the first time she laughed—how could she laugh without xir?—the guilt that is chasing her.

It's not cheating, she tells herself. *It can't be cheating.*

But then she remembers the phantom hands, the phantom tongue, the burn of scratch marks on her back, relishing the bruises. Her traitorous mind wants to etch every moment into memory.

A servant serves eggs and bacon, perfectly cooked with a slight maple aroma. *A servant? When did they hire one? Has the business truly become that profitable?*

Pa sits beside her, carrying a mug of coffee in each hand, both steaming hot and with too much milk. "Seems you made quite the impression last night. Here."

"I, umm, I'm sorry," she says, sipping the creamy coffee before realizing how hot it still is. "I hope I don't make things awkward with—and I hope we didn't wake you... you see... she left early and—" There is no point in one's life, Caitlin knew, where discussing one's sex life with one's parent was not awkward.

"What? Oh. Her. No, don't worry about that," Pa says, stealing a strip of bacon from Caitlin's plate.

She tilts her head. "Then what are you talking about?"

"This," Da says, handing her a perfumed envelope, her name on the front in florid script.

She gasps when she turns it over and sees the seal wax. The crest of the Royal House of Fola. An invitation from Prince Cian to a garden party hosted by Baron Rivers and his new fiancé, Lady Marianna Gradae. The count has been looking for some rare items from overseas to present to his bride-to-be, and he thought Caitlin would be a perfect guest for this party, as she is charming and alluring, and she might provide the baron with the opportunity to browse the Peddigree collection.

"Prince Cian," Da says. "After you slipped off, he asked me about you. I believe he intends to court you."

"Did you tell him how impossible that would be?"

Da sighs. "It wouldn't matter."

THREE

Fights and Friends

*A*FTER LEAVING THE SHORES of the Veil, the Ástfríður only wore xir ahnhörn on their wedding day. Otherwise, xie kept it in a small box tucked in the back of a closet. It might seem crass to treat such a treasure that way. Half-forgotten, gathering dust, mingling with old coats, brooms, and dustpans, the etcetera that one might collect over the years. It was moot; one could tell xie was Ástfríður even without it. Xir eyes were too round, almost too large. Xir nose was softer, xir chin sharper, and xir mouth smaller. The sun reflected off of xir skin in rainbows, glimmers, and flashes even from a distance. There was no mistaking xir. Xie had boarded a pirate ship that was returning to Fayn, expressing xir desire to see more of the world to the captain, and joined their crew. For some years, xie accompanied one ship and then joined the crew of another for several more years, partaking in the undiplomatic negotiations just as much as in the drinking. Until xie met Caitlin.

Caitlin was settling accounts with the captain when she saw xir that bright and brisk spring afternoon. Everyone saw xir. Everyone wanted to both stare at and look away from the Ástfríður disembarking from that ship; all wanted to bask in the iridescence of xir skin, watching as xie set down a crate, xir hair sparkling in the salty wind. Xie was a star descended from the heavens, and Caitlin wanted to catch xie.

Caitlin struggled to stay focused, inspecting the crates, haggling with the sailors or, more often, pirates. Later, Caitlin would ponder if she always knew what would happen at this moment. The Ástfríður's arrival on one pirate ship could mark her as a potential guide for other pirates wishing to navigate the maelstrom guarding the Isles. Most of those who came and went at Whick were respectable, or as respectable as pirates can be. Later, when she looked back, Caitlin would further chide herself for assuming that she knew those who came and went well enough to believe they wouldn't harm Brenna.

The Ástfríður approached Caitlin as she finished her transactions with the captain. "Are you Mistress Peddigree? They said you were the one to speak to... To be honest, I'm new to this town."

Caitlin stepped back a little, mouth falling open. "I..." She wanted to come up with something witty. Later, of course, a thousand flirty replies would come to her. But for now, Caitlin was speechless. "Yes, you can call me Caitlin, though. Everyone else does. How can I help you?"

"I just arrived and am not wanting to go back out to sea right away. Are there places to stay here?"

"Of course, there's an inn about five blocks away. Down that road—" Caitlin changed her mind and took the Ástfríður to the inn herself. "I'll show you the way." It wasn't because xie was gorgeous, xir smile confident, xir chin high, and xir eyes gleaming. It wasn't because Caitlin was already smitten with xir. It couldn't be because of that. Caitlin was welcoming, forging a relationship with a potential buyer or seller or, at the very least, a new resident of Whick. It wasn't because xie kept trying to flirt with Caitlin.

Maria nodded in greeting to Caitlin before taking another round of drinks to a table full of regulars, the crew of the Red Sword. They weren't the most boisterous of the pirates who came and went, but they tried to be, slamming their hands on the table whether they won or lost a round, clinking their glasses in endless toasts—to Muriel, to the sea, to Charlie's pet rat—and singing purposefully off-key. The Ástfríður looked them up and down, almost imperceptible, but skilled merchants and business people were often excellent at discerning these sorts of things; haggling was an art. Caitlin led the Ástfríður to a table in a corner to wait for Maria to return.

"So are you the..." the Ástfríður paused. "The mayor?"

"I'm a director of the port."

"Ah," xie leaned forward. "So, you do dealings with everyone here, resident or transient. A real gem this town has." This wasn't the confident, playful flirting from the dock; it was soft, warm. "You've been here your whole life?"

"Yes, my fathers were both employees of different merchants, but kept running into each other and fell in love. They moved here to establish their own business together and have been here ever since. I started helping them before I even finished my schooling."

"They are lucky to have you. And this is what you want to do?"

"I guess. What about you? You've come a long way from your home. What is your hope?"

"I am not sure yet; I'm copper. There are places out there I want to see, so for now, that's what I am doing." This was the first time that the Ástfriður displayed anything but confidence. Xie looked down at the table, and xir eyes saw something far away for Whick. "For years now, I've been traveling with sailors," xie said. "Seeing much of the coasts of Fayn, the coasts of Garcelon, of Sua—strange lot, those hell cats—and even as far away as Janeuq. But little of the lands."

"So, where do you hope to travel next?"

Xie brought xir hand to xir chin, looking up. "No clue. That's the thrill, isn't it?"

"I guess," Caitlin said; she'd never considered that the sporadic nature of pirates' travels could be thrilling in their own right. "I've never traveled, or at least not much."

"Would you like to change that?" The Ástfriður grinned, eyes alight, fire reflected from metal. An invitation, but Caitlin couldn't tell how serious that invitation was.

"I must run the business here. I can't."

"Does this business consume your life? What do you do for you?"

"I have a lot of responsibilities. It doesn't leave much time for anything like traveling."

The Ástfríður cocked xir head and squinted at Caitlin. "It doesn't have to be traveling. How do you spend your free time?"

Caitlin almost spat out her mead.

"Why are you laughing? It wasn't a joke." Xie was serious, leaning over the table to get closer to Caitlin.

"I go over inventory, schedules for shipments, accounts, negotiations."

Xir shoulders sagged. "Why? Why do you do all of that? All?"

"My fathers trust me; who else would do it?"

"Anyone else! You can train others; you can delegate some of that responsibility." Caitlin shifted in her seat and pulled at a stray thread in her sleeves. The Ástfríður backed away. "Look, I'm sorry, Caitlin; I didn't mean to get like that."

"It's fine," Caitlin said.

"Do you play poker? I got a deck of cards on me."

Caitlin laughed. "How much money are you willing to lose, Mistress…?"

"Brenna. Just Brenna. My people do not have surnames. And you have no right to be asking that, Mistress Mayor."

Caitlin had learned how to play so she could entertain the crews of ships; hospitality went a long way to building favorable relationships. But Brenna was more than someone she hoped to do business with.

"Another winning hand," xie said, scooping the coins from the center.

"Is this how you paid your way around?" Caitlin asked, setting her cider down. "How you fulfilled your obligations on that ship?"

Xie winked at Caitlin. "Sometimes I sing or dance, too. You don't have to keep throwing your hands. I like you too much to have my pride hurt."

Caitlin had been throwing a lot of them. She was exceptionally good at that sort of flattery; let the captains and crew think they had at least one thing over the person they wanted to swindle.

Caitlin won the next four rounds. "That's m'girl," Brenna said. She looked into Caitlin's eyes and smiled. "That's m'girl. You don't need to be so shy."

"Alright then." Caitlin grinned and raised an eyebrow. She sat taller. "Let's keep going then." Something in Brenna's eyes inspired a confidence that had nothing to do with impressing clients for the sake of business. She was incredible at haggling, fantastic at asserting herself to get the better deal, to impress a captain or crew. Caitlin wanted Brenna to like her and like her for herself.

The table filled with more people, pitchers, and rounds. Brenna out-drank them all and won more matches than anyone else aside from Caitlin. Xie received requests from more than one person to share a room that night. And when Maria came by and informed the two that the entire inn was full, no beds at all, they offered more earnestly.

"I have a guest room," Caitlin said.

"Well, who can refuse that offer?"

She knows she needs to study politics with haste, paying attention to more than just which nobles might be interested in purchasing what goods. She needs fluency in the language of the upper class; to dress the part of a socialite and gentry, a different sort of formal than the kind she used to conduct business. She needs to memorize the names of nobles and be able to recall the names of both their compatriots and those they quarreled with, if possible. While she has no desire to entertain a courtship with the prince, she intends to make the most of this party as a businesswoman.

And she knows only one person she could ask to help her with this. And if he cannot help her, at least he can help her commiserate her misfortune.

The sign above the door engraved with the sigil of Andraste makes no sound as Caitlin pushes it open, finding the waiting room empty and reeking of alcohol.

"Who is it?" Diarmuid calls from the back.

"It's me!" Caitlin says, hanging her rain jacket next to the door, glad that she isn't interrupting anything.

He forces a half-smile and throws down a dirty towel into a bucket next to the spotless exam table. "I'm still swamped, you know."

Caitlin looks back at the empty waiting room; the blinds closed, the reception desk tidy, and the floor still damp in spots from mopping. "Is that so? I just wanted to see you."

"Really?" he scoffs, pouring alcohol on a fresh towel and wiping down the counter.

"Yes, really. Diar, what is wrong?" He touches his arm, his skin cold to the touch.

"You would not understand." He jerks away from her and scrubs at an invisible stain, refusing to look at her.

"You're my friend; I hope you know you can tell me anything."

He chuckles. "That's just it, isn't it?"

"Pardon?"

He glances over his shoulders, a frown tugging at his lips. "You have more important people in your life than me."

"Diar. Tell me. Is this about the party?"

"Yes, it is."

"I invited you to go to it with me. You said you couldn't. I told you that I wanted you there."

"Not your fathers' party. Baron Rivers's party. You were invited and you're going to attend."

"You have heard about… How… What about it?"

"How? The entire city knows. He wants the whole country to know that the prince has a new target. You're about to have many people more important than me. How can the object of the prince's affection have any time for a physician?" Another towel lands in the dirty bucket and Diarmuid collapses into a chair, hunched over.

"I didn't ask for this. I don't want him. I could count the reasons I want nothing to do with that spoiled brat, but that would take more time than you have."

"You are strange, Cait. You've given everything to your fathers, to their business; why would you not stop at giving your hand to someone to further their business dealings?"

"Giving what?" She asks, throat tight and hands balled into fists. "What? First, the prince won't propose. Second, my fathers would never ask me to, even if that happened."

"They don't *have* to ask you. You'll do it, anyway. You don't want this, they know you don't want it. But you'll do it, anyway, if you think it will help their business. They don't *have* to ask you. You'll choose to do it." He grabs a cloth and wipes down instruments, turning his back on her.

She struggles to find words to both deny his accusations and ask him for the same comfort he had given her last week; she had sat in the waiting room while he finished his last patient, and somehow, he knew why she was there and had hot chocolate prepared. Her fathers had left her house, and she ran not far behind them, racing to Diar's clinic, in such a rush that she did not even clear the table. He knew somehow that her dinner with her fathers would not go well. He held her while she cried and cried and cried. She never even told him what she was crying about. And yet. She wants that comfort again now. But she can't ask for it from the Diar that is standing before her now. She swallows the lump in her throat. "You aren't being fair to me."

His head drops. "And you're not being fair to yourself, either. Listen, I am sorry, Caitlin. I had a rough day, and I was taking it out on you. I know that isn't an excuse, but—"

She does not want to consider what Diarmuid was suggesting any more than she already has. "I need to go home. I have work to do before the night is over."

The dice scatter on the exam table, and Caitlin pulls the daels on the table towards herself. "Surely these dice are weighted," Diarmuid says, frowning as the silver pile in front of Caitlin doubles.

"Me? A cheater?" Caitlin says, grinning. "Never, absolutely never."

"I'm sorry, what's the correct terminology, then?" Diarmuid says, leaning back in his chair and glancing out the window.

"It is 'lucky bastard.'"

"You're a lucky bastard."

"Yes, I am. Thank you!"

"You can be insufferable. I think it's safe to close up for the day, doesn't seem like Aine or Kegan are gonna stop by despite saying they were going to. Why don't I grab us dinner with my last gold dael as thanks for keeping me company?" He stands and offers her his arm.

Caitlin, glad that the awkwardness between them had dissipated, accepts it. "Are they patients of yours?"

"Friends and patients. I have a tincture ready for Aine, but I guess we can drop it off to her on the way to the tavern?"

"That is fine by me, I need the walk, and it's a lovely evening."

Diarmuid leads them from his clinic, locking the door behind him. The stop at the patient's home is quick, Caitlin not even getting a look at her as the door opens and slams shut again almost immediately. "Everything okay?" she asks, as Diarmuid takes her hand again.

"It will be," he says, and leads her to a noisy tavern that she had never noticed before, but Diarmuid seems to be acquainted with everyone there, nodding and smiling and waving to every other person before they sit down. She likes the tavern right away; it's dimly lit with mismatched tables, full of laughter and clinking mugs and smells like stale ale. *Just like home.*

A young Calla approaches their table and plops a plate of potatoes and vegetables down in front of Diar. The Calla's ears are flat, and the azure fur on their tail is puffed up, but the smile on their felinesque face could almost pass as genuine. "Your usual, here. You haven't been around lately," the Calla says to Diar, ignoring Caitlin. A statement. A question. An accusation.

"I've been busy, Jocelyn."

The Calla flicks her tail and glances at Caitlin. "With that?"

"Her name is Caitlin."

"Do Sharidan or Valen know?" Jocelyn fidgets with the pendant on the long, silver necklace she is wearing, a blooming lily, the same as Diarmuid wears on his coat.

"This isn't the sort of relationship that they need to know about."

Caitlin raises an eyebrow and crosses her arms.

Diarmuid runs his hands down his face. "Jocelyn, please. We can talk later. But for now, here, for Saoirse." He pulls an envelope out of his pocket and hands it to her, along with some coins.

"Sure. Fine. Whatever. Whenever you're done in the hay, make sure you've picked it all out of your hair before you come to talk to anyone." She spins on her heel and saunters away.

"Hey, wait, Caitlin hasn't ordered…" He sighs. "And she's gone. I'm sorry about that, Caitlin." Diarmuid flags another server and orders way too much food for just the two of them.

"Girlfriend?"

"No! Oh goodness, no. She's from—I'm in a club, I guess. Haven't been to the meetings lately. Been too busy with work and with—"

"—me. Too busy with me. And Sharidan? Valen?"

"Club leaders. Don't worry, I'm not hiding a family."

"What kind of club?"

"It's more of a social thing. But for some, the club is family. Especially for those that don't have any other."

"I see." Caitlin leans back slowly in her chair and taps her forefinger on the table.

"Tomorrow, then, I suppose," he says as he gestures for her to take the food.

The topic that they had been avoiding for the last month. Caitlin shivers. The reason they were meeting every day, the reason that he was filling her in on how cruel the various nobles were. They'd been acting like he was telling her for no reason; acting like she isn't about to attend a formal party at the personal invitation of the crown prince. Pretending that he had a vendetta against every noble and needed an outlet for his frustration. "Tomorrow."

The subject of their conversations since their argument has skirted the unwanted predicament Caitlin is in. The list of the prince's many love affairs and romances is long. Some lasted a few months, maybe a year. No one is placing bets on Caitlin being the one he would marry; not because of her lack of nobility, nor her background, nor even the fact that she is a widow. There is simply no point in betting at all anymore. He might keep up this game, this hunt, of ferreting out the most beautiful, or the most alluring, or the merriest woman until he can no longer put it off as the crown is now on his head. Many lament the fact that his father will most likely not be attending his wedding.

This is both reassuring and terrifying. Nobles have flung their daughters at him. A few have flung their sons, too. Which is how he came to be best friends with Sir Liam Downing and Sir Connor Gilroy, and how those two came to fall in love with each other. But all were hoping for a proposal from the prince at first, regardless of gender. Or hoping for maybe a few months of extreme favor. Soon they all realize what the game is, yet keep sending their daughters in. That daughter is always later offered to a duke or a duchess as a consolation, still a most advantageous arrangement for families looking to rise in the ranks. Caitlin knows her fathers would never ask of her that sacrifice. They would not ask her to be a pawn, to be passed around to curry favor. Diarmuid's words echo in her head, though. *You would do it anyway if you thought it helped the business.*

If this prince only treated women as a fad, he would grow tired of Caitlin. She is sure that she will be no more than that commoner woman he tried to flirt with at a party. Forgotten within the month.

It will be easy to push him away as she had done at her fathers' party. Doing so while not insulting the others at his garden party would be the hard part. Looking rude and uncultured would not be helpful in currying her own favor on behalf of the business. This garden party will be a business venture, nothing more.

"My elusive lady," the prince says as he approaches Caitlin at the arched entrance to the sprawling gardens, taking her arm and leading her inside. "I am so glad you accepted my invitation."

This is a new sort of diplomacy, a change from any of the varieties or tactics Caitlin previously employed with a customer, to barter, to complete a deal, to prevent a brawl. There will be no bartering fabrics or ceramics; no discussing their weights, their worth, and if rivals show up here, she is not in any danger from swords or fists; but these nobles wield weapons just as lethal. The currency here is intangible but perhaps far more valuable.

Those she dealt with in the past were no more 'proper' than she was. Her peers, for all that you could be peers with captains, traders, travelers, pirates, and privateers, never cared much for flowery flattery.

The grass is almost too well kept to be real, the roses nearly too perfect in their blossoming and the wisteria trees more fragrant than they had any right to be on the gorgeous summer day. The fountains reflect rainbows onto the immaculate walkways, and the oak branches create the ideal amount of shade. She usually has no opinion on decorations, interior or exterior. Though everyone else is spending much of their time airing their own opinions.

"I was most happy to receive and accept your invitation, your Highness. As heir to Peddigree Shipping, I would never turn down an opportunity to talk business with those who wish to do so. Where is the honorable baron today?"

His head tilts ever so slightly, an eyebrow-raising imperceptibly. But he quickly draws himself up. "A lady who is loyal to her family and does not shirk her duties. So, the rumors are true."

He is baiting her. Having no experience chasing men and, to her knowledge, no experience being chased by them, she has nothing to go by to gauge the caliber of his attempt. "I am a businesswoman through and through."

"And what does a businesswoman do when she is not working? Surely you must have some leisure time." His hand slides behind the small of her back, and leads her away from the crowd, instead of toward it. More than a few words—none that a noble lady should know but that are part of the standard vocabulary for a sailor—claw at her throat.

"As you have said yourself, I do not shirk my duties."

"Your responsibilities cannot be so great that you cannot enjoy time away from them."

"And yet they are." She closes her eyes and takes a deep breath, hoping she is playing this correctly. She is a hard-working woman; she must appear to the upper classes as the professional businesswoman they will happily transact with if her fathers—soon to be her—business is to grow. But she must act plain enough that the prince will drop her within the week.

"Ah, I see the weight of them on your shoulders. Gentle lady," he stops and turns her to face him, his hand not leaving her back. Flinching away from his stare, his face too close, is not something she can do, though she wants to slap him and run. She meets his gaze. "Gentle lady, I insist you take more time for yourself. You found time to be my guest here; surely you can find time to do so again."

"I came here most selfishly, my lord. I came here on business." Her years as the wife of a pirate taught her quickly how to show no weakness, to keep a straight face while nervous. Though this is the first time in over a decade that she must put effort into this façade.

He takes a step away from her, his hand leaving her back, and throws his head back in laughter. It is not the polite chuckle of the nobility; the only thing Caitlin has to compare it to is the laugh of a captain after pulling a prank on his rival.

"You keep bringing it back to your business. Your fathers really should be proud; they would hand the business over to you even if you were not blood, I should think. Well, in any case. If you do not take time off yourself, I shall have to order you to do so. Next week we shall have fun; I shall teach you what leisure feels like."

"My lord, I am quite serious—"

"You are very serious, yes. Overly so. If I, in all my royal duties, can find time to attend parties and go hunting and ride through the countryside, how can you not? It is a royal order." He pulls her closer to him again and tilts her head up to face his. "You are so beautiful."

Caitlin swallows as he holds her longer than would be proper for any noble to when courting another. Smirking, his eyes hold the same mix of joviality and cunning as captains playing cards. But none of their camaraderie.

"My lord?"

"Ah, well. I suppose you will want to speak to the baron."

Cataloging inventory is easy—silks, spices, metals, clay, raw materials, or finished products; the ever-shifting contents of any shipment, any item in any of the storehouses. The names, the numbers, the weights, the worth of so many things, and tomorrow those numbers will change again.

Cataloging people is difficult, though at first it may seem like such cataloging would present no issues. People rarely change; their names often stay the same, their relations remain consistent, their residence and homelands and accents rarely diverge. Surely it would be easier than keeping inventory of items. But meeting so many people in a few hours does not lend itself to accurate and comprehensive internal ordering.

He leads her to Baron Rivers and Lady Marianna; the two are beautiful together; the deep russet brown of the baron's hair complimenting the honey-gold tresses that cascade down Lady Marianna's back. His sharp face and square statue contrast with her soft features and plump physique. They find the baron having a conversation with Allil Fola, Duke of Hern, the prince's uncle. Lord Hern bears a striking resemblance to Prince Cian, but he does not linger in his nephew's company, excusing himself promptly after a curt nod to Caitlin. The baron has a fascination with foreign oddities. Knick knacks and bobbles. He wants to purchase trinkets, if the business has any, for his sweetheart. He has heard they travel most of the world now, and he regales her with many stories of his own travels as assistant to the ambassador and the baubles he purchased in Alsha Dhabu and Arrinhu. This is not about commerce; it is an interest in collectibles, the same as he might express at a Ysdá market.

The prince leads her to countesses and earls, to third daughters hoping yet to make a place for themselves, second sons who want to gain more favor to compensate for their lesser title. They eye her under hooded lids and assess the extent of her interest in the party—many asking about business but not paying any attention to the details. People have less curiosity about recently found artifacts of gold and gems than they do for her. Caitlin is the rarity. Caitlin is the oddity.

The prince's presence at her side distracts everyone from actual conversations with her about trade deals; everyone now knows her invitation is just a pretense for the prince to show off his latest quarry.

While most of the gossip at this party revolves around Caitlin, the party-goers speak of other matters, too.

"I heard they were planning to raid—"

"Same men as last time—"

"—and no one knows how many got away—"

They speak in hushed whispers when they think the prince can not hear them.

"They need to learn their place."

"They are lazy; they shouldn't complain."

"This is how it has always been; this is how the priests and priestesses tell us it should always be. They should realize they are insulting the gods."

"If they want a rebellion, we will give them the defeat that comes with it."

"The king is far too forgiving of them. Their children should watch every one of them hang."

The wine tastes like poison, and the cake like ash. She has been evaluating the monetary worth of the flatware and the plates. Calculating how much it can sell for, and how much the baron paid for them. The figures in her head were based on material goods.

But these lords were calculating lives. The palace was far from Whick, far from any consideration Caitlin had to make previously; the only need for interactions with the government was sorting out incorporating a business, buying the license to sell and trade, paperwork to leave these shores and return to them. In all the business dealings, in all internal abstraction, never was a life considered collateral.

Brenna. Her Brenna. Her wife. Her face appears in Caitlin's mind, though this is not the place. This is not the place.

Prince Cian takes her hand. "You seem to have struck my guest speechless, Baron Rivers. Caitlin, you have never heard of stag hunts? Fox hunts?"

"Oh, oh. No, my lord. I haven't." She blinks and shakes her head.

"Ah! I know what we will show you on Saturday. Do you have anything sturdier to wear? I would not want you to stain your gorgeous gown. For then, you might have to take it off." He laughs at his own terrible joke.

"I have something that will suit." There was no way out of this now. She sighs and looks away from him.

"Fantastic."

The party ends, and the prince finds every reason to tarry, to stay just a moment longer, but eventually concedes that she must return to her fathers. She ignores them when they ask her how it went; she ignores them when they ask her what is wrong, and she ignores them when they shout after her, asking her where she is going.

She wants to ask them for help, ask them to send her back to Whick, to hide her from him, to send her overseas, somewhere, anywhere but here. Instead, she locks herself in the guest room, tears off the dress, and sobs.

FOUR

ROYALS AND REBELS

"The seams are fraying," the Duchess of Clare says, picking at the embroidery on the cuff of her sleeve while they wait for the stable hands to bring them the horses, the sun slowly rising on the horizon. Prince Cian had invited Caitlin to a "small" excursion. Small. But the hunting party is composed of far more people than Caitlin had expected it to be.

Aelena Fola, the Duchess of Clare, is his cousin and the daughter of the king's deceased brother, Tómas Fola. Caitlin notices a theme; the Fola family all share the same silver-blond hair and ice-blue eyes, but Lady Clare's eyes have more chill than the rest. She is the tallest of the hunting party and the youngest, but with her eyes perpetually crinkled in disdain, she could fool anyone into believing that she was the oldest. She appraises Caitlin upon her arrival as if she were staring at a rotten fish and says nothing to her, apparently deciding that Caitlin is not worth her time or attention. Instead, she chatters to anyone who will listen that the dressmaker had not sewn the embroidery on her gloves well, the greens in the morning breakfast were too wilted, and the invitations were made on inferior parchments. What was this country coming to?

"We do not need to have this conversation before our guest," Princess Eleanor says. The prince's older sister is equally annoyed to be part of this hunting party, but Caitlin guesses that is because of her proximity to Lady Clare and not her disdain for Caitlin; the tension between the cousins fills the air. Princess Eleanor greets Caitlin kindly enough; she smiles sincerely as she takes Caitlin's hand. The glare she throws at her brother afterward, though, would send anyone else fleeing. But Prince Cian, in all his pompous assery, is unfazed.

"Don't you dare insult the table linens again; I told you last night that I am taking care of that." Caitlin recognizes Sir Liam as one of the men who had been with Prince Cian at her fathers' party, although he looked far less disheveled today with his long umber-brown hair tied back neatly and his shirt properly buttoned. Keeping his chin high, he swaggers over to the duchess and claps her on the back. "Now stop worrying."

His husband, Sir Connor, winks at the duchess. If he had been at the party, she had not seen him. His golden bronze complexion glows in the sun, making him appear younger than she knows he must be and more awake than anyone should be at this hour if they had spent the previous night drinking.

She rolls her eyes and crosses her arms. "You had better be."

"Don't be so sour," Liam says. "You'll never catch a lover that way."

Princess Eleanor sighs. "Cut it out." The princess shares the same unnaturally pale blond hair and ice-blue eyes as her brother and cousin, but her eyes are soft and welcoming.

Princess Daya is just as warm in her greeting, taking Caitlin's hand gently in both of hers. She is the smallest of the little party and the eldest by a decade. Her tight-fitting jacket and collared dress shirt make her appear more elegantly masculine than Liam and Connor. She seems more open to sullying her clothes than Lady Clare, and unlikely to complain about the quality of said clothing. Caitlin likes her immediately. The sun makes her deep golden skin sparkle, a sparkle that is not unlike that of the *Ástfriður*, and her face is spotted with flecks of amber freckles. This princess from Qaewi had once been a potential bride for Prince Cian but had fallen for his sister instead, and Caitlin had to agree that it was a better match for her.

"Fine." Lady Clare says, arms crossed. The stable hands meet the party at the end of the garden, several horses and hounds in tow.

"Have you ever seen such a beauty?" the prince says as he takes the reins of a black stallion. "I named him Lightning. He is the fastest in the country. Come, let him smell you." As soon as Caitlin gets close enough, he puts his hand on her back and pulls her close to him. "He won't bite."

Caitlin obliges him and does not protest when he pulls her even closer.

"This one will be yours for the day." One youth hands the reins of a small chestnut mare to Caitlin. She appraises it; the horse is nearing her time for retirement but is otherwise in spectacular health and has a beautiful coat. The reins are fine leather; Caitlin can't help thinking about the price this would fetch. As the rest of the party mounts their own horses, the prince gestures for Caitlin to come to his side. "We are hunting foxes today." He grins at her, clearly expecting some sort of response, but Caitlin can't figure out what that response would be.

"Let the hunt begin; I can't wait to bring home the best catch!" Princess Eleanor raises her hand to the sky, grinning wickedly at her wife.

"This will be my, let's see, the sixth time this year bagging one before you?" Princess Daya swings a quiver over her shoulders, her eyes twinkling. "We both know who the better huntress is."

"Ah, but my catches are always of better quality than yours," Princess Eleanor retorts.

"You are entitled to your opinions, wrong though they may be." They both laugh and kick their horses into a gallop.

The prince narrows his eyes, a dark and sour look on his face. "Well. Let us get to it." His petulance is grating. He kicks his horse, and the rest of the party falls in line behind him, the sound of the hoofbeats echoing across the field.

The forest north of the palace is sprawling; dense enough for the fauna to feel safe but too thick and lush during the height of summer for horses to be unguarded. These lands belong to the monarchy, but the king has given Sir Connor permission to take its lumber and game. A privilege many others could only dream of.

"You cannot tell me that you do not enjoy this." The prince chuckles as he halts, leaping into the brush in search of the rabbit he had shot. His sour mood fades away as he gets the first catch of the day. It is not the fox he wanted, but he brags regardless. He pulls the arrow out and tosses the rabbit into his game bag. "See how the arrow pierced the heart? Don't you like the rush? The thrill?" When Caitlin does not respond, he continues. "You will understand when you get your first catch."

"Cian, let's go. You can still brag and show off on horseback." Sir Connor winks at Caitlin; his jovial laugh carries through the woods.

The duchess rolls her eyes. "You will scare the animals away like that! Why am I always surrounded by idiots?"

The prince helps Caitlin back in the saddle. She wants to push him away, but she knows staying within his good graces is vital for both her and the business she will inherit. Hold him off, but keep him happy enough so that, when he ends this farce, his opinion of her will still be favorable. She holds back a sigh and allows him to lift her up. His hands linger on her thighs as she settles on the horse. "Not every woman looks as beautiful with her hair tousled from the open forest winds as she does inside the walled gardens."

She blinks at him, unsure what to say at all. Caitlin hopes that this silent rebuff of his compliment will put him off a little and make him second-guess his affection. But he chuckles. "A modest lady? What wonderful world have I entered?" He tugs on his reins and takes off again, sending the hounds forward.

The princesses continue teasing each other and accumulating their share of small game, each showing the other their catch and keeping a running tally. When they both surpass the prince in the number of prey caught, everyone's excitement dampens. Princess Daya lowers her bow a hair's breadth when she sees her brother-in-law aim for the same fox and waits a fraction of a second after he lets his arrow loose to shoot hers. His arrow pierces the heart, though not perfectly. Princess Daya's arrow clips the fox's tail. "Well done, my sister! You might have had this one yourself."

"Do not believe I am not chiding myself, too. But the catch was yours from the start." He takes it as a compliment. He does not see her scowl; a scowl quickly replaced with an enormous smile.

He holds his catch high and grins at Caitlin. "Impressive, my lord," she says. "I could not have made such a catch."

"We will not leave these woods without you having a prize of your own!" He jumps off of Lightning, tosses the reins to Sir Liam, and climbs behind Caitlin. The party takes off at a slow trot, everyone now quiet as they scan for one last piece of game. Caitlin makes no comments as the prince holds her hips tightly, sometimes running his hands a little too far up or down for her comfort. She tries to control her breathing lest she turn around and punch him square in the face.

"Shh. Right there. See it?" The prince points to a squirrel.

"I do."

Deftly, he gets down from the horse and puts his bow in her hands. Caitlin knows very well how to shoot game and does not need the prince's help at all. Yet she allows him to adjust her hands and fingers, grimacing; he is doing it all wrong. "Now pull back. Wait... wait... Let it loose," he whispers in her ear.

Even hampered by the prince's help, she does not miss.

As the beautiful summer day presses on, sun bright and not a cloud to darken the skies, they make their way to a clearing to picnic. Every time the prince tries to boast to Caitlin of his prowess, of his strength, of his intelligence, his cousin mentions his past paramours. "Remember when you brought Captain Halloran here?" "You had a cake like this when we had a party with Lady Muiris." "Did you help Lady Shennen bag a fox once? Or was that Lady Marianna?"

Each time she does this, his irritation increases. Princess Daya, ever tactful, attempts to redirect the conversation to a topic that Prince Cian will find more agreeable. But she can only do so much.

Tiring of her games with the prince, the duchess says to Caitlin, "You are from a merchant family?"

"I am, your Grace." She rubs her forearm, still stiff from holding the bow, while the prince pours her some wine.

"Does your family work with any of the garment makers?"

"Some, yes."

"Do you sell to Sir Liam's business?" The duchess elbows him, but he ignores her.

"I am not sure, your Grace. I usually deal with silk merchants; my employees handle cotton, wool, and other fabrics. What sort of garments does your family make, Sir Liam?"

"Oh, it is not my family that makes garments. I have factories." He plops a grape into his mouth and then presses another grape to the lips of Sir Connor, not interested in irritating the duchess.

"Have you always worked for your fathers?" the duchess presses.

"I have, your Grace." She sips the wine, too floral for her liking, watching the duchess over the rim of the glass.

"And is it not just shameful that they have kept this rose hidden away in some small town?" Prince Cian puts his arms around Caitlin. "I hear they came here often yet never thought to bring you with them!"

"I preferred to be at home, at our headquarters in Whick," Caitlin says.

"Home? Is this not your home now?" Prince Cian leans in closer; the smell of his musky cologne and perspiration makes Caitlin's stomach churn.

"Was there something that kept you there?" The duchess cuts in, brow furrowed.

"I liked it there," she says, wishing she could run away. No business deal is worth being caught between two predators like this.

"There was not a person who kept you there? Anyone? A wealthy merchant's daughter surely must have had at least a few overtures over the years," the duchess continues, a wolf ready to pounce.

"I am much too busy with my duties."

"You had no sweetheart? No one at all?"

Prince Cian looks back and forth between Caitlin and his cousin, equal parts angry and skeptical.

"If you are asking me if I have some lover waiting for me in Whick, I must tell you I do not. I observed the full mourning period before arriving in Eoi last year."

"I heard otherwise," the duchess grins, making eye contact with the prince.

"I do not know what you may have heard, but there has been no one in my life since my late wife passed away."

"You wound me, cousin!" the prince says. The duchess scoffs. "Have you no feelings for me? I am insulted that you would think this peerless maiden would deceive me! My dearest lady, tell my cousin how daft she is."

"Yes, Mistress Peddigree. Tell me why someone as intelligent, clever, and beautiful as you would have no suitors besides my idiot cousin."

Caitlin takes a deep breath, calmly thinking through the best way to proceed. Does the duchess think she is playing him for a fool? Leading him on while pushing him off? It would humiliate him. That was indeed what she was doing, but she did not have anyone else waiting for her in the background. The best she can hope for is that he will tire of her sooner than he had the others. "I had no reason to believe any feelings I might have for someone would be reciprocated; I would not dream of harboring emotions for one who would never return them."

"Ah! You should indeed dream, my rose. You should always hope and believe."

The prince is in a sweater temper as they ride back from the picnic. His advances grow bold as they continue toward the palace; he sings—badly—all the bawdy songs he can remember and asks others to join in. He boasts of his talents, trying to impress and amaze her. But each attempt is now accompanied by touches or meaningful glances. He talks about what he wants for the future, for the days when he will be the most loved king, the golden ruler, the jewel of the kingdom, the monarch that will reign forever in memories and history books.

But his speech on the meaning of kingly love slows when the rain starts and then ceases when the guard at the northern gate tells the party that they cannot enter the city.

"I am the prince! This is my capital; you will let us in!"

"Your Highness, that is the problem. You will want to go in another way."

"This is my goddamn city; I will go in whichever way I want."

"My brother," Princess Eleanor says. "I want to take our horses on another quick run; I think they are still antsy. Please go on without us." Princess Eleanor turns her horse, and Princess Daya waves at them before they take off.

He nods in dismissal as they leave. "Open the gates. I do not care what you say the problem is."

The guards hesitate but do as they are told.

"I see nothing wrong," Sir Liam says.

"The guards think too highly of themselves," Sir Connor responds.

The duchess glances over her shoulder at the retreating princesses, hesitating for half a second before following the prince and his companions.

They come upon a large crowd gathered around a dais, the harsh smell of torches lingers in the air even as the rain quickens. Half a dozen guards are trying to pull people down from the dais while protesters toss pamphlets out into the mob, chanting something that Caitlin cannot make out above the din of the guards barking orders. Sirs Liam and Connor move to the front of the party and part the crowd. Someone screams, and as more shouts join in the chorus, the crowd descends into chaos. Caitlin's horse rears up, tossing her from it. As she hits the ground, she rolls and is carried away by the riot, the taste of blood harsh as her lip swells and her nose bleeds. She spins around, flinching as pain shoots from her ankle, looking for her horse, but someone presses a pamphlet into her hand and then dashes away. Pushing her way further into the crowd and still not seeing the prince or his companions, she decides that her best course of action would be to retreat home.

"What are you doing here?" a familiar voice says. Diarmuid turns her around to face him. "It is dangerous to be here, especially for you!"

"I didn't intend to be here! I just want to get home now. I think I sprained my ankle."

"You bloodied your face, too. Where did you intend to be? A duel?" He holds her face between his hands, examining her nose and looking at her eyes.

"The prince invited me to a hunt, and we were just returning; I fell from my horse. I don't know where the rest of them went."

"No concussion, but this is still no good." He scowls.

"Well, just let me get out of here, then. Take me home."

He runs his hand through his hair and sighs. "No, you need to get back to the prince. That is the safest place for you, much as I hate to say it. I'll help you back there. And give me that pamphlet."

"Why are you here? What is this about?"

"Not now."

"Diar, you owe me answers later."

He doesn't reply, just grabs her arm and drags her behind him, leading her closer to the dais. "There he is. Now play nice."

She runs to the formation of guards that surround the prince and his friends. "Find her! Now!"

"We don't know..."

"Prince Cian! Please! I'm here!" She looks back over her shoulder, but Diarmuid has disappeared, and with him, the chance to leave. She has no choice but to return to the hunting party.

"There she is! Get her over here; she is not to be hurt."

A guard scoops her up and puts her on a horse, and then the party and a handful of royal guards make their way to the palace as thunder cracks and the sky opens up.

"You never mentioned your date with the prince." Diar is waiting for her when she arrives back home in the late evening after the storm has finally dissipated; a knight named Sir Sarah Dermont had escorted her in a royal carriage because the prince was so concerned about her safety. Diarmuid is scowling, slouching in a chair in the back of the office, and tapping his foot. He does not even wait for her to take off her jacket. Caitlin is growing weary of moody men, and Diar is not helping her escape that.

"Hello to you, too. I'll put on some tea. Sit straight. You'll be in pain later if you don't."

"No, you sit," he plops a bag from the ground on the table and pulls out medical supplies. "Hold still while I patch you up."

"The doctor at the palace already did," she says. "I am fine."

"That doctor is a hack. He doesn't even know how to disinfect wounds properly." Diarmuid pours alcohol on a cotton cloth and raises an eyebrow.

"How would you know?" She says, trying not to flinch every time he wipes at a scratch, the scent making her dizzy.

"You never got a look at the king's arms? Oh, never mind. Hold still."

"I am trying! Do you worry about all of your patients this much?"

"Only the ones I like. So, all of them, yes. I have a debt to repay. There. Much better."

"Thank you," she says. "Now, can I get you tea?"

"Fine," he says, sitting down again in his chair and resuming his slouch. "I'm sorry, Caitlin. Everything is just a mess, and I can't do anything about it. Thank you," he says, taking the mug she hands him.

"Tell me what is going on. What was that all about?"

"It doesn't matter what it was about." He throws his hat to the ground. "It doesn't matter, and you should not concern yourself with it. Not with you being so close to the prince."

"It is not by choice," she says, taking a tentative sip of her chamomile tea.

He raises an eyebrow. "Did you fathers demand that you accept the invitation?"

"Well, no, but I can't just turn down the prince; it would jeopardize the growth of the business."

"When was the last time you put your wants over what you thought would benefit the business?"

"No, don't change you the subject. You will not do this. You will tell me what is going on." She punctuates her statement with a flick of her spoon against the edge of the sugar bowl and then tosses the spoon down onto the table. She doesn't want to think about that question, not when the last time someone asked it...

"Fine." He pulls the pamphlet from his coat pocket and hands it to her.

"Textile workers upset with dangerous factory conditions, long hours, low pay... I had heard that this was what they were protesting about." She flips through the pages. "But some of these things, what they are asking for... Farmers unhappy at their lords? Taxes paying for palaces? This could be construed as treason."

"Which is why you can't have that pamphlet and why you should not have tried to escape at the demonstration today. If you'd taken off..."

"What is a 'parliament'? On the last page? The king ceding some power?"

"Silly, isn't it?"

"These pamphlets make it sound like today was supposed to be a peaceful demonstration. But it got very violent."

"There are a few different players behind this. The ones today were the ones who think change can happen peacefully." He rolls his eyes. "That if we ask nicely enough, we'll be given what we want."

"But it became a riot. How is that 'peaceful'?"

"That's a brilliant question. But it wasn't supposed to be violent. I am guessing they were provoked."

"By who?" She flips through the pamphlet. "Are these things true? Is it really this bad? It can't be, surely."

"Yes, it's all true. There are farmers working from sunup to sundown, and more than half of their harvest must go to their lords or the king. And you have seen what that is spent on. There are people in those textile mills and garment factories who are being worked to death. They are dying, so the factory owner can make a few extra coins."

The duchess picking at a stray thread, commenting on the table linens. Liam saying he was working on it. The comments at the garden party that the people asking for better were upsetting the gods. "But the violence..."

"Do you think people shouldn't be furious when the wealthy and privileged consider them disposable? Weighing a life against a larger profit? Calculating how much a life is worth?"

Brenna. Xir murderers... the people willing to kill for the chance at finding some mythical port and a road to riches.

"I don't think you can change those sorts of things," she says. "It's just how the world is. How it's always been."

"It's not something that can be changed peacefully. But it can be changed."

"Is that what the other groups involved believe?"

"Our meetings are much more secret."

"Your meetings? You're part of it?"

"Of course I am. Now, do you see why I was so worried? What I am involved with... and who you are gadding about with? You caught in the middle of that..."

"What does your group plan to do?"

"I cannot tell you. But I want to. I have been wanting to for a while now."

"Why? If you claim you can't tell me because you want me to 'be safe' then—"

"It's not that. You must earn the trust of the leaders. And right now? I trust you, but do you think they trust someone who spends their day frolicking about with the prince?"

She stares at the pamphlet. *Brenna. The worth of a life.* "Is this… The club?"

"Ah. Yes, it is."

"I see. Why did you join? When? Is it why you overwork yourself with your patients?"

"It's a long story, and I am exhausted. I will tell you, but not today. If you want to meet the leaders, I can try to find a way for you to prove you're trustworthy."

"I don't know…" It's too much. Each lap of a wave upon a pier is different but predictable. The sea is only chaotic for those who don't know her, for those who don't respect her. Caitlin much prefers a storm on the horizon to an earthquake, shattering her into pieces, scattered shards of her being taken by those who want something from her.

"I understand." He sighs, shoulders sagging, and stands up.

Her chest squeezes, and she reaches out her hand to take his. "It's not that I don't care…"

He squeezes her hand. "I know. I get it. Although, I am a little relieved."

"Relieved?"

"It is your choice, Caitlin. Not a choice you make on a whim. You would be in greater danger than anyone else. But it has to be *your* choice. If you had decided so easily, I would have wondered if you were just doing it out of a sense of obligation."

"But wouldn't my current position make me a perfect asset for your group?"

"Yes, it would. But there are some things—some people—that are more important to me than my cause. And if you choose not to join, well." Without another word, he picks up his hat and bag and lets himself out of the back door.

The door clicks shut, and she buries her face in her hands. She wants to go home; she wants to crawl into bed next to Brenna. Removing the pins from her hair, she lets it cascade over her shoulders. Going back to Whick is all she wants; things made sense there.

He arrives without fanfare and with an entourage of knights a discreet 20 feet behind him. Although he claims he wants to disguise himself as a commoner, his clothes still give him away as someone of noble birth. He hides his distinctive near-silver hair by tying it up and tucking it under a wide-brimmed hat, but there is no way to disguise his eyes blue eyes. Anyone who looks at him for more than a passing glance will immediately know him for who he is.

Despite this, Caitlin mounts the horse behind him, and the two head to the market, hoping they will be there early enough to avoid the large crowd. It has been nearly two months since she got lost in the protest and four months since he started courting her. But he has persisted in his pursuit. The late summer air is heavy with the smell of storms, clouds lingering in the sky and threatening the vibrant green trees with angry winds. Caitlin hopes the storms will at least hold back their fury until after her outing with the prince. The thought of his anger at the weather's disobedience sends a shiver down her spine.

Despite the early hours, the market is already overrun with people. The prince dismounts from the horse, assists Caitlin, and then hands the reins to a knight. "I am so glad, my lovely lady, that you agreed to accompany me to the market today. I am sure you are used to seeing far grander things in your own inventories, but I enjoy sneaking into the market like this, and being among the people I will one day rule, especially on the days when the man with the caramel apples is here. Have you been here before and had one of those apples? I must get you one if we can find him."

"I have, at least once a month. I love coming here for fresh produce and essentials, and the apples, too, yes."

"You mean you do not have servants? People who run these errands for you?"

"I suppose I could hire some if I wanted, but how would I know then that they chose the freshest eggs or the fluffiest bread?"

"You enjoy checking for those things? I suppose it is in your nature, then." He throws his arm around her shoulder and leads her into the crowd. More than once, a beggar approaches them, only to see the prince's eyes and think better of it. And more than once, a peddler approaches with flowers or trinkets and drives an even harder bargain once they recognize the prince; he pays twice as much as he should have for roses and daisies. Caitlin's arms are full of flowers, bees chasing after her, when they hear the woman scream.

"Thief!"

"Stop!"

"After her!"

"Help! Get her!" This last voice is one that Caitlin unfortunately recognizes. The priest who had harassed her a year ago. She had seen both him and the woman he taunted multiple times since that incident. Though, luckily, never at the same time.

The prince hesitates, looking between Caitlin and the direction of the shouts. "Stay put!" He snaps, and out of nowhere, a knight appears beside Caitlin, as if she'd always been standing there. "Sir Dermont," the prince says to the knight, "protect Lady Caitlin."

The knight bows to the prince before turning her attention to Caitlin. "My lady, do not worry, you are safe with me."

The shouts continue. Curiosity gets the better of Caitlin, and she sprints away from Sir Dermont before the knight can say anything to her. From a distance, she follows behind Prince Cian, shoving past curious onlookers until she arrives at the scene. A priest is gripping a woman's hands, preventing her from leaving despite her struggling, and Caitlin realizes it is the same woman from last year. She wants to assist the woman, but at that same moment, Cian steps forward and she takes two steps back into the crowd.

"What is going on here? I demand to know," Prince Cian says, tearing off his hat and shaking his long, near-silver hair free.

Both the priest and the woman stop their struggle and stare at the prince.

"Answer me! That is a royal order!"

The priest raises an eyebrow and attempts a clumsy bow while still clenching the woman's hands. "Your Majesty, this woman is a thief! She has been stealing from honest, hard-working people. The market is not safe while this menace walks among us! She shirks her divinely ordained responsibilities to work hard and instead—"

"I do not have all day; concisely explain what happened."

"Yes, of course, your Majesty. This woman was flaunting her figure to distract the hard-working people from her disgusting sleights of hand! By robbing them of their money and goods, she blasphemed against Culain!"

The woman is sobbing. "Please! I didn't do it. I'm innocent! He's lying!"

"Are you accusing a priest of Culain of lying?" The priest hurls her to the ground and kicks her in the stomach. "How dare you! Of all your crimes, that must be the worst. Have you no respect for His Holiness Culain!?"

"Enough! I will hear both sides." The prince points at the woman, and another knight steps forward and grabs her. "Gently, do not harm her further."

The woman still struggles while the knight binds her hands behind her back. "Please, your Highness, I am not a thief. It is true I have no money, and I cannot work, but I am no thief! He is a liar; he has been trying to frame me for crimes ever since I rejected him!"

"Harlot! Liar! I have taken a sacred vow of celibacy! Whore, it was you who approached me!"

"Sir, what is your name?" The prince rubs his forehead.

"Brother Conmhac, your Highness. At your service."

"Ma'am, your name, please."

"Morrin. My name is Morrin, your Highness."

"Brother Conmhac, Mistress Morrin. I do not care what history you have between you. What I care about right now is what she stole and proof that she did."

"Of course, your Highness. If I may?" Brother Conmhac motions to Morrin.

"You may."

The priest approaches Morrin slowly. If Caitlin had not grown up with less-than-reputable traders as mentors, she would have missed it. The priest draws something out of his own pocket and drops it in Morrin's before making a show of patting her down. "What's this? I think there's something in this pocket," he says to the knight.

The knight reaches his hand into the woman's pocket and pulls out a gold bracelet, holding it up in the air. Morrin grows pale.

"That's mine!" A young woman shoves her way through the crowd. "That's mine! It says my name on the inside of it! 'Etaoine' is engraved on the inside!"

The knight inspects the bracelet, squinting at it with a grimace. "Your Highness, it is hers."

Morrin falls to her knees. "I did not steal that..."

Someone taps on Caitlin's shoulder, and she whirls around to find Sir Dermont behind her, brow furrowed, mouth tight. Caitlin points back to the scene unfolding. Sir Dermont crosses her arms and shrugs, keeping a silence that Caitlin has grown accustomed to. Certain that the knight will not betray her, Caitlin looks back at the woman, now being forcibly dragged away, screaming still that she did not do it, that it was some mistake.

"Your Highness, when will she be executed?" The priest shoves his hands in the pockets of his robes.

"Excuse me? Why would she be executed?"

"You heard her yourself; she refuses to work!"

"As far as I am aware, that is not a crime. It is stupid. But stupidity is not a crime."

"It is a crime against Culain! It is written in his holy book! Thou shalt work!"

"Even so, it is not a crime to the Crown, and even if it were, it would not be one worthy of execution." Prince Cian crosses his arms.

"I thought House Fola were devout followers of Culain. I thought Culain had divinely blessed the House of Fola and granted them wisdom to guide them in ruling this land! Or am I wrong? Is there another God, young Prince, that you follow? Have you instead given your piety to Andraste? Maddyn? Shea? Fianna? Which of the Túdae can bless your family as Culain does?"

The prince clinches his fist, sneering at the priest. "My family shall never turn its back on Culain. I am angered that you would even insinuate such a thing."

"Your behavior says otherwise, especially since you started consorting with a low-born commoner who does not know her place. If you want to prove your loyalty to Culain and your devotion to His Temple, execute Morrin and cease your association with that sea-swallower!"

Caitlin gulps and Sir Dermont takes a step in front of her. The priest has called her 'sea-swallower' more than a few times, always as an insult. But the venom when he says it this time sinks into her bones.

The prince's porcelain face turns scarlet. "I think that there is far more between you two than her rejecting you. I can see why she would do such a thing."

"Maybe Muriel or Iden... That wench from Whick has converted you, hasn't she?"

The prince raises his fist.

Caitlin shoves her way through the crowd, hoping to reach Cian before he punches the priest. She may not like him, but she did not want to be the subject of further gossip. She did not want to cause a brawl in the market square.

The prince takes a step toward the priest. And then another, and then he lunges.

Caitlin dives in front of him, slamming into him before his fist reaches the priest's face.

"Caitlin!" Prince Cian says as they both crash to the ground. "What are you doing? Why didn't you stay put? Why are you here?"

She scrambles off of the prince, her face burning vermilion. "Oh gosh, I am sorry, my lord."

"Why would you do that?"

She turns away from him, head buried in her hands. Perhaps this will cause him to lose interest. "It was not worth it, getting into a fight... in front of everybody here."

He laughs and grabs her hand. "You wish to protect my reputation?"

"Well, I..." Her stomach drops. This is the prince who cannot be denied what he feels he is entitled to. He won't let her go now, not when someone just challenged him over her. His anger at her disobedience cannot compare to the rage the priest now faces for trying to take away one of his toys. He releases her and turns his attention to the priest, lip curled.

"You are lucky that my lady cares more about decorum than I do, Brother. I hereby order your arrest for insulting the royal family."

The priest laughs while Sir Dermont restrains him. "Oh, you do not know what you are doing. Sweet, spoiled child. You will regret this. Father Nael will hear about this. And when you realize your folly, your penance shall be Morrin's execution." He laughs even as Sir Dermont ties him to her horse and drags him to the dungeons.

The rest of their outing is uneventful, but the prince never allows her to be more than a foot away from him. Outwardly, he shows no signs that anything unfortunate has happened, but Caitlin catches the way his eyes narrow whenever someone gets too close to her.

The end of the day drawing near, Sir Dermont finally returns and informs him that although the woman most likely was framed by the priest, and despite what the priest had said to Prince Cian, King Tarmon has released the priest, and at sunset, Morrin will be burned at the stake.

This won't bring Morrin back; she knows this. *This won't bring Brenna back.*

She knocks on the door.

This isn't truly getting justice for her. This isn't getting justice for xir.

She wrings her hands and waits for Diarmuid to answer.

It's only been a week since the execution. If she can at least meet these leaders, maybe it could ease some of the pain in her gut whenever the prince puts his hand on her back. Maybe it could fight off the chill whenever she hears one of the prince's friends disparage those less well-off.

She shivers, pulling her shawl around her. Autumn is approaching quickly.

"It's late," he says, opening his door. She falls into his arms. "I have missed you, too. But can I close the door first?"

"Oh, yes, sorry. Do you mind...?"

"Take a seat in the kitchen. I can warm up some tea for us. What's wrong?"

"Last week..." She sets her shawl on the back of the chair and sits down. "There was a woman. Morrin."

"Ah. You knew her, too?" He asks, rifling through a drawer.

"Yes, how did you?"

"From the organization. Well, she wasn't part of it, but we helped her."

"I see. I ran into her sometimes at the market and gave her money now and then. She seemed very destitute."

"She had a hard life." He measures out the tea leaves into a satchel and puts them into a kettle of boiling water, the smell of lavender and honey wafting through the air.

"What I saw, though, the way it all happened. I just... I want to go to the next meeting."

"The next meeting?" Diarmuid says. "Did you speak to your fathers about this? Is this what they want? Or what you want?"

She wishes he would stop asking her that question; it reminds her too much of that summer they spent sailing and those vacations they planned without telling her fathers, those days she was too "sick" to go to the pier and help manage the docks. It reminds her too much of the *Ástfriður* who told her too often that she was more than a dutiful daughter.

But whoever she was, aside from Heir to Peddigree Trading, died the day Brenna did and was buried beside xir. She has nothing more to live for.

"There's more to this than just Morrin. What else happened?"

"I am not talking about it."

"Did he hurt you?" He sits next to her at the kitchen table, holding out his hand.

"What? No."

"If you want to talk to the leaders, I need to know if there is something going on—."

"I can't! I can't talk about xir!" She covers her mouth with her hands, face burning crimson.

"Xir?"

"It. I can't talk about it. Forget it. I'm leaving. Never mind, just never mind about everything!" She leaps from her chair, grabs her shawl, and makes for the door.

"Wait!"

She halts mid-stride and turns around.

"Caitlin, my Caitlin. Wait. Please." His voice tight, eyebrows wrinkled, not even blinking.

"What?"

"I won't pry anymore."

"Brenna." She collapses to the floor and buries her face in her shawl. "Xir name was Brenna. My wife. I am sorry, I can't. I can't say anything more. Please."

"Rebecca. Her name was Rebecca." He joins her on the floor, close enough that she can smell the harsh alcohol he uses to clean his instruments, close enough that she could reach out and grab his hand. Too close. "My mother. She died when I was young. I understand if you cannot say anything more about Brenna. But I will always be here to listen if one day you want to."

She relaxes into his chest, cheek pressed against his soft wool sweater, listening to his rapid heartbeat. "I want to join your organization. It's my choice. I promise."

"I'll talk to the leaders, see if you can at least attend a meeting, and what you can do to earn their trust. If that is what you really want."

"It is what I want. And besides," she says, wiping away her tears on her sleeve. "I am sure he will tire of me soon, and I'll no longer be in that much danger."

He smiles and kisses her forehead. "I don't know how anyone would ever tire of you. But I hope he does."

"He will." She squeezes his knee.

"I am hungry. How about some soup and cards?" He stands up and offers her his hand.

She takes it. "That would be wonderful. I hope you're in the mood to lose some money."

FIVE

PHYSICIANS AND FIRES

*T*HE GUEST ROOM WENT *unused.*

Caitlin ripped off her blouse the second that she closed the bedroom door, and Brenna didn't waste any time shoving her against the wall. Xir knee crept between Caitlin's thighs. "Does this count as free time, Ms. Businesswoman? Or is this part of negotiations for you?"

"I..." Caitlin shivered as she spread her knees to accommodate Brenna's advances, lost in Brenna's green-gold eyes.

Brenna held a hand over Caitlin's mouth while the other fumbled with the latch to Caitlin's belt. "What sort of trade deal would you like to come to with me? Because I have one in mind. Do you want to discuss it?"

As xie pulled the belt free, Caitlin let her skirt fall to the floor, eyes never leaving Brenna's.

"Do you barter in leather?" Brenna asked.

Caitlin nodded.

"Perhaps we should take our negotiations to a more comfortable location." Brenna lifted Caitlin up, carried her to the bed, and pressed her into it, a hand on the small of her back.

Caitlin knew better than to say something at this point. Brenna ripped off her stockings. The cool air shocked Caitlin; even if she wanted to say something, she could not remember how to speak. "Do you barter in cotton?"

Brenna's finger slowly crept up to Caitlin's thighs, and both hands grabbed Caitlin's hips and pulled her forward before slipping xir thumbs into Caitlin's undergarments. "Do you barter in silks?"

"I..."

"Because I would like to barter all of the above. What do you say?"

"Yes, please..."

"I have heard that some of the best negotiators are silent. If you are such a negotiator, tap your hand three times, or kick three times with your foot. Do you understand? Good. Let's see how my negotiating skills match with yours." Brenna took the stockings and bound Caitlin's arms together, and affixed them to the bedpost. Then xie slowly unbuckled xir own belt and set it on the edge of the bed, never breaking eye contact. "Is it the person who shares their wares first that has the upper hand at first? Or is it the other way around?" Brenna mused, one hand under xir chin

Caitlin smirks. "Why should I give away my secrets?"

"I believe I can persuade you to."

"Try, then."

"I think I will." Brenna ran one finger slowly down Caitlin's neck, traced it down her spine, down one of her thighs before making its way back until it was hovering achingly close to Caitlin's sex. Caitlin twitched, pulling against the restraints. Too much, it was getting to be too much and yet not enough. Brenna had been so close to touching her, having xir hand exactly where she wanted it. And Caitlin had missed the opportunity to put her own hands where she wanted them to be on Brenna.

"How shall I try to get you to talk, to say something that would spoil a deal, or end with you overpaying on goods?" Brenna pulls xir hand away, waiting.

Caitlin bit her tongue. She wanted to ask for more; she wanted to beg and whine and plead. She did not want to give Brenna the satisfaction of hearing her moan.

Caitlin is shocked out of her contemplations by a sting on her bottom. Brenna's hand connected again and again, little taps interspersed with slaps. It was too much. The taps grew harder and quicker. "What part of transactions is this? Does this part have a name?"

Caitlin writhed, wanting to lean back, to lean into Brenna's body, into Brenna's hands. Each circle and tap made her hotter and warmer. The vibrations ran up and down Caitlin's body. Brenna stopped. Then leaned to whisper in Caitlin's ear. "Do you want to keep being an excellent negotiator?"

Caitlin nodded and moaned. She was pent-up lightning; she was a dam ready to burst; she was a goblet about to overflow.

"That's m'girl. I hope you realize that I currently have the upper hand." *Without warning, Brenna grabs Caitlin between her thighs, her thumb resting at the apex of her slit.* "This might be the best item in your inventory, and I intend to have it."

Caitlin's breath hitched. Eyes closed, she pressed herself into Brenna's hand. "Oh, please," *Caitlin said, all thought of remaining silent gone.* "Please."

"I hear that sometimes you give a potential buyer a peek at the wares, showing off only a selection of what might be." *Brenna pulled xir hands away completely and backed away from Caitlin. Her eyes grew wide as Brenna picked up her leather belt.* "I was only showing you a fraction of what I can offer, too." *She spanked Caitlin again with her hand, each strike making it warmer, more sensitive.*

"Are you ready? Remember what I told you earlier? Three times."

Caitlin nodded.

The first strike came, and Caitlin floated instantly. She was engulfed in a mist of sea salt and metal when the second strike hit. When the third strike landed, she stopped thinking about anything else, just the heat and yearning. "I like to see the other person's reactions when I first show my hand. Gauge what they might be thinking. And I think you want another glance or two at my offer. Am I right?"

Caitlin nodded vigorously. Brenna cupped a hand around the wet and glistening spot between Caitlin's legs, one finger entering Caitlin. Slowly, xir finger slid in and out. "And I think I am getting a good feel of what you offer, the prize of your inventory." Just as quickly, xir hand pulled away, and the belt met Caitlin's skin again.

Each strike, each grab, each word whispered in Caitlin's ear sent her higher and higher.

"Are we close to the pinnacle of our negotiations? Are you ready to shake on the deal?"

"Yes, yes, yes." Caitlin's voice was breathy, light. She could remember only one word. "Yes."

"Yes, what? What do you want?"

"Please. Please, take me."

Brenna's hand reached between Caitlin's legs again, fiercely, mercilessly. Incandescent fire coursed through her body, through her mind, and through her heart as she reached climax.

"Slowly, m'girl. Deeply and slowly. There you go." Brenna undid the restraints and massaged Caitlin's wrists. "Do you have a bath?"

"Yes, I do."

"Let's get you there then."

They found that they had far more to haggle over still after the bath, though.

Caitlin is not sure what she is expecting, but it is not the nondescript row house in the impoverished Nuabhir district. It is nothing outstanding, no more or less than the surrounding houses. He holds her hand as he knocks on the door four times. "Stop fidgeting."

"I am not." She takes her hand from him and pushes both deeply into her pockets, but she almost regrets it as it's chilly for an early autumn evening. She rolls her eyes at him. The door opens, and the person answering looks Caitlin up and down. They are young, no more than twenty. "She's safe?"

"She's safe, Tyn."

The youth opens the door further and waves the pair in before closing and locking it. "Myles wants to see you. He's upstairs," Tyn says. Diarmuid's mouth presses into a tight line, and he gives Tyn a thumbs up.

The home is warm, if a little worn. There are scuff marks on the wooden floors; the paint is chipping; the rugs have seen better days. But, to Caitlin, it feels like home, the home she had shared with her wife. This house she has been in for less than a moment feels more like home than her current residence. The smell of coffee and muffins wafts from down the hall, and the sound of people chattering happily accompanies it. Diar puts his arm around Caitlin and leads her to the dining room. "Take a seat," he says, pointing to an uneven table with several chairs around it, none of them matching. He squeezes her hand and then disappears up the staircase, each step creaking.

"Oh! You must Diarmuid's lass! You're all he's been going on about!" The Calla beside her rests her chin in her palms and looks at

Caitlin as if she is the most intriguing object. She is small, her russet feline-esque ears and hair a startling contrast to her striking yellow eyes, with only a thin vertical pupil.

"I am Caitlin; not his 'lass'."

The Calla's sleek tail flicks behind her, ears perked forward. "Excellent! We could use someone new to play with!"

Diarmuid returns. "Aine. She is a comrade, not your new toy. Here, you said you needed more." He hands a pouch to Aine and walks away once more, winking at Caitlin. *So, this is the patient he had to see the other day?*

Another Calla sits down across from Caitlin, tossing their long pale blue hair behind them and handing a glass of water to Aine. Their strikingly dark sapphire eyes are full of merriment.

Aine slumps in her chair, opening the pouch, scooping out a pinch of powder, and sprinkling it into the water. "No fun." Her ears swivel out to the sides and flatten, her face falling.

"You are his lass, though?" The newcomer asks, long ears perked up.

"I am not his lass!"

They both smile at Caitlin; she knows that she is, in fact, their new toy.

Everyone makes their way to the cozy basement once they have all had their fill of sweet pies and sandwiches. As the meeting starts, the levity disappears, though. A Calla with forest green eyes and short, burnt orange hair hands out meeting notes as people claim chairs, couches, and spots on the floor. "Sharidan," Diar whispers in

Caitlin's ear. "Xie is one of the leaders. The other is Valen, the dark bronze *Ástfriður* in the corner, with the white hair."

"Who was the Calla I was talking to earlier? The one with the Greenwood tattoo?"

"That would be Kegan, and the Evenstar Calla is Aine. They are inseparable. Aine adopted Kegan, so to speak. They make a game of 'initiating' newcomers."

"I noticed. A few months back, when we went to the Singing Sparrow for the first time…"

"Oh, I'm surprised you remembered. But yes, same Aine and Kegan."

"The pins… everyone seems to have one just like yours. The lily, is that…?"

"A symbol? Yes."

"Ah, so that means your friend at that other tavern one time… Jocelyn?"

"Yes, indeed. She isn't here today, though."

"Does everyone get one?"

"Do you want one?"

"Well…" She can't meet his eye.

"We'll see," he says, patting her on the knee. "You haven't passed the test yet."

"There's a test? Is this the study guide?" She flips through the meeting notes and is astounded by the sheer scope of poverty, neglect, and suffering this group is up against. Homelessness outreach, childcare for factory workers, food distribution, education initiatives, and medical care; all listed meticulously with updates. This isn't just riots and protests, it is a movement born of desperation towards an uncaring government that ignores its people at every turn.

Caitlin leans back into the couch. She has never had to worry about any of this, has never gone hungry, never been cold, never lacked for a physician. A numbing weight settles in her stomach as she realizes how little she knows of what is really going on. She thinks of the gold and silk and spices that have passed through her hands, the prices they fetched, the wealthy people she has negotiated with, and the sums of money involved.

Her heart pounds in her chest as she learns about the struggles the Red Front has been forced to endure while continuing to provide basic services to those who have been abandoned by their king. How they operate covertly to help those whom the king has deemed unworthy of his help or protection.

She can barely breathe as she remembers all the derogatory comments made by Sir Liam and Lady Clare, comments she had been willing to ignore. A cruel and callous disregard for life. People are nothing more than tools: if broken beyond repair, others are always ready to take their place.

She tries to concentrate, to listen to Sharidan and other Red Front officers discuss their plans to help a starving nation and a sick kingdom. While she had been warm in a spacious house dancing with Brenna and playing cards with colleagues, people starved.

The members of the Red Front speak with a mix of hope and sorrow. Hope that this is the start of a beautiful tomorrow, planting the seed so their grandchildren can enjoy the shade. Hope that the people who made their money in unethical and unscrupulous ways will tumble from their perches and plummet. One day, somehow, the aristocracy can no longer tax their people into poverty, and the king will no longer have power over an entire country. Their sorrow that, until then, people will suffer.

Sharidan announces that the meeting is over, reminding people to check the schedule on the way out.

"No." Diar squeezes her hand as she stands up. "Stay. We aren't done yet."

"But—"

"Stay."

She adjusts her dress, glancing around as people prepare to depart. Aine and Kegan catch her eye—they are among the few still seated, seemingly in no rush to leave. They share an amused glance before sauntering over. Leaning in close, Kegan whispers in Aine's ear.

Aine smirks. "You really are Diarmuid's lass if you are still here."

"I've told you—"

"She isn't," Diarmuid says. "You've had enough fun, for now, I am sure."

"Fine, fine, fine," Aine says.

He rolls his eyes. "I'm going to grab water. Please don't torment her while I am gone."

"Grab me some?" Aine says, pulling on Diarmuid's sleeve.

"And now you are ours!" Kegan says when Diarmuid is no longer in sight.

"What is going on, though? Why are there people still here?"

"He didn't explain?" Kegan says.

"No, he's kept me in the dark."

"There are factions, and they don't always see eye to eye. This meeting is just for the faction we belong to."

"Factions?" Caitlin looks around to see who else remains, remembering what Diarmuid had first told her. Sharidan and Valen are still there. Besides them, there is a pewter *Ástfríður* with short fiery hair reclining in the corner, a woman with bright freckles and purple hair tied into twin braids reading a large book, and an older woman with bronze skin and long hair the color of freshly fallen snow shuffling a deck of cards.

"There's so few. Not compared to how many people were crammed in here before."

"Maybe not. But it's the faction that Sharidan and Valen belong to. Myles hasn't decided to take his faction and splinter off. Yet."

Diarmuid returns and hands Aine a glass of water, scowling at Kegan.

Valen enters the room again, their short hair a mess of waves and tangles and yet shining brighter than a star. "Thank you for staying. I promise to keep this brief. We have a new supplier. They will deposit the items in the second stronghold."

"What are they talking about?" Caitlin asks Diarmuid.

"I'll tell you later. I want you to meet them after."

Valen brings out a map and starts putting red pins in it, seemingly at random, and they make no remark as to what they represent. "Seraph," he says, nodding to the woman shuffling cards.

"I understand," she says before turning her gaze to Caitlin. Her bright green eyes pierce into Caitlin's soul, and Caitlin cannot look away. She is being judged; every sin was written upon her face, and Seraph was weighing them. Seraph blinks, glances at Valen, and nods.

"Saoirse?"

Without putting down her book, the younger woman replies, "Twenty-five, thirty-seven, eighteen."

"Thank you," Valen says, marking something down on a scrap of paper. "And Imogen?"

"Five, nine, four, seventeen," the *Ástfriður* says, barely audible.

"Thank you. Kegan?"

"Three," Kegan says.

"Fifty-seven," Aine says.

"Eleven," Diarmuid says.

"Very well. Sharidan will tell you who to meet."

Sharidan enters the room and points to Seraph, then motions for her to follow. One by one, Sharidan calls the members to speak with them alone. Diarmuid pats Caitlin's hand before it is his turn.

Valen approaches, brows knit.

"Yeah?" Aine says. "You're here to talk to Diarmuid's lass, yes?"

Caitlin does not have the energy to protest the appellation.

Valen laughs, their silver eyes full of mirth. "I suppose you could say that. Come with me."

She follows them to a small room off to the side of the main room, just as messy as her own office, smelling of green tea and lemon. "That bracelet...Do you know what it is?"

"Yes. It is from my wife."

"You are married?"

Caitlin hesitates. She knows this bracelet, Brenna's gift, allows her many freedoms with the *Ástfriður* that others do not have. A symbol that she is to be treated as if she herself were *Ástfriðuri,* and privy to their secrets. "Was," she says at last. "I am a widow."

Valen hangs their head, the gaiety gone, their mouth stretching into a thin line. "How?"

"I...Well..."

Valen gestures for Caitlin to take a seat and closes the door to the office. "I'm sorry, I shouldn't pry. It is plain that this is still a difficult subject. But our kind..."

"I know, I know..."

"I suppose you do. But that's not why—"

"Xie was killed." It comes out as one word. "Three years ago. The mourning period is over, and yet..."

"I'm so sorry. Thank you for sharing. It is a blessing to know that your Brenna was so loved. Again, that is not why I wanted to speak to you."

Caitlin wrings her hands, forcing back tears. "What did you want?"

"I know that Diarmuid trusts you, but I also know that you are being courted by the prince. I trust Diarmuid, he's told me that you do not want to—"

"No! In fact, I am trying to get the prince to leave me alone!"

"Diarmuid said so as well. But not everyone here is so sure of where your loyalties may lie."

"You just let me sit in on the meeting, though."

"Hmm," they say, steepling their fingers. "Did you understand what we said? Well, in time, you may be trusted with more vital information." Valen glances at the bracelet again, chewing on their lip. "While I trust you, you need to earn the trust of everyone else first."

"I understand."

"So, you will join us?"

"I don't know. I told Diarmuid I would listen to what you have to say; I didn't promise more than that."

"Well, thank you, that is all."

She rises and makes for the door.

"Wait. If you don't mind, I have a personal question for you."

She turns back to Valen. "Yes?"

"Brenna. What was xir metal?"

"Copper," is all that Caitlin says.

They chuckle. "I should have guessed if xie was married to you."

"Diar," she says, grabbing his hand as they enter the frosty night. "Why? How did you end up here?"

"Sharidan," he replies, barely audible over the sound of their footsteps on the fallen leaves.

"Sharidan?"

"Xie recruited me. Xie paid for my medical schooling on the condition that I join."

"What?"

"It's a long story."

"I'm listening." She pulls the hood of her cloak forward as a light drizzle falls. "Tell me."

"My mother, Rebecca, she was sick. And my father had very little money. He was even worse at marketing his wares back then if you can imagine that."

She squeezes his hand. "Go on."

"We couldn't afford to go to a physician. There was a medicine woman, a Sister of Andraste, but by the time my mother finally admitted that she was sick, it was too late." He pauses mid-stride. "It was preventable. The medicine, if we'd had it sooner... It was too expensive. And the Sister could do nothing."

"I'm sorry..." she says. She turns so that she is directly in front of him. If the night were not so silent, she might have missed it. A small cry, lasting not more than half a second. If the moon were not so bright, she might have missed it. His bottom lip trembles almost imperceptibly before straightening out into a tight line. If she did not know better, she might have mistaken his tears for raindrops. She reaches her hand up, wanting to comfort him, to touch his face.

His own hand snatches hers before she can, though. "I am fine. Let's go."

"I didn't mean…"

"I know," he says. "But it's cold. I want you home before you get sick."

She bites her lip and keeps walking.

"Anyway, I left my father behind and traveled to Janeuq, to Haut Ven. There is a medical school there, but I couldn't afford it. I took on odd jobs around the school, though. Hoping to have money to attend eventually and to pick up whatever knowledge I could just from being there.

"I was in town that day, trying to barter what little money I had for some food. There was a scream behind me, and I turned around. Sharidan was in the middle of the street, clutching at xir leg. I could see the blood quickly spreading on the ground. I ran to xir and provided what little medical assistance I could. I wasn't very good. But I knew enough to stitch a wound and disinfect it.

"I carried the xir to a tavern, where I could staunch the bleeding. Xie was very thankful and asked how much xie owed me. I wanted to lie, to give a high number, to get the money I needed to buy more food and to save for classes."

"Did you?"

"No, I told xir the truth. That I was not a physician. I was just some kid who hung around the university a lot. Xie told me to come with xir to xir townhouse. I was shocked and followed without question, letting xir lean on me as we made our way up the street.

"I didn't know such luxury could exist. It was grand, it was huge."

"Sharidan? We are talking about the same Sharidan that just spent hours talking about how the wealthy are complicit in subjugating the poor? That Sharidan has a mansion in Janeuq?"

"Not exactly. It belongs to xir family, a vacation home of sorts. Xir family has all but disowned xir, but, like a cat, xie has ways of coming and going as xie pleases undetected. Xie treats the family's staff well, so I think they keep xir secret."

"Like a cat, indeed."

"They may have disowned xir, but that does not mean xie lacks money and funds. Enough to pay for me to go to school. Xie sat me down and explained only a hint of what xie was involved in. I learned later that xie was there to talk to *Alliée Rouge*, the Red Front counterpart in Janeuq.

"In time, xie came to trust me and gave me all the details. In exchange for paying my tuition, I was to be the Red Front's lead organizer on their healthcare initiative. I couldn't say no. I could help keep so many alive, prevent so many other children from losing a parent. But I could save every patient that walks in the door, and it would never be enough to repay Sharidan."

"You have a big heart."

"I studied hard, so hard. But still, I lose some of my patients. An expensive education and still just a mediocre physician with bad bedside manners."

"You aren't mediocre, don't say that. Sharidan is quite wealthy to be able to pay that," she replies. "Xir accent isn't Janeuq, where is xie from then?"

"I believe somewhere in Sua, I know xie studied at *Khidima Alam*."

"Are you joking? That university is nearly impossible to get into unless you are Sua nobility!"

"Precisely. I believe xie took on a Calla name when xie came here. Xie passes for Greenwood. I am afraid to ask what xir Qatu name is, though."

"Is Sharidan also the source of money that is used to provide all of the material goods?"

Diar shakes his head. "I cannot tell you that. I do not even know where all of the funding comes from. Just that there are several wealthy donors."

"Do you expect me to be one?"

"I expect nothing from you. Nothing except that you remain safe."

"I feel so bad, though. I never knew any of what was happening, I never imagined... I feel so guilty." Caitlin stops in front of her door. "Come inside, please...?"

He smiles and follows her upstairs, plopping himself in the large armchair. "Stop. Stop feeling bad. Stop with the guilt. It is unproductive. If you decide to donate money to assuage your guilt, you might as well just leave."

"I just... How could anyone forgive me," she says, stooping over the stone and marble hearth, filling it with logs.

"I said stop. You cannot buy forgiveness. You cannot buy absolution. You were ignorant, now you are not. Your ignorance was through no fault of your own. But now you know the truth. Now you can do something about it. And you must do something because it is the right thing to do, not because you want to make yourself feel better."

"Where do I start, though?" She pricks herself on the edge of a log, grimacing to hold in her cry. She can't let Diarmuid see. Not that she is hurt and not that she is being so childish.

"I wouldn't have brought you—I wouldn't have told you all that I have—if I didn't think you would know."

"I see." She strikes a match and sits on the rug, still unable to face him.

"I was afraid when you started your... relationship... with the prince that you weren't the person I thought you were, that I hoped you were."

"I didn't ask—" Her face burns, but it has nothing to do with the sparking embers.

"I know, I know that now. But I feared, for some time, that you might end up disappointing me."

Disappointing? Something doesn't sit well with the way he had said: "disappointing." She wants to ask him more, but she does not know what words to use, her eyes watering and her throat stinging. *From the smoke. Yes, from the smoke.*

The aroma of roasted vegetables permeates the room as she moves around the kitchen, but her focus is on the Red Front. Sharidan gave up everything—status, money, and safety—to join the cause. And Diarmuid's constant dedication to his patients, his constant worry that he was not doing enough...

She tosses a pork bone into a boiling pot. There had to be more to it, though. All of the talk was about providing services. They spoke not a single word about protests, rallies, or violence at the meeting. But the way Diar had spoken about the "faction" he was part of... There had to be more to it. Diar had spoken about danger just in being acquainted with them. Why would anyone object to a few people handing out soup and free medical care? Each of the Twelve Orders had their own cause that they oversaw. Each went out once a month to provide services to the poor and less fortunate. If the priests and priestesses could do it, why would anyone object to commoners doing it?

Banging on the door draws her out of her thoughts. *Who would come by at this hour?* It was far too late and on a weekend night. *Maybe it is Diarmuid?* She hopes it's him; it's been a week since she attended the meeting, and she hasn't seen him since that night. She puts a lid on her pot, removes her apron, and rushes down the stairs.

She swings open the door before even checking who it is. "Where've you been?"

"I did not know you missed me that much, my lovely lady," Prince Cian says. "Enough to drop all formality?"

Her stomach tightens. "I am sorry, your Highness." She bows, her unkempt hair hiding her blush.

"Tell me, who was it that you believed was calling upon you?"

"Oh," she says, straightening and leading him to her office, the only room in any sort of state that is not a disaster. "Oh, an assistant. He's very late with something he was sent to fetch. Something very important and urgent."

"You would talk to someone that way? An employee?"

"Well, some assistants are not known for showing up when and where they are supposed to, and one can only handle so many disappointments."

"My dear, I know exactly what you mean. I had not thought you were capable of losing control of yourself like that, however. Strange. You almost seemed human."

"My lord, before we continue, I must attend to the kitchen. I was in the middle of making some stew."

"Oh? My lovely lady wants to cook for me? I have already eaten for the day, but suddenly I am famished, and only food made by your hands will satisfy me. Lead the way; I am so curious to know what my lovely lady looks like in a kitchen."

She tries to look past him onto the street but sees no coach, no guards, no knights lurking in the clear night. Her stomach churns, but she leads him upstairs to her living quarters. He is dressed in what he probably believes to be "commoner attire" and has his hair concealed under a hood. But he still carries himself like a prince.

"I must ask, my lord, what brings you here at this hour? I am hardly in a state to receive visitors." She takes his soft cotton cloak from him and hangs it next to the door.

"Can a man not call upon the woman he loves?" He pulls up a stool and leans against the wall, lacing his fingers behind his head.

Loves? "Of course. But the hour is late, and I am unprepared."

"I could not possibly go another day without seeing you. And you were so distressed at our last meeting. I could tell that my father's decision weighed heavily on you."

She ties the apron around her waist. *Morrin.* "Yes, it was distressing."

"I will not be like that, I promise you. I will not be the king that my father is. I remember his early days; I was still a child then. But I remember he used to be just, kind, forgiving. I know I can seem aloof and self-centered. But I am not without empathy or compassion."

"I know, my lord." She can think of nothing else to say while she whisks flour into the pot, the clang of her spoon banging on the pot almost drowning out his voice.

"Something happened when he took the throne. Something changed him when the scepter was placed in his hands and the crown set upon his head. Power. Power changes people. I do not want to be changed, not like that."

Caitlin stays silent. Any answer to this question could be the wrong one. *What could she say that would not come across as also criticizing his father?*

"When I am king, there will be no protests or riots. I've read the pamphlets. I've heard their chants. I will do everything I can to stop them and ensure they have no more reason to chant or protest. My father, I love him, I do. But... I won't change; I'll be a good ruler. I will ensure they have no reason to complain. What do you think, Caitlin?" He asks it like a pupil seeking approval from a teacher.

She freezes. He knows what they want? But...

"It is fine, my lady. You can speak freely. Speak to me as if I were a normal man, complaining about his normal father."

"You are steadfast, my lord. I cannot imagine that the crown will change who you are." *Not a lie. He is very steadfast in being a bullheaded, stuck-up, arrogant ass. There is no way the crown could make him any worse.*

"Your talents are wasted as a businesswoman. You are far more suited to politics and diplomacy."

"My lord, I am flattered," she says, setting the spoon down and facing him. "But I have no aspirations."

"You do not? No, of course, you do not. You cannot see further than the path your parents set you on. I wonder if you've ever asked yourself what it is that you want."

Brenna. That first day, that first night, and every night after that. A question Caitlin had to answer. *'You,'* was always her reply. What she wanted was Brenna.

"I want what is best for my family. That is enough for me," she says. "Isn't that what most people want?"

"I suppose. I should not be chiding you, truly. I am also following the path laid down for me by my father before I was born. Can you forgive my hypocrisy?"

"There is nothing to forgive, my lord."

"How silly it must seem for a prince to complain about his station. Never once have my parents asked me what I want; I must live the life they want. Every other person in this nation has a choice; they can choose who to marry, where to live, what their goals and ambitions are."

"But the smith's son does not have a choice, nor does the butcher's daughter." She adds in butter and whisks it furiously. "And desperate people may take jobs they hate to ensure their children have food. And marriages of convenience or circumstance happen far more often than you can imagine."

"Well, it has been at least two decades since someone has scolded me so thoroughly." He laughs. "I find I quite enjoy it."

"I am not surprised." She cannot take back the words, so she presses on. "There are no shackles on you. Is there someone holding you at knifepoint to marry someone you dislike? Your parents did not force you to marry Princess Daya, even though that was the plan. And if you do not want the throne, you are more than free to hand the crown to your sister and do whatever you please."

"Yes, yes, I do enjoy this! Please, my love, tell me more of my flaws. I desire your honesty."

She sets the whisk aside and removes the pot from the fire. "I have nothing more to say, my lord. I meant no insult."

"Why do you not bring out that fire more often? Why do you hide it?"

"It does a businesswoman no good to lose control."

"Yet you have done so twice tonight. I shall count myself lucky to see such a rare event."

"If you choose to see it that way. I am rather embarrassed by it. Excuse me, I will be right back. I just need to fetch the silverware." She hides in the closet for as long as she dares. *She has insulted him twice tonight, and he thinks he is lucky? What will it take for him to discard her?*

"Your home is very plain," he says as she enters the kitchen again, the best spoons she has clutched tightly in her hand.

She squints at him, taken aback by the comment. "Excuse me?"

"I mean no criticism. But you do not have decorations, personal touches, knickknacks, or mementos. You must surely have traveled the world and seen so many wonderful things; why don't you have souvenirs? Where was your next destination?"

"Home," she says, not realizing until after that she spoke.

"This is not home?"

Brenna. Brenna is home.

"You ask a question you will not like the answer to."

"Whick, then. That is where you are from, correct? You still consider Whick home?"

She looks at her feet. *Why is he here?* Why is he asking her these questions? Why does each word he says a hot iron in her gut? "Yes, my lord."

"Cian. Please. Call me just Cian."

She gulps. He stands up and, in three quick strides, is beside her, engulfing her in his arms and holding her tight. "It is no crime to be homesick. I do not fault you for it."

She sobs, wishing she could hold it in until he was gone. *Why do you always do what your fathers tell you to do? What is it that you want?*

You, Brenna. Only you.

"Shhh. It will be fine," he says, gently running his hand down her back. "Why don't I take you there? We can sneak out tomorrow; no one has to know. We can spend a week there, you and me. Would you like that?"

"I... I cannot do that, I am sorry. I have to..."

"You have to be the obedient daughter, I know. I know. I apologize for imposing upon you, my lovely lady. Why don't I finish making dinner then, and I can serve you?"

Too confused and disoriented to reply, she allows herself to be sat in a chair and watches as the Crown Prince of Fayn ladles soup into bowls and places a perfectly plated meal before her. "My sister would make a wonderful queen," he says, jolting her out of her stupor.

"I am sure she would," is all she can think of to say in reply.

"She would probably be better than I, truth be told. Maybe I *could* abdicate. Maybe find myself a cozy cottage in some port town. Live a quiet life. Maybe a garden, maybe some cats. Maybe a beautiful lady and a few children?"

She drops her spoon. *Is he...?*

"Forgive me. I again troubled you. But, if that is what you want, a quiet life, mornings that smell like salt, and evenings that are cool with ocean spray? If that is what you want, well. I could make it happen. Give you that life; just say the word, Caitlin."

Diarmuid called upon her the next morning, apologizing for his absence; he had to go out of town unexpectedly, he says, but claimed he could give her no more information than that. He invited her to an early lunch with some of the other Red Front members and then to help them with some charity work on the edge of the city.

She took his arm with more than a little hesitation; she had stayed up too late talking to Cian. At one point, he found a wine bottle, helped himself, and insisted that she also partake. Her head spun as they walked, but she did not regret joining Diarmuid once she got there.

She falls into a pattern as autumn progresses. During the week, she works. On Samdá, she attends parties, hunts, and galas with Cian. And on Ysdá, she enjoys herself with her new friends.

"Umm, here..." Caitlin says, handing a bag of food to the old woman who answers the door.

"Is this all there is this week?" the woman asks, adjusting the colorful knit blanket draped over her frail shoulders.

"Kayla, hello," Aine says, approaching the door with a second bag.

"Oh, Aine, thank goodness, the grandkids will be so happy."

"How is your wrist?"

"Oh, same old. Every time I think it is better, I hurt it again," she says, tapping the blanket.

Caitlin slips away, feeling awkward, and stands waiting by the cart.

"Did you think she would bite you? What was that about?"

"I just don't know how to talk to them."

"Them?"

"The people we are helping, I just feel—"

"As people, you talk to them as people. Just treat them as people," Aine says, drawing her flask from her hip and taking several gulps, her upbeat nature ever-present, joking with the people they were helping and making mischief amongst us volunteers. "You are too used to negotiating, not giving, I take it?"

Caitlin looks away sheepishly.

She had feared people would resent her or think she was bragging if she spoke of her own life of plenty when they had nothing. But the conversations Caitlin has become less stilted and transform into the chatter of friends. She trades stories of childhood escapades and listens as young girls ask for advice on love and older gentlemen tease and joke.

"Come, let's go to the tavern after we finish up here. How about that?" Aine says, looking into her flask before turning it over in disappointment. Going to a tavern, Caitlin learns, is something of a mainstay. At first, this was uncomfortable, too. How could they possibly sit down and enjoy themselves, eat warm food under a roof? How could they do this when there were people without?

Caitlin hesitates.

"You can't help everyone," Aine says, throwing a bag over her shoulder. "You deserve this just as much as they do. And you need it if you are to do this. You cannot spend your time on this guilt. You need time to recharge. You will run yourself to the ground if you don't. You will burn out, become depressed, and then cynical or apathetic. You cannot do that. So, you sit back down, and you order more wine, and you play cards and make jokes."

Caitlin sighs. She has received this lecture several times, and by now, she does know why it's necessary. She learns to dance with her new friends in dimly lit taverns that smell like stale beer and relaxes enough to shout over the din of crowded bars to tell her bawdy jokes. Sometimes she glances next to her, expecting to see Brenna scrutinizing xir cards. Sometimes she thinks she hears Brenna chuckling as the dice clatter on the table. Sometimes, she swears she feels Brenna's soft fingers graze her back as she listens to Saoirse and Sharidan bicker over the poker rules. Of course, xie is never there. *I'm doing this for you,* she says. Your life was worth so much. *Greed should not have robbed me of you.*

"Very well. I think I can get away from the office for a little longer."

"Good girl," Aine says. "I'm gonna take this back to the house and get some more water. Meet you there? Would you mind finding

Kegan? Oh! And if you get there first, order me pickles! Lots of them!"

"No problem." Caitlin packs up her own satchels and boxes and finds Kegan waiting for her on the next street over.

"So, that volunteer at the school this morning?" Kegan says.

"What about them?"

"They were flirting with you," Kegan says, tail flicking. "I've been waiting all day to ask about that."

"They were not flirting with me."

"They were too! You really are dense; you act like you don't even realize it when people are flirting with you!"

"Stop it! They were absolutely not flirting with me!" Caitlin's hands are full of empty boxes, so she jabs her shoulder into Kegan's.

Kegan trips, nearly careening into a pile of leaves, but catches themselves and bumps into Caitlin. "Yes, they were! And you were flirting back!"

"I was not!"

Kegan's pale blue tail flicked back and forth. They smile and tilt their head to the side. "If you say so."

"You can be insufferable."

"But you looooove me."

Caitlin rolls her eyes. "My point still stands."

"C'mon. Let's get these back and then meet up with Diar and Aine for the regular round."

"Sounds good to me. But please don't sing again this time. We almost got kicked out."

"Not my fault that they don't like my songs."

"Kegan."

"I know, I know. You grew up with pirates, and somehow my songs are too lewd."

"You can't just start singing about—"

A chorus of terror echoes down the alleyway as they turn into it. There are people rushing towards them, not even looking back behind them to see if whatever has scared them is following.

"What's going on?" Caitlin yells to them as they race past.

"Guards! Royals, searching for something! Get out!"

"Oh, no!" Kegan drops the boxes and bags they are holding and dashes down the alley.

"Wait! Kegan, come back!" Caitlin chases after the Calla, but soon the air is full of smoke, making it far too hard to breathe. She can't push her way through the throng of people running the other way. Kegan is fast and dexterous, bouncing over people and leaping over objects in their way, but Caitlin is slow and clumsy and quickly loses them.

"No, no, no, no, no!" Even over the cacophony of the frightened masses and the shouts of Royal Guards, Kegan's cries could be heard.

"Caitlin, they found us! We have to get people out, though; we must see if there...Aine...Aine..."

Flames rise high above the street; the headquarters of the Red Front burning quickly and brightly, fire spreading to the houses next to it.

"No, Kegan, we have to run!" Caitlin grabs Kegan's wrist and tries to pull them away. "Kegan, please."

"You run, then!" Their eyes narrowing, their tail bristling. "I'm going to save our friends." They dig their claws into Caitlin's arm until she releases them, and then Kegan dashes away.

"Kegan, no!" Caitlin can barely breathe; the smoke is only growing darker, thicker. She tries to clear it by waving her arms in front of her, but it is no use. She reaches the back entrance to the house, and she finds Kegan standing in front of the gate. They are not moving, rigid, and only the slow blinking of their wide eyes gives any indication that they are alive.

"Kegan. We can't go in there. The fire, it's too big, and there are guards swarming."

"No." They shake their head. "No, no! Caitlin." Their knees give out, and they fall, their hands balling into fists. "No."

A gruff voice echoes down the alley. "I heard something; are we sure no one was going to get out the back?"

"We poured too much gasoline back there for anyone to get anywhere within the garden."

"Well, I'm going to check it out, anyway." The clack of the guard's copper-toed shoes is louder than the screams of the fleeing crowd, pounding in time to Caitlin's pulse.

"Kegan. Stand up." They don't move. Caitlin lifts the Calla to their feet.

"We have to save them! we have to save them!"

"We can't do anything if we're in the dungeons or dead."

They nod, finally relenting. The smoke covers their retreat, or at least Caitlin hopes so. The guard rounds the corner, but she sees him only as a shade, not even sure if he is there. She hopes he can't make them out, either.

Six

Love and Lies

*I*T WAS LATE WHEN *they woke up. Brenna holding Caitlin, wrapped in light cotton blankets. Caitlin stirred as Brenna pulled a stray hair away from her face and kissed her on the top of my head. "Good morning, sweetheart."*

Caitlin wanted to stay next to Brenna, to cuddle in closer. Wanted to savor the light spring breeze from the window, wanted to savor the scent of Brenna's hair, the softness of xir skin, the taste of xir mouth, wanted to study each curve and angle of Brenna's body until could draw a map of it. Wanted to silence the thousand racing thoughts in her head. Why had she done that? Losing herself, disconnecting from reality. A liminal space, just Brenna and her. Their bodies. Mouths. Hands. Hair being pulled, lips being bitten, nails tearing into backs.

Brenna had let Caitlin devour her, and Caitlin let Brenna ruin her body repeatedly.

"Mmmm, do you want to play again?"

Shaking her head, Caitlin jumped out of bed. Brenna frowned. The light of day told Caitlin that she'd slept far too late. She raced to find a dress in the wardrobe; she needed to get out there; she needed to attend to —.

"Whoa, slow down; what is up?"

"Ships are coming in!" Giving up on a suitable dress, she pulled a blouse out of her dresser and pulled it over her head, backward.

Brenna squinted. "Yes, that happens here."

"No, no, no! I need to get down there; there's no one down there that can—" She ripped a skirt out of the dresser. It did not match the blouse.

"Yes, there are. And the difference ten minutes will make is negligible. You can get dressed at a regular pace, eat a proper meal, get washed up. You do not need to rush."

"You don't understand! I shouldn't have done this; I don't know what I was thinking. I've never done this before." She riffled through the wardrobe again, huffed, and snatched yesterday's jacket from the floor.

Brenna grabbed Caitlin's hand and pulled her up against her chest. "I don't know if 'this' refers to having sex, sleeping in, or having someone in your bed still in the morning. But there are other employees in your business, ones that you trusted enough to hire. One late day will not make or break this business."

"But my fathers' will..."

Brenna stepped back from Caitlin, and one hand snaked under her chin, making Caitlin gaze up at her.

"Your fathers won't disown you. And I am sure they will not scold you for being a little late. Others can manage it for a little while." Xie kissed Caitlin lightly on the cheek, too close and so far from her mouth. Caitlin could not resist, and the two tumbled back into bed for another hour.

Brenna was right. Caitlin's reports managed the business at the docks, made the negotiations, kept the accounts in order as cargo was loaded and unloaded. Her employees had successfully completed all the morning's work. And they had done it well. She looked around at what anyone else would label 'chaos' and saw it was all in order, as well as she would have done herself.

"See?" Brenna came up behind Caitlin as she was reviewing some inventory paperwork. "Everyone got along fine. There are no fires, no yelling, no screaming. I see no one rushing up to you now that you are here with an urgent issue. No one panicking. No one has raced to you to let you know your fathers are looking for you."

Brenna stayed a week. And then two, and then a month, and for some reason, xie never found a reason to see if the inn had open rooms. They visited it every night, and Brenna became everyone's favorite drinking buddy. Caitlin would slip away after a few hours, and Brenna would follow her an hour later once xie had won back all xie had lost gambling.

"You're bringing Brenna home a lot. There're no rooms for her anywhere else? And she has not found a suitable ship to join as crew?"

Pa said with a laugh, throwing back a swig of ale, swinging his feet over the side of the dock.

"We keep forgetting to look," Caitlin says, staring intently at her apple.

"It doesn't appear the two of you are looking too hard for a room, nor that she is looking too hard for another ship," Pa said.

"You like her a lot," Da said, gentle as ever, tucking some papers into his pocket and joining them on the side of the dock for lunch.

"Yes, I do," she said, gazing at the sapphire-blue sea.

"Bring her around for dinner tonight," Da said.

"We surely got them this time." Sir Liam slowly places grapes in his mouth, sitting on the blanket. His long brown hair is tied with a leather strap, but it does nothing to stop the late autumn wind from making a mess of it.

"That is what you said the last time," the duchess replies, her own nearly-silver hair tied up in a tight crown braid. She is the only one who thought to dress for the weather with a layered wool dress and a large velvet cloak. The duchess usually prizes fashion over function. There is gray haze all around, but the prince does not care, so the rest of their party pretends that they also do not notice the nip in the air and the scent of rain and decaying leaves on the breeze.

"Yes, but this time is different," Sir Connor says, raising a glass of beer and leaning back, smiling as the wind tussles his shaggy black hair.

"Because they burned one building down?" Lady Clare crosses her arms. Whether in response to the cold or because she is angry is anyone's guess.

"Not just one," Princess Eleanor says. "They burned an entire neighborhood down. An entire neighborhood! Do you want people to sympathize with them?"

"Sister, sister. This isn't the place for that talk." Prince Cian's arm is wrapped around Caitlin's waist, and he keeps pulling her into his chest to place dates in her mouth. "It is such a beautiful day."

"Such a warm day, bright and clear. Everything smells so fresh. It is truly a beautiful day here," Princess Daya says, turning her face to the overcast sky and taking a large breath in. "It feels so good to be alive on days like this."

"Here's a toast to that!" Prince Cian shouts.

Caitlin raises her glass along with them, and while Prince Cian may have missed the flicker of a scowl on Princess Daya's face, Caitlin does not. As she sets her cup back down, Princess Daya looks directly into Caitlin's eyes and tilts her head to her. Caitlin nods back before taking a sip of her wine.

"It was so easy; they had infiltrated my factories," Sir Liam says, taking a second flask from his bag. "Those bastards had talked to our tenants, and they came to me with a list of demands! They tried to lay it out all nicely, claiming that better working conditions would make them better workers or some line like that…"

"You do not agree?" Princess Daya asks, picking at a block of cheese.

"Why would I care? I had a manager find out who had been organizing that. From there, poof! We found their nest." Sir Liam says, and Sir Connor clinks his flask against Sir Liam's.

"They'd been talking to the farmers, too. Trying to get local mayors to stand up to the lords. They wanted an audience with the king!" Sir Conner flings his arms out. "These people need to learn their place."

The prince sets down the plate of cheese and dates. "I said no more talk of this. I do not want today ruined. Set aside talks of riots, protests, or demands. I do not want to discuss it here; this is a day for leisure." He pulls Caitlin closer and kisses the top of her head. "I just want to enjoy the day with my beautiful lady."

Caitlin pulls back away from him; if the gods truly smile down upon the royal family, they have a strange way of showing it. She stands up, making a show of wrapping her arms around herself to fend off the chill.

"Where did this come from?" Sir Liam stands and looks at the dark clouds rolling in, the cold of a storm biting all of them.

"I wanted this to be the perfect picnic for my beautiful lady." He stands up, pulling Caitlin close, wrapping his own arms over hers. "We should get back to the palace. I wanted this to be the perfect day. It should not storm today."

"Brother, there are some things that you cannot control. The weather is one such thing. It is not yours to command." Princess Daya laughs, but it does not reach her eyes.

"My wife is correct; you act as if the clouds and rains are disobedient. Let's get home where you can order things to your liking."

He places Caitlin on his horse and climbs behind her; his breath on her neck is cold. His hands, as Caitlin is all too used to by now, roam along her back and waist as he makes a show of searching for the reins. She wants to recoil from his freezing touch, but she knows that her fate will not change by continued attempts to push him away.

This picnic was not just another attempt to impress her but to put on a show to the entire kingdom that he was in love. Finally, truly, happily, forever in love. However, at this point, everyone thought he won Caitlin's heart. The whispers about his infatuation had long ago turned to bets that ran the gamut of how long he would woo her before casting me off to when he would announce the pregnancy. But all of those bets are called off as they enter the palace.

She is gorgeous. A small button nose, sharp jaw, but tempered with soft cheeks and large eyes, all on a beautiful heart-shaped face. She is standing in a corner with Conlaoch Byrne, Earl of Berah, and his son, Lord Tynen. But when the prince is announced, she turns around; her loose, dark auburn hair shining as it catches the light from the candles.

"Your Highness, it is good to see you so well." Lord Berach sweeps his hands out in the deepest of bows.

"I have not seen you at court recently, Lord Berach."

"No, Your Grace. I've been busy on my estates." There is a slight quiver in his voice, and he looks to his left for a second to the beautiful woman who shares the same deep emerald eyes as the two Byrne men.

"Ah, and who is this?"

"This is my daughter, Lady Arlina."

"You have kept such a rose hidden away from court?" The prince kisses the top of her hand.

In the span of a second, coins change hands, and previously placed bets are altered. Caitlin feels the eyes of everyone in the room lingering on her and then flicking to Lady Arlina. *She is of noble birth;* she hears some whisper. *She is far prettier; Caitlin was always just an eccentric distraction, anyway,* some mutter. Others respond; *besides, he could not marry a widow.* She hears mumbles of derision and scorn; *I am surprised he has stayed with her so long; that a common girl could hold him for this long, good riddance to her, she sought a seat above her station.*

They look for worry in her face, they are looking for fear, for jealousy. But Caitlin just looks between the man who claimed to love her above all others and the woman he will supplant her with. All she can think, though, is that she will be free from this charade, finally.

But then Lady Arlina looks at Caitlin directly. This new beauty at court, the woman whose father wants to use her as a pawn, this beautiful woman who the whole court is now hoping will supplant Caitlin, this beautiful woman who has a controlling and haughty brother, a brother who pushed her into the path of the prince, to see her take Caitlin's place, this beautiful woman looks at her and smiles.

And behind those eyes, Caitlin sees the same resignation that lives in her own heart. The same acquiescence to fate, to the duty of parental interests. Lady Arlina knows what will come and is just as resentful of it.

"Lady Arlina." Caitlin knows that she will not be introduced formally to her, so she takes it upon herself to do so. She must. Something is driving her to spend even a second more in the presence of this woman. "Do you play cards? The princesses and I have been looking for someone to join us as a fourth while their ladies-in-waiting are away from court."

"Ah, my beautiful lady." The prince put his arm around Caitlin, not an act of love but a show of possession. "You are always looking for new friends. One of your many charms. Yes, please, join the games with us tonight, Lady Arlina. I cannot deny my beautiful lady a new friend."

And all bets are off again.

"We don't know how many got away. We have several safe houses throughout the country; it might take a while for them to send us word safely. It would be wise for them to stay there for several more weeks. But at this point, we assume those who have not reported in are dead." Diar had shown up unexpectedly after dinner. Caitlin had not heard from him since the fire. She had tried to contact him, but he either wasn't getting her messages or ignoring them. For all that he is her best friend, she is irritated by his propensity for moods and disappearing acts.

"Any other news?" Caitlin sips at the lukewarm tea; it does little to ward off the bitter cold that permeates her home, but she does not want to interrupt the conversation by making more.

"Those whom I have spoken to are going to ground, too. I assume they have also passed along messages, warning people to stay low." He cleans his glasses on his shirt and slumps back in his chair.

"Does staying low mean doing less charity work? Wouldn't that be conspicuous if suddenly that stopped?"

"Some people are on both sides of that argument. I think some of them will continue it." He puts his glasses back on and runs his hands through his hair.

"That argument?" She raises an eyebrow.

"Never mind that for right now."

"Is there word on finding a new headquarters?"

"A new one? What do you mean?"

"Well, the one that just burned…"

"Oh," he says, face turning scarlet. "That wasn't our headquarters. That was a test for you."

"What?"

"I trust you, Caitlin. But many others don't. If that place went up in smoke, or if guards showed up at any of the coordinates spouted off at the end of the meeting, well. We would know where it came from. And so, many believe it was you."

"I can't believe this!" She slams her mug on the table so hard that it shakes, the spoon rattling in the sugar bowl. "Is that why it's taken you so long to come to see me?"

"I don't want the royals or the Front thinking you're playing spy for the other side."

"And so, you steer clear of me for my protection, and I am assuming everyone else for suspicion."

"Yes, and no. Most everyone is staying clear of each other. It's not personal, but some suspect you."

With a huff, she takes her teacup to the kitchen. She leans against the counter, arms crossed, waiting for the water to boil. She can't go back in there just yet. *A test? And he stopped talking to her because a few people thought she failed it?* She burns her hand, grabbing the kettle without a mitt, cursing under her breath.

Diar hangs his head, eyes fixed on the floor, as she walks back in. "I'm sorry."

"You didn't talk to me for weeks. Didn't even bother to send a message that you were alright. Friends talk to each other. Friends discuss things, friends are open and honest with each other. What have you been?"

"Caitlin, you don't understand," he says, leaning forward, reaching for her hands.

"Then tell me!" She jolts back. "Then talk to me! Do you believe me so unable to think for myself?"

"There's so much you don't know."

"Then tell me!"

He looks down at his own mug of cold tea and then back up at her. "Fine. You're right."

"Promise me."

"I will."

"Good. Now, what is this about people suspecting me as a spy?"

"You must know that your volunteer work and your affiliation with the prince has been noted. And that has not stayed just in the neighborhoods you visit."

"I had not realized that anyone had made a connection."

"It has not gone unnoticed by the royals, either. Has anyone mentioned it?"

"Well, Princess Daya had said we could all do some charity together, bringing their attendants. Make it some sort of event, though I don't know if she wanted to do it as something advertised in advance."

"The king and prince would certainly want it to be such, prove they are as charitable as they want people to think, charitable enough that commoners are whining over nothing."

"I don't think that is what the princesses are trying to do." She frowns.

"They are royals," he says with a shrug.

"They are wonderful people; they've been very kind to me." *Far kinder than anyone else at court has been.*

"Royals still uphold a power structure, one that favors them over us."

"I like them, maybe..." She cleans dirt out from under her fingernails. "Maybe I could get them to realize..."

"Too dangerous right now. Although it has been mentioned by some that you could be *our* spy."

"Bring you information from the palace? I rarely have access to anything. And I'm trying to extricate myself from that viper's den, not further ingratiate myself. For what purpose? What would you need a spy for?"

"For one, I'm not asking you to. Others have brought it up. And second, we still don't know how they found us or how much they know."

"It was Sir Liam, the factory owner."

"What? How do you know that?"

"He was bragging about it. He has been enraged about his workers asking for safety measures."

"See, this is why others would ask you to spy."

"Do you want me to?"

"It's your choice, only yours."

"So, there are those that both suspect me of selling out a volunteer organization to the royals but also want me to spy? Spy for what? There's something more going on to this. This is more than protests and volunteering, isn't it?"

"I want to tell you, but I must talk to Sharidan and Valen first. This is a decision above my head."

"I am just confused why they would torch an entire neighborhood over some protests and charity work. Sure, some demands are radical, but there is nothing illegal happening. So why?"

"I'll talk to Sharidan and... No more talk of this, for now? Please? Let's get drunk and take a walk down to the harbor."

"That sounds nice, you know. I haven't talked to someone who has only half his head up his ass in a while."

"I have never been to the palace before," Lady Arlina says, sitting at the cherry round table in the corner of the princess' rooms. "The weather in Berach is not particularly enjoyable, but I hear it is often sunny in Eoi." She looks at the other women, her eyebrows raised. Prince Cian had wanted to go on a hunt again, but the weather had been too poor, and then his father had requested his presence for some matter or another. Princess Elizabeth had asked Caitlin if she wanted to join them for cards; her attendants were still away, and she and Eleanor required company. They had bumped into Lady Arlina as they left the Great Hall and invited her, too.

"I can say that it is nicer here than in Whick." She sits next to Lady Arlina, and the crackling of the fire on her back is not the only reason she suddenly feels so warm.

"Yes, you are a merchant's daughter! It must be so nice to live close to the sea," Lady Arlina says, smiling wide.

"I can take you some time if you would like," Caitlin says, her breath hitching.

"I would love that!" Lady Arlina says, her round eyes widening as she moves her chair closer to Caitlin's. "Do you go on the ships often?"

"Not as frequently as you would expect," she says, dealing out the cards. "We usually play for keeps, by the way."

"And I usually win." Princess Eleanor scoops up her hand with a flourish.

"You keep telling yourself that, sweetie."

"Daya is a sore loser." Princess Eleanor sets her cards down and removes her shawl. "So sometimes I let her win."

"You only ever win when Mistress Peddigree is your partner." Princess Daya places her cards face down and pulls the plate of sweets towards her, picking out the caramel squares and leaving the rest.

"Daya, dearest. Let's see if we can win together."

"So that makes Lady Arlina my partner?" Caitlin says, accepting the glass of wine from the maid and savoring the tannins as she sips.

"Well, then, I feel pretty lucky tonight," Lady Arlina says, flipping through her cards. "I promise not to disappoint you."

"I have never considered myself lucky, but if others believe so, who am I to dispute?"

"Why have you not come to court before?" Princess Eleanor sorts her cards. "If you do not mind my asking."

"My father kept me isolated. I grew up at the Temple of Aife. He has only just realized I am not ten years old anymore."

"What were you doing at the Temple of Aife? Call," Princess Eleanor says, smirking at Princess Daya.

"Studying, mostly."

"Double. Oh? What were you studying?" Princess Daya asks, her eyebrow raised over her spread of cards.

"Law, primarily."

"Which Temple? The one in Eoi?" Caitlin mulls over her next card before placing the queen of hearts on the table. "Royal flush."

Princess Eleanor throws down her own hand and slumps back in her chair. Princess Daya lays out a spread of spades.

"We won." Lady Arlina smiles. Princess Daya picks up the cards with a huff.

"If we had been playing just the two of us, you know I would have won." Princess Daya scowls at her wife.

Princess Eleanor shrugs. "Of course, sweetie."

"I was at the Temple in Laocre," Lady Arlina says, passing the cards at the center of the table to Caitlin, her finger brushing Caitlin's hand.

"Why law?" Caitlin shuffles the deck, ignoring the tingle on her palm.

"Once, I had hoped to be an adviser or lawyer."

"That reminds me! Would you please answer a question I have been wondering about my whole life? The Laocre temple has vast lands, and they keep rather secretive about that. If all the teach is law, why do they need so much land?" Princess Daya says, counting the rest of her dael as Caitlin deals out the cards again.

"I could not say," Lady Arlina says. "Truly, a mystery."

"It is rather interesting; even the king's advisers could not hope for such an extensive and exhaustive education in law. How laws have changed, theories of law, foreign law, international law. With Aife being both a goddess of war and law, makes sense, for war is often the creator of law," Princess Eleanor says.

Lady Arlina inspects her cards, rearranging them in her hand, not concerned with commenting further.

"Why did you leave? Was it your father?" Caitlin glances at her cards, far too enthralled with Lady Arlina's tale to give it any actual thought. "Are you here to find a suitor?"

"Of course not!"

"That is a shame. I am sure you will have at least a dozen marriage proposals by the end of the week." Princess Eleanor glances at Caitlin. "The court will be sullen and miserable for months if you snub everyone."

***

The prince's personal secretary is waiting for her at the door when she returns late in the evening from a business meeting with wool sellers from the Galiven region of Garcelon, sellers who had been all too happy to provide her with the finely dyed wool cloak she now pulls more tightly around her. Winter is just a few weeks away, and these Garcelonian merchants could not have picked a better time to arrive stocked with their finest fibers. "I have a letter and a gift from the prince," is all that he says as he hands over the items. He shifts his weight from one foot to the other, clearly waiting for a response, and she waves him into her home. It would not be polite to let the man stand outside in such frigid weather.

My dearest Lady Caitlin,

It grieves my heart every moment we are apart; I am struck with such a heavy melancholy. That such a bond could exist defies all logic. I cannot bear it any longer. I extend an invitation to your most beautiful self and your ever-diligent fathers, Sir Teige and Sir Rían Peddigree. A dress should accompany this message. Pray, do accept this invitation. It is most urgent.

Most Humbly Yours,
Cian

He does not use his title, and even though she does not hold a title that would afford her "Lady", he uses it nonetheless. His saccharine letter offends her: the writing juvenile.

The letter set aside; she sets the box on a desk and opens it. The dress, like his letter, is overstated, past grand and into gaudy. Accompanying it are a pair of equally offensive shoes and a circlet.

"Will you be in attendance tonight, Lady Caitlin? And Sir Teige and Sir Rían?" The secretary says. If he is nervous, he does not show it, maintaining a neutral face and even tone despite this being a most awkward situation. The use of "lady" feels like sandpaper in her ears, and her fathers have never been granted any title, either. Prince Cian has been calling her 'lady' for some time, but his staff is using it, too? And the same courtesy extended to her fathers?

She pulls the dress into her chest and beams. "How could I ever say anything except 'yes'?"

"Very well, Lady Caitlin. I shall inform his Highness." He doffs his hat and leaves.

She marches upstairs to her living quarters, the offending garments bunched in her arms. Tossing them onto the floor, she stomps to her kitchen and opens a bottle of wine, drinking directly from it.

"Caitlin? Where are you? Heavens, what are you doing?" Da asks as he and Pa walk in only a few moments later. "Did the meeting not go well?"

"It went well enough; the deal is as good as sealed. That," she says, pointing toward her living room, "that *thing* on the floor in there is altogether another sort of deal. One that I want nothing to do with anymore. I'm done. I'm done!"

Da picks up the items off of the floor and hands the letter to Pa, crinkling his nose as he holds out the dress in front of him.

"Tonight? All of us?" Pa says, running his hand through his ash-black hair.

"I am supposed to wear that dress this evening. I would rather drown than wear it, let alone attend whatever this event is."

"You cannot cancel on the prince," Pa says.

"I know, I know, it would be bad for business," she says, flinging her arms in the air and spilling some of the wine.

"No, Caitlin. It has nothing to do with the business."

"Don't say that. Everything is business with you. That's all you care about. And that's all you want me to care about." She takes a large gulp of wine, not caring as some dribbles down her chin.

"That is not true. Please, do not insult us by putting words in our mouths. If this were an invitation from a business partner and you wanted to cancel, even if it were the most important deal we have ever been offered, we would not stop you from canceling."

She rolls her eyes, knowing the lie for what it is. "I don't want to wear that dress."

"I do not blame you, dear," Da says, holding it at arm's length. "The materials hardly complement each other, and what is this frill supposed to be adding? Beads and embroidery? Who made this atrocity?"

"Someone that the prince hired, and I am not going to ask any more than that," she says. Dizzy, she collapses into a chair.

"Well, there is no getting out of attending this event, but I think I can find a way for you to wear the dress while not having to wear it," Da says, setting it down on the dining table. "Where do you keep your sewing supplies?"

"I'll grab them," she says. "But he told me to wear it..."

"No, you're not going anywhere. Stay seated, I will get them," Pa says. She does not argue, just tilts the bottle again, disappointed to realize it's empty.

"He requested that you wear it, and you still will wear it. Technically."

"I would risk upsetting him," she says. "But I have been doing nothing but trying to politely upset him for months now." She frowns, brows furrowed as Pa returns and sets the notions next to the dress. "You think you can fix it?"

"Here, we can pull out the beads and add some of this trim on the sleeves," Da says.

"Oh, that's brilliant," Pa says, pulling out spools of threat from her basket.

"Why do you think he wants this? Why not send a regular courier? Why send a dress? Why hasn't he tired of me? Why is he still doing this?" She pounds her fist on the table, knocking over the container of pins. "Why!"

"No one else has caught his eye, I suppose," Pa says. "He's made his way through half of the eligible noblewomen, and the other half are probably not as beautiful as he wanted."

"I heard there is a new beauty at court." Da takes a seam ripper to the frills around the sleeves.

"Lady Arlina, daughter of the Earl of Berach."

"Yes, that's the one. He hasn't shown interest in her?"

"He was taken with her, yes." Caitlin's heartbeat quickens, Lady Arlina's face clear in her mind's eye.

"It is strange then that he has not started chasing her." Pa sits down next to Da and hands him shears.

"She's very strong-willed, well-educated, well-read; she has goals and dreams. She studied law and does not want to find a partner.... She's far too headstrong for him."

"So are you, Caitlin." Da looks up from his alterations work. "If you wanted to be."

"That was a long time ago. That was before I had so many responsibilities. Seriously, what does he want with a widow? There are dozens of women in their twenties, younger and more gullible."

PART TWO

SEVEN

Assignments and Assassins

Xie was just as animated as Pa, joking and laughing and, to Caitlin's annoyance, making terrible puns. Xie fit in right away. Caitlin would not have asked her fathers if she could bring Brenna around. And they had never offered to have one of Caitlin's partners over before. They somehow knew that Brenna was different. Walking back home from their dinner with her fathers, hand in hand with Brenna, Caitlin knew that her fathers loved xir just as much as she did

A year had gone by since Brenna had arrived and then accidentally stayed. Xie was no longer a novelty; nearly every ship that came to the port had seen xir. Xie had put aside xir copper circlet, woven like a wreath, with a tall horn adorning it. Xir ahnhörn. If nothing else had given xir away, the ahnhörn did. But xie didn't wear it past that first day. When Brenna and Caitlin stopped pretending that the inns were all conveniently full, xie put it in a sturdy box and placed it in the back of their closet.

Xie had been harassed a few times, people cursing xir for xir people selfishly hoarding their wealth or claiming that Ástfriður were devils who haunted the seas and controlled the waves; some said that the Ástfriður who came over and stayed were greedy or uncivilized. Some people believed they had the power to lay curses, a magic that could stop a person's heart, or that the Ástfriður could sink ships with just a thought. There was a litany of reasons that people would want to hurt Brenna. But the ones that concerned Caitlin the most were those who wanted to take xir on their vessels and force xir to navigate to secret ports or beaches, the ones of which only the Ástfriður knew. Ports that would allow them to sack the Veiled Forests and plunder the Isles of its treasures.

Xie had been lucky that xie had found honorable captains as xie had traveled Ahnlisen. But it was never captains at the Whick ports that would make those comments, but the crew. No one would upset the most profitable dock owners in Fayn, the ones who ran the port with the most traders and cargo. To take Brenna, now firmly known as the partner of a Peddigree, would be to risk their current fortunes for one that might not even exist. And, more importantly, after a night at the inn, they knew they would never let anyone harm xir for their own love of xir.

Xie decided it was time for Caitlin to see more of the world. A vacation, xie called it. They rode to Sanras, a city on the edge of a forest, on a warm and clear summer day. It was so much larger than Caitlin had imagined. There were so many shops, and cuisines, and fashions;

a creative's dream, an artist's alcove, a musician's heaven. The streets were festively decorated, and the placards in front of storefront's all brightly painted. Her mind was appraising everything's value—the dresses that the sprightly dancers wore were made from cotton and were made by an expert seamstress. How much would they sell for? The silk shirts adorning the thespians giving a street performance must be worth— "Stop it, sweetheart."

"Stop what?" They had made it to the center of the town, a fountain at the center, the goddess Fianna presiding over it. The square was full of people milling about outside of shops chatting, seated on the fountain ledge showing off their new purses or jewelry. The scent of pies and cakes and prime meats tempting even the most ardent spendthrift. It was as busy as the ports, but somehow it seemed less orderly. Musicians were singing about heroic deeds, and poets were teasing lovers with sonnets. Artists were on the edges with makeshift stalls, some selling paintings or small sculptures. This truly was Fianna's square.

"You aren't negotiating with any of the people here. Stop acting like you are."

Caitlin blushed, looking away. Caught again.

"No need to look so glum. Come here!" Xie pulled her closer and then spun her around, skirt flying. Caitlin laughed and laughed and laughed as xie spun her again and again. "We're here to have fun, sweetheart!"

Both overcome with dizziness, Brenna sat Caitlin on the edge of the fountain. Xie kneeled on the ground before her. She patted the spot next to her. "What are you doing? You look silly down there."

She saw them before she heard them. A small band made its way towards them, singing of the goddess Muriel and the oceans she ruled over. Oceans that would unite lovers from different sides of it.

"Will you?"

She would not know the full meaning of this ritual until Brenna explained it on their wedding night. Xie pulled three coils of copper from xir pocket.

"Will you, Caitlin, marry me?"

"Of course. What else would I say?"

Brenna smiled, holding the strands of copper coils close to xir chest. Without touching it, the copper bent itself, curved itself into a perfect intertwining circle, a whole and unbroken bracelet. No seam, no scratches, no weak spots where it might have been melted, or welded, nothing to give away that it had not always been shaped like this. It was magic. Magic, which was a myth, which wasn't real. Which couldn't b e real.

And yet, Brenna slipped this magic-forged bracelet over Caitlin's wrist. "Ahnií, eil stre ástrielta san. Beloved, I will show you the stars."

She had expected there to be some sort of extravagant party going on, something the entire court would be in attendance for, something spectacular or, more likely, gaudy. Although perhaps it would not have been if it were the king hosting it. Despite the lightly falling snow, she is led to the rose garden. Prince Cian is waiting there, seated near a gorgeous fountain, flanked by his mother and father on one side and his sister and sister-in-law on the other. Looming near the rose bushes are two priests of Culain. In the distance, she hears a band playing a haunting and lilting melody. At the top of the fountain is a statuette of the goddess Muriel, with engravings of waves, moonlight, and stars around the base.

"Here she is, my gorgeous lady, she who has stolen my heart."

She smiles at him through veiled lashes. "My lord."

"And Sir Teige, Sir Rían, thank you for joining us tonight. You must know how happy your Caitlin makes me. She has been an incredible blessing, as I am sure she is to you, too. Culain, in His wisdom, granted you such a gift in your daughter."

She does not hear her fathers' replies. There is something tugging at the edges of her memory, something pulling her away from this time and this place. Something that does not belong here.

He places his hand around her waist—how often has he done this?—and leads her forward. She leans into him and lets herself be guided to the fountain's edge. Her stomach lurches. *This is wrong, this is very wrong.* This is the wrong person, the wrong fountain, the wrong players, the wrong stage, the wrong day, the wrong weather; all of it is wrong.

Not here, not this. This is a farce; this has to be... don't let this be this.

He kneels in front of her. No one meets her gaze as her eyes dart wildly around, pleading for someone to stop this, screaming for the nightmare to end. *Not this, not thi*s. The damage is already done, though. The comparison between the dream and the nightmare already taking root in her mind, the paradise of the past, the paradise she lost. The association is made, and memories have no care for feelings.

"I have been called a playboy before," he starts. "People have called me fickle or too picky." She swallows. She does not want this. The music crescendos, a sweet violin singing as a siren might. "I realize now that I was waiting for the right person. I had been searching all these years, for one thing, for one person. And then I met you; I did not even know your name at first. But I saw you in the crowd, and I knew. I knew you were meant to be at my side. I know you felt it, too."

She nods, but it is not an acknowledgment of his words: it is an acknowledgment of her fate. She has never had any control over her life. All she has ever wanted, and the world has stolen it away. Her mouth dry, eyes wide, and body numb, the icy air unable to penetrate her fear. How did this happen? She'd done everything right; she'd done everything right! She had worked hard. She had a beautiful home, a beautiful wife, family, and friends that were family. Someone stole that from Caitlin, stole xir from Caitlin. She had come here, rebuilt, despite wanting so much not to have to. And now, someone is stealing that away from her, too.

"I never want to lose you; you have seized my heart, you have penetrated my defenses, and I am naked before you. I have had advisers, friends, family," he continues on, "tell me that this was not proper.

That I might have had fun with you, but it was my duty to marry for the good of the kingdom, my duty to find a person of noble birth, or align myself with a foreign ally through marriage. I was told repeatedly that a king's consort must be raised to it, that it is not a station that can be taught. But I know they are wrong, Caitlin."

The lump in her throat grows, eyes sting with tears. At least, if she cries, he might take it as joy and not sorrow. Not grief. Never grief. She cannot not grieve a freedom that she never had. The hands of fate are not her own. She had struggled so hard against it. But fate has always been determined to find her, to steal from her what measures of happiness she has tried to make for herself. The world has ripped Brenna from her arms, and apparently; it is not done striping her of happiness.

"You have wrought a change inside my heart, and I have the resolve now to stand up to my advisers, to make my own road, to carve my own fate." For the first time since he began his speech, his eyes wander away from her, glancing almost imperceptibly at the priests. "And I want you to carve that path with me. You and I—we—can change the world together. We shall be free of traditions of birth and marriage. I want to be free to show them that you are bright and smart and will make a clever and intelligent queen. Show them that the monarchy does not need to stagnate, that we can find our happiness and claim it, take it. You make me so happy, Caitlin. I want to make you happy, too. For the rest of our lives."

She nods while he takes her hands in his own. She glances at her fathers, seated next to the king and queen, waiting for them to tell her what to do. But neither moves even in the slightest. The prince gazes at her, and she looks into the eyes of her jailor, her captor. The person who holds her fate, her freedom, more firmly in his hands than she can comprehend.

"They told me I could not have you." Again, a quick glare at the priests. "You were a widow. You might be too old to give us a child, you might be too wild for a refined court, for many have heard of your younger days with pirates and thieves, that maybe you still are partial to ruffians, that your loyalties to your fathers would be placed before your loyalties to me. They told me these things and tried to change my mind."

She told him these things in so many ways, so many times. Protesting when he called her "Lady", pushing back when he called her graceful. When Sir Liam and Sir Connor would make their jokes, she would bring up stories of the sailors she sang with. The many times she tried to dissuade him, prove to him that his advisers were correct. Gently, at all times, and humble to the last. Never make it sound like she was complaining of his affections, just that she was not worthy of them.

"Caitlin, I do not care. This is my life, and this will be my kingdom. If I do not decide my own path now, what good will I be as king? I love you, no matter what anyone else may tell me. I would love you if I were a merchant who met you on business. I would love you if I were a peasant and you a fellow villager, my station, your station, matter not. So, marry me, please, my lady. By my wife, be my queen."

She straightens her back, false confidence in the face of fate. "How could I ever say anything but 'yes?'"

The band plays a lively tune as he pulls her up and swings her around. *Not this, not this.* Her cheeks cool as her tears dry. "Can you imagine," he whispers in her ear as he dances with her, "a whole life together."

"No. I never could have imagined this. Never had I thought that this was possible."

He leads her in a merry step dance, his closet company joining in. The smell of chocolate wafts through the air as servants wheel a chocolate fountain into the garden, and the sound of glass clinking echoes as toasts are made; everyone is laughing and chattering and speaking of the many happy years to come for the newly engaged pair and for the kingdom. Everyone except Caitlin.

"I want to tell you what is going on," Valen says, their posture rigid in their chair. Their normally opalescent hair hangs limply around their face, dull and gray.

The Calla and *Ástfriður* who sit across from her are de facto leaders of the Red Front. As such, the elegant Valen and leonine Sharidan are tasked with much of the behind-the-scenes work, as well as ensuring the safety of the members. Both now don the same bags under their eyes and the same creases on their foreheads, and Caitlin knows it is not because they are still recovering from New Year's celebrations.

Aine and Kegan's dining room is cozy, warm, and welcoming with its dark brown walls and open stone hearth, a dozen mismatched trinkets lining it, keeping away the harsh cold of the storm starting outside. Kegan and Diar sit on either side of Caitlin while Aine makes coffee and sweets in the kitchen, the sweet smell tempting Caitlin even though she and Diarmuid had a full meal before they came over. Kegan's usual chipperness has faded since the fire; they ignore jokes and do not take part in the usual teasing, and not even Aine can bring them back from their depression.

"This is not the first time Kegan has watched their home burn down," Aine had discreetly told Caitlin when she arrived. "But this was the first time that they lost someone they loved because of it."

They have all taken turns checking in with them, bringing them food and tea. But they watched as Kegan pulled away. That Kegan is socializing at all is hope enough that they might come back.

"Yes?"

"Your work with us in direct service has warranted that we trust you, and we hope that you trust us enough to do what are about to ask of you."

"Ask of me?" A pit forms in her stomach.

"We are creating an army. We are stockpiling weapons. We are recruiting from the whole of Fayn and from Garcelon, Janeuq, Qaewi, Sua, and as many as possible as far as we can. As much as we can."

"For what?"

"To topple monarchies, to throw down kings, to dismantle oppressive regimes, to liberate the people."

"That's a huge undertaking..."

"It is. But we need a society where everyone has their needs met. A society with no impoverished families, no struggling elders, no starving children, where food and resources are not hoarded just for their greed."

"This really is about more than just the protests..."

"It is. Not everyone here agrees with our methods, though. There is a smaller faction that keeps trying to convince me and Sharidan that there are other ways. Those peaceful protests, petitions, meetings, letters... They think we can beg nicely, that if we just ask nicely enough, maybe the king will assent to some concessions and cede a smidgen of power to the people."

She thinks of Sir Liam again. He would laugh in the faces of workers who asked to be treated with any kind of dignity.

"The system has to fall. Diarmuid says you can be trusted. And I trust him. So, I trust you to help us. Will you help us?"

Caitlin swallows. She is not thinking about the specifics of what they might ask. Instead, she sees the faces of the men who killed Brenna and the priest who condemned Morrin. "I don't understand what I could do," she says.

"We've worked so hard to make people see the monarchy for what it is and to see that there is a way to improve our lives. The people you've helped? They will see you being a princess as a sign that royalty can be kind, can be charitable, can be benevolent. And endorsement of the system we want to destroy," Valen says.

Caitlin looks between Diarmuid and Kegan. Diarmuid, clenching his fist in frustration or anger, she can't tell which. Kegan, impassive. Aine sets a mug of coffee and a plate of cookies in front of Kegan, squeezing their shoulder, and returns to the kitchen.

"We need the people to love you, though, if you are to be a spy," Sharidan says, their dark orange tail twitching. "It is a very delicate line."

"A spy," she says. An informant, bringing them vital information that would shape their strategies, details from private meetings, from senior advisers, and from the king himself. Being elevated to princess-to-be came with greater positions, higher obligations, and larger responsibilities. All of which will grant her access to the hidden agendas as the nobles now vie for her favor.

"Our plan is that we will get information from you, whatever you can get to us. Whatever you can do internally to turn their attention away from our activities, to tie them up in other affairs. But the people must love you so that there is no way that the prince could discard you easily," Valen says. "And, if we can pull this off, you will endorse our new government when the time comes."

"This is an awfully thin line to walk," she says. A spy and a symbol.

"It is necessary." Sharidan looks her squarely in the eye; it is not a threat though, just a firm statement of fact.

Kegan sets their hand on Caitlin's thigh. That they have lost confidence in the leadership to actually keep the members safe is obvious, and Caitlin does not blame them.

"And if I am found out?" She shifts in her chair, crossing her legs.

"You won't be," Valen says.

"You will make sure of that? The prince is not the kindest when he is angry, and I doubt I will be treated with more mercy than others." Caitlin accepts the warm mug from Aine as Aine serves the rest of the group.

"We have plans in place to ensure you don't get caught. Like Kegan here." Her head whips around, and Kegan flinches away from Caitlin's gaze. "You will name Kegan one of your attendants, and having another asset inside will help keep you safe."

"With all due respect to Kegan, I mean this as no insult, but Kegan would stick out at court. Wouldn't someone a little more," she pauses, searching for the right word, "mild-mannered, be better able to pass in a royal court?"

"We had considered that. And Saoirse had been suggested when we first started considering this. But Kegan is our brightest code-maker and linguist. They can create ciphers that are all but uncrackable and crack ciphers that others claim to be that secure and speak several languages."

The faintest smile passes across Kegan's lips before they resume their stoic observations. "Regardless, another Red Front member will have easier access to the outside world. They can request time to meet with their family and use that to report back to us, and letters they send to 'family' will not be as well scrutinized as yours. Their coming and goings from the palace will be unremarkable."

"People will surely ask how I know them, however. What my relationship is to Kegan, how long, all that."

"You could say that they are a fellow leader in Peddigree Trading." Sharidan continues their steady eye contact, but their tail twitches almost imperceptibly.

"A story anyone could look into and know for the lie it is."

"Have you been asked for your list of potential attendants? I am assuming that the prince will have his own list, and many others in the court will be wanting their daughters to be one of your ladies or maids." Sharidan sits up straighter, biting into a cookie and letting the crumbs tumble to the table, and Valen leans back in their chair, lacing their hands behind their head, content to allow Sharidan to take the lead here.

"No, I have had no word of that. So far, it's just the small circle of friends."

"Well, Kegan can be hired at one of the larger ports. A position overseeing it if at all possible. A job similar to your current one."

"Taern's Keep is our second largest. It has a lot of international trade and good relations with Suan traders."

"Perfect!" Valen says, still reclining casually. "We can make arrangements tomorrow for Kegan to travel there, and you can ask your fathers for the official paperwork hiring them."

"And how am I supposed to know Kegan if they are working in Taern's Keep? How am I supposed to put together any sort of plausible story that I personally know them? Placing them in Taern's keep might be strategic in proving that they are an employee of repute, but what about a personal connection strong enough that would want me to make them an attendant?" Kegan keeps their eyes down; they are in a similar, terrible situation. Their life is about to change drastically from what they thought it would be; from what they wanted it to be. Upended just as thoroughly as Caitlin's, and both staring down further changes.

"You could say you hired them from a frequent trader in Whick, that you've known them a long time as someone you had frequent interactions with for years." Valen tugs at a lock of their dirty hair.

"I suppose that may work better than anything else I can think of."

"Then it is settled." Valen springs up again and extends their hand to Caitlin.

"No, it isn't. You're forgetting two very important things," Diarmuid says, pulling Valen back into their chair.

"Yes?" Valen raises an eyebrow.

"Kegan and Caitlin have not agreed to the plan."

"But you—"

"He is right," Caitlin says. "We cannot agree to a plan without the full details. Now that we know what this would involve, we can discuss it and decide. But I have not yet agreed. Kegan has not yet agreed."

"Caitlin, this is our chance. This is necessary. We won't get another opportunity like this."

"No. It is Caitlin's decision; it is Kegan's decision. You cannot force them into this." Diar smacks his fist hand onto the table. "We cannot ask people to do that which is beyond their ability." His eyes remain trained on the leaders of the rebellion forces he has been with for years. Leaders he looks up to, trusts, follows.

"I will do it. But Kegan has to decide their part, too." Caitlin takes Kegan's hand. "They have given so much already to this cause. You cannot ask more of them in good conscious."

"I will do it, too. I will do it. Promise me that Aine stays safe." Kegan turns to Diarmuid. "Make sure she stays healthy. She doesn't like that mixture at all, and I have to force her to drink it sometimes. You have to promise me that you make sure she stays healthy."

Diarmuid nods solemnly.

"Good. I'll scratch your eyes out if I find out she's fainted even once."

Diarmuid nods again.

"I am going to pack my things. Let me know when I am moving out." They bound out of the dining room, their footsteps echoing on each stair.

Caitlin gets up to follow them, but Diarmuid grabs her hand, shaking his head.

"I am sure you have your own things to take care of, Caitlin. How can we help you prepare?"

"Valen, may I speak to you alone?"

Sharidan cocks xir head to the side, but Diarmuid stands and leaves without a word.

"Please?"

Valen smiles. "Of course. What do you need?"

"I have... I have Brenna's... xir *ahnhörn*. I have... I don't know how to get it back..."

"You have...? Oh." Valen slumps. "You know, then."

"Yes, our wedding night, xie explained."

"It is rare for any of our kind to share that information with outsiders. But xie gave you a gift, didn't xie? You aren't an outsider."

"Yes, the bracelet, and then when we... Our wedding. I am sorry, I can't..."

"Do not worry. I can handle it, if that is what you are asking. I just need to know which clan Brenna belonged to in this life."

"Mountain-at-Dawn."

"Oh, that makes sense. You either fall in line there, or you leave. I left, too. It saddens me that we never crossed paths in this life. Perhaps in our next, we will. I can get xir *ahnhörn* back to Mountain-at-Dawn, and they will make preparations for Brenna's next life. I'll make sure of it."

She replays the conversation over and over in her head. It is a bitterly chilly night; she cannot find enough blankets to stave off the cold. She needs to be awake early for yet another meeting with the head of staff at their operation in Taern's Keep about Kegan's employment.

But she can't stop repeating every word from her date with the prince that morning.

He told her that he was gifting her with her own title, her own lands, her own estate. She will now be the Duchess of Laocre. Lady Laocre. He had asked his father to create a new title. Laocre had been lands held by the crown, but now they are hers.

"I forgot to mention, but you will need a regnal name," he had said, taking her hand.

"A what?" She squints at him.

"A royal name. A regnal name. For when we take the throne, but you will be given it when we make the formal announcement. I have picked 'Gráinne' for you. Princess Gráinne, but of course, I will still call you Caitlin. It is just for formal ceremonies and occasions."

"A new name?"

"Sweetheart, you will still be 'Caitlin' to me; do not worry."

A new name: she'd already agreed to the engagement, she'd already agreed to help the Red Front with their plans, she'd already agreed with her fathers to go through with this for the sake of their business.

She is drowning, gasping for air. But that's impossible. How can she be drowning? She's lived her whole life on the water, on boats, on beaches; she is of and from the seas. Why can't she swim? A ship. She needs to find her ship. But she doesn't know which way is up or down, and saltwater is filling her lungs. Where is her ship? She does have a ship, right? She has to. She is the wife of a pirate; surely there is a ship. Surely her wife will save her…

She is the wife of a pirate; she is. She won't drown. She won't.

The dais is decorated in cloth of gold, richly embroidered with the royal seal and the personal coat of arms of the Royal House of Fola. The thrones upon it are not as ornate as the ones in the audience chamber but nonetheless trimmed with elaborate carvings and crushed velvet. The dais looms in the distance, the early spring sun reflecting from the awning, illuminating it with an unearthly glow, a supernatural glow.

While she has not been given a crown, a silver circlet sits on her brow. It weighs down on her; it presses against her memory. Brenna had had a circlet far more beautiful than this. Their engagement did not involve a procession to the palace, it did not need the people's approval. They'd had all the approval they could want, more clearly part of the fabric of the town than royalty could ever be to the capital.

Her gown is simple compared to what he had sent her for the proposal; it is delicate, soft velvet, and subdued, the same pale blue as Prince Cian's eyes, and only a little lace lining the hems of the sleeves. Surely someone else selected it, someone in charge of ceremony and rituals. Someone with far more sense than Caitlin's new fiancé. It is so different from the gown she had worn when Brenna and she had told her fathers. Her wedding to Brenna… but now she must look forward—or dread—to a second wedding.

Prince Cian sets his hand on her thigh. "It will be fine, my beloved. They already love you." She glances away, not trusting herself to say anything at all. "Lady, look at me." He grabs her chin and lifts it to bring her eyes to his. "You are gorgeous, you are kind, you are going to be the jewel of the kingdom. Head up. Take pride in who you are. Show them that you are proud and will love them as they will you."

Keeping her head up, a smile on her face, looking forward as if towards the future, says, "Yes, sweetheart." The horses are spurred into trots, and the procession makes its way through the streets of Eoi.

"Long live the king" and "Bless the Lady Laocre" ring across the crowd, acceptance from the people. Roses are thrown towards the carriage, cheers of congratulations accompanying them. But some in the crowd scowl; arms crossed; appraising the occupants, leering in dismissal. She meets the eyes of people she knows to be part of the Red Front along the way. What Valen or Sharidan told people about her and about this plan, she does not know. But she hopes it is as little as possible; this secret being revealed would take any advantage they have away.

When they reach the dais, a footman opens the carriage, and Prince Cian steps out. When he comes around to help her out of the carriage, the expectant faces of the crowd stare back at her. His smile is radiant but not the face of a man in love. He wears the expression of a child who finally got the toy he had been asking for or an old man who is relishing a meal full of foods that his doctor had forbidden him from eating. If the people have any commentary on his sincerity, they do not share it. She bows her head as he takes her hand, but then he lifts her up in his arms, her skirts fluttering as he spins her around before setting her gently back on the ground. Cheers ring out, a princess they can love because she is a princess that their finicky prince can love. He holds her close and kisses her forehead as the crowds continue their joyous cries. Her eyes stay fixed on the ground, fear and anxiety mixed in with the desperate hope that she can fool a country as well as she has fooled Prince Cian.

Behind the thrones of the king and queen sit the extended royal family. King Tarmon's brother, Allil Fola, Duke of Hern, and his wife, Doireann, Duchess of Hern, their daughter Lady Elwen, and her husband, Sir Nait Loughlin. The king's sister, Maeve Fola, Duke of Dontaue, has chosen not to marry at all. And his niece, the Duchess of Clare, Aelena Fola, whose father, Tómas Fola, passed away years ago. All of the direct descendants of King Dunlain and Queen Maele bear the same striking pale skin, translucent blue eyes, and near-white hair. Despite Queen Maele being a political match as a member of the Royal Family of Janeuq, none of her children inherited her green eyes, ebony hair, or golden-brown skin.

Her feet hurt in the tight slippers, and each step up the stairs is agony as she resists the urge to lift her dress where it trails, turn around, and run. Instead, she leans against Prince Cian for support. Another tableau: grace and dignity where she feels she should have none.

King Tarmon and Queen Isleen rise from their thrones. The queen embraces Caitlin, warm, gentle, and nurturing. "They love you, dearheart," she whispers into Caitlin's ear. Caitlin's meetings with her soon-to-be in-laws had been brief. While Princess Eleanor's marriage had been a political match, the queen was thrilled that both of her children were still with loving partners. She fancied that her own marriage was a love match, even though it was arranged. The queen's faith in the power of love, especially the love between her son and Caitlin, is naïve, in Caitlin's opinion. Naïve and dangerous.

King Tarmon steps forward, arms outstretched, his chin-length white hair blows in the wind, and his equally white beard is freshly trimmed. His narrow and deep-set eyes are the same ghost-blue eyes that all of the Fola House have. A stark contrast to his Garcelonian wife, with her golden eyes, tanned, umber skin, and dark chestnut hair.

"My loyal subjects! We are pleased to announce the engagement of—"

The fletch of an arrow embeds itself deep into his chest, and a bloody rose blooms on his golden coat. He coughs once and collapses into the arms of the queen. There is nothing but silence and his gasps for air. For three awful heartbeats, everything is frozen.

When the queen screams, Caitlin feels the anguish in her own bones. Guards descend, pushing the rest of the family back and rushing him away from the crowds, away from the madness that is breaking out. Princess Eleanor grabs Caitlin's hand and drags her away from the edge of the dais. "Let's go! Caitlin, let's go!"

She shakes her head and follows. Looking back at the crowd again, she sees Aine sitting stoically on the top ring of the giant fountain at the center of the plaza next to another Calla. She blinks, but both Calla are gone.

EIGHT

Dangers and Dukes

For security, they move Caitlin in with Princess Daya and Princess Eleanor. Lady Arlina had offered one of the rooms from her family's suites, too. But in the end, she is royal now and therefore deserving of royal suites and personnel. It has been a week since the king was shot, and there is still no word on his state of health nor on who the assassin is. The celebrations that had been planned after the official announcement of the engagement have been canceled, and feasts, parties, and other events are put on hold.

There was confusion over whether she should have personal guards and who they should be. Some argued that the people seemed to love her, so why would she need half a dozen at any given time? The king was clearly the target. And many thought the prince might still discard her, so why waste the resources? Of the ones who thought he might discard her, many of them had daughters who might tempt him.

In the end, Caitlin is given six guards, all of them women trained in the art of combat and led by Sir Sarah Dermont.

Prince Cian is taciturn, and Princess Eleanor spends most of her time in her private chambers. Daya leaves her alone and is instead always praying at the Temple of Andraste on the palace grounds. Everyone is on edge; the footsteps in the halls are quiet, and ghosts may as well inhabit the gardens despite the fact that spring is the perfect time for romantic and courtly garden strolls. Empty, which was why Caitlin spends much of her time in them.

When she does have company, it is Priestess Samaire of the Temple of Muriel. She is short, even for a Calla, and keeps her long ocean-blue hair in a loose braid, and, despite being the head priestess of the enclave at the palace, often eschews the diaphanous white and azure robes in favor of loose trousers and a billowing shirt. Their conversations are rarely about religion or politics. Instead, they talk about sailing—Samaire had been a sea captain herself before deciding to find other ways to commune with the water.

Caitlin appreciates her company, glad for normal conversations with no hint of ulterior motives.

But her peace does not last long. Eventually, nobles, peers, knights, and politicians all find her in the garden.

But most importantly, Lady Arlina finds her. "Does it truly always smell like fish and salt? How can you stand that?" Lady Arlina asks, laying on her back on a blanket, hands folded neatly on her chest.

Caitlin sits back and admires the trees above them, wisteria about to bloom. "Yes, but the smell of alcohol at the taverns makes you forget."

"Oh, you visited taverns often?" Lady Arlina rolls over, propping herself up on her elbows.

"Often enough to know all the secrets to games of chance. But I don't let that influence my card plays when you aren't on my team."

"A princess-to-be? Playing cards with ruffians and pirates?" She plucks a piece of grass, spinning it in her fingers. "I would not have figured you for that."

"For what? Those 'ruffians' were clients and business partners!"

"You traded and dealt with pirates?"

"They prefer the term 'aggressive barterers' nowadays." She reaches for the plate of dates and plops one in her mouth. The garden is in full bloom; the seasons and their changing do not care if the atmosphere of the court is gloomy, the flowers still sprout, the trees still grow, the wind still carries the scent of new life, and the hatchling sparrows still sing in celebration. For Caitlin, these brief afternoons with Lady Arlina are the only respite from the cage that is closing in around her.

"I am sure they do. And yet the prince still wants you, a woman who's gotten drunk with aggressive barterers and other riffraff of the sea."

"I've also dealt with less than scrupulous traders from other countries. However, I do not think he knows the half of it. Peddigree Trading Company has a reputation that is well cultivated and protected."

"And the prince only knows half of that reputation, I take it."

"That is the truth of it." Why she feels secure enough to be this vulnerable with Lady Arlina, she cannot tell. Her stomach does not drop from anxiety when Lady Arlina approaches her; her heart does not beat loudly in dread. Spending days with her drinking tea and eating biscuits does not solve any of the problems outside this bubble, but it is a bubble of safety, nonetheless.

"By now, I am sure someone has looked into it," Lady Arlina says.

"Perhaps." She sits up and grabs a bottle of wine from their basket.

"But there are many ways people make trades, many just as—questionable as aggressive barterers."

"Oh?" Caitlin says.

"Some may trade in information, some in power, some in hearts, some in sex."

"Do you trade in any of those manners?"

"You forget, the acolytes of Aife educated me. Trading in physical goods is probably the only manner in which I cannot barter. Knowing the law is to make it."

"You shall have to teach me sometime."

"You must promise to return the favor."

Caitlin sips her wine, a wicked grin on her face. "Oh, I would very much like that."

"Lady Laocre," Lord Dontaue says, taking a seat next to her and beckoning to the little spaniel that follows her everywhere. Though she would never say it out loud, Caitlin finds the duke to be the prettiest of the royals; her soft jawline and heart-shaped face are not hidden behind make-up, and she eschews the court finery that is favored by most of her relatives. She wears unadorned dresses and plain shoes, and her hair is often in a simple braid. Her understated beauty shines as she approaches Caitlin in the garden.

In her fifties, she is still single and seems to have no inclination to change that. She is the close confidant and dearest friend of her sister-in-law, Queen Isleen, that seems to be the only companionship she requires. She has seldom left the queen's side since King Tarmon was shot. If you heard Queen Isleen's voice echo down the hall, Lady Dontaue's airy laugh will follow it.

"Your Grace," Caitlin says. It is difficult trying to figure out where she fits in terms of obeisance and the royal hierarchy. She inclines her head to the duke, praying that she is not expected to curtsy.

"I thought I might find you here," she says. "When I visit the princess' rooms, you are always absent. I have been told you enjoy the flowers, though."

"Yes, your Grace. I find them very pleasant, especially as they reach peak bloom."

"I know with things so chaotic right now that you must surely need more comfort than ever. Still so new to this world, and your fiancé is preoccupied with the illness of our king."

"I do not find it so overwhelming. I have had little trouble adjusting since this became my new home."

"New home?"

No one had proclaimed it, no one had even mentioned it directly to Caitlin herself, but she glances at the guards standing just a little away from her; she will not be leaving. "The wedding may have been postponed, but it has not been called off, as far as I know. Why should I not already consider this my home?"

"Oh, wonderful!" The duke claps her hands, smiling. "Long have I waited for my nephew to settle down, and with everything going on, many had assumed that you might have found this new life and the danger that comes with it too much. Many had feared that you would call off the engagement."

"Had they, indeed? Were you one such?" Caitlin leans into a rhododendron bush, inhaling the earthy and sweet scent, pretending it is the same bush that grew in her yard in Whick.

"Never! Oh, never, my dear! You know, I think my secretary purchases often from your fathers. She told me that the newest silverware for the estate came directly from an *Ástfriðuran* metalworker! Your fathers are the only ones I know with such connections. I have not had the—"

Brenna. Caitlin does not want to hear the rest of what the duke says. Before her now is the duke as she appeared on the day of the assassination attempt, superimposed over the down-to-earth woman. The one who had dressed in more layers of fabric than could be practical, the jewels in her hair, on her fingers, all casting a glaring light that chased it away. All Caitlin can do is hold her breath, keep as much air in her chest as possible, clinging to the floral aroma. *Brenna. Brenna.*

"—you never know where you will find friends, you know?"

"Oh, yes. You are right, your Grace," she says, turning back to face the duke, a smile she knows does not reach her eyes.

"Then we are friends?"

"We are friends." Caitlin wishes she could say anything else.

Another week passes, and still no improvement in the king's health, no change in his status in the month since the assassination attempt. The cage closes ever tighter around her every day that passes with no assassin caught, but Caitlin is granted permission to ride so long as Sir Dermont accompanies her and the weather is fair. The horse she is gifted gives no protest as Caitlin holds her breath and leads him out of the stables to do a thorough examination away from the overwhelming stench made worse by the midday heat. Saddling his own horse outside of the stable is Lord Berach, his bushy eyebrows knit in concentration. "Ah, my apologies! Good morning, Lady Laocre."

He receives no obeisance from her, and his smile wavers, his deep-set eyes darkening.

"Good morning," she says, checking the musculature of the chestnut stallion, its coat far too soft for it to have ever needed those muscles for work.

"Are you going for a ride, also? It is much too stuffy in there, and there is nothing we can do but wait. I figured the air might help to keep my nerves at bay." He climbs atop his horse, a well-bred and well-fed mare with a gentle temperament contrasting harshly with his own.

"You do not seem to be one who is prone to nerves," she says, finished with her assessment of the stallion. Suan, expensive, and in fine health; a horse made for war and speed.

"You think so?" He tilts his head. "Would you care if I joined you? I would not want to hear of an ill fate befalling someone as precious as yourself."

"If you insist."

For the smallest of seconds, Sir Dermont frowns.

"Where are you going today?"

"I think just around the north paths. Do you find that agreeable?"

"As ever, my lady."

Not being in the mood for conversation, she takes off at a fast trot, hoping to remain at a distance. Her efforts are for naught; he soon matches her speed as they approach the wooded paths in the north. Her gaze remains steadfast ahead, her posture stiff and showing no inclination to turn to face him, deftly avoiding the branches and pleased with how softly her horse steps, barely breaking a twig and giving away no sound that would alert wildlife. His horse, on the other hand, clomped and huffed at every fallen branch, sending the songbirds fleeing.

Attempts to dodge or hide away from the rest of the court keep going astray and this is not a day Caitlin particularly wants to have company. Prince Cian had been overly annoyed the night before, and she had spent too much time soothing his bruised ego after he lost a sparring match with Sir Liam.

"You are dedicated to your position in the royal family. Even after learning intimately of the threats the nobility faces, you are still here."

The air rushes out of her lungs, and her blood pumps loudly through her veins. A conversation she had been having with too many people, with far too much frequency.

"Yes, your lordship. What reason would I have for leaving?"

"If you were my daughter—"

She pulls the reins and circles to face him. "Yes? If I were your daughter, you would say what? What would you have Lady Arlina do?"

His eyes widen as he scrambles to halt his own horse. "I would—well, it is entirely different."

"Answer me. If your daughter were engaged to the prince, and her life might be in peril? You would have her do what?"

He swallows back words that Caitlin knows would be laced with lies. "I would have her—"

"Break off the engagement? Secret her back home in the dark of night?"

"Well—"

"Were you expecting me to hurry back home to my fathers?"

"No, Lady Laocre. I can see that you are as strong as expected of a future queen."

"Thank you, your lordship." She nods and brings her horse back around. "I think I should like to enjoy a faster ride on my own. I wish you a pleasant day."

He blinks and waves a farewell as he steers his own horse back toward the palace.

"You should take more care, my lady," Sir Dermont says. The burly knight with closely cropped copper hair rarely speaks. When she does, she chooses her words wisely and always with good reason. At that moment, Caitlin does not care.

"I understand."

"I fear you do not truly."

As much as she is hiding away from the bustle of the court, the prince is equally absent. It is to be expected that he spends long hours with his father and even longer ones with the queen, helping to oversee the governing in the king's absence. But Caitlin fears that something more is going on.

He is as sweet as ever; he comes to bid her goodnight every evening, and at dinner, he ensures that only the finest of wines and choicest of meats are laid before her and brings her jewels and flowers. He even procures a small puppy from the palace kennels to be her companion, a sibling to Duke Dontaue's. "Only the best for my princess."

"You are looking pale, my love. Are you not getting enough sun?" He takes her hand as they walk together through the ancient stone corridors of the palace to the Great Hall. She wants to laugh at him, for he has grown pale himself, gaunt and pale.

"I am getting more than enough sun, my lord. I have been taking regular walks in the gardens with Sister Samaire and Lady Arlina."

"Ah, and I trust you are getting along well in my sister's rooms?"

"Of course, my lord. We play cards or dice every evening with Lady Elwen and are sometimes joined by a few other ladies."

"Who else?" He might be accustomed and therefore unaffected, but the shuffling of feet and the whisper of fine fabrics as everyone in the Great Hall rises as the prince walks to the head table still unsettles Caitlin.

"Well, Lady Shennen and Lady Marianna, of course. But sometimes Lady Arlina visits, Lady Muiris, or Captain Alice."

"Lady Clare does not join you?"

"Sometimes, rarely." No one enjoys it when the duchess joins them, Caitlin wants to say but bites her tongue.

"There will be quite the schism when you have your own rooms. Which room shall everyone flock to?" He sets his glass down, leans back, and smiles.

"I suppose, my lord, but I could not say."

"We shall have to find you your own ladies. I shall have my mother put together a list of suitable candidates. Only the best, my love. You should always be well attended to."

"Thank you, my lord."

"I am sorry, sweetheart, I have not been around more often." He pulls out the chair for her and servants rush from the back door to present wine and pies. Her stomach growls at the smell of duck and cranberry sauce. "It is so busy, and I am trying to keep my spirits high for my father's recovery. When he is well again, I promise I shall make up for every lonely hour that I have not been at your side."

"Ever my charming prince," she says, the same knot in her stomach that is always there when she must play at being love-struck. "Forever, my charming prince."

He clears his throat. "Oh, there is Lairde Elwee. Have you met him?"

A Calla swaggers in the main doors to the Great Hall, a smirk adorning their chiseled features, but their confidence is betrayed when Lady Shennen passes them by on her way out. "I have not met him."

"Zie is a diplomat to Garcelon, newly appointed and just returned. I must speak to him. It pains me to leave your side, but my responsibilities are paramount."

"Of course," she says. She watches him leave, enjoying the tartness of the cranberry sauce with the crispness of the white wine and chiding herself for being concerned about how pale the prince is. It's just the light, she tells herself.

The door creaks open, and a healer motions for Prince Cian to enter. The prince squeezes her hand and follows the healer. As a dutiful princess-to-be, Caitlin waits outside for her fiancé to return from his visit to his father. She has finally been allowed to accompany him to the king's grand chambers but is only permitted to wait outside the private bedchamber. He had insisted that she be allowed, pointing out that despite the circumstances, it was on this day last year that he first met her, and today was supposed to be their wedding, and he will not spend a moment of their anniversary away from her side.

As the prince enters, three men leave.

"Ah, I am glad to see you looking well." A tall and gangly man in white robes holds his hands to her, with a cadre behind him. She recognizes him as one of the priests who had been at the proposal party. "I do not know we have been formally introduced. I am Father Nael, and with me today are Brothers Sloan and Sheath."

Brother Sloan is tall, has wide shoulders, and sandy blond hair, while Sheath is short with pale orange hair and far too young to have even a hint of facial hair yet and looks like he might blow away in the wind. She rises and shakes the priest's hand, catching the scent of oak and cedar. "It is a pleasure to meet you, your Eminence."

"The king is doing well. He is improving steadily now. But there is something else I would like to discuss while you are here, Lady Laocre."

"Of course."

"We are the representatives of the Church of Culain here in the palace. We would like to welcome you to attend our services. You will always be a guest of honor." His chest puffs out, and his shoulders are thrown back. The other two survey their surroundings with the sort of curiosity of a child in an adult's bedroom.

"I appreciate that, Father."

"Am I correct in that you worship Iden and Muriel?" He keeps his gaze uncomfortably direct, and Caitlin tries to match it.

"I have no formal affiliation with any of the factions of the Tudáe." A phrase she is accustomed to saying. She is only shocked that the priests of Culain have not approached her sooner.

"Oh, forgive me. It is just that you have been seen with Sister Samaire so often I had assumed your allegiance to the water goddess was clear. And Iden overseeing trade, and your family—"

"I understand your assumption, your Eminence. But I am not beholden to any one god. And I believe it prudent, as a future queen, to show love and compassion to all, regardless of their patron god."

"Ah, a most generous thing to say. I might remind you that the Church of Culain is to whom the royal family belongs."

"I am aware."

"As a future member of the royal family, I wanted to let you know that we shall consider you part of our family, too. And we always make sure to take care of our family."

"Thank you, your Eminence."

"I shall be looking forward to it. I must get back to the temple to lead this evening's prayers. May Culain shine His light on you, Lady Laocre."

The queen hurries in as the priests exit. She sits next to Caitlin and places her hand on Caitlin's knee. "He is improving? Did they say?" For all that the king is hard and selfish, the queen is kind and caring. In the weeks since the assassination attempt, she has taken even more interest in welcoming Caitlin into the family. She wants to consider Caitlin a daughter, despite Caitlin being far past the age where she might take comfort in such a relationship. Any hesitations the queen may have had about Caitlin's status as a widow without noble blood or landowning title had disappeared. This trust is something Caitlin does not want to lose or take for granted.

"Yes, Your Majesty. They said he is doing well."

"I knew he would recover; he is strong. He always has been." That such a fragile woman could marry such an overbearing boar of a king and call it fate confuses Caitlin. It is said that they were a love match. Queen Isleen had accompanied her older sister to Fayn as her attendant. The older of the Garcelonian princesses had been King Tarmon's intended bride, a marriage that had been in the making since both had been mere children. But then he saw Queen Isleen and demanded that the marriage contract be rewritten for him to marry the younger sister. A love match, a story of a king recognizing his soulmate the second he laid eyes on her and claiming her despite all the obstacles that were in the way, re-writing law and tossing aside tradition to have the hand of the woman he was destined to be with.

That is what would be said, Caitlin realizes, of herself and Prince Cian. A prince saving a woman from grief, plucking her out of the common masses to be the queen she was meant to be, taking her as his bride even as everything seemed against him. A love match, indeed.

But for the queen, it was not an act. Caitlin could never pull off the sort of grief the queen expresses now. She knows that this is not pretend on behalf of the queen. Her heart really is broken.

Lord Hern comes into the antechamber. "Your Majesty, Lady Laocre. Excuse me. Your Majesty is needed."

"Of course." She grabs Caitlin's hands in both of hers. "We must be strong."

Sir Dermont, the only knight that was allowed to accompany Caitlin to the king's rooms, ever stoic, does not take her eyes off Lord Hern until he is out of the rooms.

A cry from the king abruptly breaks the quiet, and the silence descends again just as suddenly. A priest of Culain opens the door and runs out; a large porcelain decanter is clenched in his hands, a white cloth wrapped around the top. "Oh! Lady Laocre! I was not expecting you to be out here. I suppose you are waiting for news?" He shifts back and forth as he speaks. "Well, he is doing very well. Very well, yes. Your fiancé should be out soon. I must go for now, though. May the sun shine upon you." He scurries away without even another glance.

The next day, Sister Kiandre approaches Caitlin at dinner in the Great Hall. "Lady Laocre, I do not believe we have properly been introduced," the Calla says. Her sunshine-blond hair makes her long ears seem taller and sharper and disguise none of the movements that could give away her thoughts. Her tail swishes back and forth as Caitlin extends her hand.

"You have not stopped to pray at the Temple of Andraste for the king's health." It is a statement. The priestess takes a seat next to her, not seeming to care that she was not asked to.

"I have not."

"Are you still a follower of Muriel?" The priestess grabs Caitlin's plate and pulls it toward herself, inspecting the meats and testing the carrots.

"I do not know who told you that, but I have equal respect for all of the Tudáe."

"You are already versed in how to speak at court," she says, now stealing Caitlin's wineglass.

"I am a businesswoman in my blood."

"Silly how easily people forget that, though. Isn't it?" Not bothering with a fork, she picks at Caitlin's dinner.

"I suppose."

"You stopped being the architect behind your fathers' success and started being an ornament."

Caitlin is unsure if the Calla with sun-kissed skin is toying with her in the way all Calla excel at so easily or if she is this bold and brash all of the time. Caitlin suppresses a chuckle; she would get along well with Kegan.

"Does it bother you?" Sister Kiandre scoots closer.

"Pardon?"

"You were the dutiful daughter, and now you are expected to be a dutiful princess, a dutiful wife. Is that what you wanted?"

A lump forms in Caitlin's throat. *Brenna. Always Brenna. Only, entirely Brenna.*

"You hold your tongue well. You don't need to, not with me."

"Oh? I have heard that so many times. I am glad there are so many at court who are so willing to give me their confidence."

"Or, rather, expect it in return." Finished with Caitlin's dinner, Sister Kiandre wipes her hands on the tablecloth and reclines in the chair.

Caitlin nods.

"I can understand your hesitation. Tell me. Were you one of those children who dreamed of marrying a princess, marrying a prince, or a duchess? Is this not the happy fairy tale you spent your days imagining?"

"I am a widow, I dreamed of growing old with—"

"Silly how people forget that, too." The Calla plucks a chicken leg off of the tray of a passing servant. "It is hard, isn't it? To find your entire life upended, the future you wanted snatched away from you. Having a new life placed before you and no chance to reject it. Nothing to do but accept the change." She lifts a wine glass to Caitlin in a toast and then quickly downs the entire glass.

"I suppose."

"It is hard knowing that your life is not your own. Knowing that you can do nothing to change it. Especially when one hates change so much."

Caitlin wants to down a glass of wine, but Sister Kiandre has ensured that she can't, so she beckons to a servant.

"You were with the prince visiting his father the other day, yes? Watching as doctors and priests came in and out while sitting in the antechambers, looking pretty and appropriately worried."

A servant offers Caitlin a tray of glasses, and she plucks two from the tray, handing one to the priestess.

"No need to seem so shocked." She waves her hand in dismissal, and her ears prick forward. "Tell me, what did you think of the priests of Culain you saw?"

"I, I suppose they seemed concerned but hopeful for the king's recovery."

"Interesting. Not what I asked, though."

"I'm not sure I understood your que—"

"I don't trust them."

This Calla is just as frustrating as Aine and Kegan, Caitlin decides. But in such a different way. Is it their custom to only ever be this blunt and yet give nothing away at all? "That is a very undiplomatic statement, especially from one who just complimented me on such a virtue."

"Let me see. Lord Berach wants you to step back so he can push Lady Arlina forward, obviously. Baron Rivers wants you here so that he can continue to amass his own favor. He may be newly titled, but he has higher aspirations. Aspirations that the nobility of blood are fearful of. He may be marrying Lady Marianna after the prince discarded her, but he has no intention of his only claim to status being through her. The Duke of Dontaue is hoping you are as easily cowed as you seem. She seems kind and welcoming, but she knows how to spin the webs of intrigue. The Marquess and Marquise of Artair, Lord Ruben Gallagher, and his husband, Lairde Finn, have a younger daughter, even though Prince Cian spurned their eldest already. And I am sure he has contingency plans should that not work out." Sister Kiandre takes a large bite out of the chicken leg.

"Why are you—"

"Shh. I'm not done yet," she says, still chewing. "Sir Nait could go either way on your presence here. He's married into the royal family, but I feel he wants more than just the hand of one of the king's nieces. Although Lady Elwen certainly is a beautiful lady and has a far better disposition than Lady Clare. Let's see. Sir Liam and Sir Connor will go along with whatever Prince Cian wants and would have no problem disposing of you the second Prince Cian wants to. And all of them have, in one way or another, found a reason to converse with you, I am sure. And many more, besides."

"You are very knowledgeable about who I speak to."

"The Duchess of Clare hates you, so she has no reason even to approach you. While she wants you gone, she knows at this point that you will stay. She has you figured out far more than you think. Princess Eleanor and Daya love you. They know you are going nowhere, too. However, for reasons different than everyone else, they wish you would leave. They love you that much." That last sentence is spoken with a softness that Caitlin did not think this feline could express, even from just the half an hour she has known her.

"I should not have to tell you that there are many young ladies who wish sincerely to be in your place. I should note, though, that there is one who wishes sincerely that you were no longer engaged to him for very different reasons. I don't think she realizes it herself yet."

"Is there anything else you wish to share with me? Again, you have my admiration for your skills as a spy. I cannot say how much I believe in your information. Everyone here seems thrilled that the prince has found such a devoted wife and that the kingdom will one day have a beautiful queen."

"Do they? Fascinating. And are you?"

"Am I what?"

"Are you planning on being a devoted wife and beautiful queen?" Sister Kiandre leans in, and her words are as light as air but whisper sharp.

"Are you always like this?" Caitlin laughs.

"Like what? A cat? Yes."

Caitlin rolls her eyes.

"Don't trust anyone, Lady Laocre. Not even me. Especially not me. You can have allies here, but this court does not allow you the luxury of friends."

"Excuse me?"

Sister Kiandre smirks. "Lady Laocre, please join us tomorrow at the Temple. The Sisters of Andraste would be honored to show our future princess how we pray for a powerful kingdom led by a brave royal family."

"I shall see what I can do."

The Calla stands up and turns to leave. But at the last second, she looks back over her shoulder. "And don't let any of the priests of Culain know that you are visiting us. Though nothing escapes my notice, you should be able to make your presence unknown to them. They should not be trusted."

"Excuse me?" Caitlin's mind flies past the incident in the king's rooms and the unexpected and unsettling meeting with Father Nael and the brothers that he brought with him.

"Tell me, did you notice them holding any items that might look like artifacts of their religion or worship?"

"One of them left carrying a white porcelain vase, that was all."

Kiandre knits her brows but then waves away their confusion. "I shall see you soon. And be careful."

Nine

Splinters and Sisters

"Snake eyes." Princess Daya laughs, and Princess Eleanor slumps in defeat. "I win again."

"And I shall ensure you live to regret it," Princess Eleanor says, removing her sunhat and throwing it at Princess Daya. She misses, and it flies out of the gazebo and lands in the fountain.

"Where is Lady Arlina?" Lady Shennen says, her dark brown tail swishes suddenly, and she turns to lean over the railing, glancing down the rhododendron-lined path. "She is usually here at this hour." The Calla had once been Cian's paramour. Several former and current attendants to Princess Eleanor had once been the object of the prince's affections. Caitlin expected to be met with some sort of hostility when she had moved in with the princesses, but Lady Shennen showed no animosity, Lady Marianna l was now happily engaged to Baron Rivers, and Amelia Devlin, Marquess of Muiris, seemed more than content to live out her life unencumbered by permanent commitments and happy to let the Devlin family inheritance and title fall to a niece or nephew. Strangely, Lady Iomaire, formerly Lady Iomaire Rorick, had escaped his gaze. She had to have been the most beautiful and well-educated of the princess's attendants, and yet not once had Cian made advances on her. But now, she is with her husband in Tsvetokrasa.

"I could not say. I have not seen her at all today," Lady Muiris says. While Lady Arlina usually dines privately with her family, she still joins them for their gambling games regularly. She has been absent for the last three days, and Caitlin's mood has plummeted. She taps her cards on the table and contemplates the mug of mead in front of her.

But sunset is approaching, and even though the days are growing longer as summer nears, they cannot wait outside for her for much longer. "I am sorry I am late tonight!" She hurries to take a seat next to Caitlin at the table set out in the gazebo, looking rather disheveled and a crease on her brow.

"Lady Arlina! We have missed you! What has been keeping you from us?" Lady Shennen says, ears perking up.

Lady Arlina looks down at her knotted hands in her lap. "Family business."

"Oh! What kind?" Lady Shennen asks, leaning forward. "I want to know the details!"

"It is just, well. Disputes over property, you could say. My father's properties and such."

"Oh, in trouble with other claimants? Someone wanting to take some of his lands? Disgruntled second cousins?"

"Well, more like he is trying to sell some of his property. It is really not all that interesting, truly."

"Ah, oh well, then. Do you want us to deal you in?" Lady Muiris asks, her turquoise hair pinned neatly in a crown braid, but her shaggy bangs had gotten free and now hang in her eyes, with her constantly trying to brush them to the side. Yet another former lover of Prince Cian, although, like many, she seemed relieved to be free of him.

Lady Arlina nods vigorously. "Please do. May I be on Lady Laocre's team?"

"Of course! As long as you aren't on my wife's team," Princess Daya says, handing over the cards.

"I do not need a fantastic partner in order to beat you, my dearest," Princess Eleanor protests.

"Lady Arlina, did you see Lairde Samise Elwee on your way here?" Lady Shennen asks, analyzing her cards.

"No, I am sorry."

"Drats. I shall never catch zir if I never see zir."

"You cannot catch someone who doesn't want to be caught," Lady Muiris says.

"I can catch whatever and whoever I please." Lady Shennen sticks out her tongue.

"Like you caught that visiting noblewoman from Qaewi?"

"I did catch her in the end. Sort of."

"Caught her in the act, more like it."

Even as the evening goes on, the crease remains on Lady Arlina's brow, and she does not stop fidgeting. When crickets announce that dusk has become night and a shawl no longer suffices, Princess Eleanor and Princess Daya reluctantly retire. Arlina stands but hesitates as Lady Muiris and Lady Shennen follow the princesses. "I should go, I was just hoping that—"

Prince Cian and his entourage stumble into the gazebo, bringing with them the scent of ale and mead. "Have my sisters retired already?"

"Yes, my lord. You just missed them," Caitlin says.

He shakes his head. "Either they retire early, or I stay up much too late. I cannot figure out which it is. Either way, my beautiful fiancée is up still. So, I can kiss her goodnight."

Caitlin does her best to feign pleasure in his kiss. When he breaks away, he turns immediately to face Lady Arlina. "Ah, there is another rose still awake. Are you going to keep my sweetheart company much longer? Or can I escort you back to your family's rooms? Your father seemed concerned earlier about your whereabouts."

Lady Arlina's eyes widen. "Well, I was planning on staying longer. I had some things I still wished to discuss with Lady Laocre."

"You women and your secrets. Very well. I bid you both a good night." He bows deeply and, with too many flourishes, a performance before he wanders back to the palace.

"Are you alright?" Caitlin asks.

"Please. Let me stay here, just for a little while longer." Her voice quivers and cracks as she speaks.

"Of course. What is troubling you?"

"I cannot say. I wish I could. Can we talk of lighter things?"

"Yes, but perhaps we can go inside. I fear the bugs are much too fond of me." Caitlin leads her back to the palace, and they slip inside her room. They talk about how the stable boy looked at a nobleman's son. Neither was older than fourteen, but both agreed that they were the perfect match for life. They talk about the newest wares Caitlin's fathers have traded from a country far to the south of Sua and across the sea. They talk about anything but the politics and scheming. In the end, Caitlin asks her to stay the night. *She seems so relieved*, Caitlin notes. Whatever awaits her in her own rooms, Caitlin does not want to imagine.

The first day of summer is one of the holiest days for the Order of Yseult—the goddess of the sun, the harvests, and prophecy—and there is a public parade to celebrate. The king rides out on horseback, waving to the crowds as if he has come back from war triumphant; rides as if he has no fear of another assassination attempt, showing all that he will not be so threatened; he will not be intimidated.

But when he returns to the palace, his attendants rush to him, a stretcher already waiting, and he is taken back up to his chambers, gasping for air. The king has survived but has not recovered.

This is the first of many excursions that the royal family makes to prove that they fear no protesters, rioters, or assassins, and Caitlin is not exempt.

A terrible fire had broken out at a factory on the western side of Eoi, a fire that had spread to the surrounding neighborhood, taking out nearly three blocks of businesses, shops, and residences before the blaze was finally under control.

The Temple of Andraste in Eoi has taken in many of those without homes, and Princess Eleanor, Princess Daya, their attendants, and Caitlin have all been assigned to assist. They are there to prove that the king is benevolent and that belief in the gods is all that is required to have their needs met.

And so, a week after the Solstice Celebration, Caitlin walks under the gossamer gates of the Temple of Andraste in Eoi, taking in the splendor and the squalor both. The Temple of Andraste on the palace grounds has two small rooms and a sanctuary; the Temple in the city is larger than many manors, and it houses hundreds of people.

"Welcome. I am Sister Aoife." A dark-furred Calla with clear, blue eyes greets them. Caitlin knows she has seen this Calla before but cannot place it. "I regret that the High Priestess is not here today to receive you. She has been called away unexpectedly. I assure you that she appreciates your assistance in these trying times."

They are led through the Temple, the royal entourage standing out as their footsteps echo across the corridors in contrast to the silken footfalls of the priestesses, into what was once a magnificent hall with towering marble pillars, polished hardwood flooring, and a ceiling painted to imitate a clear night sky. But it has been transformed into a temporary shelter and medical clinic for the homeless and wounded.

At least a hundred people mill about, all bearing the same look of shock and hopelessness.

"It was intentional," a young woman says as Caitlin changes the bandages on her burns.

"There's no way it wasn't," the woman's older brother says, squeezing her hand as the young woman winces while Caitlin pours alcohol over the foul-smelling, infected wound.

"Who do you think started it?"

"Well, I think it was the workers. They were upset about the changes to the schedule," the brother says.

"They burned the whole factory down because of that?" Caitlin asks, head swimming both in confusion and from the amount of alcohol fumes she has breathed in today.

"Pardon Clive, my brother is ridiculous," the woman says. "I think it was the managers and owners. They wanted to put the workers back in their place for complaining."

Clive crosses his arms. "That's stupid, Aisling. That would be cutting off their nose to spite their face. What do they get from destroying their own factory?"

"I hear that the Gilroy-Downings are being given a significant amount of money from the king himself to make up for the losses and rebuild! Isn't that right, my lady?"

Caitlin's eyes widen, heart-racing, looking between the bickering siblings. "I have no knowledge either way. I apologize."

"We aren't getting anything," Clive says, leaning further back in his chair. "We're told we can stay here until we find a new place to live. But the fire took both our parents and the bakery I was apprenticed at. How are we going to find a place to live? It's not fair. I don't care who set the fire." He pulls a marble out of his pocket and tosses it into the air but does not bother to catch it. "It's not fair."

As they finish with the last of the patients for the day, Sister Aoife gathers them to take them on a tour of the rest of the sprawling, meandering grounds.

"I am one of the head instructors," Sister Aoife stands unnaturally still, her tail not even twitching as she speaks, pointing to an archery range at the bottom of the hill A group of Evanstar Calla are laughing and yelling, but all of them hit the practice targets. "I also teach hand-to-hand combat, in addition to archery. But in my capacity as the overseer of protection, I do very little hunting. I do not set loose my arrows as often as some of us, although I consider that a blessing."

"I, too, believe that that is a good thing," Princess Eleanor replies.

"Morale has been low here, and knowing that there are royals who care for us, and respect the Goddess, has lifted our spirits." She speaks slowly, considering each word.

"It has been an honor, Sister Aoife."

There is much ceremony for their departure back to the palace. More Sisters than Caitlin thought a temple could even house line up before the dark stone walls and trumpets sound as they get into the carriage, as much a charity trip as a demonstration of the generosity of the royal family.

As they pull away, Caitlin catches the eye of Sister Aoife, standing on the ledge of the wall, arrow cocked. From her perch, she can take out nearly anyone who dares get too close or display even the slightest suspicion.

"Oh, how I've missed you!" Diar says as she opens the door to her fathers' mansion, and he leaps inside, hugging her so fiercely that she can barely breathe.

"Please." She pushes against him. "Let go."

"Oh, I am so sorry." He stands back, his hands on her shoulders, and looks at her as if seeing a ghost. "I did not think they would ever let you out of there. In all of these months, I thought you would never come home again, and I would not see you unless we toppled the monarchy."

"Yet. Here I am," she says, leading him through the mansion to the dining room.

"Here you are."

"Are the others going to be able to make it? Aine?" She pulls out a chair at the large mahogany table for him.

"And Sharidan, Valen, Myles, Jocelyn, Tyn. Saoirse. Imogen? A few others, I think."

"More than I expected, to be honest," she says, sitting across from him and smoothing her silk skirt. "And Kegan?"

"Yes, Kegan is already in town. They were promoted rather quickly, and your fathers recalled them back to Eoi for an in-person briefing of the business in Taern's Keep."

"So, we will be doing this." She takes a deep breath. "When I go back, I am sure to be moved to my own rooms and given my own attendants…Kegan among them."

"Your fathers sent out invites formally, so this seems respectable from the outside. There are now a lot of new charitable organizations with proper names and structured operations."

"I am sure there are," she laughs.

"Myles and Imogen now run an organization that helps the poor gain employment," he says, fiddling with the buttons on his cuffs.

"Of course. The factories absolutely must have more workers," she says, rolling her eyes.

"Of course! More people to exploit. And Tyn and Jocelyn are running some sort of organization around raising awareness for something or other. Because it is the awareness that is important, not the actions."

"All legitimate endeavors and not a hint of any sort of underlying anti-monarchy motives."

"Precisely."

"And all run by the exact type of reputable people that my fathers' would be interested in giving large charitable donations."

The rest of the attendees to this meeting arrive in pairs over the next hour, and no time is wasted once all arrive.

"We cannot continue to rely on strikes and riots; our noble benefactors cannot continue to fund the long stretches of unemployment that the strikers face, and suspicion falls upon them. Where are they finding the money to survive those stretches of time? And the strikes are not working," Saoirse says, her hands flying wildly to emphasize nearly every one of her words.

"But we are making in-roads. The factory owners are considering meeting the workers' demands," Tyn replies, his palm rubbing his forehead.

"For how long, though? For how long? A week? Two? And then it's right back where we started, with them having considered it and decided against it," Imogen says, slapping the table and almost knocking over her glass of water.

"We need to take more radical actions," Diar says. "Pleading for our rights and dignity is not working and will not work. We won't ever be able to ask nicely enough for them just to hand us our demands."

"Diar is right. We need more decisive action," Sharidan says. "We have tried everything, everything we can so far to peacefully bring out a society that is just and equitable. But the powers that be will not listen."

"No, we haven't," Myles says. He is the second eldest in the organization and normally acts as a kindly grandfather figure to everyone. Today, though, he is more curmudgeonly. "We can continue what we do and keep recruiting people to our cause. We can hand out flyers and write letters to the lords showing how their actions and policies are not just hurting us, but hurting them, too. And we are still waiting for the king to grant us the audience I requested. He hasn't heard about that idea I told you about. The parliament."

"Myles is right. We must give the king, nobles, and businessmen a chance to respond. If the businessmen keep overworking the workers, the workers become less and less productive, and it only hurts the businessmen in the long run. We just need to find better ways to tell them, better ways to make them understand, they will realize it eventually," Jocelyn says.

"Here we go again," Imogen rolls her eyes and sits back, their bronze hair catching the light of the setting sun pouring in from the window.

"No. They do understand. They have always understood," Saoirse says. "They just do not care. It is more beneficial overall to keep us impoverished and too desperate to care and organize."

The arguments continue, tensions rising to a low boil as afternoon becomes evening, only ceasing when Caitlin brings in snacks and refreshments. From the way Aine and Kegan are slouching in their chairs in the very back, neither paying attention as Kegan sprinkles powder into Aine's water, Caitlin suspects that this argument has been simmering for some time now.

Abruptly, Valen rises and pounds on the table. "Enough. This isn't why we are here tonight. Caitlin is here. We would like her to share information that might help us."

She does not know what information is and is unimportant, so she shares everything. With each detail she provides, though, she can see that some members are wary of the information she is providing, squinting at her, brows knit. *Do some still doubt her loyalties?*

"And what of the assassin?" Saoirse asks, flipping a long, purple braid over her shoulder. "There has been no word from the palace except that the king and his family are once again safe. Does that mean the assassin has been apprehended?"

"What do you mean? Wouldn't you know if they had been? Surely if your archer did not report back, you would know?"

Sharidan clears xir throat, fingers tapping the table. "The assassin was not one of ours."

"Not officially, but I have my doubts," Myles scoffs. "You and Valen wanting to take more extreme actions... Like with that factory fire you started!"

Caitlin blanches. *Had that boy Clive been right?*

"Myles. Hold. Your. Tongue. We have discussed this. You either trust us on this, or you don't. I keep being told you trust us, yet you question us on this and too many other issues."

Saoirse clears her throat as Valen and Myles stare each other down. "We truly do not know; it was not one of ours. And neither was that fire. We were hoping you could provide us with more information on both."

"No." Everyone is leaning forward except for Aine, who is wincing as she drinks deeply from her flask. "I have no information on either."

The princesses and Caitlin continue to tour the city every few days, stopping at physicians' offices, schools, and even individual homes, creating the appearance of a nobility that cares about the people. Playing the part of the concerned royal family, dedicated to protecting the people over which they reign.

"We need to show them that they need not threaten us, that they need not question us, that they need not worry; for we shall provide them what they need," Prince Cian says as they climb into the carriage for another day of outreach.

"Of course, and our people are so easily assured by these trips into town, these days where we show our faces and seem to them to be as human as they are," Princess Daya replies.

"Yes! Exactly!"

"I am glad you have thought this through. We know how frequently you are correct in these matters," Princess Daya replies.

"Yes, and do not forget it, and have fun," he says, slamming the carriage door closed and watching them leave the palace grounds.

"If he believes that this is enough to win over anyone... Just how ignorant does my brother believe the people are?" Eleanor says as the carriage pulls away. "Although they may accept our charity, they know exactly why we may be there."

"I know, beloved." Princess Daya takes her wife's hand in her own. "Ah! Look over there! What is going on?"

A crowd had gathered at the center of the market square, the usual haunt of acolytes of Culain. But there is something else there drawing people's attention. A bright tent has been raised, azure blue and white streamers fluttering at the top. Standing outside, a young boy calls for people to queue in an orderly fashion.

Princess Daya leans out of the window of the carriage. "I think it's a traveling Seer!"

"Do you want to, love?"

"I do not need someone with the Sight to tell me that I have found my fortune," Princess Daya says, pecking Princess Eleanor on the cheek. "But I can think of a few questions I would like to ask. What about you?"

"I suppose we do have some time. I can deny you nothing."

Caitlin follows them outside without a word. The Sight is not something that is common, and many believe that it is a scam. She would have said the same until Brenna showed her magic. Many of those who do claim the Sight, however, ensconce themselves in the halls of the Temple of Yseult.

The line is long, but besides the boy calling for order, another dressed in azure and white robes entertains the crowd with tales of fantasy lands filled with wise sages, clever mages, and the mischief and sorrow caused by them.

Caitlin almost misses it when it is her turn to enter the mysterious tent. The Seer is veiled similar to those consecrated to Yseult and burns the myrrh and lavender incense that are found in Her Temples.

"You find yourself in the position where people might believe you have great power and luxury," the woman says, voice both young and old, timeless and ancient, before Caitlin can even be seated on the cushions. "And some may wonder what you gave up, what you sacrificed to obtain such a fate. Many wonder what you traded for such a fortune. For such things are rarely free."

What she traded. What she gave up. *Her wife. Her life.* "Everything," Caitlin says.

"You gave up everything for this future you do not want? You gave up your choice, your voice, for a fate you do not desire? No, you gave up everything long before you came to these crossroads. But why?"

It is raining when Kegan and Aine arrive; one last summer storm. Once more, Caitlin smells the earthy-rain and laments that it does not carry with it the scent of sea salt. *What has she traded for such a fortune?* What has been traded is never something she has control over, to begin with. It is not a trade; it is theft. Somewhere in her life, the sails of her ship had been torn, and she is now at the mercy of the winds, the mercy of the sea. What the sea gives, the sea can take away. Caitlin is being tossed about, propelled into directions she has no say in. She can catalog the price of anything, can inspect cloth and metal and spices and lumber and ornaments and gowns…Trading is her entire life.

What value does a future have? What value do her desires have? What had she sought that required that she trade Brenna? She does not remember making such a trade. She cannot recall such a bargain. What had she coveted that she was willing to trade her home? What had she desired that she was willing to trade her freedom to the selfish prince? There was nothing in the world that was worth the price of her freedom, her home. Her Brenna.

The sea does not change. No, sailors say, the sea does not change though the rest of the world might.

The rain drenches the dress that she was given, one of many at the palace. The cloth was imported from Janeuq. The beads; Sua. The thread was Fayn, though. Captive spiders weaving anew every night, only to have their efforts stolen in the morning. And it is getting ruined.

Aine offers her a shawl as the two meet her at the door. Caitlin shakes her head and waves them into my fathers' home. There is a gust of wind, and for half of a second, Caitlin thinks she tastes just a hint of salt lacing through the cold air.

"Kegan is all packed, all that is needed is for you to arrive and summon her. Do you think that it will be any trouble?" Aine says, collapsing into a chair near the fireplace while Kegan shoves past both and heads to the kitchen without a word.

"I do not believe so. It should be fine."

"Good, good. You know that we are like family to each other, that kit and I."

"I understand. I know the danger that we will be in. And I will do everything I can to ensure the danger does not come to fruition for either of us."

"Why?" Aine asks.

"Why what?"

"Why are you doing this? You're walking into a den of wolves, and I can't figure out why. As far as I can tell, you've no reason to hate the monarchy; it's taken nothing from you. Quite the opposite."

Caitlin's chest tightens. *Brenna.*

"Well?"

"It seems like the easiest way out of my engagement."

"Don't make like of this. You're in charge of Kegan's safety, and I need to know you aren't gonna slack. Why?"

"I do not want to talk about it."

"That's what I'm worried about. I don't see a spark in you. Every other member has a spark, and I don't see yours. I trust Diarmuid, you're his lass; he says you're good. But I still got my own eyes, too. And this is about more than the mission. This is Kegan's life."

"I really can't..." *His lass? This again?*

"I started life with nothing, a sick mom and a depressed dad and a grumpy sister." Aine plucks a wooden wren figurine from the table next to her, a gift from Diarmuid's father, and examines it. "I clawed my way to stability, and it was only after Diarmuid helped me with my sickness. I have a stake. Kegan started with less and only found their way to something resembling a home by the skin of their tail. They have a stake. Do you catch my meaning?"

"I have my reasons."

"I need more than—"

"Here," Kegan says, rushing back into the room and handing Aine a tall glass of water. "I only put a little in it. Don't make that face at me!"

Tomorrow. Tomorrow. What is Kegan trading for this prison? A chance at freedom, they will endure this cage as the price for a cause they believe in truly. They are trading, possibly, their life that others may find a tomorrow free of the tyrants that rule their lives today.

Caitlin was forced into this confinement the moment Prince Cian had seen her at her fathers' party; this is no noble cause she values enough to trade away a life outside of a golden cage. But. Tomorrow.

"Kegan," Aine says. "Would you mind fetching me something to eat, too? Do you mind, Caitlin? Something with salt?"

"Of course, as much as you need," Caitlin says, but Kegan is already skipping away, footsteps echoing through the mansion.

"Caitlin. I must tell you this, it could save your life, and it could save Kegan's. Kegan does not know it, and none in the Red Front know it either. Promise you will not share this information."

"I promise."

"It was not the Red Front that sent that assassin. This is true. But I know the assassin."

"Wait. Was this Fiadh Róisín?" The assassin leaves no trace that no one knows how to hire, but everyone wishes they did. She's a myth, she's a fable. She's nobody, and she's the one who dines with nobles and pours poison in their cups; the leader of the Siúlóir Scáth.

Aine laughs. "No, and I don't think she would work with the Red Front, anyway. The real assassin? They are a guard at the Temple of Andraste. I cannot share more than that."

"Aoife…"

"Aye. That's her. They have their own goals, their own aims, and their own reasons for wanting the king and, eventually, the prince dead. We work for different causes, but in this, we are in agreement. While the Red Front is in disagreement internally, Sharidan, Valen, Diar, and others know that we must move from a resistance movement into outright rebellion. In this, we agree with the inner circle of the followers of Andraste. If you need help, if you need assistance, seek Priestess Dierdre or Priestess Kiandre. You can trust them. Mostly."

"What about the connections that Valen and Sharidan say they are working on?"

"This is one of them. They know Kiandre and Dierdre are the enemy of our enemy and will make this concession. But Sharidan and Valen do not know everything. And they don't need to."

Caitlin swallows, averting her eyes and watching a small spider in the corner build a web, wondering what Aine might be keeping from her, too.

TEN

PREMONITIONS AND PROMOTIONS

"I TOLD YOU WHERE you should be. And yet you were not there! You were not anywhere near there. Where were you? When you didn't come back to your rooms that night, I assumed you had been successful. But now I realize I was wrong. Where. Were. You." Caitlin does not mean to eavesdrop, but she can not bring herself to knock on the door while Lord Berach yells at his daughter. Frozen, her hand an inch from the wide, engraved wooden doors, she waits. His voice ricochets through her head, and bile settles into her stomach.

"I told you! I was playing cards with the princess—"

"Is that where I told you to be? Why did you go there instead of where I told you to be? I had set it up so perfectly for you. Yet I have learned that you shirked your duty. Your duty to me, to our family—"

"Please, Father. Please."

Caitlin's hand hovers inches from the door. *Just knock, just knock.*

"I told you to be somewhere, and you expressly disobeyed my command and ran off to play some silly card game!"

"Please, I don't want this—"

"Is that where you continue to be when you go missing? You disobeyed me, and then you lied to me?"

"I never lied!"

Just knock.

"But you never told me the truth, either!"

The sound of a hand on a cheek; she knocks, and a page opens the doors.

Arlina's face is red, and the sleeves of her dress are dark and damp. She sniffles while bowing before Caitlin. Lord Berach barely nods his head at her. "Excuse me, I do not mean to interrupt what looks like a private family matter. But I have royal business that surely takes precedence."

Lord Berach thrusts his chest out. "The Byrne family are ever at the service of the king. I assume that you are here to inform me that the king or prince requests my presence."

"No," Caitlin says. She lets silence fill the space where she might have addressed him with a title. Not even the courtesy of 'my lord' passes her lips. "I am here to talk about Lady Arlina and offer her a position as one of my attendants. But from what I overheard, you have plans for her to serve your family, and so I—"

"Wait, your ladyshi—"

"I am speaking," she raises her voice. "I was saying that I understand how important familial obligations are and would not put you in a position where you must sacrifice your family needs for mine, as it is apparently upsetting that I had specifically requested that Lady Arlina attend to me and the princesses that evening. A maid had to track her down, but I am so thankful we found her. Alas, it was apparently upsetting that your daughter's presence was requested personally by their Highness's and myself. I was truly hoping that Lady Arlina would be my primary attendant. But I do not want you to have to forgo important family needs. I bid you a good day."

The sound of her dress rustling as she turns on her heel cannot mask the low, quiet growl when he lets go of his breath. "Your Highness! If you would please wait."

She looks over her shoulder and raises an eyebrow at him. "Yes?"

"The matter, for my family—it is a rather inconsequential matter."

"It did not sound that way."

Lady Arlina stands frozen behind her father as Caitlin challenges him. Caitlin will not let her live in these rooms, in this suite, with a father who spoke to her so abusively. To see a man so used to getting his way—so used to being one of the most important people in the room—squirm in front of a woman he considered silly and unimportant just a year ago is shocking, but the fact that he is willing to trade his daughter's happiness for his own gains is not. His sudden obeisance and deference to her has nothing to do with shame for his actions, only regret that he has been caught.

"I understand, my lady, why you might think that. I am tired, and coming from a tense council meeting has harried me. It is not as big of a deal as I was making it out to be. My daughter would be honored, I am sure. Would you not, Arlina?"

She sweeps a magnificent courtesy. "I am truly glad to hear that you want me in your retinue, Lady Laocre."

"Then it is settled. I expect you to start within the week." Caitlin's tone remains stiff, cold, and unbending.

She may choose most of her attendants, but aside from Kegan and Lady Arlina, she does not know who to pick or how. The nobles who want to see how quickly she will be cowed and how easily she can be manipulated have made themselves known. She does not know where others stand, though. Picking one person might seem like a slight to someone else. Where she had kept her dealings with competing importers discrete from the other, she cannot hide who will receive what and what will be perceived as favoritism.

The room smells fresh as if walking through a garden after a beautiful spring rain. The crystal chandeliers and the textured frosted glass windows send the light from the candles shooting through the room in rays of blue light. The temple in the palace is not as ornate nor as large as the one in the city, but there is a certain charm here that the one in the city lacks.

"Welcome, Lady Lacore." Sister Kiandre motions for Caitlin to follow her to her office. "I was wondering when you would visit." She smiles, and her tail vibrates. She claps her hands together. "And you've brought friends!"

Caitlin laughs. For all that the sister plays the spy and has an ear in every room, she knows when to hide her thoughts and when it is safe to be open with them.

"Yes, I am sure you know Lady Arlina, and this is Lairde Kegan. Lairde Kegan used to work for my fathers, but I begged my fathers to let me steal Lairde Kegan away." Both Calla take each other in before pricking their ears up.

"We are here for more than one reason," Caitlin says.

"That is always the case with anyone who comes here. Anyone who walks the walls of the court always has more than one reason for anything that they do. And what are yours today, Lady Laocre?" Sister Kiandre sits down at her desk and spins the star globe sitting on the corner. The office is too small to have additional furniture, and the priestess does not suggest alternative seating.

"I was told that you might be a good person to consult about whom to choose for my attendants."

"Oh, this is indeed an important question you have put before me. Have you fully thought through the implications of this?" The Calla leans back in the chair and rest their legs on their desk, unconcerned with decorum.

"I think the best person to consult with would be the High Priestess."

"Ah, I see. She is at the Temple in the city?"

"Usually, yes, but today she just happens to be here. Follow me." She springs to her feet and leads them to the sanctum.

There is no accurate way to tell how old an *Ástfriður* is. Their cycle of reincarnation already leaves open the question of immortality and if you should start counting from their first birth or from each new incarnation. Either way, Sister Dierdre could be as new as the first bloom of a lilac or as old as the moon. She has clearly taken on a Fayn name when she arrived here, and Caitlin cannot figure out why she has dedicated her life to a Tudáe god. She wears not a single metal adornment, no bracelets, no necklaces, not even a metal hairpin to hold back her long and thick mane. The slope of her nose, the length of her fingers, the flecks of gold in her eyes, and the brilliant sheen of her silver fur—glowing like starlight on ice—gives her away. She stands before the silver altar, hands folded in prayer.

"Sister, Lady Laocre is here to see you."

"Come in, child. Sister Kiandre has said much about you." As graceful as a river, the priestess approaches. Her words give nothing away.

"I hope all of what she has said is good. Lady Arlina, Lairde Kegan, if you wouldn't mind waiting outside?"

"Of course, my lady," Lady Arlina says.

Alone in the room with the priestess, she says, "Though I have been a unique presence at the court, I had always hoped to be an impermanent one, if I may be honest with you. And so, I never much played politics. I was told by a friend that I could trust you, a friend whom I know from other places."

"A certain laconic Calla?"

"Precisely. I need to choose attendants. I want to choose wisely. If not for me, then the peace of mind for our mutual friends. I have a feeling I know who my enemies are, but I would like your help in identifying friends."

"You want to know who would report to us as a spy and not to Culain or the king?"

The blood rushes from her head so quickly that she becomes lightheaded; she was not expecting such bluntness. She takes a seat on the bench before the altar. "I would prefer no spies at all, to be frank."

"Everyone is a spy, everyone reports to someone else, everyone is always gathering information for their own personal gain. After all, you yourself are a spy. Are you not?"

The silence speaks for her.

"Ah. I will help you in choosing your attendants. But the advice will cost you."

"What information would you have me report back to you in exchange for this advice?"

"And you say you are not adept at navigating these waters."

"It is precisely because I am well versed in bargaining that I have survived at all."

"What has Aine told you of me?"

"That your aims are the same, though methods and reasons differ. I take that to mean, for now, we can be allies."

The *Ástfriður* wanders around the miniature sanctuary, pausing at a globe in a corner. Contained inside of it are the entire heavens of the night, stars suspended as if in the sky itself. "Our aims are the same. Our methods? No. Our motives? We shall see. I shall help you; I request that you provide information that I cannot obtain otherwise. I am not asking for anything additional to what you are already doing, just that I have access to all the information that you pass along. The same that you would give to Aine. If you provide the information to me, I shall pass it along to Aine for you. That is the agreement I came to with the leaders of your movement."

Negotiations always have prices that both parties conceal. A silk trader being less than honest about the quality, a merchant claiming the origins of a material that was false, the purity of the object is said to be higher than it was. However, it is easy to check the veracity of their claims if you have a keen eye and the nerves to call out someone you want to stay on friendly terms with.

"Alright then. Now, as for my attendants. Who would you pick?"

"Lairde Kegan, I trust you had a wonderful stay with your family in the city; we missed you," she says, looking at them over the rim of her teacup.

Her rooms are full of all the accouterments she could ask for; thick rugs, large hearths, soft sofas and comfortable chairs, intricate tapestries lining the walls, and grand tables large enough to accommodate extravagant parties. Since she has moved into them, Caitlin has not had a moment alone. Primarily, her retinue comprises suggestions from the priestess and Queen Isleen; some are enemies to keep close, and others potential allies that could be won.

"I did, my lady," Kegan says, sitting on the plush sofa before the crackling fire, leaning in far too close to be safe.

The other attendants continue their activities, reading or writing or losing badly at chess, as Kegan sits next to Caitlin at the table, Lady Arlina moving her chair to make room. "We have a lot of shopping to do for the wedding. Lady Laocre has already asked the other attendants for recommendations. Would you mind writing some of your suggestions? I am also soliciting the opinion of the princesses."

"There is a set wedding date now?" Lady Muiris puts down her embroidery and leans forward. She's sworn off any suitors since the prince discarded her. Apparently, she never wanted him anyway. She's now the court flirt and also a court gossip. A rather useful person to have as a lady-in-waiting, one who was easily convinced to leave her temporary appointment to Princess Eleanor for a permanent appointment with Caitlin.

A lump forms in Caitlin's throat.

"I did not think that they would pick one until the king is fully recovered," says Lady Ronai. Lady Ronai's family, the Rorick family of Caibre, have long been favorites among the royal family. Her father, the Earl of Caibre, had been on the king's council as the Lord Privy Seal until he retired a few weeks ago. Her older sister, Lady Iomaire, had been one of Princess Eleanor's attendants until her marriage. It is highly speculated that Prince Cian will appoint Lady Ronai's brother, Lord Brennin Rorick, to his own council once he is king.

"Many of the royal staff are overwhelmed with the planning and making preparations," Lady Emerie says. The daughter of the Lord and the Lairde of the Artair march, Ruben Gallagher, and his husband Finn, her intentions are well known; she seeks the prince's attention. While her fathers may be the ones orchestrating it, she is enthusiastic about her mission and not the least dissuaded by the prince's rejection of her elder sister, Lady Caragh, nor that there is now an official wedding date. Sister Dierdre thought it best to keep the most ambitious of those vying to supplant her under her nose.

Caitlin sips her tea, admiring the turning of the leaves from green to gold outside of the window.

"Three months time is not enough to plan a wedding this grand." Lady Arlina sets her hand on Caitlin's knee. Since Prince Cian could not have their wedding on the anniversary of the meeting, he set it for the anniversary of his proposal.

"Sweetheart! Light of my life!" Prince Cian barges into her rooms, his friends in his wake.

"Look at what you have done here! Rooms fit for a queen, and attendants as lovely as flowers surrounding the most beautiful of roses."

"My lord," she curtseys to him. "I had not been expecting such a delightful surprise this afternoon!"

"My father's slow recovery has left so much responsibility on my shoulders," His speech is slower than usual, and though he speaks the words with genuine joy at seeing her, she can tell that he lacks the physical energy to match the fervency of his feelings. The six simple steps he takes towards her consume what energy he has; his pallor and gait give him away.

"Come, darling." His hand is icy in hers as she leads him to a seat and sits on the floor beside it. "I have missed you." Remembering every gentle touch, every sign to show that she cared for Brenna when they were sick... here, being used, now, to comfort her jailer.

"Have you had supper? I would very much like to dine with you tonight."

"I have not, my lord."

He laces his hands through her hair and then grabs the back of her neck firmly. "Excellent." It is said sweetly, a tender promise contrasting with an aggressive gesture. Pulling back his hand, he winces and then passes off the expression as laughter. "Gentlemen! You have heard the lady; my presence is needed. And a true prince could never deny his sweetheart a single request. I shall send for you once we are done."

His attendants and hers leave, and servants are sent to fetch a meal. He is slow in getting back to his feet, and when the food arrives, he does not complain about it, not the temperature of the soup, the seasoning of the vegetables, or the texture of the pudding.

Her betrothed pays it no mind, consuming his dinner as if he has a thousand other places to be, and he needed to be at all of them yesterday, his fork being used as a shovel.

"Your attendants all seem well picked. I am curious why you did not choose all the candidates my mother put before you."

"I did not want to seem to play favorites. And I truly do not need a dozen attendants."

"My Caitlin. My beautiful Caitlin. You have more cunning than I think you give yourself credit, a shrewd mind hidden behind a calm facade. You truly are not like other women."

If he were any other man, and her wine glass not empty, nothing would prevent her from throwing her wine at him and storming out. She silently seethes. 'Not like other women.' What does he know of women at all? He has discarded all of them before he could even know them. He speaks as though all women were butterflies flitting about a garden, only caring about the shine of their wings. It is he that preens and shows off. He means it as a compliment. He believes that she should be flattered that he sees her as less than inferior. Unable to express her rejection, she takes a deep breath and holds up her wineglass for an attendant to refill it.

"Your mind is special. Though I admire your looks, I wanted you for your cunning. Thank you, again, for affirming that my love is well met."

"My cunning?"

"You are always calculating something in your head, are you not? Do you think that I missed that? I will need that from you. I will need your skills when we are king and queen."

Caitlin tries to recall all of the details of their picnics, their dinners, their strolls through the garden. Never once in all of his time courting her has he even hinted that this is his aim, that he wants her for anything else than her looks, which, by all accounts, are not spectacular compared to some of the other beauties he has played with. She recalls the night he proposed, laying out why he should reject her and why others would not accept her.

"I want you on my council."

"My lord," she says, ready to protest.

"I will not accept no as an answer. Unfortunately, I must get back to work." He stands slowly, winces, and squeezes her shoulder before leaving without another word.

He has lost weight, grown pale, and is weak in a way that one would think could never touch royalty; they so loudly proclaim to have the fortune of the gods. Yet, there it is. The arrogant and self-absorbed prince; shuffling slowly away. Weighed down by something she does not even want to guess at.

"I just need a night of distraction," he says, dealing the cards to those at the table. Prince Cian has bags under his eyes and creases near his mouth that were not there months ago.

Despite being ill, King Tarmon still makes regular public appearances, yet he comes back more drained than he had left; the priests of Culain are often not far behind him. He regularly excuses himself early from events and defers to Prince Cian in many decisions advisers press for. He insists that this wedding be more extravagant than his own. The spectacle would surely mend the unrest in the kingdom and the factions breaking out in his own court.

Dukes and earls are constantly making their suggestions to Prince Cian, rather than the king, in many matters. What did he think of Sir Eloi Cariveau, the newest ambassador from Garcelon, expected to arrive this winter? Had he given thought to the trading issues with Qaewi? Would he recall the diplomats currently in Tsvetokrasa now that three priests of Culain had been murdered there by the elusive assassin, Raisa Tassia? The air around him is full of "if I may be so bold—" and "I was hoping you had given thought to—" and gratuitous clearings of throats.

The most frequent of those seeking his attention are the priests of Culain. Their focus on him soon eclipses even their attention to the king, and they seem to materialize out of nowhere whenever they need him, appearing in hallways that were surely empty just moments ago. With every passing day, they appear more and more nervous and more and more insistent that Prince Cian attend to them in private. Soon, it becomes common for them to barge into Caitlin's chambers in search of him.

She takes her cards and wonders if he thinks they will not find him here tonight. She is worried, but she is unsure what she is worried about. Preoccupied, she forgets to throw her hand.

"Another winning hand, my cunning Caitlin,"

"I concede, though, that you were more skilled. I just had luck."

"And what luck Lady Laocre has. The luck to meet the kingdom's most talked about prince," Princess Daya says.

"Yes," Lady Emeire says, eyes downcast. "Such luck. I wish I had luck like that."

Prince Cian beams and throws his arm over Caitlin's shoulder, pulling her close. That he continues to be oblivious to Princess Daya's jabs after his request for Caitlin to be an adviser is astounding. He had shown Caitlin that he was just as adept at plotting as the rest of the court. *Surely, he would have picked up on this by now?*

He shuffles the cards and slowly deals them out, eyes lingering on each of those at the table, tossing a card one at a time. On the third round, he tosses a card to Lady Arlina but misses; the card falls in front of him. He grimaces for a single second before smoothing his face into a smile. "Ah, a moment, page boy," he raises his hand. "Over here. Water." On the inside seam of his shirt, Caitlin sees a dark red stain. Only a drop, smaller than a coin. But there. She shakes her head. *Was his shirt stained with blood this morning?*

"You need water, your Grace?" Lady Emeire leaps from her chair. "I shall fetch some; no need to bother the servants!"

"Spirited young woman, is she not?" Prince Cian laughs as she disappears.

"My lord, here is your water. I brought the wine, too." She turns her attention to Caitlin. "I hope you don't mind, my lady."

Caitlin shakes her head.

"Now, then. Let us see how lucky everyone is this time!" He raises his cup.

An insistent knock echoes through the room. "Damn it all. I am not here, you have not seen me, and you do not know where I am. Let me know when they are gone," Cian says before sprinting to Caitlin's bedchamber.

Father Nael and his apprentices do not wait to be announced and let themselves in after the third knock. "Your Grace," he says to Caitlin. "I am sorry to interrupt you, but it is a matter of great importance. Where is his Highness?"

Lady Emeire slips around the table and tiptoes out of the main chambers and into her personal room, Caitlin wishes she could follow suit. Heart pounding, she says, "I do not know where his Highness is, your Eminence. Have you not checked his rooms?"

The acolytes fan out, each taking a side of the room, hunting for something or someone. "Lady Laocre, Culain values honesty in His adherents. I find it," he pushes her aside and stands next to the table and lifts the cards the Cian had thrown down, "admirable that you are so loyal to your fiancé that you would lie when he asks you to. You must truly be in love with him. But there are some people you do not lie to."

He tosses the cards to the floor and stares at the others still in the room. "This is a private conversation. I suggest you leave."

Lady Arlina rushes to her chamber, but Princess Daya stands tall, squares her shoulders, and walks out calmly, Princess Eleanor following her.

The priest advances on Caitlin while his acolytes flank her from behind. "Now, I understand that you were not raised properly and know little about the Tudáe. This is not a fault of yours, but your fathers. I do not blame you. But you are being given opportunity after opportunity to grow and bask in the light of Culain. I am happy to help you along your path of learning. And today, I shall teach you your first lesson."

Caitlin steps back to place herself between the priest and the door to her bedchamber, but she trips on her skirt, falling to the floor. Father Nael pays no mind and leans down to continue speaking with her, the air around him filling with the scent of burning oak. "Gods are to be obeyed above princes and kings. As Culain's representative on this earth, you are to obey me before the king or prince. So I ask you again, where is Prince Cian?"

Caitlin shivers, noticing the ceremonial knife tied to Father Nael's belt, speckled in blood and engraved with a symbol she's never seen before; a tree growing out of a chalice.

"If you want to sit on the throne beside him, you need *my* approval. Right now, you have it. But if you do not move aside, I shall withdraw it."

She rises to her feet again and steps out of his way, heart pounding.

Before the priest can grab the handle, the door opens, and Prince Cian steps out. "Do not be mad at the Duchess of Laocre. I have been feeling unwell. She was only trying to preserve my health." His eyes sweep the room, taking in the scattered cards on the floor. "What is so urgent that you interrupted a family gathering and disrupted the rest of a sick man?"

"I should not have to remind you of your *royal* duties, your Highness."

Saying nothing, Prince Cian pecks Caitlin on the cheek and then walks out of her rooms, Brother Sheath and Brother Sloane tailing him. Father Nael straightens his back, clasps his hands in front of him, turns on his heel, and leaves Caitlin standing, confused in the chaos.

ELEVEN

Flowers and Foes

"This is it? The jeweler you chose, Lairde Kegan?" Caitlin steps out of the carriage and approaches the door of a small shop nestled between an apothecary and a tailor, fanning herself. It is nearly autumn, but the heat of high summer clings to the air, insistent and constant.

The sign is weather-worn, but "Evoy Emporium" is still legible on the placard next to the door. "This is the one, my lady," they say, holding the door open. "I spoke to the shop owner, Seraph."

The attendants browse for jewelry themselves, while the Duchess of Clare stands with her arms crossed just outside of the door. Her presence was not requested, yet she insisted on coming along. She spent much of the last few months away from court, apparently taking up residence in the courts of Garcelon. She only recently returned. But now she is a shadow, ever-present yet barely noticeable.

It is apparent she does not want to be here as much as Caitlin does not want her here. Yet she demanded that she join.

"Ah, my lady. You do us a great honor to grace our humble establishment." Seraph is nearing 80, each wrinkle etched deeply, with a harshness that speaks to her being grumpy even before she inherited the trappings of the temperament so often reserved only for small but fearsome grandmothers. "I can show you the best of our gems in the back if you would like."

Lady Arlina raises an eyebrow. Caitlin shakes her head, and Lady Arlina goes back to inspecting a necklace while Caitlin follows the older woman.

"Wait. I know you," she says, sitting in the cramped but warm office. Shelves line each wall, floor to ceiling, and not one of them is empty. There is a desk in the corner, but no way to use it as the chair has boxes stacked on it, and the desk itself is covered in several inches of stacked papers. "I've seen you before."

"Yea, you have girly." Seraph Evoy smiles as she picks up a mug from a desk and sets it before Caitlin. "It's from Qaewi. Drink up. Should still be warm."

"You were at the first meeting I attended..."

"Yup, I was." She spots two lily pins sitting on a worktable in the back corner. *Of course.* Seraph opens a box on the table and methodically removes several fine pieces of jewelry, placing them before Caitlin. Caitlin's eyes widen in awe at the spectacular gems and stones Seraph places before her.

She laments that she did not know of this shop before today; Red Front or no, her fathers need to set up a business relationship with this woman. The gems in the store's front are magnificent enough in their own right, but these must be the ones Seraph reserves for bribing and buying. "You truly keep an expensive collection."

"And you yourself once had a collection, more eclectic but just as expensive. Do you doubt my sincerity? I do not doubt yours."

"I do not doubt you."

"Good. I have no news. There continue to be arguments about approach and strategy, so not much is being accomplished right now. Myles and Tyn keep proposing this parliament idea that the king will never agree to."

"I am sorry to hear that."

"It is only half of a solution! The king would still be king. Myles thinks that this idea would be more likely to be enacted. If you want my opinion, why would someone with power ever willingly cede it, even a smidgen of it, when such concessions would not benefit them in the slightest?"

Caitlin shifts in her chair uncomfortably.

"You do not agree with my stance?"

"With all due respect, I just do as I am told. I have no place in the arguments."

"Is that so, girly?" She reclines in her seat and taps her cane on the floor. "Is that what you think? Tell me, what do you think this whole business is about?"

"Well, overthrowing the monarchy."

"And the result would be? What should come after that?"

Caitlin looks down at her hands, wringing them over and over.

"Well, girly. Keep doing as you're told, then, if that is what you want."

"It's not what I want! However, I was given very little information about this mission. I feel out of my depth. I am not as well-read. Diar gave me some philosophy books on the subject, but it was far too abstract. And there are many things I am unprepared for."

"How so?"

"I feel like vital information has been withheld from me. No one spent any time giving me any more information on the key courtiers and advisers than I already knew."

"What information would you have wanted?

"I don't know! More information on the clergy! The priests have been obnoxious and threatening; no one told me anything—"

"Was that information withheld from you? Or did you not think to ask those questions before you accepted the mission?" Seraph taps a single finger on the table.

"I didn't know what I didn't know. How was I supposed to know to ask about that? If I had known—"

"You wouldn't have taken the assignment? You would have found some way to smuggle yourself out of the country to escape the marriage?"

Caitlin buries her face in her hands. "I don't know! Maybe?"

Seraph leaves the room, and Caitlin wonders if she has somehow failed a test, heart pounding loudly in her chest. The older woman reappears with two steaming mugs. "And this stuff," she says as she sits back down, "is from Sua. From Esiri, specifically. It's not poisoned, so don't look at me like that. Anyway, do you see any jewels in here you want to wear on your wedding day?"

She glances around, but then she sees it: a gold circlet. Delicate, so thin that one might be afraid to hold it lest it bend out of shape or break. But Caitlin can tell that it is the pure, strong, and magical metal that only comes from the Isles of the *Ástfriður*. Seraph turns, eyes following Caitlin's gaze.

"Beautiful, isn't it? You're probably as keen-eyed as me and know that's what it's for, aren't you, girly?"

"Yes... I know it." Her breath hitches, words catching in her throat.

"Spected as much. You're quite the negotiator, gotta know your wares and the values of others."

"It's not that...it's... Never mind. I have little to tell you that wasn't already sent via Kegan and Kiandre. Well, Prince Cian says he wants me to be an adviser."

"Adviser, eh? Think you can manage that?"

"I will do as I must," she says, determined not to fail any more tests.

"Hmm. Do you know what you want?"

Her gaze is searing, a fire that one would not think could exist in a person as old and as frail seeming as she. There is a storm in her; a storm that she has harnessed, has dominated, and now directs as she pleases—the tornado following her will, instead of blowing her off course.

"I cannot decide today which jewels I should buy. I shall have to visit again."

"Hmph. Consider it carefully, girly."

Kegan hands over the gold dael to Seraph as Caitlin walks back to the front. Money whose purpose will never be to purchase jewels. Lady Arlina grabs Caitlin's elbow. "Are you alright, my lady?"

"I am fine." Caitlin lifts her head high and eyes straight forward.

"I was not truly asking a question, my lady. You are not well."

"I will be fine."

"Would you like a bath drawn when we return to the palace?"

Lady Arlina's hand on Caitlin's elbow is scorching when all Caitlin wants right now is ice. She wants not the fires of change but the stasis of winter. Winters so long ago. This inferno, the people asking her to keep it blazing, feeding it... stoking it higher by her own desires. She did not truly volunteer to be standing on this pyre.

She did not want to be at the intersection of so many paths, so many people beckoning her to walk down the path that they wanted, her flames following behind.

"Yes, Lady Arlina. Please, I would like a bath. But I want a cold one."

There are far too many outings, such as the one to Seraph's shop. Both the Red Front and the royal family encourage Caitlin to patronize many other merchants, shops, establishments, temples, and anywhere else that either thinks will benefit them. For the Red Front, she gathers and dispenses information, and for the Royal Family, she shows the people that the monarchy was not afraid of some small malcontents; there is no reason for protests at all. She becomes known as "the people's princess," and there is no one in the court who wants to do anything but encourage that affection. Being seen and being seen happy in the city is vital to maintaining the image of a benevolent king.

And she wants nothing to do with it.

Yet she gives coin where she is supposed to, gives information as she is expected to do so, makes friends wherever she can, and wins the trust of everyone she must.

Caitlin is thankful that at least one of the people she must report to is located in the Royal Palace. It is easy to arrange meetings with Sister Kiandre. Having to arrange journeys to the city requires guards, and schedules, and horses, and dresses, and the subterfuge is not worth it, in Caitlin's opinion. Not when she can tell everything to Sister Kiandre.

"Trust no one. Not even me," Sister Kiandre had told her. Regardless of convenience, she must continue to pick which bits of information to give to whom.

"You are sure that you have seen blood on his clothing?" Sister Dierdre is visiting today and meanders around Kiandre's closet-office while Caitlin leans against a shelf. The autumn equinox was a week ago, but the Sisters of Andraste have spent the entire week celebrating the Ascendancy of the Moon. That the priestess made time for her is a miracle that she does not want to take for granted.

"Yes, multiple times now. Do you believe he is sick with something?"

"Our bargain was that I pass the information you give to me on to our mutual friend, and in exchange, you give me information that I want to know. Nowhere in there did I mention that I give information to you. Do you have anything else with which you can bargain? What else could you have that I want?"

"I do not know…"

"No need to answer that. If there is something I want, I will let you know."

"I see."

"There is one bit of information that I will give you freely, but only because I was asked to." She stops pacing and looks Caitlin in the eyes. "Our mutual friend is ill."

"Aine? Sick?"

"Well, more sick than usual. There was another factory fire. She was there that day and got caught up in it. Someone later found her passed out. She's making a recovery, but it's slow."

"I am not sure that this is a good idea," Caitlin says to Kegan. "People already ask why you seem to be away from court more often than you are here."

"I must do it, please. She is sick and I cannot... I need to see her. I've already arranged it." Kegan fiddles with a whittled swan. A gift from a budding carpentry business when she and the rest of her ladies shopped for decorations for the wedding. A gift that has been useful in establishing another line of communication. Kegan now regularly receives letters from their 'family,' letters with hidden meanings they can easily decode with ciphers hidden in wooden ornaments. "Come with me. I know you miss him, too. It will be 'benevolence work', or whatever the king calls it."

She turns away from Kegan and approaches an open window, a gentle breeze carrying the scent of late-blooming hibiscus. She watches the stable boys lead two black stallions out to the courtyard and hands the reins to Lady Clare and Ambassador Cariveau from Garcelon, who had arrived in Fayn earlier than expected. His predecessor had taken a turn for the worse and left the court sooner than she had wanted. She had been here for decades, having arrived on the ship carrying Queen Isleen before her wedding.

"I suppose..."

"Please, she's my only family. She's the one who found me..."

"Found you?" She turns back around, brows knit.

"When I... no! It doesn't matter, I need to see her! She hates taking her normal medicine and always forgets to do her exercises and gets up too quickly, and it's been so hot out, and she..."

"Kegan, go to her. Just go. I give you my blessing and my love; take some time off to be with her."

"That's not what I was asking for."

"I know it wasn't, but it's what you need."

"No, I can't just abandon you or abandon the mission!"

Caitlin takes a deep breath and wishes that, just for once, Kegan weren't so contrary and mercurial. "You won't be able to focus on the mission until you know she's better, though."

"That's not true! I'm fine, I am, I'll be fine—!"

The cedar doors to her antechamber swing open, and Prince Cian and Lord Rorick march in, the latter glaring at Caitlin, his jet-black hair greasy and his top lip curled up at the corners. "Where is she?"

"My lord, who are you speaking of?" Caitlin glances at Kegan and nods. Kegan slinks out of the rooms without notice. *Hopefully, to pack their bags and leave.*

"My sister. She's one of your ladies, isn't she?" His face is so close to hers that she can feel his breath on her cheeks and smell the ale he must have been drinking.

"Rorick. You will not speak to Lady Lacore like that. I have already told you—" Prince Cian grabs Lord Rorick's arm and yanks the enraged noble away from Caitlin.

"And I have told you that my family matters are none of your concern." He pulls away from Prince Cian and jabs the prince in the chest with his forefinger.

"Rorick... I am warning you," he says, stepping between Caitlin and Lord Rorick.

"Get out of my way, you spineless coward." Lord Rorick shoves the prince out of the way and storms up to Caitlin again. "Where is she? That whore thinks she can just—"

"Lord Rorick. Leave. My. Rooms. She is my lady-in-waiting, and she—"

He pushes Caitlin away with a growl, and she tumbles to the floor. "That whore! Does she think she can just moon after some foreign diplomat? Where is she?"

"Lord Rorick, out! If you do not leave, I will have the guards remove you." Prince Cian motions to the two men posted at the doors and rushes to Caitlin.

"Did you not see her? Last night? No, never mind. I'll find her later." He throws his arms up and storms out of Caitlin's rooms.

"My lady, my sweetheart, I am so sorry about that. I believe his father is near his time, and it has him more of a boar than usual."

"It is fine. No need to worry. I will let Lady Ronai know to steer clear of her brother. I do not want one of my ladies abused like that."

"Ah, yes. My caring and kind Caitlin." He takes her hand and leads her to the plush sofa, brushing his thumb on her palm.

"Has he always been so..."

"Rude? Yes. He thinks highly of himself and has been in a foul temper since his other sister was married a few years back to Emyr Owen, Earl of Iomaire."

"Does he not like Lord Iomaire?"

"That is the strange thing. Lord Rorick was the one who arranged that marriage against the wishes of their father. You would think that

Lord Rorick would be happy that there were no objections from Lord Iomaire when he approached him about the match."

"Lord Iomaire is the ambassador to Tsvetokrasa, right? Maybe he did not realize how often his sister would be away. Are they close?"

"No, another strange thing. He seemed happy when she left with Iomaire for Tsvetokrasa."

"I do not like him."

"Nor do I. My Caitlin, I value your opinion on this. I am glad we are in agreement; if you can learn more about what is going on, I would appreciate it if you share it with me." He kisses her. "Are you well? You fell hard."

"I am fine. I will be fine. Thank you."

"You are right to keep Lady Ronai close to you, at least until her brother calms down. Has she done anything that might have upset him?"

"No, my lord. She has been nothing but upstanding. Your mother was wise to suggest her as a lady. She accompanies me on all of my outings. She is a kind and attentive helper when we visit the homes for the poor that the Acolytes of Yseult have established. Everyone loves her there. Which reminds me." She takes a deep breath. "The Temple of Andraste has been approached by a medical clinic in the city for assistance; there is a fever in the eastern side of the city, and the physicians are overwhelmed. My ladies and I would like to help."

"You mean to send them money?"

"No, my lord. We would like to go with some of the Sisters and assist directly."

He smiles and tucks a stray hair behind her ear, his hand hot on her skin. "Will you ever stop amazing me? Yes, I shall make the arrangements. What days are the Sisters going?"

"In five days."

"You should ask Eleanor and Daya if they would like to go, too. I am sure they would. A family outing!" He snaps his fingers, smiling like a child.

"Of course, my lord. Thank you."

"And if you hear anything about Lady Ronai, well, do let me know if something changes." He turns to leave at the same time that Lady Arlina enters the rooms, her head down, shoulders hunched in on themselves. "Oh, Lady Arlina, how are you today?"

She curtsies to him. "Well, your Grace. I hope that you are doing well yourself."

"Yes, I am. My Caitlin here just had a fall. Please take care of her in my place." His eyes wander up and down her figure, taking in every curve and every feature.

"Of course, your Grace." She turns away from him, averting her eyes. "With honor."

"Remember what I told you, my Caitlin; we must work as a team."

"Yes, he is king in all but name right now. He is the one everyone goes to for decisions," she tells Diar as she hands him a rag, the fumes of alcohol overwhelming.

He wipes down the exam table, brows furrowed. "I could have guessed that. The princesses? You say they seem to dislike him?"

"Yes, especially Daya."

"What about any of the other courtiers?" He looks over his shoulders; the door between the exam room and waiting room is still closed, but the faint sound of children crying can still be heard, as can Lady Ronai's soothing voice as she sings to entertain the scared and sick patients.

"Sometimes I think Lady Dontaue may dislike him, but I cannot actually tell. No one else seems willing to question him right now, though."

"That's a wrench in the plan." He throws the rag in a bucket of water and collapses into a chair, fingers steepled.

"What plan?" She leans against the exam table and crosses her arms.

"Doesn't matter anymore."

"Please, Diar. At least tell me. I feel so out of my depth right now."

"What do you mean?"

"I feel like I wasn't given half the information I should have been! I was told to spy, but instead, I'm trying to survive."

"You're in danger?" He sits up straighter, eyes wide.

"Did no one tell you about the priest threatening me?"

"What?! Which priest? Who?" He leaps up and grabs her shoulders, searching her eyes.

"The High Priest of Culain. No one told me that they played such a big role in the court. I knew they were important players, but they seem to think they are the actual rulers. Please, I am not injured." She shrugs away from him, hands raised.

"Someone definitely should have debriefed you with all of the information we do have. I am sorry for that oversight."

"Are you sure it was an oversight? Or did someone see an opportunity and fear it may slip through their fingers if they weren't careful?"

"What are you implying? Are you saying I—"

"Not you," she says, rubbing his arm. "But I am not sure what I would have done if someone had informed me just how many wolves were in the den."

"I see what you are saying. So, you want out?"

"I didn't say that. But..."

"You feel deceived," he says, grabbing another clean rag and dipping it into the bowl of alcohol.

"Yes. I don't feel like this was entirely my choice." She waits for him to defend Valen and Sharidan. She waits for him to justify any omissions or explain that it's all a misunderstanding.

"I hear you," he says, scrubbing intently at some dirt that Caitlin cannot see. "I will talk to them about it. Do you want out?"

"That's not possible, not now. Not anymore. The wedding is only six weeks away..."

"It wouldn't be easy, no. But, if I have to do it myself, I will find a way. If that's what you want."

"But there may never be another opportunity like this again," she says, not sure who she is arguing with. Herself? Diarmuid?

"That's more than one way to take down a monarchy."

"What if I mess this up, though?"

"You are intelligent, clever, your poker face is too good, and your genial nature gets you more allies than I think you realize."

"Arlina..." she says.

"Your lady-in-waiting? An ally?"

Caitlin blushes. "Yes, at least, I think she might be."

"For the Red Front or for you? You need both."

She nods. "I think so."

"Then keep her close. If you choose to continue the mission, that is."

"I think I can keep going. I just feel so out of my depth."

"We all are."

"Oh, I think there are a few more things you need to know. The Duchess of Clare is being odd. She follows me everywhere, but she cannot tolerate me. The feeling is mutual, mind you. But she is otherwise entertaining the Garcelonian retinue."

"Interesting. Is she angling for a royal marriage of her own? Does Garcelon have any eligible royals of marrying age?"

"I don't know."

"One of the things that Sharidan has requested is information on when nobles might be out of the country or otherwise engaged in some sort of business that would leave them unable to keep a close watch on their properties and estates. It will help us plan our movements and any attempts at uprisings."

"I see. I have nothing right now, though, except gossip. Lord Rorick dislikes both of his sisters for some reason. One of them is currently in Tsvetokrasa with her husband, an ambassador, though I doubt he would leave here to visit her. Liam and Connor have been scarce. I haven't seen them in some time. I don't have much more than that."

"Rorick? The earl or his son? We do have a small base there in Caibre. That might be a good place to start."

"Start? Start what."

"I am tempted to tell you, but it's a surprise."

The back door opens quietly, and Kegan peeks in. They have been gone a little more than a week, but Caitlin has missed their laughter. "Oh! I forgot you were going to be here today," they say. "I'm just here to pick up that powder for Aine."

"It's in the top drawer."

"I'll be back next week, by the way," they say to Caitlin. "Aine is doing much better, but I don't know if she'll ever return to where she was before."

"You do not need to rush."

"It's not that. Aine is telling me I need to. She says I am making it impossible for her 'many lovers' to visit." Kegan laughs at some joke that Caitlin does not understand.

Diarmuid folds in on himself and buries his face in his hands. "She'll never learn."

"She doesn't want to."

TWELVE

WEDDINGS AND WIDOWS

*I*T TOOK ANOTHER YEAR *for them to properly plan. Da and Pa had so many business friends to invite, and so many more regular clients had wanted to be there for the wedding when it happened. Even if they couldn't attend the ceremony, they planned to celebrate on their own in the inns. Brenna was loved; xie had lived on the waters as they had. That's as close to family as xie could have here on this side of the s ea.*

Xie had settled on something between a skirt and breaches, a formal coat, all in copper. Xie took xir ahnhörn out of storage. Xie insisted that Caitlin's dress be trimmed in copper thread. At this point, Caitlin knew. Brenna had no concept of gender, so xie had tried on as many as xie could and planned to keep doing so. The stable part of xir identity was the metal xie had chosen, the metal that all Ástfriður choose for themselves at their coming-of-age ceremony; the first time that an Ástfriður does more than use their magic to shape metal, but uses their magic to summon metal; specifically, the metal that they feel a deep connection to. Xie had chosen copper. Others took on silver, bronze, gold... And they called it from the ground; they shaped it with a thought. It was magic. Magic that the rest of the world knew nothing of. Magic they rarely practiced outside of their Veiled forests, let alone in front of non-Ástfriður.

And Brenna had done it for Caitlin. They had laws, customs, and traditions around using their metal magic, and Brenna had used the holiest of them for Caitlin. Caitlin could wear it to the Veil and be granted entrance past the port as if she herself were an Ástfriður. Caitlin could ride one of their prized horses through their woods and not be hunted or seen as an outsider. Xie had given Caitlin a gift that many would kill for. Xie trusted Caitlin that much.

On that muggy midsummer day, there were tears and laughs and smiles and speeches and toasts and dancing and lewd songs sung off-key; all of the things you might expect from a wedding where half the guests might be pirates. Ale was drunk and spilled, cake was eaten, flowers tossed, and all around was the smell of the sea, the salty brine of home.

And then xie said as they walked inside their house, "My wife, let us make ourselves business partners and merge our assets."

"Stop it!"

"Stop what?"

"We're here to have fun, sweetheart," Caitlin said as she pushed Brenna onto the bed. "Not to do business."

But after their lovemaking and asset-merging, Brenna held out a knife to Caitlin. "Let us do it according to the Ástfriðuran law, too."

The crown has spikes that claw into her head, the lace on the gown is woven around thin blades that bite her skin, her shoes are lined with crushed rocks, and her veil is a funeral shroud. Yet everyone claps and cheers as she walks up the stairs to the Temple of Culain. The golden sun at its pinnacle catches fire as she passes through the doors.

"More," she had told Lady Arlina while getting dressed. She took off her bracelet, the one Brenna had woven with metal and magic. The first time in how many years? *Not enough years.* She tucked it away in the back of a jewelry box. She wanted to wear it always, but today, she couldn't. "More wine." *It isn't enough.* She can still feel the unwanted warmth on her arm as Prince Cian grabs her elbow to lead her the rest of the way to the altar. She can still hear the crowd's murmurs as they wonder about the future. She can still smell the poinsettias that line the rows of benches. She can still see Father Nael at the end of the aisle, Brother Sheath and Brother Sloan behind him.

Anywhere but here, anywhere but here.

Diarmuid's practice, he's washing his tools and asking her which tavern they should go to tonight.

Her fathers' house. They are laughing as she passes the bread around.

Kegan and Aine's cottage. They show her their garden while Aine tells tales of Kegan's youth.

The lighthouse at Whick, watching the ships come and go and savoring the smell of salt.

In the Temple of Muriel, Samaire is letting her bath in their pond as a small retreat from the palace life.

Home. Home with Brenna. Setting out dinner, calling for their cats to come inside, cuddling up next to Brenna on the bench on their porch to watch the sea swallow the sun. Home and free.

Anywhere but here.

"This is it, sweetheart." His breath is hot in her ear, and she closes her eyes as they stop their procession before Father Nael.

Anywhere but here.

The room spins, and everything grows far away. There are people speaking to her, but they are distant and indistinct. She nods and smiles at the hazy figures around her. She follows as she is lead, a puppet at her own unwanted wedding.

Anywhere else. Somewhere else.

Prince Cian speaks of love and duty, of fate and destiny, of forevers and of eternities. He makes promises and pledges, wrapped up in the fanciful flourishes of a boy helplessly in love. He speaks of days and years to come, of passion and devotion.

Caitlin recites her own vows, not as wordy but just as elegant. Words that are poison on her tongue, words that taste like spoiled meat, words she wishes to unsay. She does not hear the cheers as she finishes hers, she does not feel his lips on hers as they seal their vows, she does not feel or see or be.

Anywhere but here.

"More wine, my sweetheart?" he asks. He is drunk. Caitlin shakes her head. "More for me!"

"I'll take some more, my lord," Lady Emeire says.

The wedding ring now adorning his finger means little to the women still determined to catch his eye and the parents wanting to force their daughters on him still. Lady Emeire has found a way to the center of the table is sat on the other side of the prince, making eyes at him. She is not deterred.

Caitlin doesn't want to consider the possibilities now. The only way out of her marriage is in death or revolution. As much as she had hoped he would discard her for someone else, she knows now that she must fight to at least keep him in love with her if she wants to survive. "That's a good girl," Father Nael had whispered to her after the ceremony. "Stay a good girl, and I will not take your fairy tale away."

She catches snippets of conversation as the nobles and elites mill about, waiting for their turn to offer their personal congratulations.

"Just because you are in the family does not mean you get a say in it. This is your last warning, Nait," Lord Hern admonishes his son-in-law.

"Father, please don't do this again," Lady Elwen says.

"Dearest, do not worry. I can handle this on my own." Sir Nait grabs his wife's hand and pulls her away from her father.

"My lady, are you well?" Lady Arlina rests her hand on Caitlin's shoulder.

"Yes, thank you. And you?" Caitlin smiles genuinely for the first time that day.

Lady Arlina winces and glances at her father, sulking in a corner. "I will be. But my primary concern is you."

"I will be fine, thank you." Caitlin sets her hand on Lady Arlina's and squeezes it. "Where is Laide Kegan?"

"I believe they are speaking with the servants or other staff."

"Hmm...." Caitlin scans the crowd.

"My lady?"

"Oh, nothing. I was just thinking."

"About?"

"It is nothing, do not worry."

"If you say so." Lady Arlina gives a small curtsy and returns to her seat.

"Where is she?" Lairde Artair grabs a glass of wine from the server before the server can offer.

"She's doing her job, look." Lord Artair points at the head table, directly at his daughter, Lady Emeire.

"Shame that it's not the pretty one that will throw herself at him. If Caragh had just listened—"

"Ruben! Stop. She may be a disobedient daughter, but she is still our daughter. She will come around."

Caitlin wishes her hearing weren't so good.

"Ah! Our new princess!" Lairde Artair approaches with a swagger and winks at his daughter.

Caitlin grins. Were they speaking loud enough for her to hear on purpose? "Lord Artair, Lairde Artair. Thank you for allowing your beautiful daughter to be one of my ladies-in-waiting. Do you not have another daughter? I could have sworn I had heard you had two daughters."

Lairde Artair blanches. "Ah, you speak of Caragh. Yes, she is away right now, though."

"Away?"

"Ah, yes..." Lairde Artair fidgets with a button on his coat. "She is a potential novitiate with the Order of Shea."

"I would love to meet her one day."

"Ah, well. The Gallagher family is much appreciative to be so honored by our beloved new princess."

Prince Cian turns to Caitlin. "Ah, Lord Artair, were you looking for your daughter? My apologies, I have been monopolizing her attention, it seems."

"Oh, no, it is fine," Lady Emeire says, her voice pitching. "I am sure whatever it is my fathers want can wait."

"She is right. It can wait."

"Ah, no. Alas, I do have to speak with other guests tonight. Though I fear all of my conversations will be the same, I shall ramble about my happiness with my bride." He places his hand on Caitlin's knee, smiling.

"Is that…" Lairde Artair shakes his head. "Is that what you have been discussing with Emmie?"

The prince chuckles. "I am truly a lovesick fool, am I not?"

"Well, many congratulations." Lord Artair bows, and his husband follows suit. "May the gods smile upon you both."

"How are you, my love?" Prince Cian asks Caitlin.

"How could I be anything other than elated right now?" She raises her glass of wine. "To a bright future."

"To *our* bright future."

"Ah, there are the lovebirds." Lady Clare stumbles toward their table and grabs Caitlin's wine.

"Aelena, wait!" The Duke of Dontaue rushes up behind her. "That is not yours."

"Aww, is Auntie Maeve afraid I will make a fool of myself? How cute."

"Stop it." Lady Dontaue grabs the glass from Lady Clare and slams it back onto the table.

"It is fine. She can have it," Caitlin says. But the royal duchesses are not paying attention.

"I know what you are doing, and not tonight. Not. Tonight."

"You have no idea what I am doing, and you are not my mother." Lady Clare trips on her gown and tumbles to the floor. Prince Cian frowns, raising an eyebrow at his aunt.

"I will take her back to her rooms. I am sorry you had to see this," Lady Dontaue says.

"If you believe that would help…" he replies.

Sir Connor saunters over and pats Lady Clare on the back as she tries to get back on her feet. "You can't keep up with us, after all. Good try, though. Good try."

"Leave me alone. All of you!" She takes off her shoes and storms out of the dining hall.

Caitlin fidgets with the ring now adorning her left hand. "It has been a long day. Will you escort me to my rooms, Lady Arlina?"

Prince Cian holds up his hand. "Sweetheart, what was that? Your assistance is not needed, Lady Arlina. Tonight is the first night of many that I shall spend with my dearest love, and I shall escort you to my rooms, my princess." The prince pats Caitlin's arm and then stands up.

"Father. Mother." He lifts his goblet toward the king and queen. "My friends, my family. Thank you for joining us today. It is the happiest day of my life, but I know I have even happier days ahead of me alongside my beloved Princess Gráinne."

Caitlin rises to her feet as he gestures to her.

"She's beautiful, our princess. Alas, the day has worn both of us out, and we shall retire. Thank you for your support and love for both of us." He takes her hand, and her retinue and his follow behind them as they walk to the prince's rooms.

"Leave us," he says as he opens the doors to his bedchamber. "I do not care what tradition dictates. I shall have my princess how I choose."

Caitlin desperately looks at her ladies-in-waiting. *Anywhere but here.* All they can do is curtsy and leave as ordered. The prince's friends and whoop and cheer as they head out of the doors.

"Now," he says once the door closes, and they are alone in the room. "Get to bed."

Caitlin nods and begins undressing.

He comes behind her and pulls her hair out of the pins, running his hands through it. "So pretty. Pretty, pretty Caitlin."

She cringes.

"Do not be shy, my love. We have been waiting for this day for so long. Do not be nervous."

"I..."

"It is time for us to make a son, my dear. Let us be to it." He takes off his coat and unbuttons his shirt.

They are interrupted by a frantic knock on the door. "Your Majesty! Your Majesty!"

"I said I wanted privacy!"

"Majesty?" Caitlin whispers.

"It's urgent!" The page boy continues to bang on the door.

"What can be more urgent than—"

"He just called you 'Your Majesty'...." she says, and he turns to look her in the eye.

"My father..." he says. "My father!" He does not put a top on. He throws the door open, pushes the page boy aside, and dashes out of his rooms.

Caitlin finds a nightgown and quickly dons it. "Lad? Are you still there?" She exits the bedchamber and sees the page boy rubbing his elbow and standing back up.

"Yes, your Highness. His Majesty left. The king..."

"...is dead."

"Yes, your Highness."

She nods and returns to the bedchamber. If the new king wants her, he will have someone fetch her. She curls up under the thick blankets and falls asleep.

It's home, but it's a place that has never been home. Her heart recognizes it, but her senses don't.

And there is something–someone?–following her. Sometimes it has limbs and crawls on all fours towards her, sometimes, it races on two legs and reaches out with long arms, sometimes, it is a swirling black mass that follows steadily. But it is always there, just at her heels.

This thing is something familiar, something she knows, and yet she knows she has never met it before.

Her legs give out, and she pulls herself forward with her arms. Everything is heavy; her body refuses to follow her commands.

The figure is featureless, a shadow without a body standing before her now. "I found you."

Her scream is loud enough to wake anyone in the rooms. Yet they are empty, so her screams continue unheard as the shadow-person in her nightmare leers over her.

It was rushed, with leftovers from the wedding dinner served at the funeral wake. The dowager queen was both calm and quiet in her grief and wild and untamed in her anguish. For as bright and unseasonably warm as it was on the wedding day, the funeral just three days later was bitterly cold, and the rain transformed into sleet and then snow as the day wore on. How do you celebrate the end of not just a person's life but of a reign?

Caitlin shivers as she accompanies Queen Isleen back from the catacombs, where she had been keeping vigil since they had laid him to rest the week before, their footsteps the only sound on the winding stone staircase. "I know my Cian will be a marvelous king," she says, taking Caitlin's hand. "And I know you will be the most loyal queen, not just to him, but to the people. You are Fayn, where I was a foreign princess from Garcelon. You are someone they will love even more than they ever could have me."

"Your Majesty..." The dank smell of the underground mausoleum clings to them, even as they make their way slowly back to the light, and Caitlin tries to speak as little as possible.

"No, I am merely 'Highness' now," she grimaces. "The Queen Mother is what I have been told my new title shall be. They are moving me to smaller rooms, and you shall be given mine."

"I don't need them... You don't have to..." She brushes a hand down the queen's arm, brushing against the dark shroud the queen still wears.

"I cannot stay in rooms with memories. And I would like to visit my niece, Queen Joanna. I have not been back home for many years. Ambassador Cariveau said they will accompany me, and Aelena has also volunteered, and, of course, I will ask Maeve."

Caitlin nods.

"Although... Many will find it strange that the late king's wife, his eldest sister, and his niece will be in another country for the mourning period. Maybe I should put it off."

"You must do what is best for you," Caitlin says, fidgeting with the ring on her left hand.

"I suppose you are right, my dear. Is that what you do? What is best for you? Is that how you have lived your life?"

Caitlin stumbles on a slick stair, and the former queen helps her back to her feet. "I think so. I think that is how I have lived."

"Would you do me a favor?"

"What is it?"

"I am afraid that Cian will fall ill in the same way as my husband."

"Ill? From what?"

"I do not know. I could never figure it out. No one would tell me. And you cannot tell anyone else. He had some sort of affliction, and the priests of Culain helped him manage it."

"What were the symptoms?"

"The most noticeable, unfortunately, was a temper. He was so kind, so compassionate. But this affliction made him paranoid, unpredictable, and angry."

Caitlin has a hard time believing that King Tarmon was ever kind and compassionate, but Isleen has always held onto that. "I am so sorry."

"The priests tried to help, but every month they would have to sequester him for a night for some sort of healing ritual. It never seemed to help, though. And from what I hear, the same thing happened to his father, too. So if Cian… If he… Please, take care of him." The queen halts on the top stair, clenching Caitlin's hands.

"Of course, Your Highness."

"Please, call my Lady Mother. You are my daughter now."

"Of course, Lady Mother."

"Is that what you do? What is best for you? Is that how you have lived your life?"

The former queen's words clatter in her mind. What is best for her? Was dedicating her life to her fathers' business what was best for her? Or marrying the prince? Is it helping the Red Front? Is it sitting in this room now, watching the nobles fuss with their new chains of office? She drums her fingers on the council table, long and sturdy oak with the seal of the House Fola inlaid in gold at the center, while they wait for King Cian to join them, gazing out into the courtyard covered in snow. It's the first Privy Council meeting of the year and the first of King Cian's reign, only a month after this father has passed away. As promised, Caitlin has been appointed to be an adviser.

Most of the council linger near the hearth on the far side of the room, huddling around this hissing fire with drinks in hand and chests puffed out. Cian took great pains to appear fair and unbiased in his selection, a mix of nobles from ancient houses and those who were only newly titled, commoners who had come to prominence through their entrepreneurship or military service.

Of his family, he had appointed almost everyone. The princesses, his uncle, the Duke of Hern, Lord Hern's son-in-law, Sir Nait Loughlin, and his cousin, Lady Clare. Lady Elwen had declined a seat. His aunt Maeve of Dontaue had been offered a chair but also declined it. She claimed her days of politics were behind her, and she wished only to spend her days in the company of the Queen Mother. She had served on Tarmon's council, and that was quite enough for her.

He had asked his constant companions, Sir Liam and Sir Conner, much to the displeasure of the nobility. Lairde Elwee was relieved of his diplomatic duties and accepted a position on the council. Admiral Aicher Halloran was another pick that had ruffled feathers, and many wondered if it was a sort of apology to the Admiral for turning down his daughter, Captain Alice Halloran.

Brennin Rorick, now the Earl of Caibre, was asked to join the Council, but he had not been granted the title of Lord Privy Seal, as his late father had been. Both Gallaghers, Lairde Artair and Lord Artair, were given seats. Lord Berach had been appointed, and despite rarely being at court, his son Lord Byrne had, as well. Baron Rivers was the youngest member of the council.

Though not an official member of the Council, Father Nael, High Priest of Culain, will attend all meetings. He is the only clergy member given such an honor. Today he is wearing the robes usually reserved for high holidays, gold adornments weighing him down. He has not spoken a single word while the other members mill about and converse over anything and everything; instead, he leans against the stone walls and gazes out of the window, the aroma of cedar and oak emanating from him.

"It's a beautiful morning," Caitlin says to Father Nael.

"Hmm? Oh. Yes, I suppose." He looks back toward the door to the antechamber.

"I must say, I was not expecting you to claim so much of my husband's time."

He glances at her and shrugs, resuming his vigilant watch out the window.

"Should we draw up a treaty to ensure we both have ample time with our king?"

He sighs and whips around to face her. "Your Highness, you would see him much more if you accompanied him to our temple. Do not forget that you are now a member of the Royal House of Fola and expected to worship as one."

"I shall try to remember that, your Eminence. I am still new to this and have much yet to learn."

"Learn quickly if you want to survive."

"You are most generous with your advice. Thank you."

The antechamber door opens, and King Cian throws his arms wide, a huge grin on his face and a glint in his pale blue eyes. "Welcome! Friends, family, esteemed members of the council. I have many things I wish to address today, but I would like first to open the floor and give everyone a chance to bring forward their own concerns. This will be a council of equals, not favorites."

Caitlin holds back a laugh.

"Your Majesty, if I can bring up the matter of the peasant revolts. There was recently an attempted uprising on my lands," Lord Caibre says. "They killed my best horse, and my father never recovered from the fright it gave him. May he rest in peace. But I can't find hair nor hide of who exactly was the leader or who all was involved."

"Was this recent?" King Cian asks.

"About three months ago, I was…" He clears his throat and smooths down his coat. "I was dealing with personal business in Janeuq."

"Ah, yes. What for? Something about a potential suitor for your sister?"

"Correct, Your Majesty. I believe my father tried to bring the matter to King Tarmon, may he rest in peace—"

Cian winces and cuts him off. "Has anyone else experienced this lately? I know my father was keeping tabs on acts of unrest, but not strict enough, in my opinion. This ends now. It never should have gotten to the point that he was—well, what's done is done. This is more than personal now."

"As you know, the workers at our factories, and others from what I hear, have been striking," Sir Liam says.

"I've had more than a few crew members, good people, all of them, desert lately. Unexpected, but I have seen none of them since," Admiral Halloran says.

King Cian nods. "My Queen?"

"Yes, my lord?"

"Have you encountered anything? On your trips to the city, or heard anything from your fathers?"

"Your Majesty, if I may—" Father Nael raises his hand.

"No, you may not." The king glares at the priest. "Queen Gráinne, continue."

"Well, my lord." Her heart races so fast that she fears that she will pass out, and it beats so loudly that she worries others will hear. "I know that there are some worries among the merchants about import taxes, especially from Garcelon. A fear that has, unfortunately, only heightened since your father's passing."

"You think that is related to the dissatisfaction of the people?"

"The increase in prices for goods that the people need may stretch their money thin."

"I see your point. However, everyone must make sacrifices. The kingdom has a budget, as should the people."

"They could just stop buying all the unnecessary things. I saw one worker come in yesterday with a golden pin on her shirt. I will admit, it is a beautiful pin of a lily. But she was one of those striking for 'fair wages' just last week. And yet she can afford a pin like that? I call bullshit." Sir Connor throws his glass of wine back in one gulp. "They need to know their place!"

"Here, here!" Sir Liam says, raising his goblet.

"He has the right of it!" Lairde Artair adds his own drink to the toast, his husband nodding in agreement and raising his already empty mug.

"You already know how I feel, cousin," Lady Clare sits back in her chair and interlaces her fingers.

The council continues for the rest of the day and into the early evening. When King Cian finally ends the meeting, Caitlin wants nothing more than a cold drink and a warm bed. But she has duties. "Lairde Artair," Caitlin says, not letting him out of the room. "We haven't had much chance to speak to each other. Your daughter, Lady Emeire, is one of my favorite ladies, and I very much would like to learn more about her family. May I invite you and your husband to dine with me sometime?"

"Well, this is certainly unexpected, Your Majesty."

"Please, 'your Highness' is enough. And is it really so unexpected? Well, nonetheless. I insist."

"Yes, Your Highness. Finn and I would be most gracious to accept such an invitation. But I would like to propose that, instead, we will host you for dinner. You could come to our estate in the city. We have an excellent art collection that I think you would appreciate."

Caitlin grins. "I would love to. When?"

"Does this Saturday work for you?"

"I look forward to it."

Lairde Artair bows to her and continues on his way.

"Would you like me to accompany you there, my lady?" Kegan trails behind her, ears pricked forward.

"That won't be necessary. I'll have Sir Dermont or one of the other knights accompany me. I want this to be an intimate affair."

"You seem to enjoy this."

"Enjoying?"

"Politics."

"More like endure. But I do what I must."

Queen Isleen's words again ricochet in her mind. "Is that what you do? What is best for you? Is that how you have lived your life?" No. She's doing what is best. This is what is best. She's always done what is best. She cannot change who she is now.

They turn a corner and almost collide with Lady Arlina. She drops a stack of papers to the floor and hurries to pick them up. "My lady! I am sorry, I didn't see you, I was too preoccupied with—"

"It is alright, Lady Arlina. Do you need help with that?"

"What? Oh, you are too kind, my lady. Thank you."

"What's this? I don't mean to pry, but is your father traveling to Garcelon in a few weeks?" Caitlin scans a letter sent to Lord Berach but sees no sign of who the writer is.

"Hmm? Oh, yes. He has a good friend there, in Linea. My brother is going, too, at the end of next month. His friend has a beautiful vineyard, I am told. He promised to return with some of the best wine. Would you like some? I could ask him to bring back enough for you, too."

"The end of next month…" Caitlin says, glancing at Kegan. "Yes, I suppose I can wait a few weeks to try the famous Linean wine."

"Excellent! I shall tell him. I must go, though, my lady. He will be most displeased if I do not bring him these papers."

"Of course. I hope that I will see you tonight, though."

Lady Arlina blushes. "Yes, my lady. I shall be there."

"I heard you will dine with the Gallaghers," King Cian says, placing his napkin on the table.

"Yes, my lord. Do you mind?" She accepts a refill on her wine as the servant clears away the dinner plates. She shivers. While their rooms are identical, the king does not keep his hearth as well fed, and this is the coldest winter in recent history. Nothing can stave off the chill.

"Of course not, Caitlin. All the better to keep an eye on them."

"You do not trust them?"

"I trust no one. We have civil unrest around the whole of Fayn, and we still do not know who the assassin was. I tell you, there is at least one spy in my court."

"You hope I can help you catch them?" She fidgets with the hem of her sleeve, the silk fabric catching on her fingernail.

"I hope you can. Accept all invitations, and issue as many as you can yourself."

"As you wish, my lord." She raises her glass, the aroma of grapes both sweet and sour. "To a new Fayn."

"To a new Fayn. Come, let us go to bed."

She stands up slowly but still stumbles. "I must have had too much wine."

He laughs. "That would be two of us. We should sleep it off." He throws off his doublet and rolls up the sleeves of his shirt. A long, neat cut runs from his elbow to his wrist. Not the cut one would get in a fight, nor one done on accident while cutting meat. It is intentional. She wants to say something, to point it out, but she remains quiet.

Is this what his mother was talking about? An illness? Or the cure for it? She pretends she does not see it and settles beside him. Nothing feels certain, nothing feels sturdy enough to hold her up. She's on a sinking ship and has forgotten how to swim. Everything is changing, and she does not feel the same. Time is unrelenting, and the path before her is fading. Dutiful daughter, wistful widow, calculating consort, resourceful rebel.

Something needs to change; this can't be how it is. The last shred of certainty in her life has been torn away. While she made this bed, she does not want to lie in it. It is not what is best for her.

PART THREE

THIRTEEN

Deeds and Desires

All winter, Caitlin does as she is told and ensures she has as many private dinners as she can with lords, ladies, and lairdes, both on and off of the council. She is so busy wooing the court's leaders that she does not immediately hear the rumors that King Cian is wooing the court's ladies. He goes missing for long stretches of time, and no one can find him.

"I miss you," she says to him as a server places their dishes. "You rarely come to see me anymore."

"I miss you, too." He digs into his food without even waiting for the server to step back, his hair still dirty and his clothes still smelling like sweat and sawdust; he did not stop at his own rooms before coming to hers. Winter has thawed, and he was eager to help repair the fencing to the jousting field that morning. The sounds of hammers still echo across the grounds even as twilight is creeping upon them.

And what priests would look for a king among workers? "I do not believe I could have imagined how stressful this king business would be. I am so lucky to have a wife who can fulfill many of my unspoken obligations. You are still gathering as much information as possible at dinners and events?"

"Ah, yes. I am."

"Good. Any interesting gossip for me? Spare me no details."

She bites her lip. The trickles of information she has coaxed out of the nobles have all made their way back to the Red Front. She does not know what their plans are, nor how they would use the information, or even if the information she provided was useful, but she has no other choice. They are her way out of this marriage. They are as much her tool as she is theirs. "Well, I do not think your uncle is fond of some of the younger lords."

"He barely tolerates me. Everyone is an 'upstart' to him."

She drums her fingers on the table. "Well, I think he might be a little too interested in seeing particular ones humiliated."

"Yes, he hates Loughlin. I am aware. Unless you mean others?"

"Yes, besides his son-in-law. He does not think highly of Elwee or Connal, specifically."

"Yes, they are rather young and were not born into nobility. You think he is planning something?"

"I could not say."

"Interesting. Did he say anything about Liam and Connor?" He barely looks up at her, continuing to shovel down his dinner.

"No, he didn't."

"He probably would not, not to you. I hope he has sense enough to know that those two are too important to me."

"You are probably right. May I ask what this other business is that you are so tied up in?" She picks at the meat on her plate. The winter has been harsh, and the meat they have been able to get has not been the freshest. Their cooks have seasoned it well, but it is still unappealing, too chewy and too tough.

"It is nothing you should concern yourself with."

"But..." She holds out her hands to him.

"Let me put it a different way." He puts down his fork and takes her hands in his. "It is nothing I want you to worry about. You are too important to me."

"You are not making sense."

"I probably am not. But stay out of it. Please, sweetheart."

She goes through the list of women he might be interested in. "I see. I do not understand, but I will do as you say."

"Thank you, my love."

Without knocking, Brother Sheath pushes the door open and enters Caitlin's rooms. "Your Majesty," he says, standing tall.

King Cian glares at the priest. "I said I was busy tonight."

The priest does not reply.

Caitlin leans forward. "What is going on?"

"Do not worry about it," he mumbles back.

"Please..."

"I said do not worry about it!" He stands up and throws his napkin at the table, face red. "It is none of your concern. Good night, my lady. I have business to attend to. I will see you tomorrow at the spring festival."

Caitlin gawks as he storms out of her chambers, the priest silently following behind him. "What did I say? What just happened?"

"Do you want to wear a pearl necklace or the silver one today, my lady?" Lady Muiris approaches with both. "I believe the pearl one would look best."

"It does not matter. Pearl, I suppose."

Her ladies finish dressing her and escort her down the long corridors of the palace. The courtiers and other nobles give them all a wide berth, something that they have not done since before the wedding. Something they hadn't done since they were still taking bets on whether King Cian would actually choose her.

"Is there something I should know?" she whispers to Lady Emeire.

Disappointment is clear in her dark blue eyes. "I am not sure. If there is, I do not know it either. They seem uneasy about something. I shall find out, though, if it would please you, my lady."

"It would. Thank you, Lady Emeire."

"The pleasure is all mine."

The guards open the doors to the council room, and Caitlin enters, leaving her attendants behind. Father Nael is the only person in the otherwise empty room, at his usual spot near the window, cracked open to let the fresh spring air in. She curtsies. "Good morning, Father."

"Ah." He looks her up and down. "You have dressed appropriately today. Excellent. You have no excuse not to attend prayers tonight at the temple."

Her stomach roars. *Be nice.* "Perhaps, Father. I shall have to see what His Majesty has planned."

"I would like to remind you that the Royal House of Fola are followers of Culain. I know you come from Whick, and have ties to Muriel and Iden, but you are a follower of Culain now, just as your husband is, and just as your children shall be, too."

"I appreciate the reminder, Father. I shall speak to my husband about his plans for the evening."

"What are you speaking to me about, my dearest?" The king bursts through the door, looking disheveled and with large bags under his eyes.

"Father Nael was inviting me to prayers this evening. I told him that I needed to ask you first. Are you well, my love?"

"I appreciate the offer, Father. But my wife and I must attend to some private business tonight." He puts his arm around her shoulder and pulls her close before kissing the top of her head. "We shall make arrangements to attend prayers together another time."

"But Your Majesty—"

"I said we will attend later. Now, we have a meeting to prepare for. My dearest, please, sit next to me. I dislike having you so far away."

The priest scowls and sulks back to the corner window as the rest of the king's council files in.

"Now. I have heard of some upsetting activities lately," the king says. "It concerns Tsvetokrasa. Their king is mad, has no heir, and his nephew thinks he can do a better job. Their queen has fled the country and is holed up somewhere in Garcelon. We must recall Ambassador Iomaire; a war of succession is brewing, and the seas near Tsvetokrasa are far too turbulent in the summer for them to make a safe journey home, so we must bring the Owens home immediately."

"Their queen is in hiding? Alone? No supporters?" Lord Hern asks, pulling papers out of his bag.

"She is from Garcelon, so I doubt the Tsvetokrasan people ever liked her," Lord Caibre says, filling a mug with ale before sitting down.

"Does anyone ever really like Garcelonian women to begin with? They are all mad! I do not blame the Tsvets at all." Sir Nait sits back in his chair and laughs.

"Excuse me, Sir Nait?" the king says. "Would you like to say that to my mother?"

Lord Hern scowls at his son-in-law. "Answer the king. Do you believe the Queen Mother is mad?"

"That is not what I meant, and you know it." He looks around the room for support, and everyone dutifully refuses to meet his eye. "Come on, it was a joke."

"I'm not laughing," Princess Eleanor says. "Anyway. Yes, I agree with my brother. We need to bring Lord Iomaire and Lady Eilis home."

"Not having an heir is certainly a dangerous situation for any kingdom and should be the primary concern of any consort," Father Nael says, stroking his chin while looking out of the window. "Thank goodness that, at least, our ruler has his wits about him."

"Moving on." The king clears his throat. "I've also heard about concerning situations here on our own soil."

"Yes, my lord. We need soldiers," Lairde Artair says.

"We were attacked just a few nights ago," Lord Artair says.

"Attacked?" The king tilts his head. "I have not heard of this."

"Yes, the people rose up and attacked our estate! They made off with many of our valuables and left a demand letter that we stop raising rents on them. We were not at home, but they came in the middle of the night. Someone let them in!" Lairde Artair slams his hands on the table so hard that Lord Caibre's mug rattles, and some of the ale splashes out.

"Thank goodness neither of you was harmed," the king says. "It is most fortunate that you were not at home."

"Fortunate? We had our best plates and many of our goblets stolen! Priceless jewels, gone! Jewels that we had hoped would be worn by Lady Emeire when she marries! Someone let these vandals and robbers in."

"We shall get to the bottom of this. Has anyone else had such attacks since we last met?"

The rest of the council shakes their heads.

"You mentioned they wanted lower rents?"

"Yes, your Majesty. We had raised rents on the farmers recently. They do not seem to like that."

"Interesting. Why did you raise them?"

"Well, things have been more expensive for us. And they have had several good harvests; we deserve a cut of that. They are farming on our lands, after all."

Caitlin recalls Lady Emeire flaunting several new gowns last week and many new necklaces.

"There are many in this kingdom that are forgetting their place," Father Nael says. "They forget that work brings them closer to Culain, and instead, they turn to thievery."

"Your Majesty, if I may?" Sir Connor asks.

"You may." He steeples his fingers and rests his chin on his thumbs.

"I cannot help but wonder if these uprisings are related to the strikes that have happened at our factories. I've been speaking with other factory owners, and their workers have also been making unreasonable demands."

"Yes, and the protests have continued to happen," Lairde Elwee adds.

"You believe they are all related?"

"Yes, and to those troublemakers, too. I thought your father burned down their headquarters. Those treasonous rats. They have to all be related," Sir Nait adds.

"It does seem that the people are being led astray from the righteous path of Culain," the priest says, looking directly at Caitlin.

"Gráinne," the king says, turning to Caitlin. "What do you believe?"

"Well." She folds her hands in her lap. "It sounds like, related or not, all parties that are causing strife right now are upset over economic and financial concerns. The workers want better wages, the farmers want lower rents, and the protesters want lower taxes. It appears they believe they do not have the financial capacity on their own to provide for their basic needs."

"Nonsense," Father Nael says. "If they were truly in such economic straits, the churches would hear of it. They would come to us for succor, and we would help them find their way back to being hard workers."

"I want an accounting from every lord on what their rents are, and from our factories, I want a record of what the profit margins are. Queen Gráinne shall go over your books. I want a complete audit. I want first to make sure that there are no errors in any of the ledgers before I address the people to let them know their complaints are ill-founded. Because if their concerns are not ill-founded..."

"Of course, Your Majesty," the nobles say one by one, each shifting and refusing to make eye contact with Caitlin.

"Your father would have—" Admiral Aicher says.

"I should not have to remind you that I am not my father. Our queen is a businesswoman herself. She will know how the books should look. As for the matter with the rebels, we have some intelligence of where their new base may be."

The meeting continues, but Caitlin pays little attention to the contents of the meeting. Instead, she notes who bickers with whom, who supports whom, and who seems indifferent. Lord Hern and his son-in-law, Sir Nait, seem at odds and yet take the same stance on many issues. However, the royal duke seems contemptuous of Lairde Elwee and cuts zir off at every chance to do so. Lord Caibre has no discernable pattern; he seems completely at odds with everyone, even himself.

For the remainder of the meeting, however, Father Nael remains quiet. When the meeting concludes, he follows Caitlin into the hall and grabs her arm. "Your Majesty. I was unkind to you earlier. I wanted to offer my hand in friendship again. We could be very good friends."

"Do not concern yourself. I am sure you are very stressed and cannot be blamed for lapses in etiquette and politeness. You do so much, maybe too much, for the kingdom, your Eminence. What benefits come with being friends with you, might I ask?"

"First, and most importantly, the divine blessing of Culain. Second, my wonderful company at dinners. Would you not join me sometime?"

She puts her thumb on her chin. "I shall have to check my schedule and speak to the king, but I believe it can be arranged."

He grins like a predator before he pounces. "Perfect."

"Do you dislike the physician in the southern district so much that you refuse to go there?" Princess Daya asks. "We haven't been here since before you were wed. I do not think it's wise to ignore an entire section of the city. That looks like favoritism."

"She is right," her wife says, pulling out a fan. Spring has only just begun, but already the temperatures are sweltering, and there have been no rains to keep the heat in check.

"She usually is," Caitlin replies, resting her arm on the ledge of the carriage, watching as merchants hawk their wares and thespians mime the great masterpieces on the edges of fountains. "But no, I do not hate him. And we are on our way there now, so I don't see why it is an issue."

"We are only going there because you have always had some excuse about why we need to be elsewhere for our charity outings. We cannot be seen to be playing favorites! Of all people, I expected you to know this."

"I know, I know! I just…" She just can't endanger Diarmuid like this. It is one thing to do charity at any other Red Front establishment, but this is more personal. She does not even feel safe saying that she knew Diarmuid prior to her ever meeting Cian.

"Well?" Princess Daya crosses her arms.

"It is just that. Oh, fine! There's a former Peddigree Trading partner that set up their own outfit and did so right near there. I would rather not see that person's face ever again." She blushes and looks out the carriage window. "Happy?"

"My, my. I did not know our new sister could hold such grudges!" Princess Eleanor laughs, the morning sun reflecting off of her golden hairpin as she throws her head back.

"I have never seen you this flustered. Tell me, did this trading partner fancy you? Did you fancy them? There is more to this than you are telling!" Lady Shennen leans forward, her tail flicking.

"No, no, and no. There is no more to it. This former associate stole a lot of valuable business, and that is all there is to it."

"I see, I see. If you say so." Lady Shennen leans back in her seat again, folding her hands neatly in her lap.

"We are almost there. And if we see any fiendish traders, I can handle it. Do not worry about it, my lady," Lady Arlina says.

Caitlin touches Lady Arlina's hand. "You are my only true friend here."

"Excuse me? Who am I then?" Kegan laughs.

The carriage comes to a halt, and the party disembarks. Lady Shennen makes a show of jumping over the holes in the cobblestone street, almost tripping on her voluminous skirts, before wiping her tail and smacking Princess Eleanor's legs. The princess closes her eyes, clenches and then unclenches her hands, and says nothing.

Diarmuid is waiting at the door, holding it open as the morning light illuminates the front of his practice. "My ladies, thank you for assisting me today. I am honored."

"The pleasure is ours," Caitlin says. She takes a deep breath and fights the urge to leap into his arms. She curtsies and lets him lead her inside.

"I am expecting quite a few patients today. Mostly children. Do you believe you are up for the task?"

"We shall do our best," Princess Eleanor says, sitting in a waiting room chair and massaging her thigh.

"Of course! I have a dozen little siblings. If I cannot wrangle the kids, then no one can," Lady Shennen says.

"Excellent. I need some help with cleaning the floors and having some of the laundry done before we open."

"I can assist you with that. Lady Shennen," Princess Elizabeth says to her lady-in-waiting. "I trust I can leave you to care for children and distract them?"

"Of course!"

"Cait... I mean, your Highness," Diarmuid says, slapping his hand over his mouth and bowing.

"No, please. When I am in the city, I am just Caitlin."

"Thank you, you are too kind. Would you help me in the exam room? You were such a help last time."

Caitlin is beet red, too scared to look behind her to see how the others reacted to Diarmuid's slip-up.

"Yes, and can Lairde Kegan help, too? I do not believe they would be much assistance elsewhere."

"Of course. And Princess Daya," he says, turning to the princesses.

"Nay! Like our sister, you can simply refer to us with our names. There is no need for such formality," Daya says.

Caitlin lets out a huge breath. Her new sisters-in-law are a blessing in disguise in her new life.

"As you wish, would you mind triaging patients as they come in? Please help bring order to an otherwise unruly waiting room."

"That is what we were born for, doctor."

"Yes, well. Let's get to it. Thank you again for your help. The fire at the factory last week has left many with injuries and..."

"Another fire!?" Caitlin freezes mid-stride.

Kegan blanches, turning away from the group.

"Oh, yes. The Gilroy-Downing factory. It was terrible. The workers were changing shifts, and somehow the main entrance doors were locked... There was so much confusion and chaos... No one knows how the fire started... It was contained to the workers' break rooms and changing rooms, so none of the equipment or products were damaged. The workers, however..."

"Is that Sir Liam's factory?" Princess Daya says.

"Yes, but he has several," Princess Eleanor replies.

"Why did we not know about it?" Caitlin says. "Cian would have at least said something to me even if Sir Liam or Sir Connor did not. I should have known..."

"We know now, though. And now we can do something," Princess Eleanor says, coming behind Caitlin and resting her hand on her shoulder.

"Yes. You are right."

"Such a tragedy, and how cruel that it... All locked inside? And it happened when most of the workers were there? That is such a horrible coincidence," Lady Arlina says.

"Yes. A tragic accident," Daya says.

"As I said, what matters now is that we can help. Let's get to it then." Diarmuid bows to the party, and Caitlin follows him back to the exam room, Kegan, still pale, at her heels. She leaves the door open and listens as the party chatters in the front.

"This is exciting! Lady Emeire will be so upset that she stayed behind," Lady Ronai says.

"Does she like children? I did not know that," Princess Eleanor says.

"She loves them!" Lady Shennen says.

Diarmuid hands her some of his medical equipment, a cloth, and some alcohol. She gets to work.

"Oh yes, she wants a dozen of her own!"

"She better start soon," Lady Arlina replies.

Caitlin lays out the various instruments neatly on the desk next to the exam table.

"I believe she is trying," Lady Shennen replies.

"Trouble obtaining the object of her affection?" Daya asks.

Diarmuid comes up behind her and hands her a clean cloth. "Do you think you could close the door, Kegan?"

"Of course."

"I couldn't stand to hear any more of that," he says. "Is Lady Shennen always this gossipy?"

"She's usually worse," Caitlin says, not bothering to look up from her work. "I wish I could have persuaded her to become one of my ladies. But so long as I spend time with Eleanor, she'll be around. The Lady Emeire she was mentioning? Her 'object of affection' is the king himself. Her fathers are on the council, and they still harbor ambitions of having a grandchild on the throne."

"You still aren't free of rivals, then?"

"I suppose not." Caitlin fidgets with the hem of her sleeve. "However—"

"My lady," The door creeks open, and Lady Arlina peeks inside. "I am sorry to interrupt. May I come in?"

"Please, come in. What is wrong?"

"My father sent a servant to fetch me. There is some sort of emergency, and he needs me. I am sorry, I must leave."

"Oh, yes. Of course, of course. I will miss you, but..." Caitlin chews on her lip. "If your father... If he..."

"Yes, my lady?"

"Please be careful."

"Yes, my lady." She curtsies and leaves. Caitlin watches the door close and lets out a breath.

"You were saying?"

Caitlin jumps, startled out of her worry for Lady Arlina. "Hmm? What? I'm sorry."

"You were saying you do not have any rivals for the king's affection? You are not in danger?"

"I feel like the damn priests are my rivals now. He spends more time with them than anyone else."

"Are they threatening you still? What do they talk about?"

"The threats aren't as obvious, but still implied. I am having dinner with Father Nael tomorrow evening, though. And what do they talk about? I couldn't tell you, I'm not allowed into their private meetings, and they barely speak at all during council meetings. Some people think that he is having some sort of affair, and the excuses for 'praying' are just that, excuses. I don't believe it, though."

"Why not?"

"Because every eligible lady—except Lady Emeire—have backed off," Kegan adds. "It seems they want to curry favor other ways, now."

"And Lady Emeire isn't an issue?"

"Ha! Absolutely not. He finds her and her family to be vipers," Kegan says. "Although, I would say Lady Emeire looks more like a python."

"Be nice!" Caitlin says.

"I am. Python's aren't venomous, and some of them look like puppy dogs. They can be so cute!" Kegan shrugs. "Where would you like me to put these?"

"Oh, you finished cleaning them that fast? Put them in that drawer, top one."

Caitlin pulls out a piece of paper from her pocket. "Anyway, here's a list I've compiled of the various schedules of noble families. When they plan to be at their estates, in the city, or abroad."

"I already gave the cipher to Tamora, so it should already be in Sharidan's hands now," Kegan says.

"Excellent. I'll get this to Valen tonight. You should know, though, that there has been some, well, infighting."

"There always is," Kegan says.

"No, this is a little more… I don't know how to say this except dangerous."

"How so?"

"You know Myles, right?"

Caitlin nods. Kegan rolls their eyes.

"Well, he and a few others are refusing to accept reality. They blame us for the factory fire. Both of them. They claim that we provoked the factory management."

"They what? The blame is on the factory owners! They are the ones that lit the fires!" Kegan says and collapses into a chair and puts their head between their legs.

"I agree. That's not how Myles thinks, and he's got Jocelyn and Tyn in his corner now. He's been meeting with more members, too. I think he is planning something."

"Like what?"

"I don't know. I think he will do something, but Aine says he is a harmless old man, and Jocelyn and Tyn are too young to know not to listen to his rantings."

"I hope Aine's correct. Kegan? Are you alright?" Caitlin puts her hand on the Calla's shoulder.

"Hmm? Yeah...yeah, I will be. I just... I don't like fires. I need to fetch some water."

"Wait—" Caitlin starts after Kegan, but Diar grabs her shoulders and pulls her back.

"Leave them. There is a lot of... I shouldn't be saying anything, but let's just leave it at this; Kegan has been through a bit that I am sure they haven't told you yet. So..."

"Give them space, I understand."

"Anyway. Lady Arlina... You seem worried about her, too. Talk to me."

"I am worried. Her father is absolutely a tyrant to her. I have no clue why; she won't share with me. But her father and her brother are both utter monsters to her. If he's calling her back for some emergency, I can only imagine how awful it will be for her."

Diar fishes the list out of his pocket. "Lord Berach, right? Ah. Yes. He'll be out of the country soon."

"Do you think that it is related to this emergency he claims to have?"

"No. Just let me do what I do best." He winks at her.

"Secrets?" She laughs. "I thought we didn't do that anymore."

He sighs. "I could say the same to you. Don't think I didn't see how you looked at her."

"What do you mean?" She tilts her head to the side. "I don't understand."

"Then you and I are both fools. It doesn't matter. It sounds like patients are arriving."

***

"I do not see why you are so worried about her," Lady Emeire says, not looking up from her embroidery. When they arrived back at the palace, Lady Arlina was still missing. Caitlin had raced back from the council meeting, hoping to find her before she had to attend to her dinner. But she is still missing. "She is an adult and can take care of herself. I am sure whatever the matter is, it warrants her absence."

"I know, I just am worried." Caitlin plays with the hem of her sleeve. "And I miss her company."

"It's barely been a day since you saw her last. She's dealing with something with her family. It will be fine," Lady Ronai says.

Don't think I don't see how you look at her.

"I have some news, by the way. I had intended to tell you privately, but I think that everyone should know," Lady Ronai says, dealing herself a game of solitaire.

"What is it?" Lady Emeire leans forward, eyes wide.

"I am going to Janeuq! Next month, but I cannot wait! To Cygne, specifically."

"Why are you traveling there?"

"To get away from my brother, of course!" She laughs, grinning at the cards she draws. "There is also a minor lord in the Janeuq court. My brother would have me make a match with him. Some political ally he wants. I shall pretend to do so, but I intend to spend my time seeing operas going to concerts, and wandering around art galleries. Maybe I will meet a poet and fall in love!"

"Your brother was the one who made the match for your sister, too, right?" Lady Emeire re-arranges her cards. "That backfired on him in the end; he really wishes to try his hand at match-making a second time?"

Lady Ronai shrugs. "Eilis is happy. That is what upsets him. Not Emyr Owen himself."

"Interesting," Laide Kegan says. "Who is the lord he wants you to meet?"

"I do not recall his name, and I do not believe I should need to. He is unimportant."

"Well said!" Lady Emeire raises a glass of wine.

The door creaks open, and Lady Muiris, her light blue hair disheveled, creeps in. She quietly closes it behind her before seeing the rest of the attendants at the card table. "Oh! You're back. Well. Is it really that late? You see..."

"Lady Muiris, have you seen Lady Arlina?" Caitlin takes in the state of dress, or rather undress, of her flirtatious lady-in-waiting. Bodice laces dangling, her sleeves off her shoulder, and her hair full of knots.

"Ah. Yes. Well... I did, as a matter of fact." She blushes.

"Is she alright? She said her father needed her for an emergency."

"Emergency? Is that what she said?" Lady Muiris laughs. "Her father has a unique definition of emergency."

"What happened?"

"Well. You see, she and...well. You should ask her yourself."

Don't think I don't see how you look at her.

"As long as she is well, I suppose. I must get ready for dinner."

"Allow me to assist you," Lady Muiris says.

"No, that will not be necessary. Thank you," she says, excusing herself to her bedchamber. She opens her jewelry box and pulls out the copper bracelet from its velvet pouch. Three strands of copper braided in a seamless loop. One to represent Brenna, one to represent Caitlin, and one to represent their love.

Even though it is so simple, the craftsmanship is so fine, and the metal so untarnished that it still stands out next to her diamonds. She slides it on, shivering at the sting of *Àstfriður* magic. She has not worn it since the day before her wedding to the king, but today, for this, she needs protection.

She closes her eyes, briefly imagining herself back at Brenna's side. The scent of the forest enveloping her, for the scent of Brenna's homeland, clung to xir so strongly that not even the salt waters of Whick could wash it away. Xir skin, as cold as metal to the touch, the orange flames in xir eyes, the laugh always on xir lips...

Opening her eyes, she makes her way across the palace grounds to the secluded Temple of Culain, eager to arrive if only to get out of the lingering heat. "Welcome, daughter," an elderly brother greets her. "Father Nael is caught up in his office and asked me to keep you company. But there is no better company than Culain. Shall we pray while we wait?"

She wishes to tell him no, but instead follows him to the sanctuary. As soon as she steps inside, she feels that too-familiar sting. Had an *Àstfriður* been here recently? But why? Dierdre being the very rare exception, the people of the Veil do not worship gods, the Tudáe, or any others.

"Are you unwell, daughter?" the elderly priest startles her out of her contemplations.

"My apologies, Father. I am just always in awe of the beauty here. I fear I shall never grow used to it."

"As well, you should not. We should always be in awe of His Radiance."

"I agree, Father. But should we not pray?"

"Forgive an old man his idle prattle. Yes, let us pray."

She speaks the words of the Maker's Prayer, hearing nothing but her own thoughts, spiraling around the questions posed by the afterimage of magic. At some point, Father Nael joins them, his sonorous voice all but drowning out hers and the other priests.

He lingers in silence after they finish, ecstasy written across his face. "That prayer never fails to move me. I swear I feel Him in the room every time I recite it. It fills me with hope for a brighter tomorrow. I am sorry for keeping you waiting, but I feel my lateness was a blessing in disguise. I so rarely get the opportunity to pray beside Your Majesty. Shall we dine now?"

She inclines her head and follows him to his private chambers, the table set for their dinner and glasses already full of wine. "Sit, eat," he commands, already dipping his spoon into the stew.

"Thank you for having me as your guest tonight," she says, taking in the room. It was smaller than she had expected, although outfitted with fine furnishings and meticulous attention paid to the fabrics and textures of the curtains and carpeting.; deep burgundy velvet and plush wool, most likely from the Alavesas region in northern Garcelon, if she had to guess. She notes that despite that, the wood furnishing is oak, not cherry or mahogany, which would be more complimentary.

"Of course, your Majesty. I would like for us to be close. I would love nothing more than to think of you as a favored grandchild. I know we got off to a bad start, but things were so hectic and chaotic, I was not my best, and I have chastised myself for behaving so rudely and begged forgiveness from Culain Himself, and now I beg it from you." His lower lip quivers, and he folds his hands in his lap.

"Of course. I was also not at my best, Father. Or is it Grandfather?"

Father Nael grins like a wolf. "Whichever you prefer, my dear granddaughter. I think we shall be very good friends."

Caitlin sips her wine, too nervous to even note the quality. "I should hope so."

"One task of a grandfather is to ensure that his grandchildren are well versed in the traditions and practices of the family, including the family's religion. I shall assign you a tutor. He shall come to your rooms once a week and instruct you further on how to uphold the teachings of Culain."

"Oh, well," Caitlin says, setting down her fork. "What an honor."

"I shall make sure that it does not conflict with any of your other duties, rest assured, my dear. Or, if you would rather, you could come here on the days of your lessons?"

"Well, I shall have to ask the king. He is very particular about who enters my rooms. Almost as particular as he is about where I go and when."

"Do not fear, I shall talk to him about that, too. I know he will agree."

"If you are sure, I look forward to my lessons."

"Good."

An acolyte stumbles into the room without knocking. Not even noticing Caitlin, he marches to Father Nael and hands him a sealed envelope. The acolyte has shaggy brown hair, a sharp chin, large eyebrows, and a jagged scar running across his nose. Caitlin examines him, and familiarity tugs at her heart. She knows this man. Somehow. And from the shiver that runs down her spin, she knows that she does not like him.

The man hurries back out again. Not a word exchanged between the two clergymen.

"I am sorry for that interruption. I was ready to scold him for insubordination, but the letter he handed me warrants the haste."

"Father, was that man ever at another Temple? How long has he been a priest?"

"No, he joined our ranks here in Eoi about 15 years ago. Why?"

"Oh, he seemed familiar. However, I do not know where I would have seen him before. He is not one of the ones that mill about on market day in the square."

"You are from Whick, are you not?"

"Yes, Father."

"We do sometimes send our acolytes out to recruit from different towns. Perhaps that was it."

"In Whick? I had not…" Her chest tightens. Father Nael is right. She had seen him in Whick. But it was not because he was there recruiting. That scar was from a brawl, from a cutlass hastily swung in the confines of a crowded tavern. That scar was acquired the night he and half a dozen other men tried to kidnap Brenna. *But that doesn't make any sense. Brenna's murderer is a priest of Culain?*

***

"Gashes on his arm?" Sister Dierdre idly spins the outer rings of the silver astroglobe on the altar, not bothering to look at Caitlin at all. She is once again visiting the palace Temple, and the sanctuary is blessedly cool.

"Yes, and long ones, too. But they are always very straight; they look intentional. He gets upset when I bring it up. He tries to hide it, but the blood sometimes seeps through whatever bandaging he has over them."

"And his mother said that his father was always sick? But it only happened after he took the throne? That does not seem right."

"Yes, and apparently, the priests were always providing help for this ailment," Caitlin says, taking a long drink from her flask.

"Now that I think about it, he was a very different man before he took the throne. Kind, compassionate." The priestess crosses her arms and leans against the altar.

"He was not always a tyrant? I find that hard to believe." Caitlin rolls her eyes and takes another sip of water, only to find the flask empty. It has not rained yet since the season's change over three weeks ago. There are talks of rationing water already and that the king's reign might be ill-fated.

"No, in fact, I believe he had plans for some sort of reform of powers. But he turned cold once he took the throne. Not sick, but cold."

"That is what Queen Isleen said, but I did not believe her."

"It does not matter. Back to the matter at hand. King Cian, is he sick?"

"I would say that Cian is always sick, but more from blood loss than anything else. Well, not sick. But weaker, less energetic."

"He doesn't come to your rooms, you mean?"

Caitlin blushes. "That is not what I meant, though he does come far less often than I would have predicted, and I am glad of it."

"Interesting. Do you not think that perhaps you should hope for him to visit more often? Make sure he is not straying? And to keep your throne, you are expected to produce an heir. The people love you, yes. But they want stability, which comes with knowing there is a successor."

"I do not believe you are correct in that."

"We all hear whispers of the strife and turmoil that has engulfed Tsvetokrasa. A throne without a clear heir is a dangerous thing."

"You say you are friends with Aine, and yet you want me to help perpetuate the monarchy? And not destroy it?"

Sister Dierdre turns sharply to face Caitlin. "We do not have the same end goals; we do not seek the same thing. I can achieve what I want with or without a monarchy. I can achieve what I need with or without democracy. That matters little to me. But I need access to the king right now, and you need access to easy means of communication and safety if you get caught."

"I do not see what that has to do with my fertility."

Sister Dierdre opens her mouth, then closes it, whirls back around, and spins the rings of the astroglobe forcefully. "You need to keep that throne."

"I see…"

"Why aren't you pregnant yet? It's been three months? Four? You should be with child already."

"You picked the wrong woman. Firstly, I do not want to be pregnant, and secondly, I do not think I can become pregnant."

"What do you mean?"

"I do not wish to be pregnant."

"I understood that, but what do you mean by you can't?"

"Once, long ago, I tried. With my wife. It wasn't possible, according to the healers we spoke with."

"If you do not become pregnant, you will lose the throne, and I will lose my patience."

"I can't!"

"But there are ways…"

"I am done discussing this subject." Caitlin leaps to her feet and marches to the sanctuary entrance.

"Fine, for now."

As she places her hand against the door, she remembers the true reason she came here. *Brenna.*

"I have one more bit of information you might want for now," she says, turning around but refusing to look at the priestess. "The priests are almost always with him, and they have been terse with me. They seem to believe I am not devout enough. Father Nael wants to set up tutoring sessions with me."

"Do it. Bring me any information."

"That is not all of it. An acolyte at their Temple, I swear he is one of the gang who murdered my wife."

"Why was she murdered?" Dierdre raises an eyebrow.

"Well, xie was *Ásfriður*, and they wanted to kidnap xir and use—"

"You were married to an *Ásfriður*? Did xie teach you anything? Tell you anything?" The priestess approaches her, wringing her hands, crossing the length of the sanctuary in less than a second, graceful and quick.

"Well, on our wedding night, xie told me everything. Or, I think it was everything. About the cycle and magic. Here. See?" She pulls up her sleeve to reveal the bracelet that Brenna had shaped for her many years ago. "Why do you ask?"

"A priest that tried to capture an *Ásfríður*..."

"He said he was a pirate, not a priest. He was hired to find a way to the Isles without detection. He was locked up, but a month later, someone came from the King's Shield and took him and the others back to Eoi for further questioning."

"And you did not follow up?"

"Any time I sent a letter, it got returned unanswered."

"They want an *Ásfríður*... What do they know?" She turns away from Caitlin, thumb tapping her chin as she approaches the altar again.

"Excuse me?"

"I was born on the Isles. I do not know if you can tell, but I am also *Ásfríður*."

"I suspected, yes. Why did you leave the Veil?"

Dierdre laughs.

"I do not mean to be rude," Caitlin says.

"You are not rude. You are naïve. The situation in which you have found yourself is far more complex than you realize. I shall share just this bit; hopefully, it demonstrates how large the web is. I did not leave; my clan discarded me."

"Discarded? I'm not sure I understand."

"The elders of my clan abandoned me on the shores of Fayn. It was my predecessor, the former High Priestess, who found me and took me in. I have lived in the temple walls my whole life, and I plan to continue to do so. I do not wish to live with the people that did not want me."

"What does this have to do with this web you speak of?"

"The *Ástfriður* have their own politics, their own corruption, their own secrets. They discarded me as part of a plot by one elder to seize power. This elder believed I was a threat or posed some impediment to their ascension. The full details of which I will never know. My predecessor could not piece it all together. I do not care, though. I am here now. My sisters here in the temple are more family than any others I could find."

"I've never heard of such a thing."

"No, I doubt even your wife would have told you. I have only one regret; I never learned how to use the magic that the *Ástfriður* are blessed with. But my remedy for that..."

"Yes?" Caitlin asks.

"They are hoarding it. It is not gold or gems that they keep from the world, but magic. One day it will not be so."

"I do not understand."

"Do not worry about it. Spend more time with the priests. I need more information."

"That is asking for more than we originally negotiated on."

"I will pay you back in time, I promise." Sister Dierdre stares ahead of her, seeing something in front of her that Caitlin cannot.

"See that you do. I must take my leave now."

Sister Dierdre does not acknowledge her, and so she slips out while the High Priestess continues to be lost in her own thoughts.

***

Despite his promise, the king does not come to dine with her that evening. After receiving the message from one of his pages, she takes a walk—alone; she stresses to her attendants—in the gardens. She chews her fingernail; it has been days, and yet Lady Arlina has not returned.

Diarmuid's words echo in her mind. *Don't think I didn't see how you looked at her.*

He cannot be right. He cannot, what he implied. No. She cannot, there is no way that she can fall in love again, no way that she could ever feel for another the way she felt for Brenna. And of all people, it cannot be Arlina. A lady of hers, when she must always play the love-struck maiden at the king's side. No, it cannot possibly be true.

But as if summoned, she turns a corner and comes face to face with her.

"You Majesty," Lady Arlina says and sweeps down into a low curtsy. "I was told I could find you here."

"Lady Arlina. Where have you been? I've been worried, it's been days… Where—"

"I am alright, my lady. The emergency is taken care of. But there were terrible storms in Berach, and my father forbid that I leave until they pass, and I believe the storms have followed me. We should go back inside."

"Yes, of course. I was so worried."

"I am here now, though. I am so sorry to have worried you."

"My lady—."

"Please. When we are alone," she takes Lady Arlina's hand in her own, "Please, just call me 'Caitlin'."

Don't think I didn't see how you looked at her.

"My la—" she says, blushing. "I mean. Caitlin. Yes, I can do that."

The sky lets loose, the first rain in Eoi in over a month, and they race back inside.

"Here, my lady, Caitlin, let me help you get into dry clothes," Arlina says.

"But you must do so, too," Caitlin replies.

"Well, I would be happy to accept your help with my clothing if that is what you are implying, but first you."

"Lady Arlina?"

"No, please. When we are alone, just 'Arlina.'"

Caitlin smiles, her stomach knotting. "Please, change. I do not want you to catch a fever."

"I already have one; it is burning in my chest, and I fear I will leave a fire in my wake from how hot my skin is, even though I am soaked." Arlina tiptoes toward Caitlin and grabs the edges of the robe that Caitlin has put on.

"Arlina..."

"I know you are married; I know how wrong this would be. You are a queen, and I am just an earl's daughter. But just this once, just here, just now. Just for tonight..."

"Arlina..." Caitlin takes a huge breath in, her heart not wanting to stay in her chest, the blood rushing through her veins. "If you come any closer, I fear I will have a fever, too."

"Is that a problem?"

Don't think I didn't see how you looked at her.

Caitlin leans in and kisses Arlina next to her ear. "Warm me up, your queen commands it."

Arlina tears off her soaked skirt and does not put on the dry garments. She pulls Caitlin in for a deep kiss, and the two stumble to the bed, each unwilling to end the kiss as they tumble on the covers. Caitlin moans as Arlina's hands slowly inch down her side and expertly tease her. She runs her nails down her attendant's back, causing her to release her own sigh of pleasure.

"May I?" Arlina asks.

"No, not yet," Caitlin whispers. She pushes Arlina onto her back and forces her attendant's legs apart. "I want to play with you first. I want to make you purr."

"Oh? Do you think I am some wild animal?"

"If you are, you will not be when I am done here."

"Is that a threat?"

"It is a promise."

Arlina grins. "Catch me, then."

The two tug and grip and scratch each other, each hoping to get the upper hand in this dance, each wanting to be the one to draw words of submission from the mouth of the other. The fire in the hearth is forgotten, but it could never match the fire burning in the hearts of the two women.

Naked and joined, Caitlin and Arlina alternate drawing out the completion from the other.

They are both so lost in their own world that neither hears the door to the bedchamber open.

"Oh, my goodness—"

The two stop and look up, wide-eyed, to see Sister Kiandre standing in the doorway.

"Oh my... umm. Your Majesty umm. See me tomorrow. At the Temple."

"Wait!" Caitlin cries. But it's too late. The lithe Calla has already vanished.

FOURTEEN

THIEVES AND THREATS

Caitlin wrings her hands, pausing outside of the gossamer doors to the Temple of Andraste in the city. She had come here by carriage with only Sir Dermont. She had told the tall woman to wait with the chauffeur. Inside of these walls, not even the brawny knight could protect her.

She takes a deep breath and enters the chilly atrium. A young acolyte greets her with a low bow. "Your Majesty, to what do we owe this honor?" She stumbles on her words, shy and nervous.

"That is unnecessary, please. Just take me to Sister Dierdre. She is expecting me."

"Of course, your Majesty, this way," the young girl stammers and trips over her robe as she turns around.

Caitlin holds back a laugh. "Thank you. You are most kind."

They make their way down the halls, stained glass on all sides, scenes of starry nights illuminating the corridors. "Tell me, do these panels mean something?"

"Oh? Yes! Do you want me to tell you?" The girl's eyes widen, and she grins. "I am the best in my class in art history and in literature! I can tell you everything!"

"Please, tell me, I am eager to know."

The girl slows down. "This one, right here? See the fire in the sky? It's from a battle! With magic!"

"Magic?"

"Magic! Yes, it used to be real! A long, long time ago! This was a magic battle. The one side was a bunch of greedy evil magic users, and they were trying to take over everything. See, this one here?" She points to a panel with a tall man standing in the center, holding a golden chalice and wearing red robes, standing next to a tall oak tree. "That's him! The evil mage from the east! And behind him, the snow mountains, see? That's where they came from!"

"Interesting. Who won?"

The girl, forgetting all propriety, takes Caitlin's hand and drags her down the hall. "Here!" She points to a pane with three women in silver robes and flowing hair holding up their hands to a full moon above them. "They beat them back and saved the whole world! Everyone was saved by these good magic wielders!"

"And where are they now?"

"Well, this happened hundreds and hundreds of years ago."

"Anyanka." A stern voice echoes behind them. They turn and find a grey-robed sister standing at attention. "We have told you before, these are just stories," she says and then addresses Caitlin. "I apologize, your Majesty. Our young acolyte here is incredibly enthusiastic, and her imagination gets away from her sometimes. The priestess waves her hand, dismissing the acolyte. "Allow me to escort you to Sister Dierdre's chambers."

"There is no need to apologize, Sister. I was enjoying the young acolyte's story. Perhaps you could tell me more about it?"

"It was originally written thousands of years ago by a poet in the Sisterhood. She was quite prolific; she wrote hundreds of epic poems, but this one is her most famous."

"Why have I not heard of it before?"

"Its popularity has died down." The sister surreptitiously glances at Caitlin. "Andraste is not the patron god of the Fola's. Therefore, it is not our stories that are favored by playwrights and artists."

"I see. And you have no fear saying this to me?"

"I do not consider you to be a Fola."

"Interesting. Why is that?"

"Because the High Priestess does not."

"What do you consider me to be, then?"

"A wild card." The sister motions to the large door in front of them. Inlaid with amethysts, sapphires, opals and lined with silver filigree, Caitlin has passed through this doorway multiple times; it still fills her with a sense of wonder. She fidgets with the lily pin over her heart, ensuring it is straight.

"Thank you, Sister. Please, do not punish the young acolyte. I requested she explain the panels to me."

The sister winks. "She is a promising storyteller. I do not want to crush her enthusiasm, merely hone it. I believe thespians will pantomime her stories in the squares someday."

Caitlin chuckles. "Excellent."

The sister bows and opens the door, announcing Caitlin's entrance before silently slipping away.

"I trust you slept well last night," the high priestess says without looking up from the paperwork on her desk.

"Can we be direct for once?" Caitlin says, marching towards the desk with her head held high. The office has a floral aroma with a hint of iron, but Caitlin cannot figure out which flower it might be. The office has no windows, not even ones of stained glass, and the high priestess does not have any plants decorating the dim room.

A panel in the back wall slides open, and Sister Kiandre slips through the hidden door carrying a tea tray. "Cream or sugar?"

"No, thank you," Caitlin says. "What did you want to speak to me about?" She sits on the other side of the desk, careful not to trip over the stacks of tomes littering the floor.

"Since you wish to be direct," the High Priestess says as she stirs her drink, "I would like to start by asking what you were doing last night. Or, rather, who?"

"That is none of your business."

"Treason is everyone's business," the high priestess says over the rim of her mug.

"Is that why you are involved in it?" Caitlin drums her fingers on her knees.

"As I have said before, what we do does not concern who sits on the throne or who governs the kingdom. We are not plotting regime change or betraying the Crown we do not serve. Our goals merely align with those who seek to do so."

"I thought we agreed to be blunt," Caitlin says. "And I could say the same myself."

"What is your goal then?" the high priestess says.

"Freedom." *Don't think I didn't see how you looked at her.*

"Is that not what you are doing with the Red Front?"

"I mean on a personal level."

"And you think you will get that by sleeping with one of your ladies? You see a death sentence as freedom?"

"No."

"If it is not Death that you seek, then why do you court Her?"

"I want to live before I die."

"I have told you before we need access to the monarchy. We need access to the crown. We do not need you specifically. If you will not be more careful, we can ensure you are caught."

"I could say the same to you."

"So, we are agreed." The high priestess sets down her tea and nods.

"What was the reason you originally called me here?"

"I have some unfortunate news to share with you, news that your friends say is too sensitive to send by any other means. One of their members, an older gentleman, has threatened to turn in the other members."

"Myles?" Caitlin whispers, stomach dropping. "But why?"

"Your friends did not say. That is all the news I have to share with you. I do not think I need to repeat myself, but I shall do so anyway. Do not get caught."

"I see. Well, thank you for informing me. I shall try to make the most of this information. Do you have anything else to share?"

"No. That was all."

"Sister Kiandre will escort you out."

As if she had been listening the whole time, and Caitlin suspects that she probably was, Sister Kiandre sneaks through the hidden door and smiles.

"You can take her all the way back to the palace."

The Calla bows. Caitlin shrugs and heads to the door, not waiting to see if the Calla will follow her. The door closes behind them, and Caitlin says, "I do not need an escort. My guard and a coach are waiting for me outside."

"Well. I do need an escort back to the palace. Would you mind being mine?"

Caitlin chuckles. "Sure. Why not?"

"I do not like how the high priestess keeps information from you," Kiandre says.

"I do not like it either," Caitlin replies. "Is there something you would like to tell me?"

"Maybe, but not here, and not today. I am not in the best mood today."

"Your Highness!" A young page throws the doors open. "Your Highness, the king demands your presence for an emergency council meeting."

Caitlin releases Lady Arlina's hands, praying the page did not see it. The princesses, their attendants, and the rest of Caitlin's are all in the city for the day. Caitlin had told them that she needed a day alone and asked only for Lady Arlina to stay. Kegan raised an eyebrow at this request but acquiesced in the end. Caitlin gave them a note as they left and trusted that Kegan would get it to the right people.

She felt guilty as she watched them all leave, but she needs a day to not worry about schemes and spying and secrets. She does not want to think about rebellion, riots, and royalty. She does not want to ruminate on priests and princes.

Alas, she is going to have to do just that. She rises to her feet. "Thank you. I shall be there shortly." The page leaves, not bothering to close the door behind him. Caitlin closes it for him before returning to Lady Arlina and taking her hands. "I am so sorry. You can stay here while I am gone. In my room…"

"Thank you, my lady. I just need a day away from my family."

"I know. Stay in my room. I shall tell the guards to admit no one. And even if your father comes looking for you, he would not dare go into my bedchamber."

Arlina smiles, squeezing Caitlin's hands. "My lady is too kind."

The lie they had agreed upon; unspoken. Both of them pretending that nothing had happened. They do not mention it; they do not dare even acknowledge it. Instead, they find excuses, some more believable than others, to keep each other close.

She redirects her thoughts away from Lady Arlina as she approaches the council room. She tries to stop her mind from wandering to memories of Arlina's hands on her skin and her lips on her throat. There are other matters, other issues, she must worry about.

Stupid, that was so stupid. They have done nothing since, but they never should have done anything at all.

The king is all alone in the room when she steps inside. His face is splotchy, his eyes are red, and his nose is chaffed. Before him is a letter, crumpled and wet. His gaze does not leave the paper as he says, "I knew my father would die someday because, in order for me to be king, he must die. I accepted that fact at a young age. But I never imagined a world without my mother. Did she know? Is that why she went back?"

"My love?" As he buries his head in his palms, she rushes to his side.

"She is dead. She is not coming back home. She went back to Garcelon to die…"

"The Queen Mother?"

"Yes, I cannot... Why? Why could she not stay here?"

"My love, I am so sorry."

"They will bury her there. In Garcelon. In Valencia. It was one of her lands as a princess of Garcelon. They are not sending her home! She should be buried next to father!"

She hands him her handkerchief and fetches him some water.

"To add insult," he says, accepting the mug, "they are taking her lands back to the Garcelon crown. They are hereditary lands; Valencia should be mine now! Those lands should be for our child!" He pounds on the table. "They cannot do this!"

The doors open again, and the guards admit the council members. The princesses are not among them. "Does your sister know?" Caitlin says into his ear.

"Not yet. So far, it is only you, Aelena, and Aunt Maeve."

"You should wait until Eleanor and Daya are here to say anything. You cannot announce this with them still in the city. They should hear about this. Privately. First."

"I hear you, my love. I do. But Garcelon has stolen lands from us; we must decide what to do. This is a matter of state. We have sent out a page to tell them to return as soon as possible, but I must start the meeting if they do not get back soon."

Caitlin bites her tongue and takes a seat next to him. Father Nael pushes past everyone and takes his usual place, standing next to one of the windows. Opening it slightly, he smirks at Caitlin. The rain picks up, but no one seems to mind the cold draft wafting through the room, the rain has been sparse, the heat often unbearable, and it is not even summer yet.

"I am sorry for calling you here on short notice. Unfortunately, I have terrible news." The council members are silent as the king explains the situation to them. Lord Hern buries his face in his hands. Father Nael says nothing, gazing out of the window as if he has not even heard the news.

"We must decide what to do. I open the floor to my trusted council to advise in this matter." The king reclines in his chair, knitting his hands together behind his head, looking up at the ceiling. When he blinks, there are tears welling in the corners of his eyes. Reaching a hand under the table, Caitlin rubs his knee. She might not like him, she might hate him, and normally this show of devotion would be just that: a show. The queen was a wonderful person who she would miss. Arrogant bastard though he is, Isleen would have wanted him at her funeral, and she would have wanted to be buried next to King Tarmon.

Lord Hern is the first to speak. "Isleen… I have lost too many of my family. She should be brought home. Can my sister and niece not do so? Have they given a reason why?"

"They have said that she is Garcelonian royalty, and therefore, she should be laid to rest on Garcelonian soil."

"But she is Fayn royalty, too. She was our queen."

"The letter from Queen Joanna says that she stopped being Fayn royalty when my father died. With his death, her title reverted to Isleen ib-Almelus, Princess of Garcelon and Duchess of Valencia."

"Have they already had the funeral, then? Did they do so without even requesting our attendance?"

"It shall be in ten days."

"So soon...I shall go. I need to be there." He looks around the room, not at anyone or anything, but as if he is searching for something—his voice cracks. "I should be there. Doireann needs to know. My wife loves Isleen as much as I do. We will go." Never had Caitlin seen him express such genuine emotion, not even at King Tarmon's funeral. No one in the room makes a sound as he rises to his feet, nods to his nephew, and leaves.

Sir Nait laughs as Lord Hern leaves the room. "A few weeks without the in-laws. How fortunate."

Cian jumps out of his chair. "Nait. Out. Now!"

Sir Nait holds up his hands. "Fine. You'd be happy, too, if you had that bastard as an in-law."

"Out."

"Well, before I go. I have to add my advice: we kick the bloody hell out of those bastards."

Sir Liam stands up and takes Sir Nait by the arm. "Get your unwanted ass out of here."

Daya and Eleanor rush in as Liam opens the door to toss Sir Nait out. "Brother!" Eleanor says, rushing across the room to his side. "What is going on?"

"This is important, and I do not know of a good way to put it. We have received unfortunate news from Garcelon. Mother has died." The king looks away from his sister-in-law, refusing to meet her eyes as she glares at him. Eleanor turns her back on him and walks out of the council room without saying a word.

"Really? Like this? You tell us like this?" She shakes her head and follows her wife out of the room. Caitlin bites her tongue. She wants to rebuke him. She wants to rub his nose in this mistake, but doing so would change nothing.

"That went well," Sir Liam says.

"Yes, splendid job," Sir Connor says.

"What else was I supposed to do?" Cian says.

"Cian, she is your sister, you dense idiot," Sir Liam says. "You really should have told her privately."

Caitlin's heart races, unsure if she heard the king's friend correctly.

"This is a pressing matter!" Face red, he slams his hand on the table.

"It could have waited an hour!" Sir Connor says.

The priest shifts uncomfortably yet says nothing. Council members look uneasily back and forth at each other as the king and his best friends glare at each other. The silence is broken when Lairde Artair speaks up. "While it is insulting that the queen is not to be returned home, I do not recall anything in the marital agreement between your father and mother regarding those lands. Have you reviewed them?"

"No, not yet."

"Perhaps it would be prudent to do so before we jump into any further discussion about what to do next."

"It should not matter," says the Admiral. "Those lands were hers. They should have gone to you, even if it was not specified. Further, by not returning the queen to us for her burial, they are violating several international treaties."

"Then what do you propose to do?" says Laird Artair.

"Take back what is ours. Of course, we have a formidable navy. I would happily lead a force into Garcelon and take back what should be ours."

"Surely, there must be a more diplomatic way. Garcelon has been our ally for generations. Perhaps," Lord Berach looks Caitlin in the eye. "Perhaps a new treaty could be signed. There will be a prince or princess soon, surely one who could be engaged and promised the lands."

Caitlin squints. Lord Berach is playing some game, although what game it is she cannot fathom. There are murmurs of agreement throughout the room. "Many of you have excellent points, thank you. I shall look at the agreement that my grandfather signed. In the meantime, I believe that I must take my leave and have a conversation with my sister."

"Would you like to appoint an heir right now? In case she kills you?"

"I do not appreciate your humor right now, Sir Liam." He stands up, gathers his paper into a pile, and taps Caitlin's shoulders. "My lady?"

Caitlin wraps her hand around his elbow and follows him out of the council room. He leads her through the winding halls to his rooms, ignoring everyone they pass along the way, not bothering to meet anybody's eyes. The queen that had wanted to be a mother to her. The queen had wanted to be a support for Caitlin.

And now she is gone. Now, Caitlin truly is the highest-ranking woman in the court.

He knocks on the doors to Eleanor's rooms, and when he receives no answer, he enters them. Eleanor sobbing into a pillow, clenching Daya's hands. When she looks up at her brother, her face is splotchy. She glares at Cian and says nothing.

"You better have a good excuse for what you did." Daya does not flinch. "Because I certainly cannot think of a good one. Well?"

"It was an emergency," he says. "Garcelon's actions are inexcusable and are more than merely a personal matter. What they have done, what they are doing, it is an insult to the entire nation. They are not sending her home. They are not sending Mother home! And they have claimed heard our lands as their own again. Those lands are being bequeathed to Queen Joanna's future child when they should be ours. They should be mine."

"Who cares? Who cares about the lands?" Daya gets up from her chair and marches towards Cian. "That is what you are worried about? Some squabble over land is not an emergency, certainly not an emergency that justifies not telling your sister about your mother's death personally, privately!"

"Yes, war is more important than private family matters," he says. Eleanor's jaw drops. "War?"

"War. They have stolen our lands."

"That is not what mother would want!" She throws the damp pillow at Cian. "Mother would not want you to invade or attack her home. Does that not matter to you?"

"I have not yet decided whether we will go to war," the king says. "But the council needed to know immediately to discuss it."

"Does Uncle Allil know?"

"Our uncle knows, yes. I informed him during the council meeting. He will travel—"

"Leave," Daya growls. "Get out."

"Fine. I'm leaving," the king says and storms off. Caitlin hesitates, taking a step forward toward her sister-in-law.

"Please," Daya says, more gently than she had spoken to the king. "We would like to be alone right now."

"Yes, of course. I understand if you—"

"We will let you know if we need anything."

Caitlin curtsies to the two princesses. She opens the door, hesitating one more time to glance at them. They are already huddled closely together again.

Although the court is, once again, in mourning, the king has a formal ceremony to welcome his uncle, aunts, and cousins back home from the funeral in Valencia. Ambassador Cariveau is not as pleasant as he had been before the queen's death; he seems uncomfortable and, at times, embarrassed. The ambassador is curt; he speaks very few words, and those that he does say are carefully selected. He neither smiles nor frowns, his face as blank as a new canvas. Except for the Duchess of Clare, he seems disinterested in speaking with anyone in the court, and the duchess has been following him around like a lost dog.

A server brings yet another glass of wine to the dais, where the king and Caitlin are seated on their thrones. Caitlin does not even bother to contemplate if she needs another glass of wine. Plucking a glass from the tray, she downs half of it in one gulp before raising it in the air and smiling toward the dancing courtiers. She wishes she could join them; she wishes she could be dancing. But not here. She wishes she could dance at a tavern, at a bar, but on top of the table, splattered with beer and littered with cards. She wishes that she was in Whick.

The doors to the Great Hall have been opening and closing all night; nobles leave with one person only to return with another. When the door opens this time, however, Lady Arlina and her father enter. Lady Arlina steers away from her father, peering over her shoulder to see if he's following her. Lord Berach, however, is not watching his daughter. Instead, he searches the crowd for someone else.

Lord Cairbre collides with Lady Arlina, both stumbling backward. He catches Lady Arlina before she falls. Caitlin wishes she could hear what the lord was saying to Arlina as he leans in and whispers in her ear. Arlina smiles, and he inclines his head toward the center of the hall. He offers her his hand and leads her out to the floor. Her emerald gown of crushed velvet and taffeta gently flows around her as Cairbre leads her into a dance.

The song is lively, short staccato notes and high fluttering trills. Auburn hair becomes a bright flash in the whirlwind of dancers. Arlina has the grace that all daughters of nobility are expected to have, and then some. However, her grace can never match that of *Ástfriður*. Of Brenna. Where Brenna was wild and fierce, Arlina is composure and patience. Arlina's movements are perfect. Brenna would have found reasons to deviate from the scripted steps and add in xir own flourishes. Arlina knows how to blend into a crowd, and Brenna refused to.

Caitlin tears her eyes away and notices that her glass is empty again. She raises her hand to summon a server and looks at her husband to see if he would like some, too. But he, too, is distracted. She follows his gaze. Arlina. He is also transfixed by Arlina. Caitlin blushes. *Did he notice that she was staring at Arlina? Had he seen something in Caitlin's eyes that betrayed her? No. He couldn't have.* Besides, there was nothing between them, not really. It had only been one night just that once, a single night where they transactionally provided comfort. Nothing more. It couldn't be something more.

Why can't she stop comparing Arlina to Brenna, though?

"What did you do?" The king's aunt marches through one of the side doors to the dais, pushing several staff members out of her way. "Why is your sister refusing to leave her rooms, and why is her wife standing sentry outside of them?"

"What did I do? What do you mean, Aunt Maeve? My sister's actions are not my concern. If she is not attending your homecoming party, perhaps it is you who caused offense." His nostrils flare, and his eyes darken.

"You did something, you said something. Did you tell her the same way you told your uncle? Were you just as uncaring with your sister? And I did not ask for this homecoming party, nor did your cousin. What is this for? The ambassador?"

The king drums his thumbs on the arm of his chair.

"Very well. Thank you for the warm welcome home," the duke says, grabbing a drink from the approaching server and raising the glass in a mock toast before turning on her heels and disappearing into the crowd.

Cian shifts uncomfortably on his throne. "I can do nothing right with any of my family members."

"We all handle grief differently; I am sure that this will be smoothed over soon. Emotions are high right now," Caitlin says and places a hand on his shoulder. She wants to slap him. She wants to tell him that he's being an idiot. Instead, she says, "Be patient, my love."

"I am the only one in my family interested in putting this kingdom before personal feelings. If they are angry at me for being a king, they are not royalty. They are selfish. If they knew what I have to do…" He rubs a hand up and down his arm, wincing.

"Tell me," she whispers, leaning in close, her lips less than an inch from his ear. "Let me carry the weight, too."

He shrugs and pulls away from her, stands up, and storms off, saying nothing further. She sits back, reclining on the throne, and sighs. She is the wealthiest woman in the kingdom, and yet she is not getting paid enough.

Arlina is no longer on the dance floor, and Caitlin cannot find her in the crowd. Lurking in the corner, however, is Father Nael. She has never seen a priest at such civil functions, only at religious events. Had someone ever actually invited him? Why is he here to begin with? He's not speaking with anybody; he steadfastly avoids eye contact with everyone around him. Whenever someone tries to approach him, he turns his back and shuffles away.

The rest of the ladies had been dismissed for the day and free to do as they pleased while Caitlin and Kegan hide in her rooms. Although Caitlin had wished that Lady Arlina would have stayed. Her father, when he had seen her in the hallway escorting Caitlin back to her rooms after the homecoming event, demanded that she assist him in some family matters. Caitlin had not seen her in the days since. All for the best; she would not have been able to talk to Kegan with others here. Maybe some distance from her lady-in-waiting would be good.

"...thinking about it, however, it might be to our advantage if there were to be a war. The more chaos, the more disorganization, the fewer lords who are at their manors. We could definitely play this."

"Maybe. Maybe." She cannot pay attention to what her friend is saying.

The door creaks open, and Caitlin jumps, quickly covering the paper she had been writing on.

"My lady?" Lady Arlina peaks her head through the door. "I did not mean to frighten you. Are you busy? I shall come back another time. I just wanted you to know that the family emergency has been tended to."

"No, wait!" But the door closes, the latch not making any noise.

"What was that about?" Kegan says.

"I don't know. I hope she is well, though." Caitlin blushes, tempted to fly out of her seat and give chase.

Kegan knits their brow, a finger on their nose, looking between the closed door and Caitlin. "Oh no. Absolutely not. You can't!" Kegan rises to their feet and slams their palms on the table. "You cannot."

"Can't do what?"

"I know that it is in fashion these days among royals to have additional bed partners, but you aren't a real royal. You will not jeopardize this mission because some green-eyed beauty smiles at you."

"It was just that once!" Caitlin slaps her hands over her mouth. "I mean—"

"You already did? You already slept with her?"

"It was just that once, and it meant nothing. It was one night of us being—"

"Selfish! You were being selfish. Do you know what your fellow organization members have been through? Do you know what I have been through? You don't know what we have sacrificed, have given up, have gone without so that we could get to this point. I will not let all of our progress be lost because you decided—"

"I have given up my freedom; I have always given up my freedom. The only person in this entire world who has ever asked me what I want is dead. I think I may have one night to be stupid and selfish."

"Stupid is right. You better make sure that it stays that way. You make sure that it is only one night. I can't be near you right now. If you'll excuse me, my lady." They lace their voice with venom, and each syllable is a barb in Caitlin's heart.

"I was there when this was signed," the woman says, pulling the folder from her pouch and setting it on the counsel table. She wears the same finery as some of the noble ladies, but around her neck hangs a necklace with a pendant of a sword crossed with a pen—the symbol of Aife, goddess of both war and law, conflict and its resolution.

Caitlin fans herself, and Lady Clare has gotten up to pour herself more water several times. Summer is still a week away, but already it seems as if summer has lasted for months. The rest of the council members are equally listless under the oppressive heat.

"I was there for all the negotiations. Since Your Majesty asked me to, I have read it multiple times. It does not mention anywhere those lands within this document. Even in the notes that I could find, there is not even a single word about the queen's dower lands, your Majesty."

"Are you sure about this?" The king has unbuttoned his doublet but otherwise shows no sign of discomfort, all of his attention focused on the lawyer.

"If I recall correctly, those lands were part of her dowry when she was arranged to be married to a Garcelonian noble. Even if they should belong to you, they would not become part of Fayn. Rather, you would be considered a minor lord in Garcelon."

"Thank you," King Cian says and waves his hand in dismissal. The lawyer stands up, bows to the king, and leaves the council room, leaving the documents spread upon the table.

"Well," the king says, gesturing to the paperwork. "I opened the floor to my trusted counsel for their valued opinions."

"We are not going to war with Mother's homeland. This is not what she would want," Eleanor says. The two princesses have reluctantly left their isolation to attend the council meeting after his aunt had given him an even more thorough verbal lashing. Lady Dontaue herself still refuses to join.

"I agree with Princess Eleanor. If you want a peaceful solution to this dilemma, which I do not even view as a dilemma, I suggest that it be through more diplomatic means," Lord Hern says while turning to look Caitlin squarely in the eye and raising his eyebrows at her. Caitlin glances away. Far too many of the royal family have made sly jabs at her regarding her fertility, or rather, lack thereof. It's only been six months since the wedding, yet they all act as if she should have produced seven children by now.

"Well," Sir Nait starts before being interrupted by his father-in-law coughing. Loughlin swallows and clears his throat. "I agree with Lord Hern."

The royal duke grins and knits his fingers together on the table.

The Gallaghers both nod their heads, looking back and forth between Cian and his uncle.

Father Nael leaves his post at the window and takes a seat next to Berach; it is the first time that he has sat at the table during a meeting.

"I was talking to my own lawyer," Lord Berach says. "One who is not as close to the situation., while that old lady—whose mind I am sure has decayed somewhat, and who may have forgotten crucial details over the years, though I do respect that at one point she was the sharpest lawyer on your father's council…" The earl takes a deep breath and glances at Father Nael. "Well, my lawyer believes that not only are those lands yours, but all of Garcelon may be."

The king cocks his head to the side and rests his chin on his thumbs. "Oh? Go on."

"You see, the order of succession in the kingdom is, to put it lightly, up in the air."

"Seems to be a running theme these days," Ciarbre says.

"Yes, well. When a royal family does not produce heirs of sound mind, these things do tend to happen." Arlina's father once again raises his eyebrow and looks at Caitlin. "My apologies. I digress. Well, your mother may not have been the eldest of the Garcelonian royal children, but when her oldest brother, the king, died, he had no heirs himself, and that left only the queen and her niece, who had been orphaned very young."

"Do you have a point, Berach?" Hern says.

"I am getting there, patience," Berach says, glancing at Father Nael again. "What I mean to say is, who really should have inherited the Garcelonian crown? The queen's niece, whose parents had never sat on the throne, or your mother, the daughter of a king and queen? I would argue that it should have been your mother."

"She never would have done that. She was more than happy here," Eleanor says.

"True." Berach holds up a hand. "She did not want it, although it should have been hers. She did not make a formal declaration accepting her claim, but she also did not make any formal declaration rejecting her claim. Queen Joanna may be a usurper."

"Have you gone mad?" Hern says. "Are you attempting to make this a larger incident than it already is?"

Berach ignores Hern and squares his shoulders, facing Cian directly. "If your mother had the more legitimate claim to the throne, with her passing, that claim should belong to you now, not Queen Joanna."

"What are you proposing, then?"

"Is it not obvious? We do not just take Valencia. We take all of it."

The Admiral grunts in agreement. Lord Caibre, Lairde Elwee, and Baron Rivers raise their glasses and cheer. Sir Liam and Sir Connor wink at each other.

Father Nael says nothing as he stands up and resumes his vigil at the window, his expression blank.

FIFTEEN

Treason and Truth

Sister Kiandre saunters away from the table without looking back, her diaphanous gray robe blending in with the dim lighting of the Great Hall. When Caitlin spotted the elusive Calla, she suspected there would be a conversation. Instead, all that the priestess did was place an envelope on the table. No words spoken.

Caitlin picks it up, turning it over in her hand, unsure what to do. The envelope's paper is thick, textured, and flecked with gold. Not very discreet. The wax seal, however, is a simple square with no insignia on it at all.

She slides her fingernail under the seam and gently opens it. She is at once met with a strong smell of flowers and herbs she does not recognize. There is a note, although she dares not open it here. She searches the room for Cian and does not see him. "If my husband asks where I went," she says to a servant, "tell him I retired for the evening."

"As you wish, your Majesty."

She slips the envelope into her pocket and rushes out of the Hall, touching her bracelet for comfort and determined to find a secluded nook. She tries to ignore the dizziness and the tingling that rushes through her momentarily as she turns a corner. Winded, she leans against a wall and examines the envelope again. The note inside is short.

Your crown is still contingent on conception.

She grimaces. What she had told Kegan had not been an exaggeration. She was giving up her life for this cause. Giving up everything. And not because it was her choice. Once, a lifetime ago, she had wanted to have a child. She and Brenna had discussed so many ways that they could make a family together despite her difficulties with her cycle.

But year after year, it got pushed off.

Not yet.

Now is not the time.

Next year.

We're still too young.

We're not ready.

The nearest Andrastan Temple that could assist them was too far away.

A list of reasons to put it off, not because they wanted to put it off. But because life is messy and complicated.

Those flowers, those herbs... What they represent... Kiandre is right. She understands the implications of the council members' sneers every week. The reason that the king looks at her differently when he comes to her chambers is apparent. People's eyes linger on her midsection, and she knows what they seek. The insinuations will become outright questions and direct accusations. There is no other choice.

She pockets them again and turns to head to her rooms.

"I am so tired of everything going to his family and his favorites. We work just as hard. Aren't we members of the council, too?" Lairde Elwee says.

Caitlin stops mid-stride and strains to hear. *Where are these voices coming from?*

"Almost all of them were given their titles in their lands years ago by Tarmon's father as the reward for defeating the Tsvetokrasans when they tried to invade. Now, those lands are just being passed down from generation to generation. None of the current lords even do anything but sit there!" Seamus Connal, Baron Rivers, says.

She whirls around and sees a flicker of light coming from an open door.

Beside Rivers are Lord Caibre and Lairde Elwee. She spots Arlina's brother, Lord Tynen, and the Admiral.

She approaches the door with light steps, barely breathing.

"He gave me a title," Baron Rivers continues. "And yet no lands to accompany it. When Cian took the throne, I hoped the oversight would be remedied. Unfortunately, it has not been."

"You're lucky to have a peerage title at all," Elwee replies. "And Lady Shennen won't do more than mess around with me unless I have more than just a courtesy title. She's distantly Suan nobility, as she's always reminding me."

"That's what this is about for you?" The Lord Tynen says. "Impressing a lady?"

"Yeah, Elwee's as smitten as a kitten," Caibre says.

"That's rude, you know, to say that," Elwee says.

"What? Is it offensive to speak the truth?" Lord Tynen laughs.

Caitlin creeps closer to the door as the roars of laughter echo. If the only reason Elwee wants to go to war is to become a war hero and be granted a peerage, zie is clueless about the extreme willingness of Lady Shennen to wed zir.

"Why are you here, though?" Caibre asks, still laughing. "Tynen, your family has lands and titles. Right? Or are they all going to your sister, and you're to be left with scraps?"

"Can't a man just want better wineries?" Lord Tynen responds. "If this is the meeting where we call dibs, I want to call dibs on Linea. And I could say the same to you, Earl of Cairbre. You already have lands and titles."

"But I have to share with my sisters."

More laughter. Caitlin risks being caught and peers inside again. Elwee claps Tynen on the back. "I knew I liked you. The full truth, though. Why are you here?"

"I'm here as my father's representative, isn't that obvious?"

"Then what," Caibre says, "does your father want?"

"What does my father want? What any good father would want: the best for his children. Unless you want his lawyer to reassess her claims...?"

"Not at all," Elwee says.

"Do you doubt my family's commitment to our desire for Garcelon?"

"How could I? It was your father that has found a reason to make it to make it all possible. We are grateful for his support."

"Then I believe you should refrain from asking any more questions."

"Right," Elwee says. "Right. Moving on. I was hoping we could start talking strategy."

Footsteps approach, and she glances down the hallway. A priest is jogging down the hallway. *Where did he come from?* No time to ponder; she scurries away, ignoring the tingle that runs down her spine.

It's been several weeks since the queen passed away, but Caitlin and her sisters-in-law continue to go on charitable outings in her name, still dressed in mourning clothes. Today's outing is at Diarmuid's clinic, where they will treat the many people who have fallen ill because of the excessive heat and lack of rain. Kegan is supposed to meet them there; it will be the first time that Caitlin will see the Calla since their argument. Lady Arlina wanted to accompany them, but her father claimed there was a family emergency and asked her to remain behind. The carriage feels empty without her.

They pull up in front of the door to the clinic, and Diarmuid himself comes out to greet them. All of the ladies quickly fall to their usual tasks without having to be told, and Caitlin follows him back to the exam room as soon as he closes the door. Kegan springs to their feet and approaches. "Ask her! Ask her what she did!"

Diarmuid looks Caitlin directly in the eye; she quickly looks away, refusing to meet it. "I don't have to," he says, taking one step toward her. "I don't have to ask her because I've always known."

"It was just that one time–"

"Stop. Caitlin, it doesn't matter how many times."

"It won't happen again; I promise it was just one night, which meant nothing."

"Don't lie to me," Diarmuid says softly.

"I'm not lying," Caitlin says. "It was just one time."

"That, I believe. But you keep saying that it meant nothing. But it did. Whether you slept with her does not change that you're in love with her. It very much meant something."

Words die in Caitlin's throat. *He's wrong; he has to be wrong.* She doesn't love Arlina, or at least not like that. He has to be wrong. She opens her mouth, wanting to deny it, tell him that he is mistaken, and ask him how he could possibly know that. How can he possibly know what is in her heart? "Oh," is all she can manage to get out. "Oh."

"Yes," he says.

"I..."

"No, do not apologize. Do not apologize for your feelings."

"No!" Kegan cries. "No, she should apologize, she's—"

"—doing what she can to survive. We all are. You can't ask someone to live in a desert and never search for an oasis."

"But—" Kegan looks back and forth between Diarmuid and Caitlin. They stomp their foot, turn around, and leave the clinic out the back door.

"Diar, I—"

"I know. I know, I don't want to hear it, but I know."

"Are you going to tell Valen or Sharidan?"

"Tell them what?"

"I meant—"

"They don't need to know your personal business. Kegan will keep their mouth shut."

"Are we...are you and I... are we... Are we still friends?"

"Why wouldn't we be?" He sweeps her into an embrace. "Why wouldn't I still be your friend?"

She smiles. "I have something else I need to ask."

Still holding her, he asks, "What can I help with?"

"We cannot force Kegan to be at court with me. That leaves me very little access to any help."

"Sharidan is working on that. We will not abandon you. For now, be circumspect in your dealings with Sister Kiandre."

"Thank you. There is one more matter." She pulls back and reaches into her pouch. "These herbs. Kiandre gave them to me."

"Oh," he says, taking them into his hands. "This is something I will need to talk to them about. It should be your choice, but they do need to know."

"I don't want to…"

"I know. You will get no pressure from Sharidan or Valen to do anything but what you feel is best."

"But I do not even think they will work. You should have done a better job vetting me before selecting me for this job."

"What makes you say that? Are you ill?"

"I was told I couldn't."

"What? When?"

"In my first marriage…" She chokes on her words.

"Oh, Caitlin." He takes her hands. "Oh, my dearest friend."

The meeting is already in progress when Daya and Eleanor arrive, sitting at the table without even caring that their brother is still speaking. Neither of them gives so much as a hint of acknowledgment of anyone in the room at all, both still wearing mourning clothing even though everyone else in the court has once again donned their usual garb.

"Nice of you to finally join us," Cian says, glaring at his sisters.

They do not acknowledge him.

"As I said, even minor lords have complained about their tenants and farmers setting fire to their barns, releasing the cattle, and otherwise causing mayhem that takes servants days to set right again."

"It is awfully suspicious," Elwee says. "These upstarts seem to be one step ahead of us."

"He's right," Caibre says. "They seem to know when the lords will be away from their estates and lands and when guards will be sick. They seem to have all the information they need to catch even the most meticulous lords unaware."

"What are you implying?" Cian says, leaning back in his chair and studying Caibre intently.

"We still have not found the assassin," Lord Hern says. Everyone, including the princesses, whips their heads around to see the duke, having aged ten years in two weeks, leaning against the back wall, holding his cane in front of him.

"You are right, Uncle," the king says. "We have not. Do you believe these are related?"

"Well, I think there are many things that are related," Sir Liam says. "Our factory workers, for example, are always on strike. They break the machines and collapse the ceilings; they creep in like thieves and make such a mess that all work stops for at least a week."

"We are not meeting any of our quotas anymore and failing to meet important deadlines with traders." Sir Connor jerks his head towards Caitlin. "I am sure she understands our plight."

Caitlin swallows and nods, unable to bring herself to say anything.

"If anyone here is trying to imply something, then it is the people," Daya says.

The king drums his fingers on the table before him, glaring at his sister-in-law. "And what would that be?"

"Please," Sir Liam says. "Inform us of what these people think since you seem knowledgeable about their wishes."

Cian holds his hand up. "Liam, stop."

"They are unhappy."

Sir Liam throws up his arms. "Who cares? They go to work, farm, and do as they are told."

"Yes," Daya says. "That is what they do, but is it what they want to do?"

Sir Connor rolls his eyes. "So, you've been reading those pamphlets that some treasonous malcontents hand out at their riots, have you? I suppose you agree with it?"

Daya shrugs but says nothing.

"You are saying that my brother, his wife… Both died because some peasants did not want to work?"

"Uncle, you know that is not what she is saying," Eleanor says, looking between Hern and Daya. "I believe she is trying to say that the people are unhappy. And we must take care in choosing how we respond to that."

"Oh, do not be that way," Caibre says. "You sympathize with them. And they know it too, don't they?"

"Rorick," Cian says.

Caibre ignores the king's warning. "You think people do not notice? How do people react when you two are out? Hmm? With applause."

"Brennin. Stop."

"And I would wager the queen does, too. People seem to love her. Why is that?"

"Brennin Rorick!" The king raises his voice, slamming the table, eyes dark. "Careful what you say. It sounded to me like you were about to accuse my wife and sisters of treason."

"Oh, come off it. Like you do not harbor the same suspicions."

Lord Berach chuckles.

Daya storms out of the council room without saying another word. Eleanor looks between her brother and the door and then back at her brother again. "I am sorry," she says. "I will talk to her. I am so sorry." She sprints out of the council room after her wife.

Caitlin's face reddens, and she is sure that everyone in the council room can hear her heart beating. *Does he really suspect her?* Does he really think that she and the princess are aligned with the revolutionaries?

Cian puts his hand on Caitlin's arm. "Sweetheart, are you alright?"

She takes a deep breath and looks the Earl of Caibre directly in the eye. "I am just fine, merely concerned about the slanderous snake across from me."

Father Nael coughs.

"Rorick," the king says. "I have one more thing to say to you. A king who does not sympathize with the plight of his people is no king at all. I am thankful my sister and my wife always remind me of that. Now, I want you out."

"But, your Majesty, I—"

"You either leave on your own, or you be escorted out, possibly a head shorter."

"Fine," he says, crumpling up the papers before him and tossing them into the fire. "I do not know why you ask us for advice if all you're going to do is take it from a commoner."

Caitlin is sure at this point that the door will fly off of its hinges with how many times it has been roughly slammed shut.

"And Father Nael, did you have anything to add? It sounded like you might."

"Oh, nothing at all. It's just been so hot and dry all summer. It is hard for me to deal with; sorry for causing a disturbance."

"Are you sure that you have nothing else to add?"

"You know my opinions already, your Majesty. I should hope that I do not need to repeat myself. So that I do not waste my breath or your time, I shall return to the Temple and pray for you."

"Well," Elwee says. "Should I ask one of the servants for more beer?"

Lord Berach grins. "We certainly need it."

"No, I do not believe you gave him cause to suspect you." The small temple on the palace grounds is empty when Caitlin arrives. Not even an acolyte can be found tending to the flowers or mopping the floors. Caitlin wonders if the Calla is actually the only one of their Order to stay here. But the emptiness suits the two of them.

"But he was saying—"

"Brennin Rorick is simply impulsive and ill-tempered. Bitter about his father's will and desperate to be as rich as he thinks he ought to be."

"But the meeting with the other council members—"

"Same thing. I would not worry about it if I were you. You have other matters to fret over. Did you take the herbs?"

"No. I did not. I will not."

"You do not fully understand what is at stake. Since the high priestess has no intention of giving you all of the information, I have decided I will give you—well, not all of it, but—the relevant information. Can I get you tea?"

Caitlin rolls her eyes. "No, thank you. I will be fine."

"Of course." The Calla does not sit back at her desk after she pours her tea, but she perches herself on the windowsill overlooking one of the many gardens on the palace grounds. It is a small courtyard solely for the use of the Sisters of Andraste. "If I were you, I would be unhappy with the way the high priestess is treating you. She expects a lot from you and gives you very little in return. I believe if you knew a little more, you would be more amenable to your agreement with us and to our plan. Maybe…"

"Maybe?"

"Maybe even join us."

"Ha! It would indeed be helpful to know more about what is going on, but I doubt I will join whatever cause you are involved in. I'm tired of the games. If the visual proof were not in front of me, I would be more inclined to believe that Dierdre is the Calla; she's certainly about as straightforward as one."

"I've heard people say that before." The Calla pulls her legs up so that she is perched entirely on the windowsill, her gaze fixed outside on a squirrel running around the fountain. "Anyway, I'm trying to tell you that there is a lot more going on than Dierdre will say."

"That much is obvious," Caitlin says, tapping her foot impatiently.

"How religious are you?" Kiandre says. Her tail flicks back and forth, and she still has not bothered to look at Caitlin.

"I'm not particularly religious, nor do I care to become such. I'll play the part, however, if it is necessary."

"Neither am I," Kiandre says, finally looking at Caitlin and winking. "I am faithful to the teachings of my Order, though." She jumps from the windowsill and approaches Caitlin.

"If you are waiting for me to ask you more, you are sorely mistaken. You're going to tell me, regardless."

"You're no fun."

Caitlin crosses her arms and raises an eyebrow.

"Fine. Fine. There is a secret sect within the Order of Andraste. It predates the birth of the goddess. Yes, the gods were not always as they are today. Centuries ago, magic was free, and people could practice it as they wished. But not everybody agreed with its use. The new gods were born from the desires of those opposed to magic. My Order seeks to restore magic to the land. Covertly, secretly, quietly. We pretend to be devotees to a god that destroyed our way of life."

"What about the *Ástfriður*?"

"You really are no fun. I was really looking forward to the 'What! Magic is a myth!' or 'But magic isn't real!' I forgot; you've seen magic. Many believe it's a myth or an exaggeration of the abilities of the *Ástfriður*. But I guess that makes this easier. It used to be that everyone could use magic; it existed everywhere, not just on the Isles."

"That's great and all. But tell me, how does my spying on the Cian for you further your goals?"

"We are not the only secret order at court. There is another hidden inside of the Temple of Culain. We believe that Father Nael and his two companions are members of it and have some bargain or pact with the House of Fola."

"Again, what did this have to do with me spying for you?"

"This other order... They are destructive. And their goals are, too."

"You say that you wish to give me more information, but all you are giving me are more questions. What do they have to do with magic? And why should I care?"

"We don't understand that part either. That's why we need you to get us more information."

"Your goals are not so much whether the king sits on the throne but whether your enemies sit behind it."

Kiandre puts her thumb on her chin. "When you put it like that, yes. I have told you what I feel is necessary for you to know you to carry out your mission for us."

"I am not sure I follow. However, I guess the real question is, what are you expecting me to do about this? All you have asked for so far is to convey whatever information I think is important, leaving me to guess what details are and are not necessary."

"This is why I disagree with Dierdre's methods. Our order has stayed secret for centuries; we have kept the secret safe. But sometimes you must take risks. I believe this is a time for risks. We will never be free otherwise. We need to know if our suspicions are true: what is the pact, how does it work, and who partakes in it? Without this information, we cannot break it."

"And you want it broken because, for some reason, this other order is your enemy? And you dislike that they are in power?"

"We share an enemy right now, remember? An enemy that we both want out of power."

"What happens when the monarchy falls? Will you seek to be the power behind whatever government the Red Front creates? Will you seek to make your own bond? Your own pact?"

"Does it matter?"

"Of course, it matters! Do you plan to replace one shadow ruler with another? Will the people be just as oppressed as they are now? Same dictatorship; different dictator."

"Earlier, you spoke of freedom in the personal sense; your freedom to love who you wish, your freedom to live as you want, your freedom to have a little house on the ocean's shores, to have cats and a garden. Your freedom from, not your freedom of. Yet, now you speak of it on a macro level. Which is it? Are you aligned with us or with the Red Front for your own selfish reasons or because you truly believe in the causes?"

"I am done with these games for today."

"Do you understand what I want now? I need more information about Nael."

"I will bring you the information that you want now that I know more about what I'm looking for. Are you finished? I have other plans for the day."

"I am finished. There is nothing more to share. Have fun with your mistress."

Numerous nobles of all ranks have come to Cian with complaints regarding riotous serfs, dissatisfied farmers, and general unquiet on their lands. Not to mention, the ongoing drought has affected the crops and produce, creating multiple shortages. And Sir Liam and Sir Connor are not the only business owners to bring grievances about their workers.

"This is getting out of hand. Whoever is organizing this is smart and most likely well-informed," Lord Berach says.

"We need assistance and permission to use greater force to bring them back in line. The rebels need to be rooted out," Lairde Elwee says.

"If you cannot keep your people under control, how will you muster a decent army for our invasion?" the Admiral says.

"I have not decided yet one way or another on that matter," the king says, his mug cupped in both hands, staring out the window and not at his council.

"This should have been over after we burned down the last factory, but they keep going on strike, and now they are destroying some of the equipment! I mean no disrespect, but this cannot continue. The assassin is still not caught, either; need I remind you? They are all related; this is all one giant issue," Sir Liam presses.

"Enough! You have all spent plenty of time airing your concerns; I have heard them. I need to think about this," he says, still not glancing at anyone else in the room. "Meeting adjourned."

Father Nael lingers by the window as the rest gather their belongings and leave. He takes a step towards Cian, but Cian raises his hand. "No. Not today. Not anymore this week."

"But your Majesty—"

"No."

"You have heard how the land—"

"I said no!" Cian tosses his mug at the priest. "Now, leave."

"If you don't—"

"Who is the king here?" He stands up, knocking his chair over and advancing on the priest. "Hmm? You? Or Me? Who gives the orders? Now go. I need to speak with my wife."

The priest scowls and hastily leaves, slamming the door behind him.

"My dearest," he says, taking both of Caitlin's hands. "I should not have to say this to you. But... are you well? Are you in good health?"

"Of course, my love. I am well." She is trembling and unable to hide it.

"Well, we have been married for over half of a year. The country needs stability. You have heard examples from Garcelon and Tsvetokrasa about what happens when no heir is waiting in the wings."

"I am not sure I understand."

"The path to peace lies with you. We need a child if we are to have any diplomatic arrangements; we need a child to betroth. And we need a child to prove our strength, to show our subjects that we are blessed, and our line is strong."

"I... I know, my dearest."

"So, I ask again, are you unwell? Any physician in the kingdom, any of them, all of them! I will get you one. Or do you think you are not getting enough food? Or is the food not good enough? Are you getting exercise? Water? Are they rationing your water? Are—"

"I am fine, my lord. It is still early in our marriage. There is plenty of time, still. I know it will happen when the gods will it."

He embraces her, but there is something off. It feels too formal, too stiff. Too forced. He runs his hand through her hair. "Tell me anything that you need, anything that you think will help. It will be yours."

"I want for nothing. If you will excuse me. I... I think I will go to the temple and pray."

He chuckles. "Father Nael is rather upset with me, I believe. Better wait until tomorrow."

"I had meant that I want to go to the Temple of Andraste for fertility..."

"Well," he says, removing his coat. The king doesn't hide the gashes on his arms anymore, and Caitlin doesn't ask about them anymore. He takes the bindings off, and Caitlin fetches a bowl, water, and towel from the cabinet and sets to tending to them, not saying another word.

"What is on your mind, my sweetheart?"

She startles. "Oh, it is nothing."

"Tell me, I insist."

"I will tell you what is on my mind if you tell me what this is about."

"I have told you before; this is not your concern."

"It is my concern, though. You are my husband," she says, choking on that last word. She hates it every time she has to acknowledge that fact. The word is wrong. It feels like poison on her tongue. "I want to help you. I care about you; I love you." *Lies, lies, lies.*

"I know, my sweetheart. I know. But there are some things that only kings can do and only kings should know about. Things my father kept from my mother, and I must now keep from you. If I had known…"

"What does that mean?"

"It means I care about you too much to get you involved in the more brutal side of reigning. Now, I will repeat this: do not ask me about this."

She purses her lips and remains silent.

"Father Nael mentioned something else, though. He mentioned that you seek out the guidance of Andraste often."

"Well, yes. They have been most helpful."

"He mused that since Andraste is the goddess of fertility—"

"Yes, sweetheart. That is why I have been seeking them so often."

Ignoring that she said anything, he presses on. "—She could also be the goddess of infertility."

She drops the towel in the bowl. "I do not understand."

"He believes they may be interfering with your ability to conceive. That maybe they are attempting to curse my reign."

"Who is this 'they'? Why would 'they' do that?"

"Many in the kingdom are unhappy with my family's divine right to sit upon the throne."

Caitlin stands up and turns away from him. "I wonder why that is."

The king pulls on his shirt. "Because they are not educated enough to know when they are being led astray by sinister forces, but for now, we must add the Sisters of Andraste to our list of enemies. Do not speak with any of them, especially in private, again. I will root out these conspirators, but until then, I need to keep you safe. No more outings, either."

"What?" She fidgets with her wedding ring.

"I need to keep you safe, and the only way I can do that is if you are here. Do not worry, my love." He kisses her on the cheek and leaves the room without another word.

Caitlin falls to her knees, burying her face in her hands. There is no getting around it. There is no avoiding it. She must bring a child into this world, not because she longs to be a mother, but because she needs to save her own life and because others want another pawn on this chessboard.

There is a knock at the door. "Your Majesty?"

Caitlin does not recognize the soft voice from the other side of the door but responds anyway. "I am fine; I will be out in a moment."

"As you wish, your Majesty."

"Wait!" Caitlin stumbles to her feet and shuffles to the door, cracking it ajar. "Wait, could you have a meal sent to my rooms? And I will also need a mug of hot water when I arrive. I wish to retire early."

The servant curtsies. "Of course, your Majesty."

Caitlin closes the door, leans her back against it, and slides down to the floor, her stomach churning as she ruminates on that pouch of flowers hidden inside her wardrobe.

SIXTEEN

RITUALS AND RITES

The Order of Culain has only three major holidays, but today—The Feast of the Builders—is the holiest. Caitlin sits at the High Table in the back of the Great Hall, observing everything before her as people settle in for the post-ceremony dinner.

The ceremony in the grand Temple is overseen by a priest whom Caitlin has never met before. He is the same age—or appears to be—as Father Nael, and although his hair has not yet grayed, the lines on his forehead are more deeply etched than the ones that grace Father Nael. His accent is not one that Caitlin is familiar with; some parts of the accent seem Tsvetokrasan in nature, like the guttural vowels. But the hard consonants are distinctly not.

The second the unknown priest had entered the enormous Temple of Culain in the city, the Duke of Dontaue had gone pale, and after the ceremony, she excused herself to her rooms for the night. It is not the priest that scares Caitlin; it is that Lady Arlina had been the woman chosen to carry the iron hammer to the altar. That is usually the duty of the highest-ranking woman of the court. It should have been her. She had been counting on it being her to have an excuse to get closer to Nael.

And yet Lady Arlina donned the green silk gown, lowered the lace veil, and presented the sacred items to this new priest. It had been Lady Arlina who had been chosen to light the fire in the hearth on the altar, and at the end, it had been Lady Arlina who held the still-hot dagger to the sky.

She cannot stop thinking about how beautiful Lady Arlina had been as she stood before the altar, dagger raised. She cannot stop watching her as she dances with all who ask, veil discarded, dress changed, but still full of the quiet strength the dagger seemed to imbue her with. Watching Lady Arlina dance, she can't help but wish it were her, gliding across the floor with elegance and confidence.

"My lady," Father Nael says, startling her from behind. "If I may, I would like to introduce you to Father Ljósa."

She turns slowly to face the priests, reluctant to look away from Lady Arlina, now dancing with the king. "Have you brought me another grandfather?" Caitlin asks with a smile that does not reach her eyes.

Father Nael chuckles. "In a manner of speaking. He has just arrived from overseas, on the border of Tsvetokrasa. He will join us for some time."

"Welcome to court, your Eminence. It is an honor to host yet another faithful adherent to the teachings of Culain. I hope you are not too uncomfortable with the heatwave we are experiencing."

"Nay, my child. I had been hoping to escape the bitter cold of my home. My health has been fragile as of late."

"I am sorry to hear that, your Eminence. If there is anything that I may do, just let me know. I sincerely wish to make your stay as pleasant as possible."

"Dear child, I thank you. I would like to be friends, as you are friends with my brother here."

"If that is all that you ask of me, how can I deny you?" She raises her glass, and the two priests exchange glances.

"That is just what I was hoping to hear."

The heat had been too much, and Caitlin and her attendants cut their walk in the gardens short. It mattered little anyway since no flowers were blooming, all having died from lack of rain. The grass is brown, the shrubs are barren, and the people are hungry. They find very little escape indoors, though.

Caitlin reclines in her chair, attempting to finish the novel that Kegan had lent her. But her eyes keep leaving the page and searching for Arlina in the room. Every time she chides herself, every time she should know better. Arlina has been away more and more, constantly called back to attend to some family emergency.

When she hears the creek of the door handle moving, she leaps to her feet, hopeful. It is not Lady Arlina that enters, however. Instead, Brother Sheath and Brother Sloane saunter into the room, not saying a word and merely motioning for Caitlin to follow. Caitlin rises to her feet, stomach dropping. "How may I help you?"

As she approaches them, she notices one priest with them that she does not recognize.

Brother Sloane clears his throat. "Your Majesty, your presence is requested."

"By whom?"

"By the king, who else? He requests your presence with him in the Temple sanctum. We will escort you there."

Kegan stands up from their perch next to the window.

"Alone." Brother Sloane glares at every other person in the room. "He requested no one else."

Something about the way Brother Sloane barks his orders sets every hair on end. "May I have just a moment?" Caitlin asks. "I fear I do not look my best and wish to freshen up. I will not take long."

Before they can object, she dashes to her bedchamber. She removes her corset and sleeves, both far too elegant for the sensibilities of Father Nael. She searches for something more modest, without embroidery or inlaid gems. Her hand hesitates over her jewelry box, wanting to open it and remove the bracelet from Brenna. It feels like a sort of protection, reassurance from a ghost.

She is going to the Temple of Culain, the place which she is sure harbors Brenna's murderer. In one seamless action, she opens the box, feels the smooth metal of the bracelet, and slips it onto her wrist, comforted and shocked by the sting of *Ástfriður* magic. She has been meaning to ask someone if some of the fixtures and ornaments in her rooms were made by *Ástfriður*, for that could be the only reason she would feel such a shock every time she puts on the bracelet. *Does the magic linger?*

She dashes to the mirror and glances over herself—perhaps the mirror was created with *Ástfriður* magic, trimmed in silver, copper, and gold. Taking a deep breath, she waits for the knot in her stomach to unwind.

"Thank you for your patience. I am ready now," Caitlin says, ignoring Brother Sloane's glare. She falls in step behind the three priests, searching for any recognition in the features of the mysterious third priest. The only thing that sets him apart from the other two is the embroidered symbol on his collar. The color is white, but so is the thread that embroidered it, making the symbol almost imperceptible. The symbol is a simple chalice and tree. She has seen it before only once, on the hilt of a knife.

As they turn the corner from the Western wing, Brother Sheath and the new priest slow their pace until they follow behind her closely. Flanked on all sides now, she feels like she's being led to the prison, not a sanctuary.

Walking across the scorching courtyard, Caitlin is grateful she opted for lighter clothing. Brother Sheath opens the door to the temple, and before she has even finished crossing the threshold, the priest behind her grabs her waist and places a cloth over her mouth.

She struggles against her captors, her hands grasping and trying to free herself. None of the priests say anything as they bind her hands behind her back and prod her further into the Temple.

She is led to the back and then down many flights of stairs; dim torches on the wall are not enough for her to see where she is going. She wonders if she will ever see her fathers again. If she has been found out, will they also be put to death? Which of her ladies will Cian take as his next wife? Who else in the Red Front may be found out if they torture her to extract more information? Or if they will simply kill her quickly? Why did Sister Kiandre and Sister Dierdre not see this coming?

They reach the last step and slink down several more corridors before coming to an open chamber with a deep pool at the center. There are no torches, yet the room is subtly illuminated. Although deep underground, plants are lining the walls, and the structure seems to be built around roots.

"Granddaughter, I am sorry if you were handled too roughly on your way here. But we had need of absolute secrecy." Face neutral, Father Nael stands on the other side of the pool.

Out of the darkness, Father Ljósa materializes and calmly approaches her. "Father Nael tells me that he has offered you friendship multiple times, and while you say you are desiring our friendship, your actions and words have said otherwise. You do not come to the temple as often as you should; you do not consult us as often as you should. You do not come to us first when you have issues or problems. How are we supposed to interpret this?"

Still bound and gagged, Caitlin shakes her head as the priest circles her.

"My sons, thank you for your assistance and discretion. You are dismissed." Brother Sheath, Sloane, and the third priest bow to Father Ljósa before exiting the room.

Despite the cold in her bones, Caitlin stands tall as the older priest appraises her and removes the gag. "We make sure that our friends live long, happy lives. We make sure that our friends are well compensated. And we ask little in return for our friendship."

"And what happens to the people who are not your friends?"

Father Ljósa howls in laughter and turns to face Father Nael. "You did not tell me how cheeky she is." He turns back to her. "I could learn to like you. Are you asking because you are worried about your life or someone else's?"

Caitlin raises her chin, refusing to look at him.

"You do not care what happens to you. But you very much care about someone else. I wonder who that is? If you want your friends to be our friends, too, we can arrange that. Who do you want us to protect?"

With each pounding beat of her heart, the faces of her friends flash before her. Lady Arlina. Diarmuid. Kegan.

"Regardless of your other friends, the matter now involves your husband. He has not been a very good friend to us lately. And we do not know why. It is the duty of a wife to ensure that her husband stays on a godly path. As an adherent of Culain, it is your duty as a wife to make sure that he seeks advice from us, not others."

"You expect the king to take counsel for me? Have you met him? Are we speaking of the same person?"

"I do believe I like you, my dear." He grins, stepping around her and untying her hands. "And yes, he will take your counsel, for he does so already. Your role as our friend would be to advise him, as you think we would advise him when he comes to you for counsel. And to report to us any impure thoughts he expresses or any unseemly actions that he takes."

His hands pull on the laces of her skirt. She jumps away, hands fumbling to re-knot the strings, screaming as she stumbles and slams into the ground.

"I am sorry, my child, I merely do not want to ruin your gown. It looks far too pretty to be damaged. This is a long time coming, but we must bathe you in the cleansing waters of Culain and wash away the touch of any other god.."

She scrambles to stand up, half-crawling away from him. "I am the Queen of Fayn! You will not touch me!"

"Exactly, and the Queen of Fayn must be baptized and cleansed of all gods, save for Culain." Caitlin dashes for the door, but it is gone. Vanished. The two priests are advancing on her as she feels along the rough walls for any sign of the door. *Where did it go?* The only thing she can feel is her heart racing in her chest, the world quiets, and she ceases to be aware of anything except the blood pumping in her veins as the priests grab her and drag her back to the pool, throwing her in without ceremony.

The weight of her dress drags her down to the bottom, her lungs filling with cold water, and she wonders briefly if she should even struggle against it. Despite the darkness and the suffocating pressure, instinct compels her to kick and push her way to the surface, her lungs screaming for air.

She emerges from the water to the chants of the priests, their voices echoing off the water, their eyes fixed on the chalices they each hold. She swims towards the pool's edge but recoils in shock upon touching the side, her scream not breaking their prayer. She takes a deep breath and places both hands on the brim of the pool, determined to make it out this time.

The pain again races through her, but she does not allow it to break her focus this time. But as she struggles, the pain worsens, pushing her to the brink, and she succumbs, sinking back into the pool. Her concentration shatters; her will dissolves.

"Stop!" Cian shouts.

Why? How?

"I said stop!"

Continuing to sink further into the dark.

"But, your Majesty—" Father Nael says, but the other priest continues to chant.

"I do not care for your reasons," Cian shouts. "That is my wife, and you do not get to decide this for her."

He is too late; she cannot reach the surface, and he will never reach her.

"But your Majesty, it is the duty of every Fola to worship Culain. It has been your duty for centuries, a tradition you cannot break."

"Well, I am!"

There is little strength left in Caitlin, not enough to fight. The priests and Cian's voices fade, and her vision darkens.

"I do not care," Cian says.

Resigned, she keeps her eyes open, watching as the water's surface grows more distant, imagining that she can see the night sky. She raises her hand to grab a star, but she is too far away. She glances beneath her as she approaches the bottom of the pool. Glowing on the floor is the pale outline of a chalice and tree. Closing her eyes, she says good night to the world.

She coughs. Suddenly, there is air again. She is not at the bottom of the pool but next to it. Cian taps her on the back, and she coughs out more water. "Keep breathing, please keep breathing."

She sits up and spits out more water. "I thought I was dead," she says, eyes locking on Cian. "Why?" She does not know which of the many questions in her mind she is asking. *Why did the priest do this? Why did Cian save her? How did he get in?* Her mind struggles to work, foggy, slow and clouded.

She is about to ask when he holds up his hand to silence her. He rises to his feet and marches to the door, suddenly back again, His clothes soaking wet and dripping. But he is blocked by Father Nael and Father Ljósa.

"Remember who is king here; it is not you."

"I am the priest. I speak for gods. And even kings must follow the order given by gods."

Cian growls and pushes the priest aside. Quicker than Caitlin would think possible, Cian returns to her side, lifting her into his arms, and carries her past the stunned priests. Still on the floor, Father Ljósa says, "Remember what happens to people who do not follow the gods' wishes."

Cian hesitates. "You forget that I know who you are. And I know you are no follower of any god."

Caitlin passes out before they make it up all of the stairs.

"He didn't tell me," Cian says. "They lied to me. They all lied!"

They are huddled in her bedchamber, the hearth alight and their wet garments drying in front of it. Sir Dermont and three of the king's guards are posted just outside the door.

"I should have realized something was wrong. I should have realized it when they first asked me, right after father…" he says, staring out the window. Caitlin does not know what to say to him, but he does not seem to mind her silent companionship.

"I did not get a choice!" Hands balled into fists, he punches a pillow. "I did not get a choice! I do not want to! But I have to! I did not choose this!" He keeps punching the pillow, and Caitlin is sure that the seams will come undone and her room will be filled with feathers.

"It was not supposed to be like this! Why did father not tell me? No one knows! No one knows what I have to do! And I cannot tell them, not anyone, not even you!" He throws off the covers and runs to the window. "Why do I have to care about this?" he slams the glass pane. "Why is this my fault? Why did father tell nothing?"

Caitlin is unsure if she should get up and follow him to the window. She wants to rest and recover from her ordeal this morning. But Cian has not left her side since he brought her back. He has not stopped rambling, his voice echoing through the room.

"I feel so powerless. I am king, and yet," he says, sinking to the floor and burying his face in his hands. "You are too pure for this, Caitlin; I should never have let you get involved in all of this. This is my fault."

He leaps up to his feet and snaps his fingers. "I know! I shall send you away. I will send you far away where they cannot get you. Where no one can find you."

"But I do not want to go away," she says. "I want to stay here." She shivers despite the unrelenting heat. Not even the setting of the sun provides relief from the scorching weather.

"But I do not know who to trust anymore! Sometimes, I do not even trust you! I do not know who is friend or foe. I had grown up my entire life believing that Father Nael was… I have to keep everyone safe. But there are spies and assassins in my court! I know there are! They could be anyone, even you! When I look in your eyes, sometimes I think I have let my doom in by the front door." He collapses back into the bed and pulls Caitlin close.

She tenses, unsure of what to do. He sobs, wiping his tears on her nightdress—harsh, gut-wrenching sobs. "I am powerless. I cannot do anything. They could have killed you."

She runs her fingers down his back, wishing desperately that it was Arlina and her bed instead.

It has not rained, but the day is markedly cooler than it has been all summer, and so Cian wants to go on a hunt. Caitlin is ready, but as she steps out of the gates, Cian puts a hand on her shoulder and glances at the two Culain priests walking past them. "I do not know how to keep you safe here. I want you to stay in your rooms. Barricade the door. Sir Dermont is not to leave your side."

"But, my love," she says.

"No. This is an order. I need to know you are safe, and I cannot guarantee that right now."

Her attendants, all brimming with excitement for the day, share hushed murmurs amongst themselves.

"But—"

"That is an order."

Her shoulders sag in defeat. A war she had not even tried to wage, one she is willing to lose.

"I shall be so alone, though. Can I ask one of my attendants to stay with me?"

He pulls her close and runs his hands through her hair. "Of course. Lady Emei—"

"I will stay with her," Lady Arlina says.

A sigh escapes Cian, his countenance dark. "Yes, if you volunteer to do so, who am I to stop you? I thank you for your loyalty to the queen."

"Enough with the sad goodbyes. Are we going or not, your Majesty?" Sir Liam says, mounting his horse. "The foxes will not bag themselves!"

Lady Emeire laughs. "Yes, your Majesty! I believe you promised to show me how to hunt, and I am a terrible student, so we need as much time as possible!"

He pulls Caitlin in for one more embrace. "Be well, sweetheart. Be safe."

He runs to his horse and leaps upon it. He does not glance back at her or even raise his arm farewell. Lady Emeire trots to his left and engages him in an enthralling conversation.

"I am sorry that you could not go on the hunt, my lady."

"I did not want to go."

Lady Arlina takes her hand, and they return to Caitlin's rooms.

They play cards, discuss books, laugh about the ridiculous rumors they have heard about who is making love to whom, and wonder what people in the past and the future would think of it.

"You can tell me, you know," Lady Arlina says.

"Excuse me?"

"What happened? Something happened. One of his pages interrupted dinner and told him something. He stormed off and nearly broke the door when he slammed it. All I heard, though, was the page saying, 'The queen.' And he did not return later."

Caitlin sits back, setting her cards down. "You were with him?"

Lady Arlina blushes. "He was at my family's Eoi estate that day. My father was giving him a tour and discussing something with him. We were interrupted while eating dinner."

"Oh, I did not know your family had an estate in the city. And you have never invited me to it."

"My apologies, my lady. I shall have to remedy that." Arlina winks, and Caitlin's heart races.

"Will you be returning there tonight? Or will you be staying here?"

"You would like to be alone or—"

"That is not what I—" Caitlin can't say it. She can't. It was just that once. She promised Diarmuid and Kegan that it was just that once. She told Kiandre and Dierdre it was just that once. A mistake, it was a mistake. A wild, intense, breathtakingly beautiful mistake.

"Not what you want?" Arlina taps her chin. "What do you want?"

It was just that once. "I want—"

"Yes? What can I get for you?"

"I want..." She rises, making her way towards the bedchamber. She cannot make another mistake; she cannot let the fire on her skin consume her. She cannot let the lightning in her heart shock her.

She cannot let the tidal wave in her breast break down the walls and drown her in this desire.

"You want me to stay."

"Yes. Yes, I do."

"You want me to remove my clothing and for you to remove yours."

"More than anything." Her breathing picks up as she struggles to get more air into her burning lungs.

"You want us to touch each other, taste each other, move inside of one another." Arlina stands up slowly and slinks toward Caitlin.

"I want you in my arms," Caitlin says, not moving, unable to even take her gaze away from Arlina's body. "I want you in bed with me."

"You want to ravage and ravish me?" Another step forward, and another. Arlina places a hand on Caitlin's cheek and looks into her eyes.

"No, not tonight. Tonight, I want to make love to you. Tonight, I want to be selfish." Caitlin shoves the door to her bedchamber open.

"So do I. So let us be selfish together." Arlina follows Caitlin into the room, closing the door softly behind her. "Let us take from each other everything we want and need."

Caitlin tugs on the laces of Arlina's dress until they come loose. Slowly, they undress each other, and each garment that falls away is met with a kiss. Trailing their lips down each other's arms, across their breasts, up the legs.

"Get on the bed," Caitlin says.

"No, that is my line."

"Is that so?" Caitlin cups Arlina's chin in her hand.

Arlina leans in and kisses Caitlin, slinking her around Caitlin's head to pull her closer. "Yes."

"Oh, that is not fair," Caitlin says when Arlina finally releases her. "Not fair at all."

"I thought we were being selfish, not fair."

How can a mistake feel this good? How can a mistake feel this right? How can a mistake smell of roses and cedar? How can a mistake taste like honey and salt and ambrosia?

They stumble to the bed and tumble on top of each other. "Yes," Arlina sighs, her body going slack underneath Caitlin. "Oh, yes."

Caitlin enters her slowly, making small motions in and out, grazing her thumb each time across that apex of nerves, eliciting whimpers and sighs.

"Oh, yes," Arlina says again, arching her back and grinding herself into Caitlin's palm. She reaches up to encircle her arms around Caitlin, but Caitlin pulls away.

"Not yet." She spreads Arlina's legs wider, pausing to take in the sight before her. Mistakes are not this beautiful. She did not remember Arlina tasting this sweet, overwhelmingly wonderful. The smell sent her floating to some new realm where there were no concerns except bringing Arlina to completion. Just this moment, just this body, just this woman. Something this euphoric cannot possibly be a mistake. She gets lost in the song of Arlina's rapture; each moan another note in an aria of ecstasy.

The king calls the meeting to order, yet several minutes pass in silence. Strange, for in the three days since he returned from his two-week trip, he has been swarmed by the courtiers. And yet, today, they are silent. "Does no one have anything to say?"

"Oh, fine," Rorick says, slamming his hands on the table. "I'll say what we're all thinking. Someone here is a traitor. Someone here is feeding information to those so-called revolutionaries. Who in this room could it be?"

Aelena readjusts her skirts, looking down as her face flushes, and the king lets out an exasperated sigh, rises and crosses the room to the fireplace, and turns his back to the table. Caitlin straightens her back and asks, "Who could it be? Well, who benefits the most from this revolution?"

Caibre sits back in his chair and crosses his arms. "Your little revolutionaries, I would say."

"My revolutionaries? Nay. Where is our money going right now? Why is it going there? Who is benefiting from the increased strife? Who is profiting?" Caitlin continues, glancing at the priests.

"Garcelon!" Lord Berach says. "If our soldiers are too busy fighting our own people, then they cannot be counted on to be overseas reclaiming Valencia and bringing Queen Isleen home."

She had come to council today ready to cause chaos, but Berach is already doing a far better job than she could. Eleanor and Daya exchange glances. "That makes no sense. The timeline does not line up."

"You believe that the people, rather than having genuine complaints, are instead being manipulated by overseas powers and led astray by foreign agents," Cian says, clasping his hands together in front of him and leaning forward.

"I think it is just as likely as your theory that someone in this room is a spy. Caibre threw out an outlandish theory. Why can I not do so, too?"

"It was not a theory; it was fact. Someone in this room is feeding information to the rebels. Her Majesty asks whose coffers are enlarged by this, and I would have to say hers are."

Cian places his thumb under his chin. "Go on."

She places a hand on Cian's knee. "My dear…"

"No, I need to hear this." He does not even look at her.

Her stomach drops.

"When a traitor is apprehended, where do the proceeds from their assets go?"

"To the Crown's exchequer," Caitlin says.

"No, I was asking his Majesty."

"Into my exchequer. Mine, not hers."

"And what do you do with it?"

"Oh, this is a disappointment," Cian says, slumping in his chair. Caitlin cannot believe she is about to be caught over a dullard's misunderstanding of accounting, a complete coincidence.

"Exactly! She deceived you, your Majesty!"

"The money goes to charity, most often," she says, clearing her throat, "to the Temple of Culain."

Caibre scoffs. "What kind of answer is that? It conveniently absolves you of suspicion, and yet you are refusing to outright declare your loyalty to the crown."

"I would think that the crown upon my head is proof enough of my loyalty."

"Are you going to be this disruptive every meeting?" Hern asks.

"What does that mean?"

"It means you're an ass," Lairde Artair says. "Things do not go your way, and you throw a fit. Even your sisters cannot stand to be near you."

Cian rises, brushing away Caitlin's hand, and paces in front of the fireplace, hands behind his back as if alone in the room in deep contemplation.

"Why you are still on this council is beyond me," Lady Clare says, sipping her wineglass.

"Your attitude," Hern says, "cost the queen one of her ladies."

"With the absence of Lady Ronai, my daughter has had to take on additional responsibilities as the Queen's lady-in-waiting," Lord Artair says. "Emmy is now always with the queen. Not that we are not pleased that our daughter serves you, but we are getting older, and in her absence, we have had less time to devote to making sure our estates are properly protected. I daresay that could be the cause of one of the attacks the revolutionaries carried out on our lands just a month past."

Elwee laughs. "I am sure you are very disappointed that your daughter has not the free time she used to have, what with all the suitors you want her to pursue."

"Can we get back on topic?" Lady Clare slams down her now empty wine glass. "To recap, Brennin Rorick is an ass. Let us move on."

The Earl of Caibre scowls. "It is not my fault you are too stupid to see the games played here. What do you think the queen and the princesses are doing when they are among the people doing 'charity work?' When they have ample opportunity to conspire?"

Liam snickers. "Ass."

"I am so, so disappointed," Cian says, turning back to face the council. "I really needed a laugh today, Caibre. I was hoping you would provide me with one."

"You do not believe me, your Majesty?"

"Let us drop, for now," the king says, ignoring the earl, "the matter of whether Caibre is an ass. I would like to hear your thoughts on Lord Berach's suggestion that Garcelon is behind the discontent among the people. I do not think they are the original catalyst, but I think the idea that they might now be aiding the rebels is... One worth considering. One at a time, please."

"You cannot be serious, cousin!" Lady Clare says, slamming both hands on the table.

"As I think about it, I believe there might be merit. I want other opinions now."

"They might be behind it," Elwee says. "However, that does not mean there is no one at court in their pockets."

"See! Elwee agrees!" Caibre says. "He thinks someone here is a traitor."

"I said 'at court', not 'in this room.' Although, you are making yourself seem awfully suspicious."

"I said we were done with that topic. Baron Rivers, thoughts?"

"Absolutely, Garcelon is behind this; they are swine," Rivers says.

"I refuse to believe it. They are our friends. Our very dear friends," Lady Clare says, frowning into her empty wineglass.

"Do you really need to ask?" Eleanor says.

"I will not even entertain the idea," Daya says, taking her wife's hand.

"They absolutely are!" Sir Nait says.

Lord Hern glares at him and coughs.

"That being said…" Sir Nait scowls back at his father-in-law, "We should attempt diplomacy." He crosses his arms, slumps in his chair, and looks away from Lord Hern.

"I cannot imagine they would be behind this," Lord Artair says, and his husband nods.

"They are right bastards," Liam says. "I would not put anything past them."

"Whether or not they are behind this is immaterial. We have plenty enough reason to crush them."

"Even if they are, we have foes at home, too," Caibre says. "But none of you actually want to attend to that."

"In neither case is war the answer. Diplomacy is," Eleanor says.

"Like hell it is," Elwee says. "They are the ones trying to start this. Why should we not respond in kind?"

"Why are you so insistent that war is the answer, though? That is the nation of my sister-in-law, the former queen. They are cousins to us."

"They do not seem to care about that, though, do they? So why should we?" Elwee says.

"I would rather not make this into a bloody mess. Tsvetokrasa's current situation shows us what it means to fight a war on two fronts. Do you want that here, too?" Lord Hern says.

The Admiral drums his fingers on the table. "One advantage that we have, however, is our navy. We do not have to worry about tiring our soldiers with long marches. We sail right up to Valencia, take it, and then head north to Merida and show them that we mean business. Garcelon caused the offense. We cannot roll over, or we will be the laughingstock of Ahnlisen."

"It is not weak," Daya says, "to engage in diplomacy."

"A marriage between—" Lady Clare says.

"With all due respect," Berach says, "that is a bargaining chip we so far do not have. We cannot bargain on potential. I am not in favor of war. But we need to consider more carefully what that diplomacy looks like."

"Except we do—" Lady Clare says into her empty wine glass, so silent that Caitlin is unsure whether she actually hears it. "Do I not count?"

The Gallaghers nod emphatically. Caibre whips his head around to stare at Berach, squinting at him in confusion, his lower lip trembling.

"He has the right of it," Lairde Artair says.

"Queen Gráinne? What is your opinion, my love?"

She readjusts in her chair uncomfortably, inhales deeply, and squares her shoulders. "Between the protests and the drought, many are seeking aid from the gods."

"As they should," Father Ljósa says.

"Yes, indeed. They seek succor for their hunger, wounds, and ailments from Temples. And while the love of the gods is infinite, the Temple's coffers are not."

"Well said," Father Nael says. "Indeed, current events have put a strain on our finances."

"And the royal exchequer is happy to donate to those coffers," Caitlin says, sitting back in her chair and folding her hands.

"And we are gracious for such assistance," Nael says.

"But that does not mean we do not need to see financial reports and accounting for where that money is going," Caitlin says. "And we have not received reports from any Culainite Temples in months."

Father Ljósa huffs.

"She has a point," Cian says, not looking at either of the priests.

"Are you saying that we are behind the riots? Causing strife for profit? Or that we are diverting that money to the revolutionaries?" Father Ljósa says.

"I am merely doing my job as the royal comptroller. We have policies and rules for our accounting, and you are not following them."

"I have heard enough for the day," the king says. "Your time and efforts are appreciated. I must think more about this issue. When I have decided on our course, I will let you know. You are all dismissed."

"Your Majesty, just one moment," Father Nael says.

Cian groans. "What?"

"I was hoping that we could address the topic of the drought today. Our reserves, and the reserves of other temples, are running low on supplies for the people. The summer was too dry for many of the crops to survive. We fear that the harvest will be insufficient. Could we discuss this topic tonight?"

Cian rubs his arm, wincing. Caitlin slips past him, hasty to leave, but Cian grabs her hands. "No. I have another meeting to attend now, and tonight, I have a date with the queen. Perhaps another time."

SEVENTEEN

Fathers and Fears

"I am sorry, my love," Cian says, "if my words and actions at today's meeting scared you."

"You need not worry. I can hold my own." Caitlin says as she steps aside and allows the king to enter her rooms.

"I know you can. That is one of many reasons I married you. Please, do not let me interrupt your dinner."

"I have not had it yet but am about to. You have dined already?"

"Yes, I am coming back from dining with the Byrnes."

"Was it enjoyable?" Caitlin gestures for the king to sit across from her.

"Quite so. That family has excellent chefs, and Lady Arlina is a delight. I do not know why her father hid her away from us."

"She certainly is. I am glad to have her as one of my ladies."

"She has been attending to you often lately, yes? Since Lairde Kegan has been away?"

"Yes, and with Lady Ronai in Janeuq, too."

"Lairde Kegan has been away for quite some time. Are they sick, or is it a family member that requires their help?"

Caitlin struggles to remember the story she gave about Kegan's absence, growing ever more anxious with each question the king asks.

"Oh, sweetheart, you miss them a lot, yes?"

"Yes, I miss them. They are like family. That is how things go in the trading business; friends become family."

"I can understand that. I feel the same way about many of the members of my court. Except for Rorick. He can go fuck himself."

"Then why do you have him on the council?"

"What better way to monitor him? His parents were on my father's council, and his grandmother was on my grandfather's council. The Earls of Caibre have always had a seat at the table. It is easier to have him on my council than not. Tell me," he says, standing up. "What made you speak up at today's meeting?"

"I thought you desired a wife who spoke her mind? But truthfully, I could not listen to another moment of Caibre's prattling."

"Yes—"

The door swings open, and three servants enter, the aroma of chicken and broccoli following them. "Oh! Your Majesty," a servant says. "We were not expecting you. What can we get for you?"

"Do not trouble yourself. I was not expecting to be here either. Thank you, though." The servants sweep low curtsies and silently take their leave.

"Eat," the king says. "I do not want my sweetheart to have a cold dinner. Regarding your question, I want a queen who speaks her mind and advises me truthfully. I was merely surprised."

"Surprised by…" Her heart races in her chest, and her stomach drops. Her mind leaps from thought to thought, Lord Berach commenting again about her infertility, Caibre's insistence that she was a spy, the fact that Cian had not defended her today or reprimanded anyone for what they said about her, how he had banned her from seeing the Sisters of Andraste or even leaving the palace to walk on the grounds, his remarks about Kegan…

"That you dared to speak up against Father Ljósa, especially after what he did." Cian gets up from the table and wanders the room, picking up knickknacks and baubles from the shelves and examining the contents of some books she has lying around. "You usually only speak of financial matters. But today, you danced on the edge of getting involved in other affairs. Why did you feel the need to speak up today? I know it was more than just wanting to shut Rorick up. You have suffered his rants in silence countless times before."

"I am not as knowledgeable on matters of international politics, nor am I as versed as some in the politics within the court. I have been observing and learning about the way things work still. But, today, I could not hold my tongue as Caibre spat his conspiracy theories."

"Sweetheart. You posited that the Temples of Culain are engaging in treason. Save your measured and considered words for the council; you have no need of them with me."

"Truthfully, do you believe that Father Nael or Father Ljósa would be working with the rioters?"

"What I truly believe is that none of the council, except maybe Caibre, are in communication with them. And if any are, they are not stroking this flame to overthrow you but rather to raise their station in the court. Which of the lords has successfully quelled the riots on their lands? How are they being rewarded?"

"I do not want to believe that any of my people are against me, commoners or nobles. People being upset with how my father ruled, I can understand. I would not call my father a tyrant, but he implemented many laws, reforms, and changes that, although good for Fayn, were," he hesitates, "unpopular. Do you believe the people are justified in their sentiments?"

"I could not say, sweetheart. I would need to study their literature and speak privately with the lords most affected to get a clear picture of what happened on their lands, and perhaps speak with the prisoners who were captured when a base of theirs was raided and razed some time ago."

He nods absently and slumps into a chair. "I do not want to believe that my people hate me."

"I do not believe that they do, my lord."

"I got an unusual petition from someone claiming to be with these rebels. He is petitioning for an audience with me to discuss a peaceful solution to the issue. He wants to talk to me about something he calls 'parliament.' Some reform of the monarchy."

Myles. It has to be Myles... "Oh? Did this petitioner say more?"

"No, he did not. But I am considering granting him an audience. I found dozens of letters in my father's files from this man, all asking for an open dialogue, but all ignored. I want to be better than my father."

"You are, my love," she says.

"Thank you, Caitlin."

"Do you think I should meet with this Myles Ronann?" He picks up a hand-carved wren sitting on the end table beside him. Its wings were spread as if it will take off, fly out the window, fly far away. "Where did you get this?" he says as he examines it from every angle. "It's well done."

Caitlin tenses, a chill going down her spine. Why is he interested in that decoration? Why, of all of the trinkets she has around her rooms, is he interested in the one made by Seth Marr? The cipher that Seraph had given her? Again, thoughts fly through her mind quicker than she can ponder them. Berach's accusations, and Cairbre's accusations, the questions that the king is asking about Kegan, and his soliciting her opinions, does he suspect? She wishes Kegan were here; she wishes she had a quicker way to convey her predicament to the Red Front. She needs an ally, yet all she has right now is guilt and loneliness.

"It was a gift from a father at..." she pauses, racking her brain for the most plausible answer she can come up with. "At the kitchen my ladies and I go to, the one run by the Temple of Muriel. He's a widower and was thankful for the food we gave him for his children."

"When was this? I have not permitted you to leave the palace."

She can't catch her breath. "Oh —"

"A month ago? A week ago? I do not follow your schedule too closely; I am often busy with other things, and I thought I could trust you."

"It was quite some time ago, my love. And I went out so frequently at the time that I could not tell you any more than that."

He rubs his hand up and down his forearm. "I know that you went out frequently and that the people love you for it. In fact, I think they might love you more than me." He sets the wren back down and grins at her. "I think if you gave the order to the people to kill me, they would."

Caitlin's jaw drops, and she stutters. *He knows, he knows, he knows! How does he know?*

He laughs. "I am jesting, sweetheart. I know you would never do such a thing, and I know that with your help and guidance, we will weather this storm and come through victorious. Now, let us go make a prince."

Caitlin no longer sees the point in the council meetings. Every single one of them is disrupted by Rorick throwing baseless accusations at her, the princesses, the Duchess of Clare, and sometimes even Cian himself. His disruptions have put the council at a standstill more effectively than Caitlin herself could have. *Maybe he is working for the Red Front,* she thinks.

Before the king can finish dismissing the council, Father Nael leaves his post at the window and drags Cian to the antechamber. Caitlin folds the documents in front of her and shoves them into her satchel, eager to leave the stuffy room. She does not make it five steps down the hall before Father Ljósa materializes behind her. She had thought it a blessing when the priests did not attend the council meeting, but it seems she must deal with him anyway.

"Queen Gráinne," the priest says. "May I have a moment?"

Caitlin swallows a scream and turns around. "Here? Or would you prefer somewhere more secretive? Secluded?"

"I would prefer to speak to you privately. However, I understand your reluctance."

She takes a deep breath. "Here is fine."

He closes the distance between them, bringing his face within inches of hers. "I understand that you may dislike me because of my methods. But I was not lying when I said I wanted to be good friends, and I was not lying when I said that people who are my friends are sure to live a long, healthy life."

"It is not that I do not wish to be friends, you Eminence, but you are correct in that I have little trust in you right now."

"By the way, have you spoken to your fathers lately?"

Caitlin's eyebrows knit in confusion. "My fathers?"

"Yes. I know they are often away for long periods. Out on a ship that could easily be caught in the storm are captured by pirates or overtaken by a foreign military."

"What is your point?"

"It would be a shame if they were to lose their life," he says, cocking his head to the side.

"Are you threatening me?"

"A little bit, yes," the priest says, touching her shoulder. "Well, technically, I am threatening your fathers. I did try to be friends with you. But it is not too late for a second chance at friendship."

"You ask too much of your friends."

"That is what the young king says, too. He was supposed to be a pliable king, compliant like King Tarmon. Nael had assured me repeatedly that Cian would be easily tamed once he took the throne. But something changed. What could it be?"

"Your Eminence, I do not know what you and my husband speak of. He does not tell me the details of his meetings with you."

"Do you know how to manipulate someone?" He puts a hand on the wall, blocking her quick escape. She glances up and down the hall, but it is strangely empty.

"I am done with this conversation, your Eminence."

"You use what they desire most. And I was told that Cian desired power most of all. Promise him power, and he will be our friend."

"Please, Father, I do my duty to keep the books and accounts of the kingdom. I interfere in little else."

"But Nael was mistaken. And I was incorrect."

"Well, I am glad that you figured that out and did not need my help. Good day," she says, but he again cuts her off.

"It is you. That is what he desires. I do not know why. But you are the key to keeping him in check."

"Father, neither you nor Father Nael know my husband well if you think anyone in the green fields of Fayn can keep him in check. He does as he pleases."

"All we ask of you is to keep Cian on a tight leash for us, as we discussed at your baptism. Keep him following our lead, taking our advice above all others, and make as many Fola babies as possible."

"And if I do not?"

"You can either be a good queen or a dead queen."

"I do not care if I live or die."

The priest roars in laughter. "I know that! Which is why I worry about the well-being of your fathers. Be a good queen and follow our orders."

"It will be a season of weddings," Lady Rivers says to Lady Shennen, their hands clasped together. The princesses have gone on some private retreat, leaving their ladies behind to cause mayhem. Lady Rivers continues reading aloud from a letter clutched tightly in her other hand. "She is some patron of the arts, this mystery woman that Lady Ronai has fallen in love with. They met at a theater while she was in Nimes! How romantic."

"Her brother sent her to Janeuq to meet and marry someone, and she did. Just not the person he told her to. How comical," Lady Emeire says.

"I suppose this means," Lady Shennen says, tail twitching, "I will have to ask her how she does it."

"Does what?" Lady Marianna asks, furrowing her brow.

"Get people actually to commit."

"Elwee still has not...."

"No, I don't know what zie is waiting for." Lady Shennen's ears flatten. "Do I not meet zir expectations? What more does zie require? Where am I falling short?"

"I've told you before, and I shall tell you again: you cannot catch someone who does not want to be caught," Lady Muiris says, leaning against a tree, her turquoise hair worn loose today. "Zie is toying with you."

Lady Shennen ignores the barb. "How did you get Seamus to do it?"

"Oh, I did not. I asked him. You should try it sometime. Taking initiative."

The morning sun is shining, and the air still has the kiss of midnight dew, but Caitlin's thoughts are as dark as the sky is bright.

"It is really not my style." Lady Shennen says, nose high in the air. "I have dignity."

"Oh! What's more important, style or Elwee?"

"A woman can have both. Love is war, and I will be the one to conquer zir."

"But if you ask, you can start planning, and we can have three weddings then this winter."

"Marianna, was it before or after your nuptials? When you lost all common sense?" Lady Muiris asks.

"You are just jealous you are not married."

"I am jealous of anyone who is not in this garden right now listening to you prattle on about love."

Lady Rivers huffs. "Shennen, you have to get Elwee to propose! You, Lady Ronai, and Alice!"

"Alice?" Caitlin looks up. "The Admiral's daughter?"

"Oh! Haven't you heard? Yes, she has found a fellow seafarer."

"Well, I am glad. I am also looking forward to a winter of weddings," Caitlin says. Not a winter of war. However, each day, war looks more and more likely. "Let us go; I must get to the council room."

Lady Rivers folds the letter back up and slips it into her pocket. Caitlin is glad that Lady Ronai will no longer be subjected to her brother's abuse and scheming; she wishes she could say the same for herself.

As if summoned by her thoughts, the disagreeable earl marches up to Caitlin and blocks her path. "Excuse me," Caitlin says, trying to walk around him.

He chuckles and cuts her off again.

She clears her throat. "I said excuse me. I have somewhere to be."

"No, you do not." He says with malice in his eyes. "Did you not hear the news?"

Caitlin rolls her eyes. "Whatever it is, I will hear about it at the meeting. Get out of my way."

"Oh, I do not think so," he says, crossing his arms in front of him. "You are not on the council anymore. The king does not want spies on his council."

"One more time, Lord Caibre. Out of my way."

Lady Muiris and Lady Emerie step forward, flanking Caitlin on either side, glaring at Rorick.

"Go find someone else to bully, ass," Lady Shennen hisses.

"I would appreciate it if you moved. I am not playing games today." She tries to get past him again, and he once again blocks her way and shoves her back, sending her falling.

"You fucking swine!" Lady Shennen lunges forward, swatting at him.

He takes two steps back, hands in the air. "Not very ladylike behavior."

Lady Rivers offers Caitlin a hand. "Your Majesty, are you alright?"

"She will not be 'Your Majesty' for much longer," Caibre says, spitting on the ground before turning on his heel and leaving without another word.

"I hate that man," Caitlin says.

"That is the consensus," Lady Emeire agrees. "Come on, Your Majesty, let us clean you up before the meeting."

"No," Caitlin says. "I am going just to like this."

The palace corridors are chillier than they should be for the early autumn day. She hurries down the hall, ignoring everyone she passes. Not acknowledging Lady, deep in conversation in an alcove with Ambassador Cariveau, she ignores Priestess Samaire; she ignores Lady Dontaue marching in the opposite direction, one of the Culain acolytes following at her heels. She ignores everyone in her single-minded desperation to find the king.

But he finds her first, stepping around the corner and startling her. He inclines his head in acknowledgment but then pushes past her.

"Lord Caibre told me that I was told I am not on the council anymore. Why would he say such a thing?" She says, grabbing his hand and pulling him toward her.

"Because you are not." He pulls away from her. "I am sorry I failed to tell you earlier than this."

"What is the meaning of this? This is not what we discussed." She approaches him and waves away her attendants, Lady Rivers and Lady Shennen.

"I have concerns—and Father Ljósa does too—about your fertility." His words are kindly spoken, but when he says the priest's name, he spits it out like venom.

"I do not understand." She steps back, searching his face for any hint of what he is thinking.

"He believes, and so do physicians, that the stress might affect your ability to conceive. He has—I have decided to give you a vacation so that you may relax and have more time to attend to your physical health. I only want what's best for you."

The ground shifts beneath Caitlin's feet. She recognizes lies when she sees them. "I see." Not knowing what else to say, she curtseys, full and florid. "I shall retire to my chambers, then to rest. Good day, husband."

Father Nael opens the council room and peeks out. "Your Majesty? We are waiting for you inside." A smug grin spreads across his face as he catches Caitlin's eye.

This time, she pays attention to every person she passes on her way to her rooms, scanning their faces and body language as if each person might hold the key. Lady Clare hurries past her, straightening her skirts, lost in her own world. Lady Emeire skips down the hall, hand in hand with a young woman Caitlin does not recognize, giggling like a girl while her companion implores her to slow down.

Somebody grabs her arm and spins her around. "Your Majesty," Ambassador Cariveau says, out of breath. "I have been looking for you. Are you not going to the council meeting?"

"I am afraid I am not," Caitlin says. "Why is it that you were looking for me?"

"I have been asked to pass along this gift to you."

"Oh?" She furrows her brow. "From who?"

"From your cousin in Garcelon, of course. The one in Merida. She sent it with one of my envoys who just arrived. Here." He pulls a small satin pouch out of his pocket and hands it to her.

"What is it?" *Cousin? In the capital of Garcelon? That can't be right.*

"That, I do not know. Though I am excited to find out."

She opens it, and a delicate silver necklace with a lily pendant spills into her hand. *They haven't abandoned me...*

EIGHTEEN

Betrayals and Birthdays

The celebration is the first time that Eleanor and Daya have been seen outside of their mourning clothing. Everyone is wearing their finest, their most colorful, and their most expensive clothing. The sound of laughter adds a perfect staccato to the band's music as the most beloved princess celebrates her birthday on this beautiful autumn day.

The weather accommodates the revelers with a bright day and a perfect breeze, and the chefs and vintners have outdone themselves. But the smile on Eleanor's face does not reach her eyes, and her steps should be light and merry, but they are heavy and stilted.

Caitlin tries to smile, but she, too, cannot keep up any facade of happiness since the day Cian removed her from the council. Since that day, people have been curt and courteous. No longer seeking her out if they want favors, always looking as if they have somewhere else they need to be.

She lurks on the periphery of the celebration, watching as Lady Emeire hangs on Cian's every word. Watching as she touches his arm or leans to whisper to him some joke that he laughs at. He seems to enjoy the attention he has received from many eligible ladies since it became known that Caitlin is no longer in favor. Caitlin wonders how he will discard her. How can he discard the woman he's wed, especially when he made such a commotion when he did wed her? She wonders if she should join the betting pool on who will replace her.

She cannot make herself feel the terror she knows she should have; her stomach is in knots, her neck is far too stiff, and a headache is building behind her eyes; she knows it but cannot feel it. Panic has risen in her chest, but she cannot sense it. She knows her mind is full of racing thoughts: has she been caught and will be hanged, or if she hasn't been caught, that an Aifen lawyer is scouring the library for a legal reason for him to set her aside out of boredom? But these thoughts are separate from her.

This is what she had once been waiting for: for him to grow bored and leave her. But now, too many people relied on her to keep his attention. She sips her wine while Cian excuses himself and walks across the garden, only to collide with a frazzled Lady Arlina. They both laugh at something he says. If Caitlin makes it out alive, she hopes that she can still see Lady Arlina.

"Does it upset you?" startled by the voice, she turns and finds Daya behind her, having crept silently beside her.

"Excuse me?"

"Are you upset to see the person who you love flirting with someone else?"

Caitlin knows that every word Daya says has at least three separate meanings. She has been an official member of the royal court for nearly a year now and involved in court politics for over two, and in that time, she has tried to take her negotiation skills and hone them into the language of politics, though she will never match the mastery with which Daya can navigate its lexicon. "My late wife flirted with other people all of the time. It never bothered me. I knew she would always come home. I knew those pretty words meant nothing to anybody but me."

Daya snickers. "That is not what I asked."

"Yes, it is. But what frightens me," she says, searching the garden for Lady Emeire, but the woman is missing, "is not knowing what the person whispering in his ear says of me."

"She loved you. I do not think anybody told you this, but the queen loved you. She had hoped you could mold Cian into a righteous king, a just king. She was not oblivious to how King Tarmon changed once he took the throne."

"Well, her hopes are dashed now," Caitlin says. "How are you and Eleanor? You have barely spoken to anybody…"

"We have barely spoken to anyone in the court, you mean?"

"Ah," Caitlin says.

"We find few at court worth talking to anymore."

"Such boring conversationalists; they all are," Caitlin replies.

"Precisely," Daya says.

"What do you think," Caitlin asks, taking a risk, "of the people demanding better conditions? Do you think they have reasonable requests?"

Daya purses her lips.

"Because I do," Caitlin says before losing her nerve. "I think they should be listened to, and they are not under the influence of anyone else. Excuse me, I fear I must speak with others here, or I will be accused of having favorites."

Daya chuckles. "Of course, would not want that."

She does not reach the next dessert table Before the Earl of Caibre bars her way. "Oh, your Majesty, imagine seeing you here."

"Why would I not be here for my sister-in-law's birthday?"

"Oh, I just thought you had other friends that you might want to be meeting with right now. By the way, your friends visited my home the other day; they thought it would be unexpected." He grins. "But I was already prepared for them. It seems they are not as organized as they once were, as if the little mole feeding them information has vanished. I wonder why that is."

"I do not know," Caitlin replies. "My biggest concern right now is that my glass is nearly empty. Now, if you will excuse me." He remains immovable despite her efforts to push past him, blocking her way once again.

"This is becoming quite the common occurrence," he says. "You think you have everybody here fooled."

"I must ask you, Lord Caibre, how is your sister doing? The sister who thought it necessary to travel abroad to evade your manipulations? Oh, sorry, that does not narrow it down, does it?"

"I am going to enjoy watching you hang," he says.

"I have heard that Lady Ronai has met a fantastic woman, and I am so happy for her. What was her name? Elana? Elena? Ah! Lady Eliane Riqueti, that was it. Has she told you of this? Are you also happy for her?"

"Fuck you; you will get what is coming!" Fuming, he storms away.

She wishes she had an ally. She wishes she had a friend. But she's been abandoned. She has received no word since the day she was given the lily pendant. She's had no communication, no attempts at contact, and she knows not how to make her own. Maybe they've given up on her, a useless spy who can't even do the bare minimum of keeping her husband's attention and trust. Maybe she was never up to the task to begin with. Maybe she should have refused rather than risk the entire movement being demolished by her ineptitude. Maybe she needs another drink.

She downs the rest of the wine in one gulp, grabs another from a passing server, and sits on a makeshift throne, raising her glass at everybody who passes by and smiling, the Merry Queen everyone loves. Trapped in a spider's web.

"I do not believe we have had the pleasure of having a conversation," Lady Iomaire says, hand in hand with her husband. The two are a beautiful couple, made even more beautiful in each other's presence. She has deep caramel eyes, complimenting his light amber ones, and her dark brown hair makes his light auburn locks stand out. His broad shoulders and tall stature dwarf her short figure and slim body, making them stark contrasts. "I see you were just speaking with my brother."

Caitlin laughs and gestures to the seats next to her. "Charming fellow, he is. Have a seat."

"Absolutely," Lady Iomaire says. "Thank you for keeping Ronai safe. I know you did not have to, and I know what my brother plotted or probably still plots."

"Plots?" Caitlin asks.

"The same thing that many noble plots. To have their family on the throne, near it, or at least have someone in the king's bed."

"Ah, I should have guessed. So that is what this is about."

"Unfortunately, yes, that is what this is about. They are persistent, especially my brother. He wanted me to chase the prince; he was the one that got me the position of lady-in-waiting to Ellie."

"I do not recall hearing any rumors of you and the prince," Caitlin replies.

"No, I told Ellie that I did not want to be yet another of his marks, and she ensured it never happened."

"That is very kind of her."

"As punishment for not following his orders, he had me married to Emyr." Lady Iomaire claps her hands and blushes, the same gesture that Caitlin has seen Lady Ronai perform countless times. "But that did not work out the way he planned."

"It certainly did not, my love," Lord Iomaire says. "He gave us an extraordinary gift."

"I hear that things have gotten precarious in Tsvetokrasa," Caitlin says.

"That is putting it lightly," the ambassador says.

"They say that the Siúlóir Scáth are behind some of the attacks. But we all know it is at the behest and pay of other nobles."

"The Siúlóir Scáth? The assassin's guild? What is going on?" Caitlin says.

"Standard royal affairs; no clear heir, uncles, aunts, cousins, all enemies. I honestly could not tell you anymore. It has gotten so convoluted, and now some of them have their own militias," the ambassador says. "And every faction is vying for our alliance. All of them promise that when they take the throne, they will reward us for our support in their claim. We are very thankful that Princess Eleanor could arrange our safe return home. I suppose this is what I signed up for, but..." He throws up his hands.

"Sometimes we sign up for jobs and yet resent the responsibilities that come with them."

Lady Iomaire puts her hand on Caitlin's. "I hope you know how truly I am grateful you have helped my sister. I believe there is someone else I need to speak to," she says. "No one should keep Princess Eleanor waiting."

"I understand," Caitlin says.

"Thank you for this conversation. I hope to see more of you."

Caitlin sits back in her chair, weary and tired, and gestures for a servant to refill her goblet.

Her exhaustion fades away as she spots Arlina entering the garden, Lady Dontaue by her side. Arlina fidgets with a bracelet on her wrist while Lady Dontaue chatters beside her, the spaniel running circles between the pair. The duke guides Arlina towards a secluded corner where Lady Clare and Ambassador Cariveau are engrossed in conversation. Arlina takes a few steps back when Lady Clare says something to her, but as she excuses herself and turns away to escape, Cian catches her arm and pulls her back into the circle. Pulling away from Cian, Arlina holds up her hands and dashes away. Lady Dontaue whips around and scolds her nephew before he storms off, too, leaving the party without saying another word.

Nightmares haunt her: her friends on the gallows, Diarmuid on a pyre, her fathers on the chopping block. She cannot stay in her rooms where these terrors join her in bed, so she races down the hall, not paying attention to where she's going. Not caring where she's going, just as long as she gets away. She remembers what Caibre says. She remembers the way that Father Nael sneers at her, the way Father Ljósa hunted her. All of these thoughts racing through her mind faster than she can run. It wasn't supposed to be like this. She'd done everything right, everything that was asked of her.

She takes another corner and realizes she's at the garden entrance. It's raining and dark, and clouds obscure the moon. She's only wearing a thin shift, but she does not care. If she cannot feel anything at all, the cold cannot touch her.

She wanders past the fountain where Cian had proposed to her. She wanders around the lilac grove, remembering when she'd got caught in the rain with Arlina. She thinks about the first time she wandered this garden, Cian trying not-so-subtly to woo her, and she too-subtly trying to put him off.

Her racing thoughts halt when she hears other voices. She creeps away from them, not wanting her solitude and silence to be broken. Two voices; she recognizes one of them as the silky voice of Lady Emeire. But tonight, it is full of steel, her cheery cadence chilled.

"This will hurt a little bit," the other voice tells her.

"Just do it."

There is something in the air, something that shouldn't be there. Something that doesn't belong here. Something she recognizes only because she lived with it for seven years and knows it intimately. The sting of magic as an *Ástfríður* weaves metal.

Lady Emeire muffles a scream and then another. Caitlin takes a step toward the sound, confused. *Ástfríður* are not supposed to use their magic to harm others; it is a magic of beauty, not destruction. And it is a magic they are not supposed to use around anyone not of the Veil; their most closely guarded secret, more valuable than anything else they protect on their isles.

"You accept the terms."

Lady Emeire hisses. "Yes."

"You have one year to provide full payment. If not..."

Lady Emeire stifles another scream. "I know."

"Are you sure this is worth it? We could just kill them for you. It would be less expensive."

"But more suspicious."

"We do not mess up. There would be no suspicion."

"I believe your boss said something to the effect when I first contacted them. But this is how I want it done."

"You want them to know it was you, don't you?"

"Guilty as charged," Emeire says, winded. "I want to watch it happen. Slowly. Painfully. I want to watch them on their deathbed, look them in the eye, and tell them that it was me."

"You are a cruel woman."

"Says the assassin that just turned my blood against me."

"That is business. I normally do not ask further questions, but please humor me. What have they done to earn such a brutal punishment?"

"Brutal? No, they are getting off easy. What they did to—when Caragh was—they are getting off easy. Let us leave it at that."

"Very well. And you are sure you will be able to pay us the remainder?"

"More than sure. My fathers are making sure I can. Ironic, isn't it? Although, it would be easier if you were to also—"

"As we have discussed, even as queen, you will not have the funds to afford that."

"If you say so…"

"Well, here is to the future queen. And the gold she will pay us."

Caitlin knows not to expect to hear the *Ástfriður* assassin slip away. Those graceful people know how to walk without a sound and know how to swim without so much as a splash. They can waltz through corridors without a whisper and apparently kill without a murmur.

Caragh Gallagher. What does she have to do with this? Caitlin does not know much about the other Gallagher daughter, only that she decided to forgo court life and take up vows at a Temple of Shea. As far as Caitlin knows, she has not been seen since.

From the way Lady Emeire talks about her sister, Caitlin had thought that there was some sort of animosity between them. It seems it was just an act. *She should have been a thespian.*

She waits until she is certain she is alone again in the garden before slipping from her hiding spot. She doesn't know if it's better or worse, knowing the true reasons that Lady Emeire wants her out of the picture. She gazes at the garden walls, wondering if she could climb them and run away.

Surely, there are still friends of Brenna's on the seas. Surely, she could find them. Surely, they would take her in. Surely, they would take her in, just as the people of Whick took in Brenna as one of their own. Caitlin chuckles at this thought.

In her many years as the heiress to Peddigree Trading, she had never outright been accused of dealing with pirates. Although, it was an open secret that she did. As an escapee from the crown, a fugitive, she would have no choice.

Still lost in her musings, she does not notice the shadowy figure lurking behind the hedge before it leaps in front of her and places its hand over her mouth. "I am a friend," the shadowy figure says. Their voice sounds feminine but somehow distorted and strange. "I am not here to hurt you. I'm here to help. Do not turn around."

Caitlin stiffens.

"You are in great danger," the shadowy figure says.

Is it that obvious?

"But your friends have not abandoned you. Here." The figure slips a velvet pouch into Caitlin's hands.

"Who are these friends?" Caitlin asks. "And what do they want in return? What do they want in exchange?"

"You are pretty smart. I am sure you can figure that out on your own."

"I must admit, I am not so sure how excited I am to be in debt to yet more people at court."

"Do you have a choice?"

"I do not know." She pockets the pouch. "Exactly how much danger do you believe I am in?"

"I would say perilous danger. More people than just Lady Emeire want you dead, including those with the ability and means to make it so."

"Such as?"

"You already know."

"Ah, Nael and Ljósa."

"Do not lose faith. The stars still favor you."

Caitlin hears the figure leave, not daring to open the pouch until she is sure she is alone again. A crescent moon hairpin and a short missive. "When you decide you need assistance, wear this in the morning, and in the evening, wait in your rooms. The stars shall shine brightly upon you."

"When I need assistance? More like when I am so desperate I have no other choice," she says.

"Your Majesty, I would like to request leave from your service formally," Lady Emeire says. The request does not come as a surprise to Caitlin. In fact, after what she has learned, it surprises her that it did not happen sooner. "I need to focus on my family affairs. My fathers are growing old, and I am the only one who can help them."

"Well," Caitlin says, standing up from her desk. "I would like to think that your fathers are not so old that they are close to infirmity and death. However, I understand where you are coming from, and besides, Lady Ronai will return home soon. I will not be short on attendants."

Lady Emeire curtsies, her unbound strawberry blonde hair obscuring her heart-shaped face. Caitlin knows that behind that sheet of hair lies a wicked grin. "Your Majesty is most kind, thank you. It has been an honor serving you."

"If you should ever like to enter my service again, you need only ask. But if you would do me just one more service, please attend dinner with me and the rest of my attendants."

Lady Emeire rises to her feet again, taking a sharp breath, clutching her chest before collapsing.

"Lady Emeire, are you unwell? Should I fetch my physician?" Caitlin rushes to the other side of the desk and places an arm around Lady Emeire. A shock runs through her body, the familiar sting of *Ástfriður* magic. What had Emeire said to the assassin? *You turned my blood against me. Can the Ástfriður control even the iron in blood?*

"I am fine, your Majesty. Thank you for your concern. I think I just have a cold."

"I truly do not mind fetching a doctor for you."

The door to Caitlin's study opens, and Lady Muiris peers inside. "Your Majesty, we are ready—Emeire! Oh my gosh," the marquess says and rushes over.

After inhaling deeply, Lady Emeire stands tall again. "I am fine, truly."

Lady Muiris purses her lips. "You should rest nonetheless."

Lady Emeire shakes her head. "It is time for dinner, and you said that the other ladies were ready, correct? Then let us take our queen to dinner." Lady Emeire laces her hands in front of her and walks, head held high, out of the study.

The ladies make their way to the Great Hall, arriving to find many courtiers mingling while waiting for the servants to bring up the meats. Caitlin scans the hall for any sign of Lady Arlina. Once again, her father had called her away on urgent business the night before, and Caitlin cannot contain her worry.

"Caitlin," Daya says, approaching Caitlin. "You are looking well today." There are bags underneath the eyes of both princesses, and Eleanor does not look like she has slept for a week. Daya's sparkling amber eyes are dull, and her gold-flecked skin lacks its usual glow.

Caitlin bites back the obvious reply. "It is good to see you. May I join you tonight?"

"Of course," Daya says, leading Caitlin and her ladies to the princesses' table, where they join the Duke of Dontaue, the Duchess of Hern, her daughter Lady Elwen, and Lady Clare.

"You missed an interesting meeting yesterday," Lady Clare says.

"We did not attend for a reason," Eleanor says. "And I would like to enjoy my meal."

"We have already been filled in," Lady Hern says.

"Yes, Nait already told me everything. Can we please eat without politics?" Lady Elwen says, tossing her long pale blonde hair—a trait shared by all in the Royal Fola family—over her shoulders, her translucent blue eyes betraying the storm brewing inside of her.

"I have not heard," Lady Emeire says. "What is going on?"

"Well, it appears Cian is leaning towards war with Garcelon."

"It is ridiculous," Lady Dontaue says. "He is being influenced by all of those young lords who just see Garcelon as potential lands they can be granted."

"It is Elwee," Lady Hern says. "Always the one leading that pack of warmongers."

"They've even tried to recruit my husband!" Lady Elwen says.

"What! No! They wouldn't! Why?" Lady Emeire says, leaning forward.

"Please, let's just leave it. You can gossip about it later, Elwen." Eleanor motions for someone to bring her a drink.

Caitlin fidgets with the hem of her sleeve, still scanning the crowd for any sign of Arlina. Or any sign of her husband, for that matter. Her stomach lurches, and suddenly, food seems like a terrible idea.

"Looking for someone?" Lady Care asks. "If you were looking for your husband, I heard he is dining privately tonight. Did he not tell you?"

"No, I was looking for someone else." Caitlin smiles. "Although I just remembered that I have some business that I forgot to attend to, and I must take my leave."

"Caitlin, please stay," Eleanor says, eyes full of worry. "Whatever it is, we can help you with it later. Please join us." Eleanor is on the verge of crying, and Caitlin desperately wants to stay, if only to be near Eleanor and Daya. But she cannot stand to be around Lady Clare right now, and she has a terrible feeling that something is going on with Cian.

"Tomorrow, I promise." Without another word, she leaves the hall and makes her way to the king's chambers. She ignores the guards as they try to stop her, pushing past them until she finds herself at the doors to his private bedchambers. She grabs the handle but freezes as she hears a woman sighing in pleasure and Cian grunting.

She knows that sigh; she knows it because she has been the cause of it before. She backs away from the door one slow step at a time until she can no longer stand to hear another sound, turns on her heels, and flees.

She has not seen the king for two weeks. And yet she's still sitting beside him, a large crown sitting on her head, wearing a dress of purple velvet lined with cloth of gold. She looks every bit like the queen that people claim that she still is. But she does not know what is happening; one of Cian's attendants had arrived early in the morning to tell her she was needed for a formal event and to be in the throne room before noon.

Cian does not acknowledge her even once, does not take her hand when they are seated, and does not look her way as the harold announces their names. She does what she does best: wave and meet the eyes of every person in the crowd, one by one. She does not show the slightest bit of weakness or fear.

"You may admit him," Cian says.

The guards open the grand doors to the audience chamber and lead an older gentleman, wiry and tall, into the room. He holds his head high as he approaches, wearing garments that would have suited him finely thirty years ago and clutching a stack of papers under his elbow.

Myles. He reaches the edge of the dais and bows deeply. "Your Majesties. King Cian, Queen Gráinne. I am honored that you've agreed to speak with me."

The king merely nods, and Myles wrings his hands behind his back. Although he holds himself proudly, Caitlin notices the slight twitch in his lower lip each time he breathes in.

"I petition on behalf of the people for better conditions in the kingdom."

"I am listening," the king says.

"Many of your subjects are poor, precariously on the edge of hunger and starvation each day. Threatened with the prospect of homelessness. Many are dying in the factories from poor conditions and overwork. The schools are not well funded. Many are forced to go without health care and die from preventable diseases."

To her left, Lady Clar snickers.

"I have heard these complaints before," Cian says. "I have read about it in these packets distributed by these traitorous so-called revolutionaries. Are you affiliated with them? Are you here on their behalf?"

"Yes and no, Your Majesty. I was affiliated with them. But their tactics grew violent, and I believe we are better served by petitioning respectfully, especially since you took the throne, your Majesty. You and Queen Gráinne are the most compassionate rulers Fayn has had. I beg that you consider reforming the monarchy and creating a council of commoners to weigh in on matters and advise you, just as your council of nobles does. I do not want to be your enemy like others in the Red Front might want to be; I want to work with you."

Caitlin blanches, her stomach dropping.

"Red Front?" Cian asks, putting his thumb under his chin. "Red Front... So, you have a name?"

Myles gulps.

"Interesting," Cian says.

"Your Majesty... I did not think it would go so far. I thought we were all loyal subjects, merely wanting to do our part as good citizens and provide honest feedback and counsel. Give you the knowledge that you need to rule successfully."

Caitlin's eyes widen in horror as she feels the contents of her stomach rising, threatening to spill out. How long had Miles viewed it that way? Or was he spewing this bullshit now to save his neck? She knew that he and others in the Red Front hoped that they could ask respectfully enough for rights. She never thought that one of them would betray them in such a capacity.

"So, you disagree with their methods but not their opinions?"

Myles hesitates.

"And yet you partook in those methods until now. These violent tactics of theirs have been going on for several years now. And yet you stayed." The king speaks with an almost disinterested calmness.

"I thought I could talk sense into them. They are young and naïve, and I thought... Well, when you took the throne, I thought that we should again petition directly. And I was right; you agreed to listen!" Sweat buds on Myles' forehead, and he shifts his weight from side to side, one hand rubbing the back of the other. "I thought I could guide them toward more appropriate methods. Here, your Majesty. I have written a proposal for how the council of commoners would function and advise you." He holds out the papers, lower lip still quivering. A guard takes the papers, and Myles collapses to the floor in a gesture of thanks.

"Thank you," the king says, "for informing me of this."

Myles lets out a relieved sigh. "Your Majesty, I knew you were gracious, and I—"

"I am sure you will provide us with much more information now. You can take him to his cell."

Myles gazes upwards, meeting the king's eyes for the first time. "No, you... but... I...." He looks at Caitlin, his wide eyes imploring her to say something. She refuses to meet his gaze. He sold them out, and for what reason, she does not know. They will torture the older man. Wring from him every bit of information he might have. She recalls the fire, pulling Kegan back away from it. The way that Liam bragged about it the following day. Valen, Sharidan. Seraph. Aine. Imogen, Jocelyn, Saoirse, Tyn...

Diarmuid.

All at risk. All in danger.

Diar... Would he give up Diar's name?

Caitlin tries to steady her breathing as two acolytes of Culain step forward from the dais and grab Myles on either side. "No, you can't... I didn't..." He looks over his shoulder one last time and locks eyes with Caitlin. "Caitlin! Please stop them!"

Heart beating in her ears, she stands up and glares at him. "How dare you! How dare you implore me to save you? You are a traitor! A treacherous vulture! You should be killed right here! I will do it myself if the king will allow it." Kill him right now before he can say anything else.

The entire room grows still, even the acolytes gaping at her.

Myles' jaw hangs slack.

"Your Majesty?" An acolyte says to the king.

"Take him away."

Myles' knees give out. The defeated defector allows himself to be dragged out of the room in silence.

Caitlin feels the gaze of the king on her, cold and calculating. Her stomach will not settle, and she forces herself to swallow her own vomit.

PART FOUR

Nineteen

War and Wounds

For hours, her maids have been asking her if she needs help, if she is ill, if she needs breakfast. Yet Caitlin sends them away with a perfunctory "No, thank you." Caitlin has lain awake every night for the last week watching the stars fade from the sky, not knowing what to do. Between what happened with Myles and with Arlina, she is lost.

She waits for word from the Red Front. She waits for Kegan to walk in the door and tell her everything is fine. Everyone is fine. She waits for Arlina, who left court the following day, saying nothing.

"Your Majesty?" Another maid says.

Caitlin grabs one of the many pillows on her bed and hurls it toward the door. "Go away!" And then she screams into the bedsheets.

"My lady?" Arlina says.

Caitlin freezes. Her mouth stops working, and she cannot remember how to speak. Another soft knock on the door. Caitlin's breath catches in her throat; the very person she would seek for comfort is the person who caused her heartache. Caitlin gulps. "You may come in."

Caitlin smooths her hair down and slap the color back into her cheeks. Quietly, the door opens, and Arlina enters, looking just as ragged and worn as Caitlin. "Are you sick, my lady?"

Caitlin wants to correct Arlina; she wants to say to her that, in the privacy of these rooms, use her name. Caitlin shakes her head, not knowing how to start. Not knowing where to begin—not knowing if she can.

"I did not sleep well." She hasn't slept at all in days. "And how are you?"

"I need—I have—there is something that I need to say."

Caitlin's stomach twists. She cannot do anything more than nod at Arlina.

"Last night and a few other times, the king and I, well..."

"I know." Caitlin pulls the blankets tighter around herself. "You do not need to say it. I already know."

Arlina takes a step toward the bed, hesitates, and then backs up against the door again. She fidgets with her necklace, unable to meet Caitlin's eyes.

Neither speaks. Caitlin has a dozen questions, and yet she has no questions at all. What could she even ask? What answers could she even need? There are none. There are no answers that would make any of this easier.

"Say something, please."

"What is there to say? I'm sure you have your reasons... But you should have told me."

"My father, my brother," Arlina starts.

"They made you?" Caitlin wipes her eyes with the corner of her bedsheets, already drenched in tears.

"When my mother died—"

"I'm listening."

"My father and brother blamed me for it. Whatever I did, it was never enough to make up for causing her death. Never enough. I did not sing well enough; I did not dance well enough; my penmanship was bad; I did not study enough. Always told that I would never be enough for anyone."

Caitlin makes room on the bed and gestures for Arlina to join her; Arlina does. Caitlin hands her the other corner of the bedsheet.

"My father told me the only thing that I had of any worth was my beauty. And look at me right now; my eyes are red; my cheeks are splotchy. I am so ugly when I cry."

"I do not mind how you look when you cry. It just hurts me that you are in pain."

"I have no right to be in pain right now; I am the one hurting you. This whole time—"

Caitlin shakes her head and puts her hand on Arlina's knee. "I am listening."

Arlina nods. "When they sent me away, they did not send me to the Temple of Aife; that is where I escaped later. They sent me to an aunt. At first, I was glad. At least my aunt did not slap me or hit me. But she did not need to; her words were as sharp as a sword, and she wielded them well. She—" Her tears still flow from her eyes, but she stops speaking, simply staring into the distance, still and silent.

"Arlina," Caitlin whispers. Arlina does not respond.

Arlina does not stir.

"Arlina," Caitlin asks again. "What is wrong?"

Her breathing is shallow but quiet. Barely blinking, she remains far away.

Caitlin runs her hand up and down Arlina's back, whispering words of comfort and safety. They are both daughters of men who saw their rise in position and power as more important than their daughters' happiness. The difference, however, is that Caitlin complied out of a sense of duty and loyalty, and Arlina out of fear.

Caitlin crawls out of the bed, squeezing Arlina's hand before she does so, and opens the door to her bedchamber. "Please fetch me some water, toast, and jam. Thank you." She creeps silently back to the bed and pulls Arlina into her chest, running her fingers through Arlina's hair.

"I escaped," she says. "I got out."

"Yes, you did." Caitlin kisses the top of her head but knows danger surrounds them. "And you are more than good enough for me."

"Thank you," Arlina says.

"We will get through this together. I promise. No more secrets, though."

The Order of Culain has only three major holidays, but today—The Feast of the Builders—is the holiest. Caitlin sits at the High Table in the back of the Great Hall, observing everything before her, including Arlina, smiling, giggling, dancing, and flirting with the king at the heart of the celebrations.

They agreed to do this, but that doesn't mean she enjoys the sight. Unfortunately, this is the best way for them both to stay safe. Or, at least, as safe as one can be at the center of a spider's web. As the queen, she is expected to make appearances at all holy festivities, regardless of which deity is being worshiped, despite the Fola adherence to the god of builders and makers. Her stomach twists, and she waves for more food.

There have been three holidays in the last month: the *Harvest Dance* for Yseult, the *Way in the Dark* ceremony for the twins—Maddyn and Dana—and the *Harmony of Life* for Fianna. A month of watching Arlina and Cian dance together at joyous festivals and celebrations. A month of him parading her around as the unofficial queen and no longer caring what Caitlin sees. A month of him being curt and cold towards Caitlin while he names Arlina "Queen of the Autumn Harvest," "Queen of Dusk," and "Queen of the Song." Everything but "Queen of Fayn."

And although the Harvest Dance was gloomy, as the harvest had been meager this year, and the Way in the Dark had been attended by more mourners than expected, as so many had died in the heat of summer. But Cian had still made merry with the could-be queen.

Last week, he made her a duchess in her own right. Arlina Byrne, Duchess of Caerhe, now afforded her rooms in the palace. There are whispers, dozens of whispers. Whispers that he has lawyers looking into his legal options for divorce. Murmurs of him seeking overseas locations to Caitlin her to. Insinuations that perhaps he has learned of some great crime committed by Caitlin. Is the queen actually a spy for Garcelon? *Is that why she does not speak in favor of war?* They wonder. *Has the queen taken others to her bed?* They ask. *Could it be possible that the queen is secretly supporting the rebels?* They say when they believe no one can hear.

Can it be that she cannot conceive?

Whatever the reason, he has all but put her aside. But it is not just Caitlin that he has cast to the abyss, but every other woman he had flirtations with, favoring Lady Rhees Caer above everyone else.

Will he execute her? Will he banish her? Will he throw her in the dungeons?

Her wedding anniversary is a few days away, and she is not sure she will be alive to celebrate it.

She is not just without friends and allies but without even acquaintans. Beside her, Lady Dontaue is lost in thought; Caitlin has tried to engage in conversation several times, but each time, Maeve gives a noncommittal grunt and looks away. The princesses made just a brief appearance, enough to satisfy etiquette, but only that.

Lady Ronai is back in Fayn, and she is the happiest Caitlin has ever seen her. She may be the happiest person in the room as she laughs while spinning in the arms of her new wife, Lady Eliane Riqueti. Caitlin offered both positions in her household, but all involved knew it was more of a formality. The two wives wanted to spend as much time together as possible.

A faint click from behind startles Caitlin, and she glances to the side and sees one of the servants' doors shutting quietly behind someone. The man is wearing robes that look like they might belong to a clergyman; however, none she recognizes. They look almost like the robes a priest of Culain would wear, but they lack any of the symbols that should be there. Instead, embroidered on the front, barely visible on the neckline, is a tree with large roots emerging from a chalice. A symbol she has seen before and knows it means nothing good. Two steps behind him are Father Nael and Father Ljósa.

Caitlin taps on Lady Dontaue's shoulder. "Is that a new acolyte at the Temple?"

"Who?" Maeve asks.

Caitlin points to the man, making his way toward Cian. "That man with Father Nael and Father Ljósa. He looks like a priest. I have never seen him before, though. Is he new? Where are Brother Sheath and Brother Sloan?"

The color drains the duke's cheeks. "I cannot say," she says through tight lips.

Caitlin raises an eyebrow.

"I am not feeling well. If anyone asks, please tell them I have retired to my rooms." She hurries out of the Great Hall, head low, looking at the floor.

Caitlin slumps in her chair and gestures for more wine. "I can get you some, your Majesty." It is not a voice that Caitlin expected to hear, yet Lady Emeire is standing beside her. Caitlin wants to laugh, wondering if this is how Lady Emeire plans to get rid of her. Perhaps she has found enough funds to buy Caitlin's death as well.

A shorter woman with messy, dirty brown hair, pale brown eyes, and a determined chin stands next to Lady Emeire. She is not wearing the fine garb one would expect of nobility, especially at a celebration like today. Despite all of this, she was the most beautiful of the pair. "Before I do, I want to introduce you to my sister. This is Caragh."

Caitlin recognizes the woman now; she had seen Caragh with Lady Emeire a few times in the corridors. This shy woman fidgets with an acorn pendant and keeps glancing under hooded eyes around the Hall, searching for something or someone.

"It is a pleasure to meet you, Lady Caragh. Please sit with me."

"Do you want me to get your wine?" Lady Emeire says again.

"I have reconsidered. I may have had way too much already tonight."

As Lady Emeire takes a seat and smooths her skirts, Caitlin catches her glaring at something in the center of the Great Hall. She follows Lady Emeire's gaze, expecting to see Cian still enraptured with Lady Arlina, but she sees Father Ljósa arguing with Cian. At the same time,

Lady Arlina looks around nervously, the unknown priest speaking with her. Father Nael stands directly behind her, preventing any escape.

"You have not met Caragh yet, have you?" Lady Emeire says, taking a deep breath, still watching Cian from the corner of her eyes.

"No, I have not. I have been told that you live at a temple?"

"Yes, I lived at court for a while. However, I felt that my calling was elsewhere. I am now an acolyte in the Temple of Shea. Well, calling it a temple is a bit of a misnomer; we are more of a small village living in the woods near Sanras."

Out of her peripheral vision, Caitlin watches Cian jab his finger into Father Ljósa's chest while Father Nael drags Arlina out of the hall, the unknown priest scurrying behind. Cian's face is red, sneering as he slaps Father Ljósa before chasing after Father Nael and Arlina, pausing ever so briefly to glance at Caitlin over his shoulder.

For the fraction of a second that their eyes meet, she swears she sees the same concern and fear as had been in his eyes the day he rescued her from the baptism.

"It is so cute," Lady Emeire says. "Each acolyte must make their cabin when they first join. Caragh has the most artistic of them." She pauses, clutching her chest and breathing heavily.

"Emeire! Are you okay?" Caragh gets up from her seat and rushes to her sister's side. "Are you sick, too?"

"No..." Lady Emeire says. The sting of magic pricks on Caitlin's skin as her attendant catches her breath. It passes as suddenly as it came; Lady Emeire drops her hand back to her lap and takes a deep breath. "I might have had too much wine, as well."

Caragh smiles at her sister. "I am going to go fetch us some water, then. I will be right back."

"How do you handle it?" Lady Emeire says, withdrawing her fan from her pocket.

"Excuse me?"

"Watching the king dance with someone else. Especially Lady Caerhe. He always goes back to her."

Caitlin searches Lady Emeire's face for any hint of malice, but she finds no smugness in her eyes nor condescension on her lips. Instead, her words are laced with genuine concern.

"How do you handle being one of the ladies he regularly discards? We all live at his whims."

"You are too good of a person to be playing these court games, your Majesty. Queen Isleen was, too."

"And you are too good to let yourself be a pawn, Lady Emeire."

Lady Emeire stands up and leaves without another word.

Every day, she hears another rumor about herself. She hears rumors that her fathers have indeed been taken captive by pirates or possibly being preemptively held for ransom by Garcelon. Every day, there are murmurings about another raid on a Red Front hideout and more prisoners rotting in the dungeons. Every day, her hope dwindles. She is no longer gathering information for any of the parties she has allied with. She is gathering information for her survival.

She lingers in the alcove near the meeting room, hiding herself behind the curtain as much as she can, pretending to be absorbed in a letter, although she hopes no one will spot her at all. She has been there all afternoon, ever since she spotted the king slipping into the meeting room this morning with a horde of priests who all seemed to come out of nowhere.

Since then, she has watched various court ladies come and go; some of the palace guards enter and then leave; many different acolytes and priests of Culain, and now, a mysterious clergyman in brown robes with the tree and chalice symbol embroidered over his heart, hovers in front of the door.

"What are you doing?" Lady Dontaue asks, coming up behind Caitlin.

Startled, Caitlin clutches the letter to her chest and turns around to see Maeve looking at her, puzzled.

"I was—" Caitlin searches for an excuse. "Waiting for his Majesty to finish with the meeting."

"It is Caeldá. Are council meetings no longer on Maeldá, or is there an emergency?"

"I do not know, but many people are there now."

"What is he—" Maeve gasps when a clergyman exits the room and races down the hall before vanishing from sight around a corner.

"What Temple is he—" Caitlin begins, only for Maeve to grab her hand and pull her in the other direction.

"I believe it is time for dinner. Let me escort you." The duke hastens her steps each second until Caitlin is out of breath from running. "You did not see those men. Do you understand?" Maeve says.

Caitlin simply stares at Maeve.

"Do you want to live or not? You did not see those men; you do not mention them; you do not speak of them or think even about them." Maeve's tone is ice and steel. Commanding, prophetic, leaving no room for argument.

"See who?" Caitlin says.

"You are learning too late and not as fast as you needed to, though."

They eat in silence, commenting occasionally on the quality of the meat and the flavor of the wine. Otherwise, Caitlin listens to the chatter of the courtiers. One lady laments that Cian is once again seeing no ladies at all and that she never even got her turn. One man complains that his older sister is getting a larger share of the inheritance than he is. She overhears snippets of people complaining about everything from the quality of their bedsheets to the laziness of their servants.

They complain about such trivial things. They complain about such meaningless things compared to the people who are hungry and homeless. She is consumed by the relentless thought of Diarmuid, plagued by the uncertainty of whether he is among the rebels who have been thrown into the dungeons. The weight of the unknown gnaws at her, leaving her restless and tormented. She wishes she had any information at all. But she is utterly alone.

The king, pale and gaunt, stumbles to the table and collapses beside Caitlin. There are fresh bloodstains on his sleeves and blood splattered across his chest. Her jaw drops, not because of how he looks, but because he is near her. "What happened? Why are you not with a physician? Let us get you to one."

He waves her off and says, "I have already eaten, but once you are done, I would like to go to your rooms together." He takes her hand and kisses it. "I need my sweet and gentle Caitlin."

She can feel the eyes of the court upon them, assessing his attitude toward her and his weakness. She nods and continues to eat. Every time she shifts to get up, he encourages her to keep eating, almost as if she were eating for him, too. He glares at anyone who passes by, searching each person up and down for something, but Caitlin cannot figure out what.

When Father Nael enters, Cian throws his arm over her shoulder and leans into her, kissing her forehead tenderly. "Is my wife not beautiful today, Father?" he calls out to the priest. "Strong and beautiful."

The priest scowls and storms back out of the hall.

"You should not do that, nephew," Maeve says.

"I am the king. I can do as I please."

"If you say so."

Finally, he escorts her to her rooms, dismisses her ladies, not even acknowledging that Arlina is there, and makes for her bedroom.

Once inside her room, he removes his shirt and exposes the dozens of lacerations across his back, chest, and arms. "I do not like anyone else to see what I give up for this land. But right now, I need to share this burden with someone. Could you please help me wash my wounds?"

She gets washcloths and water and gets to work. She wants to ask why he is suddenly speaking to her again, why he is suddenly kind to her again, why when he has all but discarded her. But she doesn't.

"Caitlin, no matter what happens, please know that I do this not just for the people but for you."

"Do what, my lord?"

"Everything. Absolutely everything."

"I do not understand."

"It does not matter. I have decided that we will go to war with Garcelon. Just for the dower lands, nothing more than that."

"I see. If that is what you believe is best, my lord."

"It will upset some people. Elwee, Rorick, and Byrne want me to take all of Garcelon. I know I can stand up to Elwee and Rorick, but I am unsure if I can stand up to Byrne."

"You are the king. It is ultimately your decision, and they must accept that."

"That is what I am told… Nael said he offered strength and security, so why does it feel like shackles?"

"Sweetheart?"

"Do not worry, love. Tomorrow. Tomorrow, my love. I will show everyone that I am king. I cannot wait for you to see. Consider tomorrow an anniversary present."

Her maidservant, Rosemarie, had knocked on the doorway too early that morning, and Caitlin shouted that she should return later. Cian had only left her rooms a few hours prior. Caitlin wanted to sleep, but Rosemarie protested that she had important news. There is to be some formal gathering in the afternoon, and Caitlin needed to wear regal attire and dress for the cold weather. Caitlin admitted the maid, allowed her to start her chores for the day, and summoned her attendants to help her get dressed. When she asked Rosemarie if the king gave any more information, the maid shook her head. A surprise, he had said—an anniversary surprise after months of open neglect.

Now, wearing too few lawyers for the chill of late autumn, Caitlin waits on the throne next to her husband, touching the lily pendant necklace she had put on almost as an afterthought. As had become custom, Eleanor and Daya are not with them on the dais, and Caitlin cannot see them even among the crowd.

She suppresses a gasp as she notices the gallows erected in the courtyard and the guards leading a line of prisoners to them. She glances at Cian, more pale and gaunt than she has ever seen him before, hoping he will say something and explain.

He rises to his feet and lifts his hands to the sky. "My loyal subjects," he begins. "I come before you on a most depressing occasion. There is a rot at the center of this kingdom, a rot which has been threatening the peace. A rot that has been disrupting our tranquil way of life. A rot that has been allowed to fester. But no more. I have found the source of the infection. I have discovered the nature of this disease, and I have come before you with the cure. It may take some time to heal, but I administered the medicine today. I administer justice."

He looks about the crowd, judging, assessing, and reading them as if looking for clues. Caitlin recognizes so many people on the gallows. First among them is Myles, looking beaten, battered, barely standing upright. There's Jocelyn, her blue hair nearly shaved from her head, and her tail is missing large patches of fur. Jocelyn; young, hopeful, and idealistic. And there's Tyn, naïve, misguided, but well-meaning. She had often wondered if he was even old enough to work legally at the factory, but he did anyway. They were hopeful and in love with each other. They should have had a future together. They had both looked up to Myles as a father they never had.

Three members of the housing committee, all of whom had given up rooms in their homes for those who had none. Several members of the nourishment program; they had shared food and broken bread with people who would otherwise starve. There was another physician; Diarmuid might have called her a rival at one point. She provided the same services on the other side of Eoi. There are so many on the gallows that she does not know. She wants to scream, jump down, and demand that the guards free the people. But she is powerless. She is the queen of the land, and she is powerless to save the people in it.

More and more prisoners are brought out. More and more faces that she knows, more and more friends that she will no longer have. She prays to any god that will listen, *not Diarmuid, please, not Diarmuid. At the very least, please, not Diarmuid.*

The last of the prisoners are brought out; one is limping, her tail docked, and one of her ears clipped. Aine. It's Aine. Caitlin wants to look away; she doesn't want to be a witness to this.

But she has to witness this; for who else can? She tries to hold in her screams. Kegan. Does Kegan know? Was Kegan there when Aine was caught? If Kegan doesn't know, what will happen when Kegan finds out? Not Aine. She blinks, hoping she is wrong.

It is Aine.

And then behind Aine, slung over a guard's shoulder and being carried to gallows, is Valen. So far from their home, they will die as Brenna died. Far from the Veil and with no one to carry out their last rites. No one to take them back to the Isles to complete the cycle. The guards throw the *Ástfriður* to the ground and kick them. Valen does not move. They kick Valen again, and still, there is no movement. A guard shrugs, grabs a wooden block, and shoves Valen's head on it. Valen is so thin, eyes glazed, pale as if they have been drained not just of their blood but their life.

Already dead.

No. No! She fiddles with the lily necklace around her throat and hopes that those on the gallows know that she is still with them. Distantly, she hears Liam and Connor cheering and clapping, celebrating as they point out which prisoners worked in their factories. *It should be them being struck down.*

She must not cry; she must not cry. She must not cry. Crying will make it worse. The necklace on her throat might as well be a noose.

Aine looks directly at her as they wrapped the rope around her neck. Almost imperceptibly, the Calla smiles and mouths one word. *Kegan.*

Caitlin nods back. *I promise.* She doesn't know how to keep that promise, but she will. She will keep Kegan, the tempestuous, reckless, rash, loving Calla, safe.

Cian raises his arm, and everyone goes silent—rather, everyone except the prisoners. At once, in unison, hoarse and old, young and sweet, soft and plaintive, but real and strong voices sing out.

> *We won't give up until our work is done,*
> *We won't give up until justice is won,*
> *Until the tyrant's fall,*
> *We answer freedom's call,*
> *We won't give up until our work is done.*

Cian tries to yell over them, asking if they would like to beg for forgiveness. But they keep singing. They keep singing until Cian lowers his hand, and the floor drops from underneath them.

Caitlin looks away; she can't stomach it. Cian puts his hand on her knee. "What is distressing you, my sweetheart? They are traitors."

"It is distressing to learn that there are so many people who do not believe in you, so many who do not see the Cian that I see."

He purses his lips and silently nods to her before returning his attention to the crowd and smiling like a 10-year-old who just won his first chess match.

"Sweetheart," she says. "I think I am going to be sick."

"Oh, oh, my lady. Of course, women are much more delicate. I am sorry; I was hoping this would be a wonderful anniversary gift. Oh, well, this is only half of my gift. You are excused if you desire to be."

She knows this is a test. But the nausea will not go away. She leaves the dais, goes behind the canopy, and vomits just as a gentle rain begins to fall. The first rain that Fayn has had in months.

TWENTY

Reunions and Revelations

The Great Hall is adorned more lavishly than it was for her wedding reception, with fountains overflowing with wine and beer, tables and pillars decked in gold, abundant food, musicians from far and wide performing their finest, and a plethora of poinsettias. Tomorrow, the first of the troops will leave for the shores of Garcelon, where an invasion will be launched to take Valencia. Probably for the silliest reason Caitlin has ever heard. Although, she had heard that Janeuq and Sua had nearly gone to war over a dog who'd crossed the border.

A platform stands where the head table usually sits. A very drunk Cian stumbles to the center. "One year ago today, we celebrated my wedding! Today, we celebrate with Valencian wine. But next year, we shall celebrate in Valencia! Today, we ready our Navy in the name of justice. Tomorrow, we will see it through in Garcelon. All of Fayn rises in pride, in honor. The people know that our cause is divinely inspired. Tonight, I want to raise a glass in celebration of Admiral. Halloran, who will lead our Navy in our quest to take back the lands that are ours and to rescue the queen's fathers, and Captain Halloran, who will ensure that our shores are well defended while her father is away, and who I now promote to Rear Admiral. I will now name our future heroes!"

Two dozen people make their way onto the stage, and the musicians cease their songs, the servers slipping to the back of the hall.

Next to her, the Earl of Berach, recently appointed Lord High Chancellor, leans in to whisper to her. "For the crime of kidnapping members of the royal family, we should be razing the entire country. Do you not agree, your Majesty?"

Caitlin nods, not knowing what to say. The ambassador has denied that Garcelon is holding her fathers and claims not to know of the official-looking correspondence from Queen Joanna claiming otherwise. But it was this news that firmly solidified Cian's choice.

"Sir Moira Branagain. She fought bravely as a young lieutenant under my father years ago when the Tsvetokrasans invaded. As of today, she is General Branagain and leading our land assault." The newly named general looks too young to have served in the army nearly half a century ago, but she carries herself with the authority of someone born into it.

"Sir Ailbhe Tuama. She also fought under my father. I name her Lieutenant General." He pauses as the chiseled, gray-haired woman marches across the stage and stands at attention before him, saluting.

"Sir Donn Corbain. Another veteran who fought under my father. I give him the rank of Major." If General Branagain was too young to be a ranked officer, then Major Corbain was several decades too old. But despite his wizened appearance, his steps are light and spry.

"In addition to our seasoned heroes, I also name as captains; Lairde Samise Elwee, Sir Ethna Mearlaigh, Lord Seamus Connal, Lord Brennin Rorick, Sir Teafa Loisig, Sir Fiona Iain, Sir Nait Loughlin, Lord Tynen Byrne, and Sir Connor Gilroy-Downing."

Caitlin listens as he rattles off the names, surprised that despite Lord Hern's insistence that his son-in-law is not involved in the war, Cian had named him anyway. As things stand, Lady Elwen is now the one the court is looking to for the next generation of Fola rulers. However, she wonders if Loughlin had requested to be part of the troops behind the duke's back.

As Cian makes his way through the list, Lord Hern scoffs, making snide comments under his breath, both about the capabilities of the generals being named and the overall necessity or, in his opinion, lack thereof of the war.

In the far corner, Caragh and Lady Emeire sit with their fathers. In the past weeks, both Gallagher men have become ill, and no physicians can diagnose the issue. Lady Emeire requested that her sister return from the Temple to help care for them. Both of the

Gallaghers had served in the army during the Tsvetokrasan invasion, and Caitlin suspects that their opposition to war today stems from their experience with it in the past.

Next to Caitlin, Lady Ronai and Lady Riqueti are deep in conversation, although, for once, it is not about their love for each other. "I told him, if he is so eager to go to war, he can die in it; one less person to share the inheritance with."

Daya, Eleanor, Dontaue, and Clare are missing entirely.

The other players absent from this tableau are priests of the Temple of Culain, Father Nael and Father Ljósa.

It is a court divided against itself. She should be pleased; the Navy and Army will be far from home, a perfect time for an armed rebellion to swoop in. She should be sending a letter to Valen and Sharidan, letting the Red Front know of an opportunity. Except Valen is dead, and Sharidan may be, too. The Red Front is done... She wants to vomit.

Cian stumbles offstage. He is pale, weak, as if the life has been drained out of him. With shock, she realizes that he's not drunk; he's ill.

The rest of the evening passes in a blur of hidden hostilities simmering into open verbal conflict. Caitlin waits at the periphery, ignored by everyone, watching as her sickly husband dotes upon Lady Arlina again. Although he looks exhausted, he scrounges up the energy to dance with her, to smile at her, and to shower her with attention. She raises a glass in a toast as the two apparent love birds dance closer. *Happy anniversary, indeed.*

Caitlin endures the merriment and revelry, the jubilance with which people prepare for war, and the smoldering anger of those who oppose it. A knot tightens in her stomach.

To no one in particular, Caitlin excuses herself as nausea overtakes her. She slips through a servant's door to the Great Hall but does not make it more than six steps before she vomits onto the marble floors.

When she put it on that morning, she tried not to think about it. She pulled her hair up as normal, retrieved the crescent-shaped silver hairpin from her box, and put it on, not expecting the sting of magic *Ástfriður* made. As she went about her day, she pushed it out of her mind, walking through corridors and gardens, talking with courtiers, and joking with her attendants. She tried not to think about it as she dismissed them for the evening after dinner, telling them that she needed to be alone that night. She tried not to think what this would mean; another alliance, another price she would have to pay eventually; she tried not to think about how much more of herself she was promising to others.

She dismisses her attendants and enters her bedchamber, only to find that Sister Kiandre already occupies it. "How…?"

"Not important. Did you give up? We gave you a means of contacting us, and you waited two months to use it?"

"I did not know it was you! All that the person said was, 'The stars are with you' or something like that. I was not exactly excited about owing a debt to yet another faction at court."

"You should have figured it out! The hairpin is a moon! It is fine, it is fine," Kiandre says, breathing deeply. "What matters is how we go from here."

"How did you get in here? Have you been able to get in here the whole time? Why did you not do so earlier?"

"Not what matters. We believe we have more information that you need, and you have more information that we need."

She takes a deep breath and tells Kiandre about the baptism, the symbol she's seen so many times, the threats against her fathers and then her fathers disappearances, her removal from the council, Cian's strange behavior around her, how Cian looked on the day of the executions, how Valen looked on the gallows, Lady Emeire's arrangement to have her fathers murdered, Cian's affair with Lady Caerhe. She left out nothing.

"You need to get back in his favor." Sister Kiandre removes her slippers and tumbles into Caitlin's bed, getting tangled in the blankets as she rolls around.

"I know that my life depends on it," she replies.

"It is more than that. We have reason to believe that the pact between the Fola family and the Blodheimr Hjart."

"The who?"

"Ah, I got overly excited. The secret order of mages that exists inside of the Temple of Culain they are called the Blodheimr Hjart.

Their symbol is the chalice and tree that you keep seeing. The order I belong to is called the Araelta. We have existed long before the gods were born and hope to continue our traditions even after they are gone."

"Mages? Magic, again."

"Yes, they practice a form of magic sourced from the planet. And we of Araelta draw our magic from the stars."

"Earth magic?"

"No, the Blodheimr Hjart do not practice elemental magic. Their magic comes from the life force of the planet itself, from the soil, from Ahnlisen."

"But only the *Ástfriður* can wield magic."

"For now. That is what the gods have decided."

"I do not follow."

"It does not matter. You need our help, and we need yours. I do not know how yet, only that your involvement was prophesied."

"Now you have truly lost me. I could follow along well enough with magic, having already seen proof of its existence in the past. But a prophecy about me? Your tale is as far-fetched as the one an acolyte told me when I was at the Eoi temple."

"Which one was that?"

"It also involved magic, and a city was being burned."

"Ah. The fall of Escnea."

"Whatever it was, it was clearly a work of fiction."

Kiandre shrugs. "What I am telling you today is no fiction, no tale. Centuries ago, the Blodheimr Hjart made a pact with the Royal

House of Fola. We believe we have now figured out what that pact involves. This pact binds the Royal Family to the land. As long as this pact remains, a Fola must sit on the throne."

"Or else?"

"The land will die. Drought, floods, storms, earthquakes, plagues, wildfires. The land will rend itself apart. If your little revolution overthrows the king, you are dooming the people of this land to death."

"So what must we do?"

"You must break the pact," the priestess says, settling on her stomach, her legs kicking in the air as she traces the tip of her finger on the embroidered blanket. "Dierdre may have said otherwise, but your assistance was foretold; your involvement was prophesied. You are the key to what we need to achieve our goals. You must break the pact. We need help from you, not the Red Front. But you're aligned with them, so we must make do.."

"So, you don't care who sits on the throne, just who stands behind it." Caitlin leans against the wall, crossing her arms.

Kiandre shrugs.

Caitlin glares at her. "What would you need me to do? What help do you need? I've provided you with all of the knowledge that I have. What else do you want?"

"That's for you to figure out. You're smart."

"I'm already in grave danger. And you want me to expose myself to even more danger?"

"It is necessary in order to take out the Blodheimr Hjart."

"This may come as a surprise to you, but I don't care about all of that. I care about getting out of this alive, I care about saving my fathers, and I care about getting my friends out of this safely. Is that something you can help me do?" Caitlin marches across the room, pulls the pillow out of Kiandre's hands, and tosses it to the floor.

"Perhaps." The priestess rolls onto her back.

"I will help, but if things go south, I need you to get me out of this alive."

"What about your revolution?"

"What revolution? It's gone. It's over. It's dead."

Kiandre taps her forefinger on her chin.

"And I need you to get Arlina out, too."

"Cute as that is, you ask for too much with that."

"Do you want the help of 'She Who Was Foretold' or not? I'm not here for your chessboard. I'm not here for your politicking; I'm not here for your ancient grudges. I'm here because I'm in danger, and I thought you could help, obviously for a price, but help, nonetheless. So, if you want me to do whatever this prophecy says I do, you need to promise me a lot in return."

"I will see what I can do." The priestess springs to her feet and jumps off the bed, her robes wrinkled.

"And one more thing. I need to know that Kegan is still alive."

"You want to rescue your fathers, save Arlina, and find out the status of Kegan, and then you will help us take out the Blodheimr Hjart?"

Caitlin turns away from the priestess. "I don't know. I'll think about it."

"You certainly do ask for a lot."

"I ask only for what is fair. I'm tired of being a pawn."

"So, you've decided to become a player?"

Retrieving her bracelet from her jewelry box, she says, "No, I've decided to quit the game before I lose it." She turns around, sliding the bracelet on, but the priestess has vanished.

Kiandre is true to her word and hasty in keeping it. Only a few days later, Caitlin arrived back at her rooms after dinner to find a note on her desk informing her that she is to ensure she will be alone the following evening.

She tells everyone that she is feeling unwell, quite unwell, and requests that her attendants instead occupy themselves elsewhere.

She pours herself a last glass of wine and enters her bedchamber.

Kiandre is on the other side of the door, but that is not what causes Caitlin's jaw to drop. Diarmuid. He is somehow, impossibly, before her. But it is not just Diarmuid. *Kegan. Kegan is here, too.* Her friends are alive and safe and here. She has no words as she stares in astonishment at the people she loves most. She is frozen, paralyzed with relief.

Diarmuid looks like he might fall apart. He's always been lanky, but now he's only bones. There are dark bags under his eyes and wrinkles on his brow that were not there when Caitlin last saw him. Kegan refuses to meet her eyes. They are impossibly pale, their long hair now a choppy mess. Their ears swivel back on their head, hissing when Caitlin steps closer.

"But, how? I can understand that you could slip past the guards just yourself, but how did you sneak Diarmuid and Kegan—"

"We can discuss that later," Kiandre says. "We do not have long."

With another hiss, Kegan storms to the other side of the room and sits on the floor in a corner, turning their back to them. Before Caitlin can call to the tempestuous Calla, Diarmuid shakes his head.

"Cait," Diarmuid says, drawing her into an embrace. "Cait. I can't believe it. When we stopped getting reports—and then with what happened after Myles—"

"I'm so sorry, I am so, so sorry," she says, listening to the steady beat of his heart. "Cian banned me from seeing Kiandre and Dierdre. I couldn't get anything to them; I've been under suspicion and not allowed to leave the palace. And when Kegan left—" Caitlin bites her tongue. In the corner, Kegan hisses. "I couldn't save Myles. I didn't want to. I might have condemned him accidentally. But he almost outed me—"

"He what!?"

Caitlin shakes her head. "It doesn't matter now. I was just so angry. What he said, what he told..." She clenches her fists, getting her breathing under control. "Anyway. I am sorry. One reason they suspected me was that the attacks were far too organized. They suspected that there was a spy. I don't think they suspected me specifically because of anything I did, merely out of political convenience. There's a lot of fathers with daughters, you see, and a flighty and fickle king..."

"I figured it was something like that. I may have to talk to Sharidan. We're rebuilding and have turned some guards to our side. We've got a bunch of members in the prison as guards now."

"Sharidan is still alive? And are my fathers in the dungeons?"

"Yes, and no. Valen and Aine... They let themselves be caught so that... I'm sorry, I can't. Not now. As for your fathers, none of our plants have seen them. But they are looking, I promise. Anyway, you need to speak to Sharidan."

"Why? There's no point. I don't want to be here anymore. I am done. I want out."

"But we have to keep fighting..."

"For what? Why? We lost. I cannot do this. You picked the wrong person. Please get me out of here."

"You made me a promise, Caitlin. Before I took you to the first meeting. Do you remember?"

"Diar... The priests stole my fathers; I do not know where they are. I need to get out before they take anyone else." She pulls away from him, unable to face him, wiping away tears on her sleeve.

"You promised to tell me why you wanted to join the Red Front. You said you would tell me more about Brenna."

"My wife," she says, still unable to look at Diarmuid. "Xie was murdered. At the time, we thought it was by a gang that wanted to know how to get to the Isles, and beyond the Veil, greed and desire for the riches they thought they might find there. But I learned a few weeks ago that was not the case."

"Oh, Caitlin. I am so sorry." He puts a hand on her shoulder, but she shrugs away from him.

"The greed I saw in the eyes of xir murderers; I saw it again in the eyes of the Sir Connor. The same disregard for the value of a life. That is why I joined."

He embraces her again, gently running his hand down her back.

"But I have learned that it was not a gang that wanted riches, but the priests of Culain." Her knees give out, and she collapses, burying her face in her hands. "They had been the ones behind the attempted kidnapping. That is why I kept fighting."

"Why do you wish to stop now?"

"I am scared; I see no way out of this. My fathers have been captured, being held who knows where. Aine, Valen... All lost. When I lost Brenna... I cannot bear to lose another."

"Kiandre will help, but she said there would be a cost, and you could pay it. We will get you out, but what must we do to pay Kiandre for her help?"

"I do not know."

"She didn't tell you?"

"She did," Caitlin says, glancing over at the priestess, who has tucked herself in the corner with Kegan, the two Calla wrapped in a blanket. "But I do not understand it."

"I will talk to Sharidan. Do you think you can hold on another month?"

"Would you be able to get Arlina out, too?" Caitlin hesitates and looks away from him.

From the corner, Kegan scoffs. Diarmuid sighs and slowly nods his head. "I cannot promise that. I can't even promise that we could get you out. But we can try. Is that what you want, Caitlin?"

The conversation with Kiandre replays in her mind. *The rituals. The magic. The pact. Without a Fola king, the land will die.*

She looks over her shoulder, ensuring the bedroom door is still closed. "What Kiandre wants me to do; she said that there is more going on than we know about, that there is some divine connection between the king and the land. They say we will fail if we don't break at first, and the whole of Fayn will fall to ruin."

"A pact? I do not follow."

"It has something to do with the secret order embedded in the Temple of Culain. Some ancient magic."

"Magic? And do you believe that? That sounds like a bunch of bullshit court politicking. Is this pact what they want you to get information about?"

"Not information, Diar. They want me to break it."

"How?"

"I have no idea."

"This sounds messy and impossible," he says, glancing over his shoulder at Kiandre.

"I know. What if it's not bullshit? What if they are right?"

"I don't like it. But it is your choice. I will support whatever decision you make, and I will make sure that Sharidan backs you up."

Choice. Her choice. What she wants, her decision to make. She can stay, dedicate herself to the mission, and commit to taking down the monarchy. This cause that she stumbled into, this chessboard she fell onto, this stage she suddenly found herself on, playing the part because she knew not what else she could do.

But she can rewrite her lines, or she can bow out.

She doesn't want to be spirited off stage; she doesn't want to be rescued. The only way to true freedom from Cian, from the monarchy, is on a path she makes. If she accepts this offer, she will be on the run for the rest of her life. Looking over her shoulder for people who would find a hidden queen quite valuable.

But it's more than that. It's so much more than that. "I'm staying."

She waits for his rebuttal, for him to ask if she is sure about that. But instead, he says, "What support will you need?"

"Kegan. I need Kegan by my side," she says softly enough that Kegan does not hear her even with their keen ears.

He nods. "Kegan, please come join us."

"I don't want to."

"Kegan," Caitlin says. "Please. I've missed you so much."

Kegan's ears wiggle, and slowly, they get to their feet and turn around. Tears are streaming down their face, "I missed you too."

Caitlin crosses the room and pulls Kegan in for a hug. "I missed you so much, Kegan. Please stay."

"I'm all alone now. Aine is gone. She's gone! And I'm all alone."

"You're not alone."

Kegan's return to court was widely celebrated; neither Caitlin nor Kegan had realized how many people appreciated the capricious Calla and their antics. As the impromptu celebration died down and the courtiers left with purses either heavier or lighter than before, Kegan informed Caitlin that a meeting with Sharidan had been arranged, with Kiandre somehow cooperating with Eleanor and Daya. The priestess had discreetly pleaded with the princesses to find a way for Caitlin to get fresh air at least, and the princesses had interceded with Cian to allow Caitlin to be seen by the people.

It is the first Sunday of the new year, and the sun is high in the sky on an unseasonably warm winter day as they make their way to Seraph's shop. When planning this trip in the morning, Caitlin could think of no reason that they should not ride there in open carriages. Lady Riqueti and Lady Ronai sit across from her, constantly forgetting that they are not alone. Caitlin wishes that she could hold Arlina's hand right now the way that Lady Riqueti is holding Lady Ronai's.

A child runs into the street, and the coachman pulls the reins, bringing the carriage to an abrupt stop. A crowd swarms the street before them, tossing garbage and rotten fruit at Arlina, chanting.

"Whore!" The carriage is pelted, the scent of rotting fruit and vegetables and spoiled meat poisoning the air.

"Slut!"

"Queen Gráinne is the true queen!"

Caitlin rises to her feet, enraged. "Stop! Stop at once!"

The crowd goes silent except for one man who cries, "But, your Majesty!"

"I said stop. I never want to hear anyone speak ill of the Duchess of Caerhe again! Or any of my attendants, for that matter."

Some in the crowd still weigh the fruit in their hand.

"That is a royal order." The words feel weird on her lips. In all this time as royalty, she has never once issued an order quite like this. She has asked for things and requested help but never ordered. Something is intoxicating about telling a crowd of people what to do and being listened to. Something is exciting about having her desires carried out. Right now, those desires are simply for Arlina to stop crying.

The crowd disperses with reluctance. "My dress, it is ruined." Arlina wipes her handkerchief across a growing stain. "A queen's lady should not be seen like this. I can go back if you wish, my lady. I shall return to the palace."

"It is your choice, but I want you with me. Tomato-stained dress or not. We can wrap my cloak around it, and no one will see it."

"No," Kegan says. "My sash will work better. Wrap it around your waist, and it will cover the stain." Caitlin catches Kegan's eyes and smiles.

Seraph greets them, and spotting a sale, she tells Lady Riqueti how much Lady Ronai likes rubies before she beckons Caitlin to follow her. Caitlin follows Seraph to the back, where she finds Sharidan and

Saoirse seated. They both stand up and pull her into a hug. "Thank you for everything."

Grief wells up in the pit of her stomach again, bringing with it nausea. The faces of Jocelyn, and Tyn, but especially Aine and Valen, come to the front of her mind. "I couldn't save them, not without exposing myself or bringing further suspicion upon me."

"We didn't expect you to," Sharidan says. "You are where you need to be, doing what you need to do, acting how you need to act. We cannot ask the impossible of you."

Caitlin opens her pouch and pulls out all of the information she has gathered, neatly organized. "The main thing is the division in his Privy Council over whether to go to war with Garcelon."

"We have heard nothing about that. Not even from our allies in Garcelon."

"Nothing? At all?"

Sharidan shakes xir head, lips tight. "Tell us more."

"He announced it at court about a month ago. The announcement was my anniversary gift. A minor lord leads the pro-war faction; Lairde Samise Elwee. The king's uncle, the Duke of Hern, wishes for diplomacy. The advance troop has already been deployed."

"What is even the issue?" Saoirse asks, rubbing her temples. Saoirse is only twenty-six but has stepped in to fill Valen's shoes. Now second in command of the Red Front, she has grown dramatically from the youth who used to skip and sing, her twin braids often hitting people as she spun around.

"The king believes he should have inherited Valencia when the queen passed away," she says, her chest tightening at the thought of the woman who had thought she could change Cian.

"Based on what?"

"The fact that they were her lands before she was wed to the king. When she was still a Garcelonian princess."

Sharidan buries xir head in xir hands. "I cannot believe this. And the king has already deployed troops?"

"Just the generals and captains."

"This is so stupid." Sharidan takes the mug of coffee that Seraph offers xir, drinking the full mug in one gulp, not even waiting for it to cool. "Did he say when he will announce it to the people?"

"Probably at the end of the month. I'm still barred from the council meetings, but I'm assuming he will also raise taxes. One argument against war is that his exchequer is empty."

"Stupid, but we can use this. Who are the leaders of the factions again?"

"The Duke of Hern is the one leading the antiwar effort. Elwee is the one spearheading the pro-war campaign. However, Conlaoch Byrne calls for more than just taking back some disputed lands. He wants to invade and conquer all of Garcelon, as do the priests of Culain."

"We can use this. Caitlin, could you increase the tension among these factions?"

"If I can get back into the council meetings."

"Good. Good. Don't worry, we will be more careful this time. Focus on returning to the king's good graces and causing as much internal strife as possible."

"Did Diarmuid tell you about what the priestesses are requesting?"

"Yes, and you do not need to worry about it. We are working on a way of getting you out before long."

"Did he also tell you why the priestesses are requesting it?"

"Yes, and it sounds like superstition and myth."

"But the harvest has been bad, and the drought…"

Sharidan waves xir hand.

Caitlin wants to say more. But what? The little clues, him being weakest when it rained, the priests seeming to materialize out of nowhere to demand that he meet, his mother saying Tarmon was cursed. Every time Cian mentioned how much he sacrificed for the kingdom… But what would the Fola family get out of such a bargain? How does this bond between them and the land benefit them? If Cian was talking about this bond any time he complained of 'sacrifice,' it did not sound entirely voluntary. But why?

"No. I am going to do as Kiandre and Dierdre ask. Not because I feel in debt to them but because I believe them and want a truly free Fayn. I do this for the Red Front. I'm staying."

Sharidan sighs, leaning back and crossing xir arms. "Well. You say you do this for the Red Front. Make sure that that is your true reason."

"I understand."

"I have another question. Kegan has been back with you for a few weeks now. I was hoping you could tell me how they are," Sharidan says.

"I would say usual Kegan, but more intense. They're angry and then withdrawn, but I've never seen them be quite this withdrawn before."

"They've been through a lot. Honestly, I don't think they should work right now. But I know they want to keep going. They don't want to let Aine down," Sharidan says, tail flicking.

"They never told me what they were. Aine and Kegan." Caitlin looks over her to check if the Calla is lingering in the doorway.

"They are not from the same clan, but Aine became Kegan's only family at a very young age. Kegan's from a Greenwood clan, a tiny village. It's a very upsetting story."

Saoirse leans back in her chair. "Then maybe you should leave it for Kegan to tell."

"Maybe," Sharidan says, tail flicking. "I don't think Kegan would tell it, though. And it's Aine's story, too, and Aine's not here to tell it."

"Please, I want to know, and you're right; Kegan would never tell it."

"Very young, Kegan had to flee from home because of some catastrophe that involved a fire, and that part I will leave for them to tell, but they spent several weeks wandering Eoi aimlessly. One night, they fell asleep under the stairs to one of our bases. The next morning,

Aine arrived there to get ready for a meeting, and she found Kegan, took them in, and became an older sister to them."

"The base that was burned down…"

"Yes, that one."

"Why are they still working?"

"We asked them the same thing," Saoirse says. "They said that they would rather be busy, that they need to keep going, that they need to see this through. That they need to see Aine's dream fulfilled."

"Would Aine really want them to continue without even a moment's rest?"

Sharidan drums xir fingers on the table, xir chin resting in xir other hand. "Kegan lost the first person who ever offered them love. And when that townhouse burned down, they lost the first place they called home."

Shouting after Kegan as they rushed headlong into the smoke. Having to drag them back out of it. Kegan screams and cries over and over. "Thank you for telling me. I will take care of them. I promise I will."

"I'll hold you to that," Sharidan says.

The leaders of the Red Front nod to her, a silent dismissal. As she makes her way out of the office, Seraph holds up a hand. "Take this," the old woman says, giving her a heavy velvet pouch. Caitlin opens the drawstrings and finds roughly two dozen rings inside—some bearing the crests of noble families, some of foreign nations.

"What is this for?"

"I hear you intend to create some chaos. This might help."

Her legs refuse to work; she can barely move them enough to crawl across the floor, sometimes not even then. But she must keep going; it is quickly catching up. She pulls herself forward with her hands, figuring out where in the palace she is, not recognizing the portraits on the walls or any of the doors that line them.

Thump. Thump. Thump. She glances over her shoulders but cannot see it, and then the thumping comes again, this time more intensely and forcefully.

"My lady!"

Does it know her name? Her legs still won't work. She is moving as slow as molasses.

"My lady, please!"

Why can't she run? Why can't she walk? Why can't she get away?

"My lady, wake up! Wake up!"

The strange corridor falls away as Caitlin takes a sudden deep breath. Her bedroom appears, and she struggles to escape the twisted sheets. As she slowly acclimates to the waking world, she hears Lady Ronai's voice, consistent, urgent, and pleading. She rushes to the door, and Lady Ronai and one of her maidservants, Rosemarie, stand on the other side. Rosemarie is wearing only a night shift and a sweater, both covered in dirt and blood.

"Thank goodness. Rosemarie," Lady Ronai says, "tell her what happened."

Rosemarie shakes her head and tries to get away before Lady Ronai drops her hand and pulls her back. Rosemarie struggles to escape Lady Ronai, crying and saying she doesn't want to. Lady Ronai insists Caitlin must know what has happened. Caitlin can tell from the insistence that Lady Ronai demands that Rosemarie comply that something is very wrong.

"If Rosemarie will not tell me, Lady Ronai, please do so."

"I found her," Lady Ronai says as Rosemarie relents and goes motionless. "In the gardens, with a knife press against her stomach." Lady Ronai pulls a large kitchen knife from her bag and tosses it to the floor before Caitlin.

"Rosemarie," Caitlin says, "what's going on?"

"I can't; I can't say, please don't make me."

"I cannot help you if you don't tell me what is happening."

Lady Ronai hands Rosemarie her handkerchief, which the maidservant gratefully accepts.

"Why can't you say?" Caitlin takes off her robe and gently wraps it around Rosemarie. "I want to help you. Please let me help you."

"I can't. He threatened me…"

"Who?" Caitlin fears the worst, terrified that the man in question is Cian and even more terrified to find out what he has done.

"I can't say! Just before he left, he said… He told me not to say… I didn't want it. I told him no. And now… Now I'm…" Rosemarie collapses to the floor, cradling herself and sobbing. Caitlin and Lady Ronai huddle around her, letting her cry until her voice grows horse.

"You can tell me who did this," Caitlin says.

"No, please. Don't make me, I just want..."

Caitlin studies Ronai's face, assessing how much she trusts Caibre's sister. "I understand. I won't ask anymore. But do you want to get this taken care of tonight?" Caitlin asks.

Rosemarie, still shaking, looks up bewildered. "What do you mean?"

Caitlin glances at Lady Ronai one last time. "I know a physician," Caitlin says. "I will not tell anyone about this if you promise the same."

Rosemarie nods and takes a deep breath. "It's already so late," she says.

"I don't want to see you in distress anymore." She is terrified that if they do not do something now, her maid will end up injured. Or dead.

"You do not mean the palace physician, do you?" Lady Ronai asks.

"No, not at all. Will you help me?" Caitlin says to Lady Ronai.

"Of course, your Majesty."

"I am not ordering as a queen; I am asking as a friend. It is your choice."

Lady Ronai nods.

"Can we use your rooms? Will Lady Riqueti mind?"

"No, Eliane will not mind, and she will not tell anyone either."

She wants to ask Kegan to fetch Diarmuid, but if Kegan gets caught, she will not be able to live with herself.

She also wishes she knew how Sister Kiandre has been getting in and out of her rooms with no one seeing her. The priestess has not told her, and she's never caught her coming or going. "Would you or Lady Riqueti be willing to go into town and fetch the physician? I can give you his card and a note. I would do it myself, except…"

"I understand, your Majesty. I will do it. May I ask, is it the physician that has the clinic associated with the Andrastan Temple?"

"Yes, it is. Thank you. Rosemarie, it will be alright."

"He is a good man." Lady Ronai escorts them to her room. The guards that they pass make no comment as the queen consoles the sobbing servant.

Within the hour, Ronai returns with Diarmuid.

Before he can say anything, she says, "Please, one of my ladies needs your help."

He takes his snow-covered hat off and runs his hands through his hair. "Of course." For just a moment, Caitlin sees double; superimposed is the image of him taking off his hat as he enters her office.

"This is Rosemarie," she says to him, setting down his bag and removing his jacket.

Rosemarie opens and closes her mouth, trying to find words. Diarmuid holds up a hand. "You don't need to tell me anything more than you want to."

"I want an abortion," Rosemarie says, determined and steady for the first time that evening.

"I can do that. Lady Ronai, is there somewhere here that I can set up an exam table? I will need hot water and plenty of bandages, too. There will be some blood."

"My wife has cleared off the dining table. Will that work?"

"Yes, that will do fine. Here, Lady Rosemarie," he says, handing her a small vial of liquid. "Drink this. It will help with the pain. It takes a few moments to work. While I get set up, Cait—Your Majesty, may I speak with you briefly? I have never made a house call to the palace, and I..."

"Oh, oh yes, of course, doctor, we can discuss payment now," she says and follows Diarmuid to the dining room.

He glances over his shoulder before saying, "And what about you?"

She raises an eyebrow at him. "What about me?"

"Do you... Need one, too?"

"What? You have to be... No..." *No. Oh my gosh, no.*

"How long?" He shoves his hands in his pocket.

"I don't know... four months. Four months ago was the last time—"

"Do you want one, too?"

"I can't! Yes, but no, but yes..." She wrings her hands, unable to breathe.

"We'll be getting you out of here soon. There's no need to keep playing at this...."

"Yes, but... A pregnancy also ensures he will, at the very least, not execute me for a few more months."

"I don't like this."

"I don't either," she says through gritted teeth.

"It's your choice."

"Is it?" She holds back a laugh.

"It should be." There are lines around his eyes that were not there when she met him for the first time three years ago. There are creases in his forehead, and he has more gray hair than anyone should have in their late thirties. "Sharidan is finding a way to get you out without the priestesses' help. It is your choice. None of the Red Front would demand that you stay, let alone carry a pregnancy you do not want. The world we are fighting for is one where people can make these choices themselves."

"I choose to continue my mission. And this aids my mission. I need to see this through."

"And after?"

"After you will have to learn how to be a good uncle, I suppose."

"I love you," he says. "I will be whatever you need me to be."

"Tell me, what day did we meet?"

"Culaidhe third."

"Three years to the day," she says, smiling.

"Technically, it's after midnight. So, it's Culaidhe fourth." He winks.

"I miss you," she says.

"I know, but I must be quick. It's your choice. It's all your choice; never forget that."

"I know. For now, I will be fine. Please, take care of Rosemarie."

"I will. Lady Rosemarie? I am ready." As Diarmuid gestures to the makeshift exam table, putting his gloves on. Rosemarie says to Caitlin quietly, "You trust him, correct?"

"I trust him with my life."

TWENTY-ONE

Keys and Clues

He promises that there will be a celebration soon, but for now, he wants to keep her pregnancy private despite being overjoyed. Shortly after she tells him the news, he reappoints her to the Privy Council, no longer concerned about how the stress might affect her health.

When Caitlin walks into the council room, she is met with both glares of animosity and welcoming smiles. Her usual chair is vacant, and everyone else has rearranged their seating so that it is clear who is on which faction. On the left side sits Eleanor, Lady Clare, Lord Hern, Lady Dontaue, who finally agreed to join, and Lady Emeire, who represents her fathers while they are too ill to attend the meetings. Daya is noticeably absent. Captain Alice Halloran, Sir Connor, Lord Caibre, and Lord Berach are on the right.

The door swings open; chest thrown back and head held high, Cian enters the room with the swagger of a man on the path to victory. He crosses the room, bends down to kiss Caitlin on the forehead, and tells her to rise. "My beautiful wife is back. The physicians have deemed her in perfect health, and she may return to work with us, making the kingdom a better place for all." He claps, and by how he looks at everybody else in the room, he expects them to follow suit. She squints, confused that he does not mention the pregnancy at all. Father Nael and Ljósa glare at her.

"And I have even better news to accompany it," he says. "As Caibre has just told me, the war is going splendidly! We have taken Valencia back. My mother's lands now belong to her heir. We continue to fortify against their counterattacks. But our troops are strong, and I know that it will be under our full control before the end of winter."

Breaking his habit of loitering at the room's edges, Father Ljósa steps forward, pulls out the chair at the far end of the table, and plops down. Absolute silence fills the air and even the roar of the fire quiets. Father Nael opens the window and stares out intently at the snow-covered courtyard.

"I believe we should continue marching north and take Linea, too." Caitlin's jaw drops, and Caibre nearly spits out his beer.

"Excuse me?" Cian says.

"Since we are in such an advantageous position right now, why should we not also take Linea?"

"Did they put something in the ceremonial wine this morning?" Caibre quips under his breath.

"They must have," Lady Emeire says.

"Maybe he drank all of the wine, and that's why he needs Linea," Sir Connor says.

Father Ljósa glares at Caibre. "I mean it. Despite our victory, they still insist that they do not have the queen's fathers. This might put pressure on them."

"Suppose I were to agree, why Linea, though? Why not march straight to Merida?"

"It would be a very natural port for us; already, we receive plenty of ships at Whick from there, but if we controlled it, if we had a trading post on the mainland, we would no longer be at the mercy of the customs officials in Garcelon for our goods." He says, stumbling over his words and pausing in awkward places. Almost as if trying to convince himself that this was a good enough reason.

Cian's face is completely expressionless, and without looking away from the priest, he says, "Caitlin, does Father Ljósa have a sound argument?"

Before Caitlin can respond, Eleanor interrupts. "Absolutely not! I believe them when they say they do not have the Peddigrees. The war is already unpopular; people were more than upset about raising an army, and they are furious about raising taxes. There is not enough money in the exchequer to keep paying the troops, and levying any more taxes will throw the entire kingdom into open revolt."

"Like they are not doing that already," Lord Caibre says.

Eleanor ignores him. "The people are starving from the poor harvest already, and there have been terrible earthquakes along the western coast for the last month, and we have yet to send any aid to those regions. They will not tolerate any more of our resources being diverted!"

Cause chaos, Saoirse had told her. "But my fathers..."

"With all due respect, I do not believe they are holding your fathers," the Duke of Dontaue says. She says this to Caitlin but glares at Father Ljósa.

The priest crosses his arms. "Do you have another suspect you would like to name, your Grace?"

"He makes a sound argument," the king says before his aunt can say anything else. "Having control of a port on the mainland would improve our economy in the long run."

Eleanor's eyes widened. "Did you hear what I said? I cannot believe this." Eleanor leans back in her chair, arms crossed, refusing to meet anybody's eyes.

Cian looks between his sister and his wife, frowning. "I can see the point you are trying to make, Father Ljósa, and I, too, am eager to find my wife's fathers. However, I am not sure it is wise to do so now when we have not even solidified our presence in Valencia first."

Father Ljósa coughs.

"Your Majesty, as I have said before, you should be the rightful heir to the Garcelonian throne," Berach cuts in. "And I am sure that Lairde Elwee will report next week that our presence is more than solidified. I have confidence in zir abilities."

"If I may," Lord Hern says, glaring at Berach. "Now that the queen is pregnant, we could try a diplomatic approach again."

"She is pregnant?" Father Nael swivels quickly to Caitlin, searching her up and down for any signs. "Well, perhaps we can ask that Linea be part of the marriage agreement between the royal offspring and someone of the Garcelonian Royal family. Do you agree, Father Ljósa?"

The elder of the priests presses his thumb to the bridge of his nose and nods.

"Uncle," Cian chuckles. "I knew I could count on you to not keep a secret."

"You are early," Lady Emeire says.

"Oh, yes. I'm waiting for someone," she says, turning away from the window. She has been waiting for an hour, watching the snowstorm grow fiercer, the screams of the wind echoing in the corridor. The weekly council meeting is still at least a quarter-hour away.

"I hope it is neither of my fathers; they are both ill again today."

"That must be hard on you," Caitlin says. "Do the physicians know what is wrong with them?"

Lady Emeire places a hand over her heart. "Not yet," her voice cracks. "I hope... I pray that they get well soon. I am so thankful that my sister can be home right now to help care for them."

Caitlin is about to reply when she spots her quarry. "I am praying for them as well. If you if you will excuse me." She intercepts Lord Hern before he can converse with anybody else as he approaches.

"Your Grace," Caitlin says. "Good day to you. I have some important things I would like to discuss."

"Your Majesty, yes, what is it?"

"It is something very urgent," she says, looking surreptitiously to her left and right before continuing, "and not something I would like to discuss in public if you understand my meaning. Would you care to have dinner sometime?"

His face lights up as Caitlin puts her hand protectively over her stomach. "Of course. Of course, in fact, I humbly invite you to dine in my rooms. I hired a new chef, and she is the best. Does Friday of next week work for you? I will tell my cook to make enough for two or three!" He laughs, patting her stomach. She wants to throw up. But if letting an older man touch her without asking first is the price to pay for what she hopes to accomplish, then it will be worth it. "Wonderful." Pretending he did not violate her, Caitlin smiles. "I am excited to share dinner with you."

He laughs again. "Yes, well, we are family."

"Precisely." Just as she is about to say more, Cian and Elwee arrive, deep in conversation. As soon as Cian sees her, he disengages and approaches her. "My sweetheart, uncle. You both look thrilled."

"Yes, my love. I was asking your uncle if he would like to have dinner with me sometime. Luckily, he agreed."

Cian chuckles and winks at his uncle before tapping Caitlin on her stomach. Caitlin is tempted to ask Lady Emeire how to get in contact with an assassin. If one more person decides that her stomach is public property, she will have many targets for such an assassin. *If only it were that easy.*

"There is much exciting news all around today. Come, let us get to it." Cian opens the door and ushers everybody inside.

As the council members step inside, an unknown priest rushes down the hallway, seeming to appear out of nowhere, and taps Cian shoulder, breathless. Cian holds up a hand, leaving for a private conversation with this priest. Before they slip away, Caitlin notices that his collar also has a barely visible symbol of a tree and chalice and shivers—the Blodheimr Hjart.

Staggering into the room, Elwee trips and falls to the floor. Before anybody can offer their help, zie guffaws. "I've either had too much ale or not enough."

Lord Hern rolls his eyes as he takes his seat. No one else laughs along with Elwee, though—of course, all of zir friends are still on the battlefield. As zie gets up and takes a seat, zie immediately reaches for the decanter of wine in the middle of the table. Instead of pouring zirself a glass, zie drinks straight from the container.

"Are you sure that is wise?" Lord Hern asks.

"Oh, shove off, old man. You are jealous."

Lady Emeire clears her throat. "What does the duke have to envy?"

"Look at him. He's old, frail, and too weak to be on the battlefield. He only opposes this war because he knows young people like me who will be the heroes. He doesn't want to watch that; he doesn't want to watch other people be made heroes."

Lord Hern shrugs.

Cian steps back inside before any more jabs can be tossed. "Well then, as you might notice, Elwee is here today to update us on the war front. But before zie does, I have a very important announcement. Because of zir heroic efforts on the battlefield, I am promoting Elwee to Major and granting zir the rank of Earl. Zie is now Major Elwee, Earl of Madigan."

Elwee stands up and bows, expecting a round of applause. Zie does not get one. Zie sits back down again, unaware that zir keys have fallen from zir pocket, and rests under the table.

Elwee reports on the successful capture of Valencia and the eagerness of the troops to march onward if ordered. Zie stresses that the Garcelonians continue to deny that they are holding the queen's fathers and insist that the letter stating otherwise was forged. Report given, zie collapses into zir chair and passes out.

"Are you sure you made the right choice in promoting zir?" the Duke of Hern asks.

The king ignores his uncle. "The other major matter that we must address is the speed at which the rebels are regrouping. Despite burning their nests and executing their leaders, they have re-mobilized and are again carrying out violent attacks and causing unrest."

"Your Majesty," Berach says, slamming a fist on the table. "My lands have been experiencing great unrest. We need to utterly crush these miscreants and imprison any who have even a hint of sympathy for them."

"I agree, which is why I appoint you Lord High Constable of Fayn. You have my permission to choose other persons to assist you in your duties. I expect weekly reports on your progress. Do whatever you need to, however, you need to. I am counting on you."

"Your Majesty, I am truly honored to be—"

Still unconscious, Elwee slides out of zir chair. "My lord," Caitlin says, "I fear I have nothing else to add to this conversation. May I be excused to assist the Earl of Madigan to zir rooms?"

The king chuckles. "You are the queen of kindness, my dear. Of course."

She snatches Elwee's keys and pockets them while lifting the drunk Calla to xir feet. "I can help, too," Eleanor says.

Together, they slip out of the council room, dragging the newly ennobled earl between them, passing an unknown priest waiting anxiously outside the door.

Caitlin is dressed plainly; she wears a dainty circlet as the only sign that she is royalty. Lord Hern, also dressed in simple attire but sporting a wide grin, answers the door and admits her. "My dear niece, welcome. Unfortunately, Doireann and Elwen could not be here today. Though they send their regards."

Caitlin does not comment on the fact that he left out his son-in-law on his list. "Thank you for having me. It means so much to Cian and me." He leads her to a small dining room and pulls out a chair, motioning for her to sit. She does so, thanking him for his assistance before softly touching her stomach.

He sits across from her, and a dozen servants come out, each bearing a different course, quickly filling the table with food. She laughs. "I thought you said you would feed me as if I were eating for two, not an army."

He laughs. "Who said that all of this is for you? I am an army unto myself."

"I wish I could have invited you to my estate in the country. I think you would like it out there. Alas."

"I am sure I would enjoy it greatly, but these winter storms will not let up."

"No, but it is more than that. It would not be safe. Unfortunately, the rebels have regrouped. The last two weeks have been nonstop stealth attacks across my lands. They come in at night into the kennels and steal the dogs. Or they come in and steal the chickens."

"I did not know; I have not heard of the other lords having this problem currently." She helps herself to a large helping of mashed potatoes, which are dry and bland. The scant crops that made it through the harvest lacked flavor; even the best chef could do nothing to improve them.

"As far as I can tell, I am the only one receiving this treatment. I wish I could tell you why. But they never seem to leave anything that would give me a clue as to the motivations for targeting me and only me right now. Although it gave Elwee quite the laugh when zie found out."

"I would not take what Elwee says with much seriousness," she says, peering over the rim of her glass.

"I know, but zie on the council. Why?" The duke throws his napkin to his lap. "Zie adds nothing. Zir mother was an excellent adviser—Aife trained!—to Tarmon before her death, and zir father excelled at diplomacy. But Samise Elwee? Did you see zir at this last one? So unprofessional."

"I completely understand."

"There are so many people on the council," Hern says while scooping dry potatoes onto his plate, "who have no right to be there. The Earl of Caibre? His family has always had a seat on the council, but sometimes, one needs to change tradition. His father may have been a good statesman. That means nothing for Brennin Rorick."

"I completely agree. Neither Elwee nor Rorick are civilized enough to be on a council that deals so seriously with the state of affairs of this country. Please do not tell Cian this," Caitlin says, taking a gamble. "But I was hoping they would find honorable deaths on the battlefield."

"Promise me you will not tell my nephew this, but I wish the same." He winks and raises his wine glasses to her.

"But let us move on to some happier topics," Caitlin says.

"That sounds like a wonderful idea. Tell me, what was it you came here to ask me?"

Caitlin places her hand on her stomach, smiling serenely. "Cian and I would like to know if you and Lady Doireann wish to be our son's godparents. It would be a great honor for us and our child if you would be the godfather."

The duke beams and claps his hands together. "Of course! How could I say no? It would be my honor." He rises to his feet. "One moment. I do believe this occasion deserves better wine than what I have out right now. I will be just a moment."

As soon as the duke is out of the room, Caitlin snatches a small ivory-carved hunting dog figure on the mantle of the fireplace in the dining room and pockets it. Next to it, she spots a sealed envelope with the duke's name written on it. With only a second of hesitation, she pockets it, too.

He returns several minutes later, proudly bearing the wine. "Tell me, Caitlin, may I suggest some potential names for the little prince?"

It is a private ceremony for Caitlin held at the Temple of Culain in the city, with only the immediate family and the godparents in attendance. She does as she is told without protest, wears the robe she is told to wear, holds the candle she is told to hold, and recites the prayer she is told to recite. Without error or imperfection, she makes it through the blessings that the priests insist she must receive now that she is pregnant.

No one was supposed to know of this, yet a crowd rushes them as they exit the Temple. Some shouting blessings for the queen, and others shouting curses for the king.

Sir Dermont grabs her arm and drags her to the carriage, Eleanor close behind. In the commotion, she loses sight of the king, but the

King's Shield surrounds the perimeter, corralling both supporters and detractors, Cian's voice carrying over the crowd to arrest and detain everyone.

"You are only making it worse," Eleanor says as Cian climbs into the carriage. "The people who love you will end up joining these revolutionaries. Your actions are turning the common people against you. These uprisings are your fault."

He bangs on the roof and the carriage, and they return to the palace. "Hold your tongue, sister. If the people are so upset about their neighbors being hanged, they should be mad at their neighbors for doing treasonous acts. Not at me for simply dispensing justice."

"You keep telling yourself that. You are a selfish, conceited, stuck-up child with a crown you have no right to wear. You have turned into our father!"

"Take that back!" His face is crimson, and his upper lip quivers.

"No," Eleanor says. "You are building your own downfall with every increase in taxes, with every soldier you send overseas, with your complicity with the business owners, allowing abuses to happen. You have sown the seeds of your own toppling."

"I will banish you and Daya if you do not take back what you just said."

"I will make it easier on you, then. I would not want you to be in a position of making yet another hard choice. I will leave." She taps the side of the carriage, and when it comes to a halt, she jumps out and disappears into the crowd.

"Eleanor, wait! Dammit." But she is gone.

Unfortunately, the letter that Caitlin stole from the Duke of Hern was nothing more than an inventory of grain stores from the previous winter. However, it would still be useful. It has been over two weeks since that fateful dinner, and Elwee has taken Lady Shennen to zir new estate. "Hopefully, zie will propose," Lady Shennen had said that morning. "I do not know how much longer I can bear this. What if I am not good enough now that zie has a higher rank at court than me?"

None of that is Caitlin's concern, though. With zir gone, it is time to see what zir rooms at court hold. There had been an outcry when Elwee had noticed the key missing, and zie blamed it on a spy being amongst them. No one believed zir, merely pointing out how drunk zie had been, and surely it would turn up any day now.

Caitlin glances up and down the hall, sure no one is coming. She inserts the key and lets herself in. She is unsure what she expected, but it was not rooms with dozens and dozens of Suan trinkets. The tapestries that adorn the wall are distinctly from the Esiri region of Sua, and the furnishings have all been reupholstered in silken Izmyri damask. The scent of masyi lingers in the air, and Caitlin wonders how the earl had procured the fragrant herb.

Making her way to zir desk, she marvels at the Suan treasures Elwee has collected, all of which would have been difficult to obtain without connections. She wants to appraise the paperweight, ink well, and quills to determine if they are imports but instead rummages through the paperwork.

A letter on extremely well-made parchment is among the pile, and it is not sealed. She opens the delicate parchment. It is written in no language she understands; she does not even recognize the lettering. She holds it up to the light, and her stomach drops—a faint watermark in the corner: the chalice and tree of the Blodheimr Hjart.

How? Why? It makes no sense. Do those priests not already have what they desire? They are the power behind the throne; what need would they have for assets and spies? Especially ones that are not known for their steadfastness. *At least this explains how zie would have the money for such lavish imports. They must pay well.*

She wants to take the letter with her for Kegan to attempt to decode or decipher. But of all the letters on zir desk, this is one she knows they would miss. She sighs and pockets it anyway.

She snatches several more innocuous ones until she finds a second suspicious letter. This one bears the seal of the Byrne family, but it is on the same elegant parchment. She adds it to her collection and slips back out of Elwee's rooms.

How many people are working with Ljósa and Nael? How much larger is this web?

She wishes she could be honest with Arlina; she wishes that she could tell her what she is doing, about her mission, about her plans, all of it. But she does not want to endanger Arlina or anyone else. A few gold daels is all it takes to buy Rosemarie's help and only a few more to buy her silence. The copy of the key to the Byrne rooms entrusted to the maids and servants vanishes a few days later. And the day after that, Caitlin finds it tucked at the bottom of her basket of clean shirts, freshly delivered by her maid.

She wishes she could tell Arlina. Both of the Byrne men are out of the city, rounding up as many rebels as possible in Clare. Arlina, now having her own rooms as the Duchess of Caerhe, has no reason to frequent the ones that belong to her family. Caitlin enters the rooms, confident that she will not be disturbed.

The office is larger than she expected, filled with more books than she would have ever guessed. But the room is undecorated and has no personal touches; the sole item that could identify this room as Conlaoch Byrne's is the oil painting of his late wife hung above the hearth.

His desk is disorganized; mundane correspondences mixed with important notes from the privy council, none of which is useful to her. She pulls on the handle to the top drawer, but it is locked. As are the other three. *Would he leave a key anywhere?* She moves aside the ink, checks under the paperweights, checks under the book stopper on the shelf, but has no success.

She pulls a pin out of her hair and prays to Bardon for this to work. The click of the springs sends a chill down her spine, and the drawer opens.

Success. Another document on elegant parchment with letters she does not recognize also bears the faint watermark of the three and chalice. She had handed the other one to Kegan, who immediately began working on it. She hopes that they have made at least a little progress on it.

Moving aside other papers, she sees a letter that catches her eye and rips it out of the drawer. A list of names and Diarmuid Marr is at the top. She almost vomits. Some of the names are crossed out, some have question marks next to them, and some are underlined; all are Red Front Members. She tears out the other papers in the drawer, her heart racing in fear and excitement. Dates and locations: the days that the high constable will visit each location to make arrests. Everyone can escape in time if she gets this to the Red Front quickly. Or perhaps Sharidan can plan a counterattack.

Pleased that this was more successful than she hoped, she places her prizes in her pocket, closes the drawers, and sneaks back toward the entrance.

"What are you doing here?"

She freezes. Arlina stands in the doorway, arms crossed, the dim light of the candles the only illumination on her figure.

"Caitlin. Why are you here?" Arlina asks again, an edge in her voice.

"I... I needed something from your father's files."

"And you could not ask him?"

"No. But I have it now, so I will just be going."

Arlina blocks the doorway. "Why? Tell me. How did you get in here?"

Caitlin shifts her weight, unable to come up with a convincing lie.

"Did you steal the key? Did you steal the key to Elwee's rooms too?"

"You do not understand."

"Then make me understand. Tell me why, tell me why. Please."

"I wish I could," she says, approaching Arlina and holding her hands. "I cannot tell you; I am sorry."

Arlina takes a step back. "You do not understand what this is about, do you?"

"This is about my life. This is about my safety. I do not know what else to say."

"And why could you not tell me that three minutes ago? Why could you not have told me that three weeks ago? Why could you not trust me with that?"

"Because I do not want you in danger, too."

"You do not understand. This is about trust. That is what this is about, Caitlin. You did not trust me."

"But..."

"There is no but here! After all this time, after all we have been through, I would think that you would trust me by now. I know that you have more going on than you tell me; I know that there are other things aside from this that you are doing. I know you are just trying to survive, but so am I. And I thought we could do so together. But if you will not trust me, why am I wasting my time?"

"Arlina, no, wait—!"

"It is too late. Leave." She holds open the door, leaning against it, foot tapping. "If you do not wish to share your secrets with me, if you do not want to work together, why should I share mine with you? I will let you find out on your own."

"What does that mean? Find out what?"

"Leave."

Caitlin sulks back to her rooms and finds Kegan in her bedchamber, papers on the floor before them. "I have some more for you," she says. "Some to decipher, but also some with information that needs to reach Sharidan and Saorise immediately."

"I can take it now," Kegan says, springing to their feet. "Are you okay?"

"Not in the slightest, but it is nothing that a nap cannot fix."

TWENTY-TWO

Dungeons and Discoveries

For the first time since she had moved to the palace, she awakens feeling rested. Carefully sitting up, she notices that the room is chilly. She listens, hoping to hear the faint sound of servants bustling outside of her bedchamber. The fire in the hearth is down to only a few embers, and the curtains covering the windows have not yet been pulled back. Hand on her stomach, she makes her way across the room and throws a log in the fireplace. Before she can turn around and open the curtains herself, she vomits. And then vomits again.

No one comes running to the door; no one barges in and asks her if she is well. No one can be heard outside making a fuss.

She wonders how women manage pregnancy without servants to help them. This is so much harder than she could have imagined.

She can find no one else in any of her chambers. But there is a single lily laid across her desk and, underneath it, a note.

My dearest love,

You were sleeping so peacefully that I could not bring myself to wake you. I confess I may have stared too long for what would be proper. After much discussion with the priests, it has been determined that spring progress this year would overly tire you. In light of our encounters at your blessing last month, it is safest for you for your health, our son's health, and for your security that you stay here where you shall be well protected. I shall miss you while I am gone on spring progress, but I cannot risk any of the revolutionaries or rebels harming you and there being no doctor to attend to you should you need it.

Your loving husband,

Cian, King of Fayn

She rushes to the window overlooking the courtyard, pulling aside the curtain. The carriages are packed, courtiers mingle about, hostlers checking the horses' shoes. In the carriage nearest to the gate sits Cian, and next to him is Lady Caerhe.

He can't leave without her. She knows this is the work of Father Ljósa and Father Nael. But she cannot let him leave without her. She knows that being alone in the palace would present her with unique opportunities to do as much snooping as she needs. But it will not give her the most updated information, information that she needs to keep her friends safe. She thought she had been back in his good graces; she thought she was once again his favorite. And yet he is about to ride away with Arlina at his side.

Without thought for propriety, she races out of her rooms, not even telling Sir Dermont, standing vigil right outside her doors, where she's going. The palace has never seemed this large, but each hallway seems to elongate, growing faster than she can run down it. She takes the stairs three at a time, almost tripping more than once. But she reaches her destination.

"Your Majesty, please!"

The King turns, jaw-dropping when he sees her. Face pale, he leaps from the carriage seat, confusion, and conflict written across his face. She marches towards him, not caring that people will see her still in her nightgown. Mouth still hanging open, he says nothing as she glares at him.

"Well? Why are you leaving without me, my love?"

He bites his lip and pulls her into an embrace. Softly, so softly that she is unsure if he even intends to say this out loud, he says, "I failed you. I have no choice. But at least this way, they will not be near you." He pulls back and glances at Father Ljósa and Father Nael, deep in conversation on the other side of the courtyard.

"My husband, there is something that I learned rather recently." She puts both hands on his chest, gripping his shirt. "You always have a choice. And abdicating your choices to others is a choice in and of itself."

His hands drop to his side, and he looks at her, eyes wide, mouth slack. He takes a deep breath, knits his brows, and says, "You do not understand, my love."

"I understand far more than you think I do," she says, crossing her arms against the morning chill, ignoring the drizzle of rain that is starting.

"I am sorry," he says, running a hand through his long hair. "If I had known... Please, stay here. Sir Dermont will keep you safe, for right now, I cannot." She is not sure if he is wiping away a drop of rain or a tear, but no sooner has he done so than he plasters a smile on his face and turns back to the carriage, sprinting toward Arlina.

Arlina, who has been pointedly ignoring every attempt Caitlin has made to make eye contact with her. Arlina leaps out of the carriage and into Cian's arms—Arlina, the king's favorite and the happiest woman at court.

The rain falls heavier, and in no mood to catch a cold, Caitlin returns inside. As she trudges back to her room, she notices an unfamiliar priest walking down the hall. A priest that seems to have materialized out of nowhere. She glances over her shoulder to see if anyone is following her, and she stalks the priest from a distance.

The priest quickens his pace, and Caitlin wonders if she is about to be found out or if he has heard her. But then he disappears into a wall. Caitlin halts. *How did he disappear into a wall?*

She spends the next several days searching the corridors. She replays the image of the priest turning and vanishing into a wall. A ghost? The palace has been here longer than the Fola dynasty has reigned, and although the Fola rulers have added their own touches and expanded several wings, parts of the palace are so ancient that its builders are forgotten. It would not be surprising the palace if it were haunted.

She turns over several facts at once. Priests always seem to materialize out of nowhere when they need Cian. Sister Kiandre spoke of wanting to release magic long sealed away. And she is still unsure what the Folas bargained for when they made a pact with the Blodheimr Hjart.

But the only magic that she knows of is *Ástfriður* magic. She waits until evening, and the few remaining servants are out of sight. Wearing the bracelet from Brenna, she tells Sir Dermont not to follow her and the knight and, thankfully, does not argue the point. She winds her way around the corridors and hallways, brushing her finger over the coil of her bracelet until she comes to a spot in the wall that has vexed her for several days.

As soon as she stands squarely before it, she feels the sting of magic. But it is not *Ástfriður* magic, or at least not purely *Ástfriður* magic. There's something else interlaced with the sting. Something she's never encountered before. Shaking, she reaches for the wall, expecting her hand to meet the hard stone. Instead, her hand passes right through it.

Furtively glancing up and down the corridor, she takes a deep breath and walks through the wall. Every hair stands on end, and her heart briefly stops between one step and the next. On the other side of the wall is a corridor, the same as she had just been walking down, but somehow entirely different. *If magic has been locked away, what in the hell is this false wall? If magic could only be practiced by the Ástfriður, who the hell made it?*

Taking only a moment to steady herself, she heads down the impossible corridor. A straight, uninterrupted path lay before her, devoid of turns or entrances. She loses track of how long she walks. She would not be surprised if someone had told her it had been an hour since she started this journey, nor would she be surprised if someone had told her it had only been several minutes. As her feet complain that she has been walking for too long, she comes across a dead end. The corridor stops, and another stone wall faces her.

Dismayed, she turns around, clutching Brenna's bracelet. But as skin meets cool metal, and the tingle of magic washes over her again, she hears voices. She turns around, and the wall has vanished, in its place as an opening to an office. She reaches forward, and the wall returns.

What the heck? She touches the bracelet again, and once more, an office is before her. She pulls her hand away, and it disappears again. These priests are somehow using *Ástfriður* magic. *Valen, Brenna...* They sought them out so that they might somehow harness their magic.

Dierdre...

This ceremony that Brenna had performed on their wedding night. *Blood and copper.* She touches her bracelet again and tiptoes closer to the office.

She peers inside, not daring to step further than the wall. Inside are two priests having a heated conversation. One of the people inside is Sheath, the acolyte always trailing after Father Nael. His face is red, fists clenched, looking at the ground as the other priest, an older man, scolds him for some transgression. She cannot understand the language that they are speaking, but she knows all too well the tone an elder has for a child who thinks they should not be accountable for their actions.

The elder crosses the room, slides open a door, grabs a broom, and hands it to Sheath. The acolyte glares at his elder, gets one final word in before he leaves, and slams the door behind him. The elder chuckles, clearly amused by the temper tantrum. He mutters something to himself in the strange language as he rummages through papers on his desk. Caitlin cannot even guess this language's origins, but she makes out three words. Rían, Tómas, and *Ástfriður*. Do they mean her father? Is this where her fathers are being held? And what about Lady Clare's father?

The elder slips an envelope in his pocket before leaving the office. She waits half a second before slipping in, grabbing every paper on the desk, and running back out. She knows she should take this to Sister Kiandre, but she is afraid that the priestess will again tell her nothing, so she prays that Kegan has deciphered the code.

Kegan is efficient in copying the additional documents that Caitlin brings back. When Caitlin rises the following morning, Kegan has a completed cipher.

"Did you even sleep last night?"

"No," Kegan says. "With these new documents to cross-reference, I made quick work of it. Let's get to it!" Their tail vibrates.

Both Daya and Eleanor have vanished; Eleanor made good on her promise to banish herself and take her wife with her. All of her attendants, except for Kegan, are on progress, so there is no one there to interrupt them as they lay out the papers on the tables.

She wonders if she will have attendants by the time that progress is over, for the king had granted Lady Caerhe the right to employ her own attendants at his expense. She is sure that Lady Emeire, at the very least, will request to wait on the Duchess of Caehre.

"This reminds me about the first time," Kegan says, their ears swiveling forward. "I did not know what I wanted to do. I just knew I wanted to help Aine. She set a stack of papers on the table, and I had no clue what they were. I spread them all out on the dining room table, thinking I would organize stuff for her, but it was all in code."

"Oh?" Caitlin sets paper after paper down on the table.

"No, put that paper over there, and that one over there, yeah, good. I was so in awe of Aine at the time; I assumed that she had these coded documents because she was some sort of code breaker. And I want to be just like her, so I set to work."

"Aine did not seem like the kind that would enjoy deciphering codes." There is no more room on the table, so Caitlin sets papers on the floor.

"No, she wasn't. While I was decoding, she rushed through the room, and half of the papers were sent flying. She was so shocked she screamed so loudly..." Kegan laughs, clutching their stomach.

"Now that sounds like Aine."

"She thought she was being attacked! Oh gosh, I miss her."

Caitlin does not know what to say, and so she says nothing.

"I am afraid to go home after this is over. Our home... I want to freeze it in time."

Caitlin's heart flutters, and she looks up from the floor at Kegan. "You want the air in there to be air that she might have breathed? And the fur in the carpet to still be hers..."

"How did you know?" Kegan collapses into the chair at the table and buries their face in their hands. "There are still fingerprints on the bathroom mirror that are hers. I can't wipe it away. I don't know how to keep going."

"Nor do I," Caitlin says, "but I don't know what else to do except keep going."

"Keep going. Keep going; I can try. So let's crack some codes." Kegan takes a deep breath and hands Caitlin a ledger, and they begin their task.

Most of the notes are mundane, talking about chores that need to be done at the temple, rats that have infested the temple kitchen, mice that are leaving droppings, and Father Nael's bed—which many suspect is part of a prank by Sheath—, and reminders the never put Sloan on the dinner rotation again.

But there are a few that stand out; many complain that Caitlin is not as tame as they had thought, and several complain about her infertility; more than a few worry that Cian seems more loyal to Caitlin than he is to the priests of Culain, and a few notes mention Arlina being more docile and pliable than Caitlin. She chuckles as she finds a note that mentions that Emeire is even more obstinate than Caitlin, and all efforts must be taken to ensure that she never becomes a serious love interest for Cian. Caitlin has to agree with the priest's assessment of Lady Emeire. There are many notes about Lairde Elwee and Lord Berach being easily manipulated by their hunger for power. And more than many notes about the Earl of Caibre being an ass. *At least we can agree on a few things.*

"Hey, Caitlin," Kegan says, approaching her with a letter clutched in their hand. "You were in Whick in the year 3010, correct?"

"Yes," Caitlin says, stretching. "Why?"

"This letter here. It mentions them trying to steal an *Ástfriður* that was living in Whick. You remember that?"

"I was there." With great effort, she stands up and goes to the window, a weight in her chest threatening to pull her back to the ground.

"So you remember it?"

It is raining, the first rain of spring. Rains that many will take to be a promise that this year will be better than last. "Brenna"

"Is that the *Ástfriður* they wanted?"

"Brenna was killed." Caitlin tries and cannot keep the quivering out of her voice. "They staged it to look like pirates were after Brenna. And Brenna fought back."

"You knew Brenna?"

Caitlin cannot bring herself to say another word; she hangs her head and sighs.

"Oh. Oh," Kegan says. "I won't ask anymore. All we can do is keep going."

Caitlin turns back around to face Kegan. "Thank you."

"Anyway, I thought it was weird, considering there's also this note about Valen's blood not being enough?"

"Yes, they might use *Ástfríður* blood for this pact."

"Well, there certainly are a lot of notes here about blood," Kegan says. "Notes about Tómas' blood, Maeve's, Cian's, Tarmon's. What confuses me the most is they talk about taking blood from Tómas recently. Didn't the Duke of Clare die a long time ago?"

"That's what I thought, too," Caitlin says, chewing her lip.

"I'd say most of them that mention blood talk about Cian not giving enough. They also complain that you are the reason he is so stingy. What does that mean?"

"I have no idea."

"I am absolutely worn out and hungry. I will be right back." Kegan springs to the kitchen, leaving Caitlin to wipe away her tears. She tries to take in deep breaths, slow her heart, and push away the thoughts clawing to the front.

Kegan sets a plate down before her. "I hope this does not cause you any discomfort." Not bothering with a fork or spoon, Kegan shovels food into their mouth. "There are a few things I don't know what to make of, though. There are a lot of words that make little sense to me. There's this one," Kegan says, using their foot to point to a paper across from Caitlin. "This one keeps talking about 'Arkae,' specifically an 'Arkae Mi'ia,' but I do not know what that is. There are also 'Audgisil,' 'Escnea,' and 'Sine.' They sound like places, but I don't know where they would be. I've never heard of them before."

Caitlin takes a bite of her bread, knowing she's heard at least one of those words before but unable to tease out the memory.

"And another thing," Kegan says, licking their fingers. "All of this sounds like magic, but Kiandre said it was locked away. So, what is being used? You mentioned something about the *Ástfriður*, is that right?"

"I believe they are finding *Ástfriðurs* and somehow using their blood to perform magic. That must be how they created the magical link between the land and the land."

"But why *Ástfriður*?"

"Oh," Caitlin says, not knowing where to start, not knowing if she can break the trust of Brenna. But she explains in fits and starts.

"So you say that Kiandre and the Araelta want magic to be free, and it sounds like these Blodheimr Hjart people are trying to use magic, too. Why don't they work together to free magic? It sounds like that's what they both want. And ask the *Ástfriður* for help instead of whatever," they say, gesturing to the papers, "this is. "

Caitlin chews on her nail, growing tired of asking questions and only finding more. Never finding answers, only questions. "*Trust no one, not even me.* That is one of the first things that sister Kiandre told me. They are lying. But what are they lying about? What else is going on here?"

Kegan reaches across the papers, steals a slice of bread from Caitlin's plate, and shoves it into their mouth. "I don't think they are wrong about the land dying if there is not a Fola on the throne," Kegan says, crumbs falling out of their mouth. "No matter what, we need to break that pact if we want the Red Front to be victorious. I say we focus on that for now."

"I understand this is so much more than we thought we were getting into. I understand if you want to leave again."

"Aine asked me that all the time. I had been through so much already, she would point out, and that I did not need to pay her back by joining the cause. That's what she was always worried about. That I had only joined the Red Front out of a sense of obligation to her for saving my life, but I joined because I believed in it. I do not want anybody to live through what I lived through again."

"So you're with me?"

"That is my choice. I'm going to see this through to the end."

"Excellent. Would you join me tomorrow for worship at the Temple of Culain?"

Kegan grains and rubs their hands together. "Oh, heck yes!"

The clergy clamor to accommodate Caitlin when she declares her intent to visit all of the Temples at least once a week to seek blessings for her son. She says that her son deserves to be gifted, that Fianna should bless her baby with the gift of music, and Bardon should bless her baby with keen insight and cleverness, and she hopes that Dana will bless her baby with the strength needed to survive and protect him from an untimely death.

Many comment behind her back that she must be terrified that she is about to be set aside if she is praying so fervently. She pretends she does not hear these whispers.

Of course, she always makes time to go to the Temple of Culain. Father Ljósa and Father Nael are still with King Cian on progress, but she does her best to note anything that looks out of place. She compares and contrasts the trappings, prayers, and rituals of all the deities to those of Culain, searching for anything out of place.

She eventually realizes that she is entirely out of her depth, having never been one for religion, and takes out the crescent hairpin.

That night, it is not just Sister Kiandre that she finds waiting for her in her room, but also the High Priestess, Dierdre.

"I must ask, how are you getting into my bedchamber?" She leans against her door.

"That is a secret we cannot share," Dierdre says, not getting up from where she sits on the edge of Caitlin's bed.

Caitlin taps her foot and holds up the letters that she and Kegan decoded: "I suppose, then, that these must then remain a secret I cannot share."

Kiandre lunges at Caitlin from her perch on the chaise, but Caitlin quickly sidesteps before the Calla can snatch the documents.

"We use a secret door that leads from the rose garden to your bedchamber. There are many such doors in the original parts of the palace; they are remnants of the ancient magic that was used to construct the palace over a thousand years ago."

"You could have been sneaking into my room for the last two years. Why haven't you been? Where is this door? Who else knows?"

"The ancient magic is volatile. It requires several items to work properly, which is why we have not been able to use it before. That hairpin you have is one of the items, and Kiandre's necklace is the other. But we only just obtained the hairpin."

Kiandre plays with the crescent moon pendant on her necklace; her face scrunched up in a frown and eyes downcast.

"There needs to be one at each end of the doorway. And until recently, all we had was Kiandre's pendant. That hairpin had to be made, and it took a long time."

Caitlin retrieves her bracelet from her jewelry box. "Right here?" she says, standing next to her mirror, the sting of *Ástfriður* magic strong. "And it is invisible?"

"How did you know?"

"I do not believe this was made with ancient magic, but *Ástfriður* magic. Or at least some of it was made with *Ástfriður* magic or from the blood of an *Ástfriður*."

For the first time since she has met Deirdre, the priestess is speechless; not the silence of concealment, but the silence of shock.

Caitlin hands some letters to Kiandre and Dierdre, pointing out the chalice and tree watermark, the strange characters, and the key to decipher them.

A crease now adorns Dierdre's brow, her lips tight at the corners as she looks through the letters. "I believe you are correct. They are using blood to fuel their magic, and they use that magic to fuel the pact." Her eyes are far away, seeing something sorrowful that no one else can. "If they are using *Ástfríður* blood to maintain the pact, then it must be an *Ástfríður* that breaks the pact."

Dierdre buries her face in her hands, takes a deep breath, and, without looking up, says, "I cannot; I do not know how. But you can."

"You are an *Ástfríður*. I am not."

"Your wife? Brenna. You said she explained things to you on your wedding night."

"She explained many things that I am still confused about."

"Xir blood is in your blood; xir soul lives on in you. Xie cannot be reborn until xie returns to the Isles."

"I made sure that xir *ahnhörn* was sent back to the Isles, though," Caitlin says.

"That is not enough. Xir soul lives on in you and will do so until you yourself visit the Veil. But until that time, you do have some measure of *Ástfríður* magic. You can sense it and feel it."

"But only when I am wearing my bracelet."

"And that is all we need."

"I cannot believe it!" Kiandre says, leaping to her feet and shoving a letter in Deirdre's face. "Look! Look!"

Caitlin glances at the document that Dierdre is now examining. It is a document that discusses the Arkae Mi'ia and Valen's blood. But she and Kegan never did figure out what an Arkae is.

"Look, here, the second meaning..." Kiandre says to Dierdre, pointing to the third line. "And here... and also here," she says, pointing at different spots on the document.

"What are you talking about?" Caitlin asks.

Kiandre grins, a grin that Caitlin has learned to hate because she knows that it means information is being withheld. Deirdre grabs the paper and holds it close, squinting. A smile creeps across the high priestess' face. "I think you are correct. This is it! This is it!" The high priestess leaps to her feet and lifts her hands into the air. "At long last, this is it."

"I would truly appreciate it if you could at least inform me of some of what is going on." Caitlin glares at the two priestesses.

"Well," Dierdre says, each word drawn out, "our suspicions are correct. The pact between the land and the crown that the Blodheimr Hjart are facilitating grants the Fola monarchs some protection and health. Which explains why our poisoned arrow did not kill Tarmon."

"That was you?"

"I thought you figured that out long ago, but yes. That poison should have been instantly lethal. He did still die, but based on these notes, I assume it is because the priest took too much blood from him."

"How much blood do they need? And how often?" She remembers all of the wounds on Cian and how often he had fresh ones.

"Some of these notes mention getting blood from Maeve and Tómas, in addition to the king, so I would assume that the pact must be maintained daily and with large quantities of royal blood."

Caitlin bites her lip. "I thought that Tómas had died quite some time ago, but some of these letters about him are dated as recently as three months ago."

"Yes, he was very close with Maeve. There was something about Maeve wanting to get married and Tarmon not approving. Tómas tried to intercede, and he died shortly after that. Many found it a little suspicious, but this does raise some questions about the veracity of that claim." Dierdre scratches her chin.

"I have some more questions," Caitlin says. "First, if we break the pact between the king and the land, how do we know we will not be making things worse? And second, what does all of this have to do with your sealed magic? It seems like both you and the Blodheimr Hjart have an interest in unsealing magic. And aside from being the power behind the throne, what do the Blodheimr Hjart get from this pact?"

The priestesses stare at each other.

"I'm waiting for an answer. I brought you a lot of information. The least you can do is give me some back."

"The Hjart are dangerous, and they should not be in power. We want them gone, and obviously, we do not want the land to suffer because of that." The hesitation between each word is enough to let Caitlin know she is being lied to. But she presses on anyway. "Then why do you not truly help us? Why don't you join us?"

"I'll say it in as plain of words as I think I can. You are pregnant. With a Fola child, a child that can be used by the Hjart, yes. But also by the Araelta. Our short-term goals align. That's where it ends."

Caitlin places her thumb on her chin. "You say that the Araelta found you? After the *Ástfríður* discarded you?"

Deirdre glares at Caitlin, standing up quickly. "I think I have an idea now about what needs to be done to break this pact. But I need to verify some things in my library first. I shall send word with Kiandre when I have a solution. Until then."

The two priestesses quietly slip out of the room to the invisible door next to her mirror.

The court has returned from their progress, and Cian is confident that, having seen him, the people will love him again. Arlina establishes her own court in her rooms, with Lady Muiris and Lady Shennen—now engaged to Lairde Elwee but with no princess to wait on—as her attendants. Caitlin is surprised that Lady Ronai remains an attendant to her. Lady Riqueti also offers to wait on Caitlin, and Caitlin graciously accepts. During the bustle of the day, Kiandre slips into Caitlin's bedchamber and leaves the note waiting for her tucked behind a pillow.

The note contains the promised information from the high priestess. What she must do to break the pact, where she must do it, and when she must do it. Caitlin's stomach turns as she reads the note, for what she must do involves a dagger and blood. She searches her pillows and finds a knife, just as the note says she will. The knife's blade is engraved with stars, and the hilt is inlaid with sapphires.

She is skeptical that this will work, suspicious that perhaps this ritual, with all of the words and phrases that she does not know, is doing something other than breaking the pact. They want to take out the Blodheimr Hjart, but if this ritual does more than that, well, she can deal with the consequences later. The note says that she must perform this ritual in the sanctum of the Temple of Culain in the city.

She wastes no time asking Cian if she can volunteer to assist the priests. Since his return from progress, has been torn between his wife, the queen that the people love, and the woman he is courting to satisfy the priest's demands.

He grants her wish, and shortly afterward, he sets a date for them.

"Your Majesty," the woman says, two children hanging on to her sleeves. "I cannot thank you enough. My wife died in one of the factory fires, and I am often too sick to work. It has been hard for us."

Caitlin places children's shirts and shoes into the box next to the rest of the supplies they are distributing to the poor. "What was her name?"

"Sarah, your Majesty."

"May the gods keep her and save her," Caitlin says, sealing the box and handing it to the woman.

"Your Majesty is too kind." Tears welling in her eyes, the woman leads her children out of the courtyard, tossing one more glance behind her shoulder at Caitlin and mouthing the words thank you.

Caitlin meets the eyes of every single person who approaches her and listens with full attention as they explain to her their plights, each pleading as if making a case for themselves. As if trying to prove that they deserve her charity. As if they are afraid that they will be turned away.

She asks for their names; the names of their family members who are overseas; their children's names, and their grandparents' names; she doesn't want to forget these people. She became a player on this chessboard to save her life, to get back at Cian, to get back at Liam and the others like him who burn their factories out of spite, to get back at Aelena and others who treat people as disposable.

And to get back at the Blodheimr Hjart for murdering her wife.

Before today, she had met with many in this situation while working with the Red Front. She handed out clothes and food and watched the children as their parents went to work. And she had continued to do so in her capacity as a princess-to-be.

But today is different. Today she meets with them not as a member of the Red Front, not as a member of the Royal family, not as someone with an agenda tied to anyone but herself. She is not tagging along with her friends. She is not playing a part in someone else's game.

She is Caitlin, a player at the table, not someone else's queen on the board. And each person joins her ever-increasing list of reasons she must break the pact.

Arlina still refuses to speak to her. She is not forcing the issue, but she wishes she had an additional friend. Knife hidden among her many underskirts; she tells Cian that she is going back inside the Temple to retrieve something. She makes her way to the sanctum and finds it empty. The note had mentioned the back room. Caitlin feels along the wall for any seams that might be the door. Instead, she finds another invisible entrance.

The hidden room is small, with a strange rune engraved on the marble floor. It is not the chalice and tree symbol she had been expecting; instead, it looks more closely related to the lettering on the coded documents.

She collapses to her knees at the center of the room. Something strange is in the air, something oppressive. It bites but does not sting. She had memorized the chant, though she knows not what the words mean. Taking a deep breath, she chants.

Words she does not know, words that taste strange, words that sound otherworldly.

She slices into her left palm.

Words that have color and weight.

She does the same with her right palm.

Words that should remain unsaid.

She places both palms on the marble floor and begins the chant again.

The ground shakes, and she expects to hear screams, but she remains bathed in silence. A shock runs down her spine, and she falls to her side. She clenches her teeth, fighting against the quaking to get back to her knees to complete the ritual.

A sharp pain tears down her back. "I do not know who you are or what you are doing. But you will stop."

More blood. *But she only cut her palms... Why is there blood pulling around her?*

"Caitlin!" Arlina. Why is she here? "Who are you? Get away from her! Help! The queen!"

Her vision swims, more screams, more footsteps.

"Oh, my gosh! You idiots!" Father Nael. She can't move. The world is fading, her breathing shallow.

"She's dying!" Father Nael says.

"It's fine," Father Ljósa says. "Arlina will be pregnant soon."

"Oh no, the king is coming..."

Caitlin closes her eyes, and the world goes black.

The first thing that she notices is the cold. The second thing is the searing touch of Arlina's hands on her forehead. The third thing is the scorching pain on her side.

"Don't leave me, stay. Please, stay." Arlina chokes with each word.

With great effort, Caitlin opens her eyes. She is not in her bedroom. She is not in the infirmary and is not sure where she is at all. The room is sparse and undecorated, with no windows and one simple wooden door. The only other furniture aside from the bed is the chair Arlina is in.

"What... where... Arlina?" She tries to roll over, but fire courses down her side.

"Try not to move, or you will pull on the bandages and open the cut again."

"What happened?"

"Someone stabbed you; the wound was not lethal, but the blade was poisoned."

"The priests..."

"Yes, the priests have been taking care of you."

"No, I mean... Later. Not here."

Another spasm of pain cuts off her next words. She is sweating profusely, but it feels as though she is outside in the snow without a coat. There is a hammering in her head and an agonizing ache in her stomach. Her world spins, and she fights to remain conscious as wave after wave of torment washes over her. She tries to form words, but her mouth refuses to cooperate. Her vision shrinks to a pinpoint, and all that she can hear is the dull roar of her blood pounding in her ears. She is not sure if she loses consciousness or not, but soon one of the Culain priests is at her bedside: his voice is so far away, his features indistinct, his movements choppy. She watches him from outside of herself, watches him touch her forehead, feel her chest, take her pulse. Watches as he touches her but does not feel his hands on her body.

"...Poison."

"Weaker..."

"...Antidote..."

More priests enter, and with them is the king.

"She's dying..."

"...the baby..."

"Save..."

"...Did anyone know...a girl..."

"...not for another month..."

"If you have to choose... The baby first..."

"...Father Ljósa, you cannot..."

"But Caitlin..." Arlina. Arlina is still here. Somewhere.

"...almost."

"...it is too soon."

"Where is Diarmuid..." the only words she can say.

"Who's Diarmuid?" Cian shouts. "Who is that?"

"Physician," she says. "No priests."

"Find this man," he shouts and storms out.

"No priests," she mumbles again.

"...it's too soon, Father..."

"...you should have known your place, girl," Father Ljósa says.

"It's too soon, m'girl." Brenna. "I'm waiting, but I can wait a little longer. Stay with that pretty girl, and when you're done here, bring her to the Veil. I can keep waiting. I will keep waiting."

The world goes dark again.

She opens her eyes, but the world is still black. Callous and cold, damp and dark. She blinks, begging her vision to clear. Her mind is full of the sounds of moans and screams and clanking metal, and her nostrils fill with the smell of decay and debris. She recoils at the putrid taste that invades her mouth.

The dungeons? Why? It must be the doing of the priests.

Cian, though, will save her. Even if he hates her, even if he is more interested in Arlina, he will save her. Even if he wants to appease the priests, he will still save her. He dislikes it too much when someone steals his toys.

She stands on wobbly feet and ambles to the front of the cell, hands wrapping around the bars and clinging to them to stay upright. Her whole body feels weird, off, strange. She touches her stomach. She is no longer pregnant. Dimly, she recalls flashes of conversation. Arlina begging them to save her, a priest saying to save only the child. Did she hear Cian say something, too? She remembers his voice in that chaos, so why is she here? Why did he let her be taken?

"Oh, the whore is awake." A guard halts in front of her cell, eyes glancing up and down at her.

"What did you call me?"

"You heard me. You thought you could go around with someone else behind the king's back?"

"I never…"

"Don't worry; your precious Diarmuid is being found, and we'll make sure he's taken care of."

"I am the Queen of Fayn; release me!"

The guard leans in, face inches from the bars. "Nay, you're Diarmuid's lass through and through." The guard winks and strolls away.

Diarmuid's lass? Aine and Kegan had called her that the night of her first meeting, and others used it not long after that, too. Diarmuid had to demand Valen and Sharidan put a stop to it.

"Wait! Wait! Come back! What's going on?" If the guard hears her, he does not acknowledge it, and no one else walks past.

Too weak to keep standing, even with the bars to brace her, she collapses back down to the cold floor. Hours pass, or maybe days, or maybe, minutes. She does not get up from the ground.

"Your Majesty, I hope you are enjoying your new rooms." That voice. She opens her eyes, and standing outside of her cell is Father Nael. "So, you are the one that those witches thought could save them? To think you were in front of me the whole time." He grins, wicked and wide. "I shall enjoy destroying the prophecized savior of the Araelta."

TWENTY-THREE

Flames and Futility

W*HEN ASKED ABOUT HER wife*, Caitlin wanted to detail each and every year: those happy years. Count each one. The year they made their home. The year they got too many cats. The year they planted a garden together—strangely, also the year they found out that neither of them was good at gardening, the year Brenna took a job at the library—also the year Brenna got fired from the library, the year Caitlin's fathers promoted her, the year they spent on a ship out at sea. And then she would pause, wanting to keep going, to keep listing years. That's not enough years, she would say to herself. There weren't enough years.

The captain said this man was a new recruit; he had picked him up at a previous port. The man had been remarkably eager to find a ship heading to Whick. Very inquisitive about the people of Whick.

What was the Peddigree girl like, and what of her wife? Were they often on the docks during the day? The other crew members were happy to indulge this man's questions; they were bragging, in a way. Proud of their friends, proud of their drinking buddies, why wouldn't they talk of Brenna in any other way? Why wouldn't they share the stories that they would admit to when in the cups but vehemently deny the next day?

"You're going to love xir," the one said.

"Xie is really good at cards; best watch how much you throw down tonight."

"Don't be surprised if xie tries to sing at some point; xir voice is beautiful, but xir language can be rather dirty."

"You'll see why we call Brenna family. It has nothing to do with xir relationship with the Peddigrees."

"So xie will be at the inn tonight?" the man asked.

"The one closest to the dock? More than likely."

"Good," the man said. "I'm glad to hear that."

Caitlin had had paperwork to do that night. She didn't go to that inn; she hadn't been there in at least a week. It had been rather busy for her. She was planning to, though. But she got there a little too late. The man was holding a knife to xir throat. Another man who seemed to have come in on another ship that day was trying to hold people off.

"Where is it?" the man asked. "Where is the other port?"

"There isn't one!" Brenna cried.

Xir friends tried to approach and help, but the men quietly lurking in the corners of the inn stood up, each armed. "You are getting on our ship, and you are going to take us there." The man said while his accomplices held off anyone approaching.

A fight broke out; these pirates would not let one of their own be taken. Brenna did all xie could on xir own to take on xir captors xirself. But in the melee, xie was severely wounded.

In the end, the plotters were rounded up—those that weren't dead—and sent to Eoi to be dealt with directly by the King's Shield. They'd been coming in slowly, never seen with each other. Quiet, and when asked, they said they were waiting. For someone, for something. For a ship, a relative, a trader. But, in truth, they were waiting for this man to give the signal. They had a ship of their own ready and crewed. If Brenna could not show them a hidden port, then they would use xir to get past the gates of the known one.

Or, at least, that was the story they gave when questioned.

"Who else is working with you?" Fire on her back.

"Who are the collaborators?" Flames on her chest.

"Who else is a traitor?" Sparks on her shoulders.

Tied down, arms outstretched, bound, immobile. Lash. After. Lash. Prod after prod. Her life has three constants: pain, questions, and priests. Pain and questions from the guards, questions they know she cannot answer, and then priests slicing her slowly. She watches from the corner of the damp and dark room as they try to rip a confession from her throat. She observes as they try to extract her soul from her body, not knowing that she has done so already for herself. They strike her.

Let me know when to stop by tapping three times or saying 'amethyst.' The whip strikes expertly across her back, Brenna having long ago mastered the art of this type of play. And again, and again and again. Each time Brenna strikes her, she whimpers in passion.

Anywhere else, anywhere else but here.

"Your precious Diarmuid was hanged yesterday."

Anywhere but here.

Another lash, and then another.

You're doing so wonderfully, my girl. You're doing so well. Brenna smiles with pride.

"Your baby has died; probably a bastard, anyway."

Another lash.

You're being such a good girl, Brenna says, caressing her.

"All of the traitors will be burned. Your little rebellion is dead."

Another strike.

Can you take a few more for me, my girl? Brenna stares into her eyes. *That's a good girl. That's a good girl.*

Anywhere but here.

"The king is having Whick destroyed. All of your friends from home are going to burn."

You're such a good girl for me.

"And all of your allies at the Temple of Andraste have been arrested."

"Are you working with Garcelon?"

"Where else do you have bases?"

Anywhere but here.

"Were you going to kill the king in his sleep?"

The creak of a door on rusty hinges. "Gentlemen, I will take it from here." Father Ljósa dismisses the guards. "I have questions of my own I need to ask."

The pain recedes only a little.

"I promise I will be gentle," Father Ljósa says. "First, how long have you been working with the witches?"

Brenna places a hand on one of her wounds.

Caitlin spits out blood.

"Is every member of the Temple of Andraste a witch? How many are there?"

She flinches, ready for a strike that never comes.

"You will die regardless, but if you give me this information, I promise your fathers will remain alive."

Shaking her head causes a bolt of pain, but she refuses to speak.

He punches the door. "I need to know what the witches know. What did they tell you?"

She shakes her head again, bracing for the pain.

"Dammit, you bitch." He closes the distance between them, leaning over the table so his face is inches from her. "What do they know about the Arkae? What do they know about Aodhe?"

Closing her eyes, she imagines that she is somewhere else.

"How did Dierdre end up among them?" He slaps her, but it barely registers. Can you at least tell me that? Why is an *Ástfríður* in their upper ranks?"

Anywhere but here. Anywhere except this cold room of hard stone, somewhere that does not smell like burning flesh and dried blood, somewhere with air that tastes like salt. Anywhere. Somewhere.

Let me take you away from here, " Brenna says, holding out her hand. *I'll take you home.*

Caitlin takes Brenna's hand, and the world goes black.

Caitlin does not notice her; she notices nothing. But the young woman presses a cool flask of water against her lips. Cold, fresh, clean.

"My name is Carys. I am here on behalf of the Temple of Muriel to help you wash away your sins, to bathe you in the healing and cleansing waters of the sea."

Caitlin acknowledges nothing that this priestess says. She drinks the water and returns to the haven she has built in her mind.

"Please, Cait," the priestess says.

Cait. Only Diarmuid calls her that. She searches the face of the priestess, looking for any signs of recognition, any hint of familiarity. And finds none. The priestess tucks a stray hair behind her ears, and that is when Caitlin sees it—a silver hairpin shaped like a crescent moon. Caitlin squints, and the priestess holds a finger in front of her lips.

"We wish to save you. There is still hope. You must pray with me."

"But…"

The priestess again motions her silence. "The stars are with you."

Caitlin looks behind the priestess to the guards standing at attention; backs turned against them.

"Pray." The priestess hands her a prayer card.

We, who are soaked in sin;

We, who *will* let the cold waters in;

We, who ask Muriel to *save* our souls;

We, who read from the sacred scrolls;

Muriel, we ask *You* for Your mercy,

Muriel, we ask to *be* at peace upon Your sea,

Muriel, we are *ready* to be free.

Caitlin reads the prayer card out loud, glancing at the impostor wearing Muriel's robes.

Carys nods. "The stars still favor you."

Caitlin wants so desperately to believe this priestess, to believe that she will make it out of this alive. But she has forgotten how to believe.

"Let me clean…" The priestess takes Caitlin's hands. "Your wounds. They are already healed." The priestess pulls Caitlin's hands closer, inspecting the white lines that once bled.

Caitlin shrugs.

"When did they most recently lash you?"

"This morning," Caitlin says. It takes great effort to remember how to move her mouth. She cannot be entirely certain that it was this morning. Time has ceased moving forward, yet all it does is move forward at ever-increasing speeds.

"How often do they lash you?"

"Every day," Caitlin says. "Every day, twice a day at least."

"And they heal this quickly?"

Caitlin shrugs.

"Interesting."

Caitlin does not have the energy to inquire any further about this priestess's confusion.

"I have one question," Caitlin says as the priestess makes for the cell door.

"Yes?" Carys says, looking over her shoulder

"Did the infant truly die?" She does not even know what to call her own child.

The priestess pauses. "I am afraid so; three nights ago."

Caitlin nods, still not sure what to believe. Dierdre's voice rings in her head. *A child that can be used by the Blodheimr Hjart, yes. But also by the Araelta. Our short-term goals align. That's where it ends.*

The priestess calls for the guards to open the door, and they let her out without another word.

The waking world and the dream world have ceased being separate places. It does not matter; both are full of nightmares and monsters. They tell her things as they torture her, things that break her, things that destroy her. It makes no difference; she broke long ago. She broke the day that Brenna died. They can take nothing from her that she has not already lost.

Each night, she hears cells clattering open and slamming shut; she watches guards walking in with prisoners and walking back out with the condemned.

She receives no more visitors and hopes for none. She wakes up. They torture her, bleed her, and interrogate her. They torture her but cannot touch what is in her mind.

She has never seen it, but Brenna has described it so many times. The Isles of the *Ástfriður*. To touch the sky of silk, the rivers as blue as sapphires, verdant green fields, and flowers that glow in silver and copper and gold. This is where she lives now. Bruised and broken, barely alive, but at home.

The Araelta told her to stay the course. Some part of her does not want to be rescued. She wants to stay here and wait for death to take her.

Even if she escapes, the rebellion is thoroughly crushed, spirits broken, resistance defeated, and fight stamped out. There is nothing left to rebuild; there is nothing to be regrouped.

She decided to abandon her life to others. It was a choice to acquiesce to being a pawn. It was her choice to stay silent as others decided for her. It was a choice to abdicate responsibility. She didn't want to raise her voice in protest.

Sometimes, when torturing her, they tell her to renounce Andraste. They ask her if the witches have cast a spell on her or if they were controlling her. If she was loyal to the king but the witches of Andraste had somehow ensorcelled her. She never replies. They tell her that all will be forgiven if she denounces Andraste. They tell her that she will be set free if she gives them the information; they need to stop the witches. They tell her that if she comes clean and sees the light of Culain, she can be reunited with her husband. She tells them nothing.

It takes her sluggish mind too long to realize what the priestess has figured out. Her blood is unique, far more so than that of any Fola. And she apparently has an infinite supply. They drag her to a ceremonial room and leave her to bleed out, too weak to even crawl off of the markings carved into the marble floor, and then she wakes up again in her cell. She doubts the priests will let her be taken to the gallows, not when they have discovered how valuable she is. And so, this is her choice. Her choice is to die.

The voice is too cheerful, too lighthearted for such a grim place. The voice belongs in the land of sunshine and the demesne of life. And yet, it laughs with the gruff guards. Caitlin turns away from it, wants no part of it.

The voice harmonizes with the screech of the cell door swinging open. "You got twenty minutes. No more."

"Of course," the lilting voice of Lady Dontaue says. "Please, enjoy the cookies and tea that I brought you in the meantime."

The guards open the door and let the Duke of Dontaue into the cell. The royal duke is accompanied by two priestesses of Muriel. Caitlin recognizes one of them as Carys, the Araelta in disguise who had visited her long ago.

The other lifts the novitiate veil for half of a second before lowering it again. But Caitlin does not need any longer to recognize the face of the High Priestess Dierdre, garbed in the attire of a newly initiated acolyte of Muriel.

She has forgotten how to speak, has forgotten how to communicate. She says nothing as the duke asks her questions that the guards have already asked. Who else is she conspiring with? What are the plans? Where are the bases?

But there is something in her voice, a wavering that makes all of her words ring hollow. As the Duke continues her interrogation, Carys surreptitiously peaks out of the cell. "We're clear."

"Good. Go grab the keys." Dierdre pulls out a flask of fresh water and some towels. "All of our temples were ransacked. Few escaped. Out of love for you, Priestess Samaire gave us sanctuary at the Temple of Muriel. You still have many people on your side."

The cool, wet towel brushes across Caitlin's face, and Lady Dontaue wipes away days, weeks, perhaps months' worth of grime and dried blood. Still, Caitlin can say nothing.

Carys returns, keys in hand. Wordlessly, she kneels beside Caitlin and unlocks the shackles to Caitlin's wrists and feet. "Can you walk?"

The only answer Caitlin gives is steadily rising to her feet, bracing herself against the wall.

"Take this. Hurry." Soft satin meets calloused hands as the duke hands her a robe; the blue of the ocean, the white of cresting waves, the flow of the morning's tide. Confused, Caitlin dons the robes and cloak worn by the acolytes of Muriel.

Dierdre fixes the hood and veil so that it sits low across her face. "Let's go."

The priestesses flank her on either side, and the duke leads them forward, winding their way around the labyrinthine prison.

They approach the chamber that Caitlin has spent so much time in. Without meaning to, she shivers. Dierdre halts, holding out her hand and grabbing Lady Dontaue. The door to that chamber was left ajar, and she has no trouble pushing it open soundlessly. It is occupied by someone else. Someone with choppy hair and dead eyes. But his hair is the shade of white that only Fola scions have, and his eyes are the striking blue that only Fola heirs can claim.

The duke turns around to see why her companions have stopped, eager to hurry them forward. Peering in, she takes in the sight of her brother tied to the rack. She drops the keys in her hand, clattering as they hit the stone floor. "Tómas."

Dierdre takes a tentative step forward, looking past the dying royal, and examines the sigils engraved on the floor.

Mission forgotten, Maeve—just a loving sister, not a plotting royal— rushes to her brother's side, taking his hand in hers. "Tómas. Tómas! Please, please... Tómas." She holds her ear to his chest and places her fingers on his neck—any sign of life, searching for anything that would signify that her brother still lives.

Barely perceptible, he squeezes her hand. "Maeve?"

"I'm here. I'm here."

"I'm sorry." Tómas coughs, smiles, and lets out a dying gasp.

"No. No, no, no! Hold on! We will get you out of here."

She shakes him, pulls at the shackles tying him to the rack, and a single drop of blood splatters on the floor.

Energy, fire, the taste of copper, and the smell of iron. It engulfs Caitlin; it envelops her in a whirlwind of power, drowns her in molten steel, and sucks the breath from her lungs.

Maeve continues to cry, unaware that anything has changed. Oblivious to the weight that now hangs in the air. Dierdre grabs Caitlin's hands. "Do you feel it, too? This is it; this is the magic of their pact! But something... No... It's something else... Something more?" The priestess scrunches her face and taps her chin. "Were we wrong?"

The only answer Caitlin can give is the shock written on her face.

Dierdre takes a deep breath in. "We do not have time for this. We need to get out." She wretches Maeve away from the dead duke's side, dragging them out of the room without another look back.

"Just a little further ahead," Carys says. "We are almost there."

"We have friends waiting outside. We will get you out of here." Carys leaps to the small door reserved for the prison staff. Their friends are indeed awaiting on the other side of it. But they are being chained up by guards.

The leader of the King's Shield sneers at Caitlin, a predator who has caught his prey. "Looks like I caught more than I expected."

The guards take great pains to inflict as much harm upon them as possible as they are dragged back into the dungeon and shoved into a cell together. Their clothes are torn from them, their arms are bruised, and their feet are scraped raw. They do not even spare Lady Dontaue, being just as vicious with the royal duke.

After countless hours, it is Maeve's voice that breaks the silence. "I cannot believe he has been alive this whole time."

Caitlin's gaze shifts towards the duke before returning to fixate on the speck of rust on the bars before her.

"How much do you know?" Dierdre attempts to cross her arms in front of her, but the chains and shackles do not allow it, so she settles for glaring.

Unfazed by the priestess's hostility, the duke says, "Far more than I probably should, but do not think I reveled in it. I assume they were using Tómas as a sacrifice when Tarmon or Cian were not well enough to provide their blood." She tests the shackles one more time, a ritual she has taken to performing repeatedly.

Dierdre huffs.

"His name was Svilen Gurov. A second cousin to the Tsvetokrasan czar, but still royal…" She repeats her attempts at removing the shackles. "My father did not approve, and neither did Tarmon and Allil. But Tómas did. Tómas knew I loved him."

"I cannot see what this has to do with anything."

Caitlin grabs a fistful of hay and, one by one, breaks the pieces in half.

"We discovered that the Scáth had been hired to assassinate him."

"Found out? I do not think so," the priestess says, voice full of venom. "They do not make mistakes."

Lady Dontaue shrugs. "I told Tómas, and he got me an audience with Father Nael, who told me about the Blodheimr Hjart. He claimed that, in exchange for a little of my blood, he and his order could save Svilen. I made the agreement with them."

"I do not believe that. Once you are marked, you are marked. The Scáth do not make those mistakes."

"I am telling you what I know." The edge in the duke's voice sharpens. "A few weeks later, his bodyguard suspected poison might be in his wine. He had someone taste it first. They did not die, but when it was tested, they found it was full of poison."

"How convenient."

"Let me finish. It had somehow been neutralized, though. The Blodheimr Hjart told me that they had been the ones to neutralize the poison with their magic."

"Again. Convenient." Dierdre rolls her eyes.

Caitlin struggles to follow the conversation, both wanting to know more and wanting to forget all that she already knows. She breaks another piece of straw.

"Unfortunately, a few weeks later, he fell off his horse. It feared something, and it trampled him. His death was covered up and never mentioned. And then, Tómas suddenly died, too. They say it was peaceful and in his sleep. But he was still so young."

"Utterly, utterly, astoundingly, conveniently coincidental." The priestess emphasizes each word by banging a shackle on the stone wall.

"Everything I have done since then has been an attempt to amass enough fortune, position, and power to buy myself out of the pact that I made with the Blodheimr Hjart."

"You did figure it out in the end? Right? You figured out that it was the Blodheimr Hjart that ordered that hit in the first place? And let you know on purpose?"

"Dierdre!" Carys says.

Caitlin wants to remind Dierdre about her own recent revelation. But doesn't.

There is no way out of this. Maeve has been fooling herself by thinking there is any way out of this spiderweb. Caitlin tosses a handful of hay against the wall.

"Does it matter? Every month, they come to my rooms. They take little but collect it in this dainty silver chalice, and I want to vomit when they leave."

"There is not enough money or power in all of Ahnlisen to break the pact you made," Caitlin says.

The bars to the cell rattle as a guard slides the key into the lock. Father Ljósa smiles. "Rise and shine, ladies. Don't want to be late for your execution. Hope you're not afraid of fire."

He sneers and waves them forward.

"All of us?" Caitlin asks. She does not care if she hangs, burns, or loses her head. But she cannot fathom that the priests are willing to lose a source of *Ástfriður* or Fola blood.

"Not necessarily. The king is willing to show some of you mercy. I suggest you take it."

It is late afternoon, but it is chilly even though it is the height of summer. The guards and executioners make no attempt at kindness as they bind her to the stake. The lawn is full of gallows and people standing on them; a swift and merciless massacre. Nearly all of her friends bound and waiting for the floor to vanish beneath them. A taciturn court occupies the dais. The gleeful smiles of Lady Clare, Sir Liam, and Sir Connor. The quiet disdain of Lord Hern and the ravenous hunger of Lord Caibre. At the center of it all is Cian, cycling between excitement, rage, and another emotion that Caitlin cannot identify. He is gaunt, his hair has lost its sheen, and his eyes are cloudy. Back straight and head high, Arlina sits next to him; a dainty tiara sits on her head. Hovering behind his throne is Father Nael. The princesses are at the far edge of the dais. Flanked on all sides by two of the King's Shield. Unwilling guests.

There does not need to be a royal proclamation; it is plain to all of the world who the next queen shall be. Unexpectedly, a nursemaid stands directly behind her, holding a swaddled infant. That child... It couldn't be hers... Everyone told her the infant had died... Then who...

The executioner makes one more loop around her waist; the people gathered in the courtyard scream her name, shouting that they love her, that she is the true queen, and that Arlina is a whore. Enraged, Cian shouts for silence. No one heeds him.

One minute. That was all it took. A cry for a physician when she was surely dying. It was not the nights with Arlina that betrayed her; it was not her love for Arlina, but her love for Diarmuid. The first person she befriended in this city, the first person who tried to make her see that she was strong enough to make a choice, that she could live and be happy despite her pain and loss. She and Arlina had plotted to survive at court, and Diarmuid fought for them to be free of it—a handful of words, and now a countless number of people sentenced to die beside her.

"There was a sickness in this land," the king says as he stands. "A conspiracy against me, against my house, against the entire kingdom. A sickness led by witches, abetted by foreign nations, and spearheaded by the woman I thought was my true love." His voice cracks and Caitlin wonders how much of it is an act and how much of it is genuine. Beside him, Arlina lets her tears flow freely. Caitlin wants to wipe them away, wants to tell Arlina that everything will be fine. Hold Arlina close, whisper the words that she has longed to say for so long, but she knows they are words that do not need to be said.

"But her duplicity will not go unpunished. Her duplicity broke my heart. And yet, I still want to believe. I want to believe that she is the kind, warm, dedicated, and steadfast woman that I fell in love with. And so, I offer her one last chance."

Silence descends on the courtyard.

"It is my belief, and the belief of many of the priests in the Order of Culain, that the devotees to Andraste are not the pious and virtuous adherents that they have led us to believe they are. Rather, they have sought to ensorcelled and enchant the people of this realm and hex to those who have stood in their way."

The crowd whispers again, hushed words and soft gasps.

"Many people have unknowingly fallen into these witches' clutches, my poor sister included. But because of the goodness and kindness of Culain, she has been saved and returned to my side." Cian turns away from the crowd, staring at his sister solemnly. Arlina dabs at her eyes with the hem of her sleeve. Standing next to her, offering a handkerchief, is Lady Emeire. The horror on her face is barely masked; her hand keeps clutching at her chest, and she is gasping as if she cannot get enough air.

Cian turns back to the crowd. "Some part of me yet hopes that the same is true for my Caitlin."

Caitlin. Not Mistress Peddigree. Not Lady Caitlin, not Duchess of Laocre, not Queen Gráinne of Fayn. Just Caitlin.

"Some part of me hopes that she too was taken in by these witches, that they cast some spell over her that turned her against me, and she can still be saved and return to the light. I do not want to believe that the hate in her heart has always been there."

She shifts her weight; she had been hoping that she would be dead by now and past her pain. She wishes he would hurry with his speech.

"I offer her this chance, the opportunity to let the priests of Culain cleanse her of the dark forces which stole her from me, free her from their enchantment, and she might live for the rest of her life safe at a Temple of Culain, in sanctuary."

There it is. That is why Father Ljósa is willing to put her on the pyre. But she has chosen to die. He thinks he has a queen in check, but Caitlin long ago stopped playing the game. Sanctuary in a Temple of Culain. Safe? What kind of sanctuary bleeds and beats its residents?

"Sweet Caitlin, it is not too late. Cast off this curse, rejoin the light. Renounce this heretical rebellion. Condemn the witches you plotted with. Denounce your Garcelonian conspirators." *Garcelonian conspirators? He should not be so thin, not with how many lies he is being fed and eating.*

He looks directly at her, his lower lip quivering, hands shaking, and eyes welling with tears.

A lone voice casts a song to the wind. The song catches, quicker than fire, and soon everybody on the gallows is singing it; the melody is clear, and the lyrics strong.

Caitlin stares past the king to Father Nael, lips set in a hard line, a challenge. Defiance. And for the first time since she has resigned herself to death, she wants to live. She wants to live to knock that confidence off of his face.

No matter what she says to Cian now, she will be burned to death here or bled to death in the dungeons. She will not be rescued; the only freedom that awaits her is death. She draws a deep breath. Smiles one last time at Arlina, searches the gallows until she finds Diarmuid, and cries, "From my ashes may the phoenix of the rebellion rise!"

The cacophony that erupts in the courtyard is equal parts chaos and a carefully orchestrated dance. The executioner approaches her. She presses her back against the stake and looks at the sky as the first tendrils of evening snake above the tree line.

Father Nael lunges to the front of the dais, waving his hand. *They miscalculated.*

The executioner leans close to her face; she steels herself for whatever insults he is about to speak. She almost collapses when the ropes fall away. "Run. Run and do not look back." A silver lily is pinned to the cuff of his glove.

The whole courtyard is alive with energy. The gallows are empty, Red Front members leaping from the platforms and climbing the dais. Underneath the gallows, a few are reaching for concealed weapons, while others in the crowd are being supplied with swords.

"Come," Dierdre says, yanking Caitlin off the platform. "We need to break the pact. Follow me." Caitlin is dragged back into the dungeon, still too shocked to comprehend what has happened.

"Wait! Caitlin!"

Caitlin wrenches her hand from Dierdre and whips around to see Diarmuid. "We have to get you out of here."

Dierdre glares at her, motioning her to follow.

"I have something I need to do first," Caitlin shouts.

"It's your choice, but take this," he says, handing her the dagger. "Meet us at the Eastern gate. I will ensure we get Tala and Arlina, too. We can only wait so long, though."

She nods and then follows Dierdre back into the prison. Distantly, she swears she hears Cian scream her name over the din, shouting for her to be free.

TWENTY-FOUR

Partings and Promises

Half of the guards are unlocking the cells to let prisoners out, and the other half have been beaten unconscious and tossed aside. Clergy run amok, clergy of every order: Muriel, Andraste, Shea, Maddyn, Yseult, Fianna, Bardon, Corrann, Dana, Iden, Aife... Cian—or the Blodheimr Hjart— does not just want to wipe out the Order of Andraste; he wants to scrub Fayn of all other gods. These acolytes and priests wrap bandages for injured prisoners and help others walk. Dierdre and Caitlin run against the tide of fleeing prisoners, dashing to the sacrificial chamber.

Unceremoniously, Dierdre shoves aside the rack, paying no heed to the corpse on top of it. "The dagger," she says, joining Caitlin again on the outskirts of the room. "Slice open your palms and place them at the center of the sigil carved in the floor. I will do the same."

The dagger is plain, bearing no symbols of any religious order or noble house. "Why?"

"You might be mortal; you are also *Ástfriður*. You were taken in as one of them when you married Brenna. Born mortal but belonging to them. And I was born to them but belong to the mortals. It is *Ástfriður* blood that this needs. Combined, yours and mine should be enough."

"I don't understand," Caitlin says, scrutinizing the blade.

"You don't have to understand; you just need to do it. This will break the link between the land and the Fola line. If you want your rebellion to win, do it. Now!" Dierdre pulls out her blade and slices open both of her palms. "After we do this, we will get your baby back, and you both can stay with us."

Caitlin takes a step away from Dierdre. "No. The Red Front has a place for me. And for the infant."

"We saved you. We got you out. You must pay your part of the bargain."

Caitlin glares at the priestess.

"Fine, Arlina, too."

The infant wanted only as a pawn. Even as the monarchy is falling around them, all this priestess can think of is ensuring they will be the power behind the curtain in whatever regime rises from these ashes. And the infant girl was to be one of the cards in the deck they hoped to stack. "I never promised you that infant."

The priestess glares at Caitlin and shoves her hands into the center of the sigil. "No matter what your plans are, or ours, if you want the

Cian gone, if you want his family gone, cut your palms and put them here."

That infant. A Fola scion. If it isn't the Araelta coming after them, it will be the Blodheimr Hjart. And if it is neither of them, it will be whatever nobles hope to find a lost heir and put them on a throne. Where in all of Ahnlisen could they go that they would not be found? Diar had promised to get them away, but—

"Now!"

Caitlin steadies herself, and slowly slices open each palm. She closes her eyes, and before she can lose the nerve, she slams her hands to the ground.

The ground shifts, and then it shakes; the taste of copper and iron fills the air. Her blood sings in some farce along with the cries of the earth. *Magic. Ástfriður* magic. A stone breaks loose from the wall, and then another. As the prison lurches, the sound of cracking walls and stone fills the air.

"How long will this take? The dungeons will collapse around us if we stay too much longer." Caitlin says, glancing at the door.

"Another second! Hold on!"

A flash of light—a current of power assaults her.

"It is broken," Deirdre says, panting. "We did it. Now anyone with the strength to try can sit upon that throne."

The earth trembles again. Thunder roars outside, so violent that it shakes the ground. Caitlin stands up and then tumbles back to her knees as the land heaves again.

"Wait... this..." Dierdre spins around on her toes, grinning. "I think this is it! We can break one of the Arkae right now. That must be why they chose here... this is what they were really doing... So clever, how did we not realize... Caitlin, we can break one of the seals on magic!"

"No, *you* can do that. We have freed Fayn from the Fola dynasty. I am getting out now."

But Deirdre grabs her hands and slams her palms back on the ground, holding them in place while she chants in that language that Caitlin has heard too often and knows nothing about.

Tremors shake the dungeon again as the earth convulses in either protest or celebration. The floor cracks and splits in two, throwing Caitlin and Dierdre to opposite sides of the room.

Deirdre raises her bloody hands above her head. "It is broken! How long have we waited... one of the seals is finally broken! The first Arkae is shattered!" She laughs a bitter and mad laugh.

The floor continues to rattle, the gulf between the two sides of the room growing larger.

"Come on," Caitlin says, snapping Dierdre out of her trance-like laugh. "If you wait too much longer, you won't be able to jump."

Too late, the priestess realizes she is trapped. "Wait, no, help me. The table! I can walk across! Please!"

Deirdre's words replay in her head, her desire for Caitlin, the infant, and Arlina to stay with them, to live with the Araelta. Another Fola to be trapped in a spiderweb. "I am sorry, but our goals are no longer aligned." She scrambles to her feet and dashes out of the collapsing prison.

The door is just ahead of her, still propped open, the ceiling collapsing. She dodges and weaves her way around the rubble, the air cloudy with dust and smelling of blood and earth. She does not look behind her to see if Dierdre is following. The priestess may have helped her, but Caitlin has no intention of repaying that debt, especially not at the cost that Dierdre claims she owes.

She keeps running barefoot across the cold, dew-covered grass. Her lungs sting, and the air is now heavy with smoke and screams. But she keeps running. The Eastern gate. Diarmuid is waiting for her. Ignoring the burn in her calves, the ache of her legs, stiff from months in a dungeon, she keeps running. Ignoring the weakness caused by months of not eating, of wasting away to nothing, she keeps running, ignoring the sounds of fighting in the distance.

"Caitlin!"

The Eastern gate. Almost there.

"Caitlin!"

Arlina!

"Cait, we're waiting for you!"

Diarmuid.

The gate.

Diarmuid is waiting on the other side, and she lunges into his arms. "I thought I never see you again! I'm so sorry, I'm so sorry I got caught. It's all my fault. All of this is my fault."

"We'll talk about this later. Come with us." She takes his hand, and they run off. Diarmuid. Arlina. Kegan. A cadre of Calla archers are scaling the brick wall and landing in the woods past the palace grounds. "Sharidan is waiting for us with horses. We're almost there."

He drags her forward, and she wants to scream at him to let her have just a moment to catch her breath. She doesn't, she can't.

"Here," he finally says, handing her a flask.

Caitlin doubles over gasping, only now noticing that Arlina's dress is covered in blood. "What happened?"

"Cian… He killed Father Nael and then Father Ljósa. He was vicious, stabbing over and over… He kept screaming that they had stolen everything from him."

"And where is he now?"

"I let him finish getting his revenge, and then I got mine." Arlina hikes up her skirt, exposing a dagger sheathed to her leg.

"You killed the king?" Sharidan says, materializing out of the shadows, tail twitching.

Arlina nods. "One strike."

"Where did you learn to do that?"

"I studied at a Temple of Aife."

"So, it's true then. Huh."

"Are you okay, though?" Caitlin asks her. They take a step toward each other.

"Absolutely. But what about you? Are you well?"

"I am now."

Diarmuid clears his throat.

Neither of the women acknowledges him. Arlina reaches into her pocket and pulls out the lily pendant and the bracelet Brenna gave Caitlin. "I hope you do not mind. I stole them." She gently places them in Caitlin's outstretched hands.

They embrace, firm, wild, without reservation or hesitation. Caitlin whispers to Arlina, "I wanted to die."

"I know."

"As touching as this is," Sharidan says, clearing xir throat, "we need to get moving. Take these horses. Diarmuid knows where to go to. The archers will cover your retreat."

"Right," Diarmuid says. "Let's get going." He mounts a horse, one that Caitlin immediately recognizes as belonging to Lady Clare. Caitlin climbs on the one next to him, shivering as night descends around them.

"Thank you," Sharidan says. "When things settle, you can come back and help us. Be a face for the new government."

"No. I am not coming back."

"Ah. Well. I understand. We asked a lot of you, Caitlin. Thank you."

"You're welcome. Just ask nothing more of me now."

The Calla lets out a noise that is a mixture of a sob and a laugh. "I am sorry, I must ask one more thing of you. As a favor, personally." Sharidan unslings the large pouch around xir waist. "It's Valen's.

They made sure that Brenna's *ahnhörn* made it home. Can you make sure that Valen's does, too?"

Caitlin grabs the bag, but before she can say anything more to Sharidan, the Red Front leader disappears into the woods so thoroughly that Caitlin wonders if the Calla also have their own form of magic. Diarmuid hands her a cloak and then kicks his horse forward. Wordlessly, Caitlin follows Arlina. She does not turn around when she hears explosions behind her.

They ride throughout the night, followed by palace sentries, royal guards, and the King's Shield. Calla archers, with their sharp eyesight and dexterity, loop back around to pick off their pursuers. Sometimes, all of them return. But as the night creeps on, fewer and fewer report back.

There are so many questions that Caitlin wants to ask, so many things she needs to say, and so many things she needs to hear. She clutches the cloak tightly around her, fighting off the chill as dusk turns to midnight.

Diarmuid stays at the head of the procession, every five minutes taking a second to glance back at Caitlin, face hard, jaw set, expression full of fear and love.

"We need help," an archer says, approaching Diarmuid.

He pulls a sword from the sheath and, saying nothing, turns his horse around and gallops behind them. The archer nods to Kegan, who then takes the lead.

She does not know how late in the night it is nor how far they have traveled. And no clue how much further they have to go. But she can feel the magic still, clinging to her skin, can still taste it in her mouth, and can still hear it in her head. Humming, alternating between discordant and harmonious, equal parts copper and iron, a miasma of sensation and weight. She can feel it dragging her to the soil; she can feel it lifting her to the stars. Calling to her in a voice that is both gentle and forceful. Both loving and angry. Sometimes, it speaks with Brenna's voice, and sometimes, with a voice she does not know but feels ancient and familiar, dancing on the edge of memory. She can feel tendrils of magic that do not belong to the *Ástfriður*; she can touch it but not hold it. It is something she has never felt before. It is something she knows that Fayn has not felt in over a thousand years.

Diarmuid returns to them, blood across his shirt and a broken arrow in his hand.

"You are..." she says, reaching for him.

"I am fine. We must keep going." He kicks his horse into a gallop, and the rest of the party does the same. Dawn is cresting over the sea. They break out of the forest and into a field. In the distance, a tiny village. She races towards it, Diarmuid telling her to run, run, go! Sitting in port: a fishing boat with her fathers! Pa, holding a tiny infant, waves her forward, calling her name. She kicks her horse, hoofbeats loud on the cobblestone as she pulls on the reins to stop just at the edge of the gangplank.

Diarmuid helps her off the horse and clutches her tightly against his chest. "I love you, Cait. I always have, and I always will. I love you in whatever capacity you want to accept that love."

"Why does it sound like you are saying goodbye?"

"Somebody has to stay and cover your retreat," he says, motioning to the tree line. The cadre of Calla jump off their horses and now spar with a wave of the King's Shield pouring out of the forest. "Somebody has to stay behind and make sure you leave port safely, and there is no one left to report your potential whereabouts."

"But you're injured. Come with us."

He shakes his head and tucks a stray hair behind her ear. "They will take you to safety. No one will find you."

"No... You'll die..."

"I have to save you," he says.

"You've saved more than enough people! Please, come with us." She clings to him, her fingers digging into his back.

"There cannot be any witnesses. I need to stay here and make sure of that."

"No, please. You've given so much for the cause; you do not need to give your life for it, too."

"There are some causes, and some people, that are worth dying for. The Red Front is that cause, and you are that person."

"No, please."

"I promised Sharidan a long time ago that I would repay the debt. I have been trying to do so, but what I have done so far is still not enough. But maybe this will be."

"No!" There have been too many losses in her life. *No!* She looks between him and the sentries that inexorably make their way closer. "No!" Kegan grabs her hand and yanks her away, dragging her up the gangplank and into her father's waiting arms. Diarmuid unties the ship, kicks the plank into the water, and shoves the boat away from the dock. He squares his shoulders, sets his jaw, and turns to face what is most assuredly his death.

TWENTY-FIVE

Hope and Home

Her fathers drag her down below deck, even while she screams, calling out for Diarmuid repeatedly. "No, I need to go back! We can't just leave him there!"

"Dear, you are injured. Let us help you," Pa says, an edge in his voice that Caitlin has never heard before.

She relents and allows them to lead her to a bed. "I have some bandages and alcohol right here," Pa says.

"And I'll be back with some food." Da's lips are a tight line, and the wrinkles on his forehead are new. But Caitlin slips into sleep before she can ask either of them the questions she has.

When she wakes up again, Pa is in the corner rocking the infant. "Da will be right back with some food for all of us."

"I thought I would never see you again," Caitlin says, dizziness overtaking her as she tries to sit up. "Is that…"

"My granddaughter?" Pa says. "Yes. She is your child."

Her child. The one she does not remember giving birth to, the one she has never met, the one she only wanted because it would provide her with a measure of safety. "Everyone was so sure I would have a boy."

"Well, everyone was wrong. Do you want to see her? I think she has my eyes, but *someone* keeps telling me I'm wrong." Pa hands the infant to Caitlin just as Da walks in with a large tray of dried meat and cheese.

"No, no, put your hand here. Yes. The other one goes there. Excellent. Look at that. Do you agree that she has my eyes?"

No, Caitlin thinks. The eyes of the child are Fola: ice blue, pale, and harsh. There is no way that this infant is anyone but Cian's. But she cannot bring herself to break her father's heart, and so she smiles and nods.

"What is her name? I thought someone said it, but I do not recall."

"Cian named her Tala. Tala Branwen of House Fola. But I believe it should be you who names her."

Her stomach churns as she notices the wisps of hair on her daughter's head are not the dark blond of Da nor the deep brown of Pa, nor even her own mousy blond. The girl has Fola hair, too. They could change her name, but there is no disguising who she is. "Aoibheall."

"Beautiful," Da says.

"What happened to you? Where were you?"

"In the dungeon in Taern's Keep," Da says. "But those revolutionary friends of yours had some guards on their side and released us as soon as they got some signal. Only a few days ago. We've been on this boat ever since, waiting for you. Someone rode ahead of you with the Aoibheall."

"That's some commotion you ended up causing. We just thought those friends were charitable folks. Did you know what they were planning? Did you know this was going to happen?"

"Did you know," Caitlin says, unsettled by the accusatory tone in Da's voice, "the conditions that the factory workers endure? When you purchased garments in cotton from factories, did you know the circumstances within them?"

"Caitlin, what do you mean?" Pa says.

"Take Liam's factories, for example. Did you know that he forced the workers to work 15-, 16-, 17-hour days? Without a break? Did you know? And if you did, why are you not celebrating that downfall?"

"Why does it matter?"

"It matters. If you knew and continued to buy and trade with these factory owners, do you consider yourselves complicit in that abuse?"

"What is this about?"

"If you knew that the royalty, the businessmen, the nobility, saw people as expendable, as exploitable, would you have wanted to be in the circle? If you knew that, would you have tried to court them? Would you have sent me to the viper pit?"

"Caitlin, you chose. We gave you the choice. You wanted to be in the circle just as much as we did." Pa says.

She does not want to admit that they were right. She does not want to admit that she had been given a choice. She does not want to admit that of all the people who used her as a pawn; she had allowed herself to be one.

"And it does not matter now what we knew and when. We are not going back."

"Now that we have discussed that, we wanted to let you know that our final destination is the Veil."

Brenna. She can take Brenna home.

"Supposedly, that was always the destination that your revolutionary friends were hoping to smuggle you to after if things got dicey. I believe Sharidan said that Valen had been setting it up beforehand. We've been assured that you, your daughter, and ourselves are welcome there. Anyone who you consider family," Da says.

"Is there somebody else you want to add to our family?" Pa says.

Caitlin is silent. She knows who she wants to mention, who she wants to ask...

"Well, if it's all the same to you," Pa says, "I like that Arlina lady. She's got spirit."

"Caitlin? May come in?" There are no doors below the deck where the refugees stay, just well-worn cloth nailed between beams.

"Please," Caitlin says as she finishes bandaging her hands again. While all of her other wounds heal quickly, those she inflicted on herself refuse to.

"I don't want to make assumptions, and I know that we are going—" Arlina leans against the empty door frame, wringing her hands.

"Will you stay with me?" She blurts out, heart pounding. "Live with me, please, on the Isles."

"Yes, of course. There's nowhere I would rather be than by your side."

"I am so broken. I want you with me, but I don't know if I would be—"

Arlina rushes to the bed and sits down beside Caitlin. "And you think I am not? We can heal together."

"I feel like I am just so damaged. I can't even look at the infant without thinking of *him*. I do not know how to be a mother to her."

"It is okay, I can be mother enough for her until you are ready. I have been trying my best since she was born."

"I am sure you have been wonderful. I also want to say that I do not regret sneaking into your father's office and stealing his papers, but I regret not telling you. Can you forgive me?"

"There is nothing to forgive," Arlina says, pulling Caitlin close and stroking her back.

"It isn't fair. Not to you, not to the Aoibheall."

"None of this is fair, but we can make the best of it. Together."

"Together."

Summer turns into fall, and they are still at sea. They might be *Ástfriður* traders, but they are still traders, and they will not let something silly like escaped royalty prevent them from making their sales.

Each stop they make, they learn more about what is happening in Fayn. The monarchy has fallen, the rebels have made a provisional government, and the nobles are all fleeing or being executed.

The taverns are full of songs about the two queens riding off to freedom in the middle of the night. Songs about the king-slayer and her spy. This makes Arlina chuckle. "I think my title is a little better than yours." She winks.

When they make port at Linea, for even the *Ástfriður* need wine, they learn that Ambassador Cariveau petitioned for the Aelena Fola, former Duchess of Clare, to be allowed to leave the Fayn and live in Garcelon. She had secretly married Queen Joanna's half-sibling. A half-sibling the ib-Almerlus family had been hiding in plain sight: Ambassador Eloi Cariveau. Sharidan could do nothing but acquiesce. Not without protest, the former duchess relinquished all titles for herself and her future children, and Sharidan gave assurances that Fayn forces would withdraw from Garcelon.

When they stop on the shores of Qaewi, at the glittering golden city of Alsha Dhabu, they learn that Daya and Eleanor escaped and are now living with Daya's mother, the dowager Sultana. It is also rumored that Lady Muiris escaped to Qaewi, too, with some lady she fancied, but that cannot be confirmed or denied.

When they make port Erzurumei in the Esiri region of Sua, they learn that Lairde Elwee and Lady Shennen are now living with a distant—and royal—family member of Lady Shennen.

When they land at Haut Ven in Janeuq, they learn that Lady Ronai and Lady Riqueti have settled in the grand city, and Lady Ronai is studying medicine. Lady Ronai renounced her Fayn citizenship, and as the wife of a foreign diplomat, Sharidan's provisional government could not detain her.

They circle the continent, skirting the northern border of Tsvetokrasa, making several stops at smaller trading posts. They learn that Maeve Fola has been pardoned for her part in saving Caitlin, so long as she renounces her titles and swears never to interfere with the democratic government. However, Liam and Connor Gilroy-Downing, Nait Loughlin, Brennin Rorick, and Allil Fola were all executed. No one knows where Doireann or Elwen escaped to.

Finn and Ruben Gallagher died of their mysterious illness on the day of the would-be executions, and Lady Emeire died just as mysteriously that night. No physician has been able to determine what killed the three Gallaghers. The only remaining member of the family, Caragh returned to the Temple of Shea and renounced all titles and nobility.

The Admiral and Captain Halloran surrendered themselves to the provisional government, stating that their loyalty is to Fayn, no matter who governs it.

Sister Kiandre spends much time with the provisional government, offering help and assistance at every opportunity. But Deirdre is missing and presumed dead.

"That is a little concerning," Caitlin says to Kegan as they discuss the news of Kiandre and Dierdre. "What if she is still plotting something? What if Dierdre isn't dead?"

"No, Sharidan is smarter than that. Xie can see right through Kiandre."

"I hope so… But so much bloodshed," Caitlin says.

"They are creating a democracy. There cannot be any nobles left to rebuild a monarchy."

"Yes, but every time I hear about someone else being executed…"

"The people being put to death were happy to let the people starve."

Caitlin sighs, wringing her hands. "I know, but the cost of a beautiful tomorrow should not be such a sorrowful today."

"Well, this is it." Kegan balances on their toes, straining to see over the edge of the railing as they approach the islands.

"Home. My new home." Caitlin smiles, enjoying the icy wind tangling her hair and relishing the sight of the verdant green trees on the shore of the Veil. *Brenna.*

"You plan to stay forever?"

"Of course. But what about you? Are you going back to Fayn?"

"For a little bit. But then I believe I'm being sent to Sua. We have allies there that want their own revolution."

"That sounds like fun."

"I think it will be, but I wish Aine were still here. We had talked so many times about wanting to go there. And I get to go, but she doesn't."

"It is not your fault," Caitlin says, brushing a hand down Kegan's back.

Kegan turns back around, facing the horizon. "She let herself get caught so that I could escape. She's never been strong. She was prone to fainting spells, weakness, headaches, and the like. She knew she could not run fast enough to get away. I was trying to carry her, but she... she covered my escape."

Diarmuid, standing tall in the early morning light.

"It's not your fault, Kegan."

"But..."

"She made a choice; it was her choice."

"I know, I know. That does not stop the pain."

"Do you think that Diar...survived?"

"I don't know."

"I love, loved him, and I was a terrible friend to him."

"You were not. Please do not think you were. He made a choice. It was his choice to make. It isn't a reflection on you."

"No fair! You can't just say what I just said. But I loved him."

"I know... And I loved Aine. But our friends made their own choices. Do you think I was a terrible friend to her?"

"No... I feel so guilty, running away when there is still fighting to be done."

"You don't have to keep fighting for Diar's sake; this is what he wanted for you; take it."

"Kegan, I love you, too. You know that? I'll miss you. You're like family now."

The anchor is tossed as the ship makes port, and the captain calls for the passengers to disembark.

"Don't get sentimental on me. I don't like it. I'm gonna go see if I can find something to eat."

Arlina meets her at the gangplank. "Together?"

"Together." Caitlin smiles. For the rest of her life, she will have a home with her family.

"Welcome, children of Fayn," says an *Ástfriður* wearing a gold robe, head adorned by a golden *ahnhörn,* standing at the front of the crowd. "I am Inge, the *Sång* of the Lake of the Mirror. Which of you was wed to Brenna of Mountain-at-Dawn?"

Caitlin steps forward, and before she can speak, the *Sång* embraces her. "Thank you, thank you for bringing xir home."

The elder touches the bracelet on Caitlin's wrist, then runs their finger along the mostly healed cuts on Caitlin's palms, looks deeply into Caitlin's eyes, and says, wide-eyed and pale, "You have no idea what you have done."

"I saved my family." Caitlin looks at Arlina, at her fathers, and the infant—her child. Aoibheall.

"Oh, if only it were just that. You have started something great and terrifying by breaking an Arkae."

Caitlin pulls herself away from the elder. She's had enough of prophecies, enough of superstition. All she wants right now is to hold Arlina.

"I did what was needed to save my family. Do not worry; I do not intend to insert myself into any political affairs again."

The elder's face softens. "Of course, child. You have been through enough. But I shall hold you to that promise."

"Please do," Caitlin says, glancing at Arlina. "I never want to leave my home again."

Also By Dax Murray

The Magic Surrendered
A Lake of Feathers and Moonbeams
Birthing Orion

SCIONS AND SHADOWS:

Shades and Silver
Stars and Soil
Coming Soon:
Smoke and Steel

About Dax

Dax writes positive queer fantasy and science fiction, worlds where being LGBTQIA is normal, accepted, and celebrated. They enjoy creating new magic systems, blending science and magic, and building kingdoms just so she can tear them down. When not writing bisexual witches, Dax can be found playing music or writing code, exploring Eorzea, petting cats, or ranting on Mastodon. Dax has a way too intelligent a service dog and a very persistent cat that, together, cause way too much trouble. Dax calls the DC metro area home. You can read more about Dax at https://www.daxmurray.com/ and find out about their editing services at https://www.enchantedediting.com. They also occasionally post new short stories at https://www.daxaeterna.ink/

If you enjoyed this novel, you can find more information about the world of Ahnlisen, including a treasure trove of bonus materials, short stories, character bios, maps, and more at stars.daxmurray.com.

Sign up for Dax's newsletter to get access to exclusive bonus content, behind-the-scenes updates, and sneak peeks at WIPs! Dax frequently puts out calls for subscribers to join the ARC team and get free copies of the newest releases before they hit shelves, so sign up today!

newsletter.daxmurray.com

You can purchase other books directly from Dax at their store, which also has planner pages and excel templates designed for authors who need help with self-editing.

https://store.daxmurray.com

Kraken Reads

At The Kraken Collective, we know how frustrating it can be to reach the end of a book and want more. Within the following pages, you will find books with a similar feel to help you scratch that reading itch and why we're recommending them. We hope our suggestions will help you find your next favorite read!

The Kraken Collective is an alliance of indie authors of LGBTQI-AP+ speculative fiction, committed to building a publishing space that is inclusive, positive, and brings fascinating stories to readers. Looking for your next great read? Check out these other sci-fi and dystopian titles from Kraken Collective authors!

Kraken Reads: City of Strife

Claudie Arseneault

If you're looking for more political back and forth underpinned by deeply personal stories, check out *City of Strife* from Claudie Arseneault! City of Strife is a mosaical, epic novel with a large and majorly queer cast, a web of political intrigue and personal narratives, and a heart of gold. In it, an elven noble's attempt to stop imperialist wizards from taking over his city will have repercussions on its inhabitants, from its richest towers to the homeless shelter at its bottom. Fans of elves, magic, and crisscrossing storylines will find everything they want within this story.

Kraken Reads: A Promise Broken

S.L. Dove Cooper

If you're looking for more political back and forth as well as aromantic and asexual representation, but underpinned by deeply personal stories, check out *A Promise Broken*, by Dove Cooper. When four-year-old Eiryn tries to call rain at her mother's funeral, others worry she might have upset the balance of the world. As her new guardian, her uncle Arèn must learn the ropes of parenting while trying to protect her from harm. Yet all Eiryn wants is to make everyone happy even as grief and fear tear at them. A Promise Broken is a beautiful tale of kindness and grief that will slip into your heart quietly and stay with you.

Acknowledgements

I started working on this novel almost as soon as I finished "A Lake of Feathers and Moonbeams," and yet I released two books between now and then (about 5.5 years....) This has been a sort of "Emotional Support WIP." I wrote most of part 1 while sitting in a hospital as my best friend got chemotherapy. I wrote most of part 2 while my own life was completely upended, and I did not even have an address. I wrote most of part 3 while in the hospital for a serious health issue and most of part 4 while recovering from said ailment.

There are people who were in my life when I began writing this that—some fortunately, some unfortunately—no longer are, and people who entered my life after I started writing this and I hope to keep them in my life while I write the next book. Suffice it to say, I do not know how to approach thanking everyone who helped shape this book in some way, directly or in—.

Thank you to Sarah Waite for the beautiful cover. Thank you, Etheric Tales, for the chapter and scene break art. Thank you, Campfire staff, for building Campfire and for dealing with all my weird bug reports, especially the intercalary days issue. Correct calculation of leap year is important! Thank you to Vane Issoton for the beautiful character portraits.

Coming Soon: Smoke and Steel

Please enjoy this excerpt from the first chapter of the next book, SMOKE & STEEL.

If you want more sneak peeks, please sign up for Dax's newsletter at newsletter.daxmurray.com

Smoke and Steel is the story of the lost princess of Sua who must claw her way back to her throne or else the revolutionaries who slaughtered her family will bring about the end of the world.

Mar'sahre'dan'i are not born; they are chosen. That is what her mother—Sumalika mat Qa'taru, Sarhe'Danu of Sua—had told her. Chosen based on strength, wisdom, cunning, and desire. Chosen for their ability to be ruthless, unforgiving, and unfeeling. In the six years since the violent insurrection at the hands of the Amyrdine Bara,

Saritrah has not forgotten those words. She turns them over as if they were stones in her mind as General Arishaki moves the pebbles on the parchment, movements deliberate, slow, but coldly calculated. As long as everyone follows his orders, tomorrow, they will take back Antalyza from the Amyrdine Bara.

If she can take back Antalyza, she can take back all of Sua. The cool night wind pricks at her skin, but the glow of the twin moons sets her eyes on fire. The lost princess; six years in exile, six years of biding her time. Six years of sharpening her claws and honing her fangs. Tomorrow will not be her first skirmish, but it will be the most significant. The sarhe of Antalyza was loyal through and through to her family, the perfect vassal, the perfect servant of the royal family. Now, she will free him from the prisons the insurrectionists have left him to rot in, proving to the world that she will be a just ruler, righting the wrongs of the world swiftly and decisively.

Distantly, a herd of camels sings into the winds of the desert. "Are the Re'u coming through?" Puzur asks. Young, ambitious, but hopelessly clueless. Sari twirls a strand of hair around her finger, willing to let him embarrass himself.

"That doesn't sound like them; that's something else," Harharu replies.

"Aye," General Arishaki says, straightening his back and scanning the horizon. His harsh voice is barely a whisper, but it has the commanding tone required for a leader. "I don't like the sound of it."

"No, it has to be some merchants or traders. Who else would be here?" Ears pricked up, tail frozen, Yangi glances around the fire, eyes wide.

Sari purses her lips. Ashur. It is Ashur. That cursed brother of hers. Her hand reaches for the royal seal, a ring threaded with a leather lace worn loosely around her neck. Always next to her heart, pried from the hands of another of her siblings when she fled the palace the night the Amyrdine Bara attacked. Ashur cannot have it.

"He's getting closer," Arishaki says, both hands brushing the sand, speaking with the dunes. "He'll be upon us within half an hour. From the north."

"Dammit." Sari reaches for *Katynna*, the bladed weapon passed down through the generations, wielded only by the *mar'sahre'dan'i*; the other item that proves her divine right to the throne and that marks her as the rightful heir to the throne. She pulls the curved blade from the sheath and raises it above her head. "To me! To me! We fight!"

She brandishes it into the night sky, racing towards her stallion, relying on the loyalty of her soldiers to follow her into battle. Fires quickly extinguished, rations hastily eaten—her followers, her believers, her trusted servants rally behind their queen, Saritrah, the next Sahre'Danu of Sua.

She rides toward the gates of Antalyza, the shining city that the Oracle of Yshuld calls home. Of all the people in her demesne that she must protect, the Oracle is the most vital. If Saritrah is their leader, the Oracle is their hope.

She steadies her breath, a trick she was forced to learn before she could walk. She will make it. She will save Antalyza not just from the savage insurrectionists, but from her brother's sharp talons. The glint of gold against the gate distracts her; a flash of light and then a shadowed figure slips into the desert. A spy sneaking out of the city? The figure creeps along the wall, staying just out of reach of the moonbeams.

But others follow, and the shrill pleas for help that are ripped from the mouth of this mysterious figure alarm her. Not a spy, but someone in distress. Four more figures creep through the gates after it. "Ari, take the lead! There's someone there," she yells, no doubt that he will follow her orders.

"Of course, my princess," he replies. His domineering tone gives way to gentleness and care. He is the only one she has allowed to address her thusly.

The shrill cries continue, interspersed with cruel chuckles. Ashur's soldiers visiting some sort of violence upon a helpless civilian. She leaps from her horse, putting away Katynna, drawing her spear in one swift movement, and stabbing at the predators before they even see her.

Their prey is small, dark hair pulled back, exposing every inch of fear etched in her face, back pressed against the city wall, fingers curled around a dirty gray robe. She is terrified, cowering, weak. But for the brief second that Sari glances into the woman's eyes, she sees a golden, radiant light. Power untapped, strength unharnessed, determination hidden beneath fear.

What a waste of potential. And yet, it is her duty to save this woman, even if the woman is too cowardly to save herself. In two graceful arcs, she dispatches the rest of the leering soldiers, sending them to meet Xana. "Hurry back inside," she says, not bothering to look at the woman as she plunges her spear into the sand and then wipes the sharp point it on her wrist brace.

"I am not going back in there," the woman says. Her voice quivers, but Sari hears just a glissando of defiance in it. A defiance that she can admire, praise, even respect. But not one she can tolerate. Not right now.

"That's an order. Get back inside. Things are about to get violent, and the fighting out here is not something a delicate flower like you should have to witness."

"I assure you, I have seen worse."

Sari laughs. This woman looks like she's never seen the outside of whatever walled garden she lives in. What, has she seen the kitchen cat torture a rat? Sari turns around. The woman still shakes, but her back is straight, and her chin is high. Just the right combination of fear and defiance for playtime but a lethal combination on the battlefield. Crossing her arms, Sari wonders if she could recruit the woman for something like armor repairs or weapons maintenance.

"Fine. Do as you like, but I don't like my work going to waste. I saved your life; pay me back by not losing it tonight."

The woman looks out into the desert, a death sentence if she has no supplies. "Thank you, ma'am. I will wait out here until the fighting is over and then go home."

"If I see you out later, I won't be pleased."

"Understood."

Sari mounts her horse, enters the city, and only chides herself for not getting the woman's name as she unleashes a fury of lethal assaults on the soldiers she meets inside. She slices her way through the throng; how Ashur acquired so many soldiers is baffling, and yet his numbers are overwhelming. His laugh echoes on the wind, mocking her as she forces her way toward his unspoken call. Haunting her as she races to answer it.

Arishaki—loyal, brave, dependable Arishaki—is already engaging her brother. Blood pounding in her ears, she takes a deep breath. Steady. Steady. You don't win by being reckless; you don't win by being hasty. Squaring her shoulders, she leaps from her horse, lunging at her brother, her sword point slithering toward his throat.

"Ah, sister dearest! I had not expected to see you here. What a delightful surprise! A family reunion. How have you been, love?"

Sister dearest, he would say before wrapping his hands around Zisuthra's throat. *How have you been, love?* He would say before dragging Zisuthra down the halls by her tail. He never hurt Zisu because he hated her; he hurt Zisu because he knew it hurt Sari.

Steady, steady. Don't let him win; don't let him get to you. She swings upward and then back down, quick and ruthless and without aim or method. He dodges easily, just as easily as he had dodged her attacks in the *iseru*. His smile just as cruel now as it had been when they were children fighting in that arena.

But this is different. She has *Katynna* strapped at her hip the royal seal concealed under her tunic this time. She has the power of the mar'sahre'dan'i. She slashes, he dodges, neither getting a hit on the other. But he is clearly winning, no sweat upon his brow, no quiver of fatigue on his lips. Her face is contorted in anger and concentration; his is as tranquil as the glow of Yludi on the full moon night.

Why can't I win? Why can't I beat him? I can't lose, I can't. I have to save our people from him; if he claims the throne, it will be worse than even those brutal insurrectionists.

"Well, this has been so much fun, sister dearest," he says, jumping backward to land on the edge of the city wall and nodding at someone behind, most likely his second-in-command. "But I have more important things to do than to toy with a little mouse. I got what I came here for, but thank you for keeping me entertained." He leaps back over the wall, a silent signal to his troops to retreat.

As quickly as they came, Ashur's army leaves Antalyza. All that remains for Sari to do is drive out the insurrectionists now.

Milton Keynes UK
Ingram Content Group UK Ltd.
UKHW010919271223
434976UK00004B/262